Heavenly Places

A NOVEL

Kimberly Cash Tate

Walk Worthy Press

West Bloomfield, Michigan

12 11 10 09 08   10 9 8 7 6 5 4 3 2 1

Cover design "Family" copyright © 2007 by Synthia Saint James
www.Synthiasaintjames.com

Heavenly Places
ISBN 13: 978-1-57794-857-5
ISBN 10: 1-57794-857-2
Copyright © 2008 by Kimberly Cash Tate

Published by Walk Worthy Press in association with Harrison House Publishers
Walk Worthy Press
33290 West 14 Mile Road #482
West Bloomfield, Michigan 48322
www.walkworthypress.net

Harrison House Publishers
P.O. Box 35035
Tulsa, Oklahoma 74153
www.harrisonhouse.com

Acknowledgements

Father, You are the One who tries the heart, so I should have known when I typed my first line that this writing process would be about much more than producing a book. You refined, tested, and established my priorities, causing me to put the partial manuscript away for more than a year as I sought whether it was truly Your will. And when I was writing, I often had no more than an hour in the mornings before bright shining faces were upon me, ready for a hug, breakfast with Bible study, and a shared day of learning. But that's the way You ordered it, and if the book was never completed, it would have been fine because You made it clear—first things first.

But then I watched, Lord, as You took that little bit of time, blessed it, and multiplied it, so that much of the book was written in my head, in snatches throughout the day, and I only needed to find a pen and get it down before it was lost. How can I not give You the glory? Thank You for leading me the long way. My life—and this book—are richer because of it.

My husband, Bill—You helped me to keep a merry heart throughout this process, which was easy since you've always got me laughing about one thing or another. I'm thankful for the grace you give me. More than anyone, you see the whole me—warts and all—and yet you keep that same calm, jovial spirit. Thank you for your love, your strength, your wisdom, and your leadership, and for giving me the latitude to do what God speaks to my heart.

Quentin and Cameron, because of you two, my days are full of flavor and drenched with purpose. Thank you for keeping life fresh and giving me an excuse to act young and silly.

To my mother, Edna Cash—I love that you are my friend and counselor, but most of all, I love that we are sisters in Christ who enjoy long, enthusiastic conversations about God and His Word. Thank you for always being there, always listening, anticipating, blessing, and bearing my burdens. And thank you for being my personal prayer warrior. You prayed over this project from the beginning, when it was a mere thought, and I know you're still praying over it in some form or fashion. Your faithfulness astounds me!

To my daddy, Earl Cash—I told Bill the other day that I must have been subconsciously looking for a husband with the same qualities as my father—easygoing nature, quick wit, a ready laugh, sports nut, and the ability to bring a smile to my face. Those qualities have enriched my life since I was a little girl. Thank you for a treasure trove of feel-good memories and for continuing to be such a loving and positive presence.

To my step-mother, Joyce Cash, who, after more than thirty years, is so much more to me than that title could convey. Thank you for the invaluable ways in which you have blessed my life, including the blessing of growing up a part of your large, loving, extended clan—the Terrell family—whom I long ago claimed as my own.

To Bridget Thomas—What would I do without you? Our friendship was born in a Bible study and has continued all these years as a sister-hood with Christ at the center. You've been right there through all the twists and turns of my life in the last thirteen years, and you even had a hand in jumpstarting this particular one. I'll never forget when you told me, after reading an excerpt of Christian fiction, "You could do this!" I hadn't thought about it before, and I'm sure God used that kernel of encouragement to get me moving years later. Thank you for supporting me in so many facets of my life.

To Anne Amado—After I moved away, I just knew the days of long discussions by the coffee pot at North Dallas Community Bible Fellowship were gone, but I'm so glad I was wrong. Well, the days by the coffee pot are gone, but the discussions are longer, broader, and much more frequent—often several times a week. Thank God for e-mail! You have such a gift for exhortation, mingled with thoughtfulness and uncanny timeliness. So often you would send an e-mail saying simply, "How's the writing? I'm praying." And because of where I was at the time, it would trigger one of those long discussions, and there you would go to exhorting. I can't thank you enough for filling my inbox with love and encouragement.

Tanya Harper—Your friendship has blessed me in many ways over the years, and one of the biggest has to be when you did me the favor of donning your editing cap and reading this long manuscript, even though you were under a deadline to complete the editing of another manuscript. You were the first to read it, and I was so nervous, anticipating the umpteen things you would tell me didn't work and the months and months of additional time I would have to put into fixing it. But when you gave me your feedback—"It's ready to go"—I nearly leaped out of my skin with excitement. Thank you for your strong encouragement. It gave me the confidence to release it and get the ball rolling.

My cousins, Melinda Carroll, Yolanda Davis, Christie Minga, Sheree Terrell Walker, Martita Williams, and Sylvia Wills—Our Heaven's Seven weekends have been a testimony to how powerfully God can move within an intimate group of women. Because of you all, I could easily imagine a character like Treva being changed through a weekly gathering of women who share an eternal bond. (Can y'all imagine what would happen if we could get together every *week*?) Christie—That word you gave me back in 2000—"Don't be frustrated if you don't have time to write; it's your season to tend to your home and your children"—helped to change my entire outlook. Thank you for letting God use you.

Toni Glymph—Long ago you shared with me the way in which God let you know that you were fearfully and wonderfully made. Thank you for being so transparent. Your experience inspired the breakthrough scene with Treva and Hezekiah.

Denise Stinson—You just keep blessing me. More than ten years ago, you took me on as a client and secured a publishing deal for me. Now, *you're* my publisher. Thank you for believing in me and for giving me wings to fly. I truly appreciate you.

My editor, Monica Harris—You have such a talent for bringing out the best in a story and its characters. Your insights made me roll up my sleeves and get back at it, and the book is better as a result. It was a privilege to work with you.

Julie Lechlider—You were delightful to work with. Thank you for the time and care you put into this book, and thank you to Julie Werner and and your entire team for the hours and hours of behind-the-scenes work that I'll probably never know about, for which I am very grateful.

Dedication Page

To every woman who has ever doubted that
she was fearfully and wonderfully made.

Chapter One

I told Hezekiah I wanted to live in Potomac or Chevy Chase or North Bethesda, someplace with cachet, where people had money and minded their own business. I didn't know this for a fact, of course—that they minded their own business—but it sounded good and gave me one more reason to tick off in favor of living there. If I had had my druthers, I wouldn't have lived anywhere near the D.C. metropolitan area. But if we had to be there, the where *had* to be Montgomery County, Maryland.

Montgomery County had seasoned money and grand old homes—or, in Potomac, breathtakingly newer homes. Exquisite shopping. And neighbors who would be concerned mostly with themselves and, perhaps, the fleeting question of how another black family amassed enough nickels to break bread among them. They wouldn't get to know me, I wouldn't get to know them. And we would revel, the neighbors and I, in perpetual aloofness.

I definitely did *not* want to live in Prince George's County—no matter how many new communities somebody built and called "exclusive." No matter how many black executives made it their home, as the realtor was fond of sharing. P.G. with bells on was still P.G. Step outside the luxury home, tip past the golf course, and the love affair ends. No cosmopolitan breeze for miles. Nowhere to go. Nothing to do. And worse—black folk everywhere who've worked hard and long enough to buy a few thousand square feet, who are happy to be around other black folk with a few thousand square feet, and who—I could just see it—would think it a wonderful thing to knock on the doors of said black folk and get to know them. I wanted no part of it and told Hezekiah so.

Well, I told him everything except the part about the neighbors because he would have scoffed. Hezekiah is a people person. In our former neighborhood outside Chicago, he knew everyone on our block, and many who resided two and three blocks over. He took walks, not as a form of exercise—he keeps his six-foot-two body fit with regular basketball runs and weight lifting—but to catch up with whomever was out and about. If he'd had his way, we would have had rolling dinner invitations starting up our side of the street and going down the other. I know because he suggested it once. He must have known it was a long shot because when I suggested he might be crazy, he left it alone.

It's not that I don't like to get to know people. Well. I won't sugarcoat. I'm not a fan of people. For the first half of my life, I cared about them too much—what they thought of me, why they thought what they thought of me. I cared about the words they said to me and would sometimes count them after an encounter to see if I could use up ten fingers. Often I needed only two. Usually it was, "Hi, Treva." On a good day, five. "Hi, Treva, how are you?"

These rude people would treat me like that when they were in my home, or I was in theirs. They were peers and parents of peers, longstanding members of my parents' social circle. We saw each other regularly at this function or that. I ached for real interaction and inclusion. From time to time I'd rehearse in my head how I might turn those five words into a conversation; it seldom worked in reality. If I said, "Fine, how are you?" I got a "Fine" over the shoulder. If I planted myself where conversation was flowing, it was worse. The laughter and banter would swirl all around me while my own interjections fell flat.

Sometimes I wonder if time has exaggerated it all in my mind. Was it really that bad? But then I remember the utter sadness that would overtake me afterward, how I would cry someplace alone because once again I'd felt the sting of a brush-off. I cried, too, because of the reason. It wasn't that they didn't like me, in the sense of judging some aspect of my personality. They simply gravitated to their own, and I wasn't one of them. They were various shades of fair with naturally straight hair and eyes the color of pools. I was milk chocolate with hair that grew—I was thankful—but needed help to get straight, and I had regular old dark brown eyes, too far on the other end of the spectrum to be one of them.

So by force of circumstance and other more painful circumstances in my own family, I gravitated as well, further and further inside myself. I could never shake the burden of caring what people thought of me, but by college the hunger for interaction had turned cold. I didn't look for friends; my focus was grades. In law school and then in the working world, the essence of that focus never changed. I was driven to succeed—yes, to prove myself. I had a vision of what I wanted to do and who I wanted to be and where I wanted to be. It had to be a posh community, an established posh community. Every major city had one. And any major city would have been fine, except the one I was from— the District of Columbia. I never intended to return, not to the city itself nor anywhere in the Maryland-Virginia vicinity.

Since Hezekiah knew I wanted nothing to do with my former home, and since we found ourselves relocating there nonetheless, I figured he could at least let me choose the county. He didn't, which meant a debate ensued—a good one, between my P.G. County-born-and-bred husband and me.

It was largely one-sided. Hezekiah refuted each of my points with only one—the cost. "We can get more for our money in Prince George's County," he insisted. I had my rebuttal at the ready.

"We can get more for our money in Chevy Chase too," I said. "Instead of square footage, the 'more' is prestige. It matters where you live. A premier address speaks volumes."

"Really," Hezekiah indulged, pulling his chair closer, hand lovingly upon my knee. "And what does it say?"

"Success. Significance. That we've risen to a higher level."

"I don't need a house to tell me that. God already did." Smiling, eyes penetrating.

"Hezekiah, the 'speaking' is not to you, it's to others."

"Oh, why didn't you say so?" His half-chuckle was ominous. "We could've dispensed with this issue long before. The P.G. house—the one we can build from the ground up, the one that would be more spacious than any on your list—wins hands down because it's smarter. It speaks to *me*. At one hundred thousand dollars less, it's calling my name."

That was it. Here I am. Unpacking. In Prince George's County. And I'm about to scream because I haven't been here but a few hours, movers still carting in boxes and beds, and some woman, a neighbor no doubt, has already stepped into my foyer.

"Hello?"

There she goes again. I am in the kitchen, rhythm broken, arm in the air, hoping the sudden silence sends this message: *Get the hint and leave.* I am not in the mood since I haven't even come to grips with being here. I certainly don't want to be bothered with a stranger who has the nerve to just walk up in my house. Granted, the door is open, but she's a trespasser nonetheless.

"Hi, is anybody home?" the persistent voice sings out.

"Take a guess," I sing back under my breath.

I resume work, pulling tightly packed swirl-accented glassware out of a box, unwrapping them, and lining them along the countertop to await a turn in the dishwasher. Quietly. I'm trying not to crumple the packing paper too much, resenting the fact that I can't. Why would the woman drop by at such an inopportune time anyway? She couldn't even wait for the moving truck to pull away.

A glass slides too quickly from my hand, making an awful ping as it catches the counter. I cringe, casting a furtive glance in the direction of the front door. I know she heard it. The kitchen sits a good distance from the entryway, tucked at the end of a slightly curved hallway, but that curve apparently does nothing to deflect sound. Her "Hello" was clear as a bell; my blunder had to be as well. *I bet she'll follow that ping and find me here. I bet she's like that.*

My eyes begin bouncing around the kitchen, hating the impression this will make if she sees it. It's a mess—boxes and contents of boxes everywhere. I know that she knows that we are in the process of moving in, but what does that matter to my central nervous system? The thought of receiving a visitor in here right now is enough to make me hyperventilate. I need things in place, special dishware and collectibles perched behind lighted glass-front cabinets. I need countertops cleared of everything but the items strategically placed there, for neatness' sake and for the sake of the tiny flecks of gold in the granite, just waiting to pop out and align themselves proudly with the burnt gold on the walls. It would be nice if one earthen-colored square of floor tile were visible, real nice if one could see the decorative tile pattern around the base of the center island. Definitely need a seasonal floral arrangement on the kitchen table, not that unsightly heap of mechanics' tools that haven't made their way yet into the garage.

And me. *I'm* a mess. Makeup's faded, I'm sure. Nails chipped. Hair has no life, just hanging limp past my shoulders. And I'm wearing a sweatsuit, which I would wear only around the house, and that rarely, when I need to roll up my sleeves and work, like today, not in front of anyone outside of my family, and certainly not in front of someone I am just meeting. When people do happen into my world, I have to be prepared so everything can be just right. Whatever I can make beautiful—my house, my hair, my clothes—I'll strive every time to do it. Helps me to feel good about myself, and even then it's hard.

I tilt my ear sideways. Haven't heard her in a couple of minutes. Maybe she won't walk back here after all. Maybe she's gone. A sigh escapes as I relish the thought.

"Hi, my name is Hope. My mommy's in the kitchen."

I groan at my five-year-old's annoying bent toward hospitality.

"Hello, Hope, I'm Carmen Nelson. This is my daughter, Stacy, and the baby's name is Malcolm."

What? Did she bring the whole family? My eyes flash to the ceiling and ricochet down. All I can do is beat a path to the foyer before Hope escorts her back here. The foyer is a much better option. Not much clutter there, so I won't feel mortified the entire time we're talking, and there's nowhere to sit, which should keep it short. I can't do anything about me, though.

Swiping a hand through my hair, I move my rubber soles quickly down the hall along the bamboo hardwood and into the domed entryway. I see her, illuminated by a single ray of sun cast through the upper Palladian window. It complements her honey-nut complexion, which is the first thing I notice—where someone sits on the spectrum. She's not on my end.

I muscle a smile and extend my hand. "Hi, I'm Treva Langston."

Carmen tightens a one-arm grip around the baby and shakes my hand with the other. She's wearing blue capri pants, a blue-and-white striped shirt, and Keds over bare feet. Her hair, pulled softly into a ponytail angled behind the ear, matches the color of her skin. I can't tell if the hair color or the texture is natural. Eyes average brown. About five-five and in good shape, given the baby in her arms. She looks youthful and energetic. Peppy.

"Hi, Treva. My name is Carmen," she says, and introduces her two children, both browner than she, the baby a much darker brown. He must take after the father.

Hope tugs at my arm, her rounded face animated with delight. She whispers, "Mommy, Stacy's my age. She's five."

I give Stacy a smile and notice that she and Hope are about the same medium brown—another habit, comparing shades—all while quickly smoothing Hope's flyaway hairs. She has several long braids, and none of them have been redone in days. I don't know when or why she threw on these mismatched clothes—red shorts and a pink shirt with blue flowers—but I sure wish the boxes to her room had not yet been delivered. The girl loves to go digging in her clothes and pull out who knows what. And look at Stacy, wearing a cute pink sundress with cute pink sandals and a cute pink ribbon in her freshly combed hair. I glance up the spiral staircase, hoping my other two daughters remain hidden. They're older than Hope, and more particular about their appearance, but I don't want to take a chance. The two of us look bad enough.

"I hope we're not disturbing you too much," Carmen says. "We saw a moving truck down the block and thought we'd walk down and welcome you. Your husband is so nice. He talked with us outside and told us to go on in and call for you."

"Oh, really?" *Why am I not surprised?*

And now that I know she's seen Hezekiah, I'm even more self-conscious. I'm self-conscious whenever someone meets him first. Hezekiah's skin is so light that I know people expect his wife to be, well, not so dark. I've seen the subtle double takes when I walk up to him at a gathering and he introduces me. Now, it *could* be my imagination. Hezekiah says my upbringing has caused me to read color into too many situations. But I might be right too. They might actually be thinking, *How did those two get together?* Or even, *He could have done better.* I wonder if Carmen did some shade-comparing of her own.

She smiles. "This is a great neighborhood, isn't it?"

I give a slight nod to avoid stammering.

"I love the green space and the mature trees," Carmen is saying. "It's so serene. You'll find it has an old-fashioned feel because the developer kept the lots to a minimum. People actually talk to each other, you know?" The baby whimpers, she switches him to another hip, fishes a Winnie-the-Pooh pacifier from a small shoulder bag, sticks it into his mouth, and continues on. "Last week a neighbor stopped by to say hi and brought homemade cookies because she hadn't seen me around in a while. Wasn't that sweet? She wanted to know if I was all right. Lots of good people around here. I really like it; reminds me of my hometown in North Carolina."

Hope and Stacy hopscotch across imaginary squares, a needed distraction as I reach for something beyond a visceral response. This might be Hezekiah's cup of tea but it sure isn't mine. Folk dropping by at will. Random acts of kindness, accompanied no doubt by expectation of reciprocity. Thrilling. What's the use of a gated community if the irritants live within? I'd prefer privacy to cookies.

Seems I don't need a response. She's still talking.

"The woman a few houses down from you is from North Carolina too, Winston-Salem. Real nice, you'll like her a lot. Where did you move from, Treva?"

"From the Chicago area."

"Oh, where in Chicago? I'm a little familiar with it."

I watch Carmen step further inside the entryway, afraid she'll plop the baby down any second and make herself at home. "In Evanston, North Shore."

"Chicago is such a beautiful city—the skyline, the lake. D.C. doesn't have a downtown like that but we love it. You'll see there's a lot to do."

"Actually, I grew up in D.C. but we've been away for a number of years."

"Really? Well, I would love for us to get together, maybe during the day when the kids start school. I live on this same street but down and around the bend at 8217."

Why does this woman think I don't have anything better to do than to sit around and chitchat? And why is she assuming I don't work?

The smile twitches but holds as I cross the entryway and stand before the opened double doors. "Thanks, Carmen. I'm sure I'll be seeing you." Carmen heads to the stroller parked in the circular drive and Stacy trails, giggling with Hope about something I missed. I urge Hope to join Hezekiah in whatever he's doing and I pick up where I left off in the kitchen.

I am working with greater intensity. Funny how a bad attitude helps you sail through a monotonous task. My thoughts are moving in tandem, fast and furious, assuring me that I really am unhappy in this fabulous new home. But I know it's not the home that's truly bothering me.

In truth (and I would never admit this to Hezekiah), buying a home in Prince George's County turned out to be the best part of this deal. The building process kept me intensely occupied, which meant less time to stew over the relocation itself. Hezekiah knew that I enjoyed decorating and would throw myself into the building of a home. He also knew that such immersion would be to his benefit, so he stepped completely out of the way and let me have at it.

I loved every minute. I loved making tough choices about layout and fun choices between hardwoods, granites, and stone. I loved picking appliances, searching like crazy for the right indoor and outdoor lighting, and even for the little knobs and pulls on the cabinet doors and drawers. I began to think maybe Hezekiah's prayers were being answered, that I was feeling more at peace with the move.

I say "Hezekiah's prayers" because the only prayer I was praying was to remain in Chicago. Even while my nose was buried in the building project, I made enough snippy comments to let Hezekiah know that I was proceeding under general protest and would have no problem chucking the whole thing and staying put. In the low moments, though, the builder would send digital pictures of the progress and I would grow excited about seeing the finished work.

One month ago we flew in for a walk-through of the completed home and were awestruck by what the builder had done. On that same visit, I met with an interior designer to implement the vision I have for the rooms and various spaces around the home. As instructed, I've already compiled notes and pictures of ideas in a nice little three-ring binder for our appointment in a couple of weeks. I've been greatly looking forward to that. I had the heated swimming pool filled a few days ago and lively colors applied to the builder's off-white walls. The Jacuzzi was made ready as well, and I was looking forward to snuggling in it with Hezekiah, maybe as early as tonight.

But whatever peace I had managed to find fled last night as I did a final walk around our empty Evanston home. All of the turmoil I had originally felt, the turmoil that had gurgled and bubbled for months, boiled over and handily engulfed me. Everything was wrong. Everything.

I couldn't believe I was actually leaving an associate position at Thompson & Klein in downtown Chicago. I could see the clouds from that office, the realization of my dreams. I could see future high-stakes litigation that would catapult me to higher echelons. I could see the federal bench from which I would one day rule. I could see the people before whom I would stand, graciously of course, with a fantastic, over-whelming, soul-satisfying smile of success that would say, "I told you so."

I was leaving all of that and heading…nowhere. No, not nowhere. Heading to unemployment, which is a definite somewhere, a *horrible* somewhere. I had thought surely by moving day that I would have secured a fantastic position at a D.C. firm. That assurance had to be what buoyed me throughout the building process. But that very last day in Chicago, another three-line form letter had arrived from a top firm telling me that they were not hiring. The enormity of it all struck me as I stood in the middle of the kitchen floor. I couldn't go without a desperate last stand.

"We can't leave," I said simply.

The car was loaded and Hezekiah had come to check on my where-abouts. Tired from cleaning the house and the garage, with a ten-hour drive in front of him, he simply looked at me, so I said it again. "We can't leave."

"Treva, we've gone over this a million times," he said. "Our house is sold. The truck is packed. The car is running. Let's go."

"Hezekiah, it's not too late. You know it isn't. Northwestern would take you back as a professor in a minute and my firm would do the same for me. We could find a house to rent until the Maryland house sells, and it should sell fairly easily since we got one of the last lots. What do you think of that house for sale over on Sheridan? It's old but we could update it like we did this one, and we could—"

"Treva," Hezekiah said calmly, "the girls are in the car. Take the time you need, then come on."

I barely said a word the entire ten hours. If I wasn't asleep, I was pretending to be asleep, the darkness a fitting serenade to my misery. By the time Hezekiah pulled into our new driveway, the sun had dawned bright and strong, but for me, it was still night.

I growl a sigh, unpack another plate, and sling it into the dishwasher, daring it to break. *God, what am I doing here? Why in the world did You let Hezekiah move us from Chicago? I was blossoming there, on track with my life. And if I had to come back, I could have at least returned triumphantly. Why have I been uprooted and stuck in barren soil? Nothing makes any—*

"Hey, Treva, guess who I found outside?" Hezekiah yells.

I jerk from my thoughts, gasp with knowing, and scurry to the foyer, feet flopping in tennis slides.

"Heyyyyyy!" My younger sister, Jillian, and I scream, hug, rock back and forth, look each other up and down, and scream again.

"Jilli, look at you; you look great!" And she does. I've known her all of her life and I'm still struck by her beauty. It doesn't matter what she wears—she's standing here in denim walking shorts, a rust colored T-shirt, and basic brown flip-flops, no makeup—she always shines.

Jillian was the sought-after one growing up, the one who blended in—her features a straight hand-me-down from our mother. The contrast never came between us; Jillian was my closest friend. But obviously, there *was* a contrast, and my mind, ever active, pointed it out on occasion. Like now, as I notice the slightly wet, wavy ringlets atop her head. That was one thing, well, one of the things, I couldn't help but envy—her wash-and-go hair.

"When did you cut your hair off, Jillian?"

"Girl, two years ago. And look at yours. You've let it grow long. Turn around and let me look at you."

I shrug and turn reluctantly. "Nothing to look at. I'm bummy today."

"Please. You don't know what 'bummy' is. Those are the cutest capri jogging pants I've ever seen, and the fuschia Tee looks great with the fuschia piping on the pants. And I see you're still working out. Got the tight everything going on. You'd better not say anything about my rear."

Hezekiah clears his throat. "Before you two get too deep...."

"All right, Hezekiah." Jillian laughs. "You know I haven't seen my big sister in three years. She acted like the Midwest didn't have planes to transport her back East." She raises a hand to my coming objection. "I don't want to hear it. I don't even know my nieces anymore. Where are they anyway?"

"No telling. Hope, the Welcome Wagon, is usually the first one at the door when company comes. But she and Joy may be in our room. They got tired of dodging movers so Hez set up the DVD player in there. Faith was working on her room last I saw her, but that was a long time ago."

"Well, give me a tour and we'll find them on the way."

We chatter our way into the living room and I listen to Jillian gush over the house I'd sell in a heartbeat.

"Treva, these wall-to-wall windows. Look at the sun you get in here. And what is that area over there?" Jillian's face is pushed against the window panes of the French doors that open to the rear of the house.

"A loggia."

"A what?"

"A covered porch, furnished like an indoor living space. At least it will be one day."

"HGTV?"

"Magazine, girl."

"Hey, Jillian, thanks for coming," Hezekiah calls out, leaning against a column just outside the living room, smiling as if there's reason.

Jillian turns, curiosity in her brow. "Why?"

"Because your sister was acting mean before you showed up, mad all over again about moving out here. Now look at her, all smiles. I won't take it personally, though."

Hezekiah's tone is light, an attempt at peace, but he must not know where I've been. In a corner. The corner he put me in while, for hours, he unpacked and organized around the house and outside the house, anywhere I was absent, to give me space. Well, I'm not a child, obligated to come out of a time-out with a better attitude than the one I went in with. Mine is worse, and as far as I'm concerned, he just rang the bell. I'm coming out swinging.

Backing a few steps to his full view—lips scrunched, hand on a jutted hip—I wait for two movers harnessed with weight belts to pass. They're laughing while carrying an antique armoire at a precarious tilt. I glare at them until they park it against the dining room wall unscathed, and turn that glare on Hezekiah.

"Excuse me? Won't take *what* personally?" I say, my voice rising. "That life, as I knew it, is over? That you get to keep climbing your career ladder but mine is kicked to the ground? Oh, but for good measure I get to wile away my time, not in a community with art galleries, antique shops, ethnic restaurants, and upscale shopping within walking distance." I fling my arms wide. "No, the best shopping these parts have ever seen is Beltway Plaza and Landover Mall, that great hustler hangout that somebody had the mercy to shut down. Why should you take any of this *personally?*"

My thoughts sound worse now that I've given voice to them. Regret is squeezing my lungs, begging me to stop. I'm feeling like a spoiled brat as I breathe in the scent of beautiful calla lilies sent this morning by the interior designer with a "Welcome" card, now perched in a crystal vase on a pedestal in the foyer—the foyer that is roomier than my college dorm room. Jillian's mouth is hanging open as she wonders, I'm sure, what happened since last we spoke and she applauded my attitude adjustment over the move. She's praying for me right now, I just know it.

And Hezekiah, who had a fabulous offer from the University of Maryland and wouldn't accept the position until he knew I had one, which I did (until I didn't) and who likely would have moved to Montgomery County if I'd had a job but never said so to spare my feelings, is staring at me with a look I can't quite figure out. He is not smiling. I feel bad, but stubbornness has taken hold. I know I shouldn't—

"And let me add this," I say, finger stabbing the air, "if all you're going to say is, 'God's hand is in this move,' save it. I'm tired of hearing it. God has a plan for *my* life—isn't that what you like to say? So let me tell you God's plan for *my* life: God would have left me in Chicago."

With that, I corral my speechless sister with an arm hooked in hers, turn from Hezekiah, and continue the tour. "Let's go outside; I'll show you the loggia. The view from the—"

My breath catches as Hezekiah rushes me with a bear hug from behind, curling me forward with his two-hundred-pound muscular frame. His whisper teases up a sudden flutter: "If God's will is for *me* to be here, which I know it is, then God's will is for *you* to be here, because we're one, and there is no me without you. I don't know what will happen with your job situation, but I've been praying and I believe God will answer. I've also been praying about the *other* situation that's upsetting you but you won't talk about. Now, if you're still mad and need space, I understand. Let me just do this one thing."

I search his eyes but it's too late. His knuckles begin to tickle my side. I struggle to free myself, hiding a half-smile. In no time I'm slumping to my knees in uncontrolled laughter.

"Stop, Hez, let me go. Seriously." My body is writhing on the floor, a slave to two knuckles. "Jilli! Are you just going to stand there?"

"I'm cheering for Hezekiah. I always said he's the best thing that ever happened to you."

"Hez, no, it hurts." I would say anything to get out from under this.

He releases me and I scramble to my feet feigning a frown, fists squared in boxing mode.

"So you're Ali now?" Hezekiah says. "Or Sugar Ray Leonard? You know he lived over near P.G. Community College when he was starting out."

"Yeah, and moved to *Potomac* when he made it big." Laughing, I jab the air as Hezekiah leans right, then left. The moment is surreal, Jillian's words echoing in my heart: *He's the best thing that ever happened to you.* Before Hezekiah, I never loosened up and acted silly. In fourteen years of marriage, he has brought things out of me that I didn't know were there, things that I like—when I allow myself. I land a left hook to Hezekiah's chest and he grabs me again.

"You know you can't stay mad at me," he cajoles, dotting my face with quick kisses, "and I know how I can help you through this. If you ever want to run for Miss P.G. County, I'll swear you're only twenty-one and single. I bet you'd win with your good-looking self."

I catch one of those quick kisses on the lips and let it linger. He's right about my not being able to stay mad with him. He's a master at dealing with me, always knowing what I need—how long I need to stew, when I need to snap out of it, and how it needs to happen. In this moment, with his strong arms around me, the night has suddenly turned to day.

This time Jillian clears her throat and I dart back to her with fresh spunk. I *will* find a job. I *do* want this house. All the time I put into building it, I ought to.

"Thanks for coming, Jill. I mean it this time," Hezekiah shouts, bounding upstairs.

"I'll see you this evening," Jillian shouts back.

"Oh, Jilli," I moan, walking through the French doors, "I forgot we planned to get together tonight. Now that I'm up to my neck in boxes, I'd rather work until it's cleared away."

"Girl, you can't do it all in one night and you've got to eat. We live only ten minutes away—on the other side of the tracks."

I give her a light shove. "Whatever, Jill."

"Seriously, come on over." Jillian admires the leaf of a shrub with great intensity. "And I think Mama's coming too."

A jolt surges through my body. I find that interesting, that my body reacts before my mind. It wants to sit down. The involuntary shaking is a clue. I look around as if furniture appeared while my back was turned, and then I remember that it exists only in my little three-ring binder. My body doesn't mind; it settles for the wide tiles of the loggia. Legs pulled to the chest, arms wrapped around the legs, head tucked inside, it is hoarding relief as best it can, waiting for my mind to catch up, decide what we should do. The spunk that endured all of two minutes is gone. Thanks to Jillian, the Grand Dame has made her entrance, bringing with her, as usual, tangible distress.

She is *the* reason I never wanted to return—Patsy Parker Campbell, whom I haven't spoken to in three years and whom, long before that, I had banished to the outermost ring of my life. I hadn't even processed yet what it means to be near her again. I thought I could put off consideration of that reality for weeks, maybe months. I couldn't have guessed I'd be dealing with it the first night.

I lift my head and ask accusingly, "She knows I'm back?"

"Is it a secret?"

"I sure hadn't told her."

"Well, I talk to her a little more than you do and it would have been unnatural for me to keep quiet about her daughter moving back to town."

"You didn't have to invite her to dinner. I have zero energy right now, and less for her. You know how she is." I tuck my head back down.

Jillian touches my shoulder, eases down next to me on the tiled ground, and sighs. "I'm sorry. She called this morning and I honestly wasn't thinking I had to be guarded, so when she asked what I was doing

I told her I was cleaning the house, getting ready for you all to come over. She was quiet—you know Mama doesn't get quiet—and I felt bad and said, 'You're welcome to come, too, if you want.'"

I groan loudly, understanding fully. The invitation didn't have to be, if only Jillian had had the guts to honor the status quo; lack of contact has worked quite well. But maybe Patsy didn't say she was coming. Jillian said, *I think Mama is coming*. Hopeful, I lift my head again. "And she said?"

"She said, 'Okay.'"

I stare at the pool, blankly at first, then with great interest. Its other-worldliness is inviting, and not just because it's a hot August day. I want to dive in, let the water swallow me whole. I want to feel the smack of a change in circumstance, the rush you feel when you don't dip toe-to-shin-to-waist-to-neck until you're completely under, but you just take the plunge. When I do that, I glide near the bottom and swim until I need a breath. I can't hear, can't see what's happening above, can't be bothered. My leg rocks side to side. It likes the idea, wants to give me a running start. The ripples conspire too, rolling lazily with the faint breeze in a come-hither fashion, promising to shut out the world. That's what I need, an escape.

Jillian knocks her leg against mine and playfully obstructs my view with her face. "Treva?"

"What."

"This *could* be a good thing. Maybe it's time for you to build a better relationship with Mama. Maybe you could begin to see her in a different light." Her earnest eyes fill my peripheral vision. "You're a new person, Treva. God has given you the strength, you know."

Jillian and Hezekiah, always quick with a pep rally.

"All things are new, Treva."

"With God in your life, all things are possible."

"Treva, God is living *in* you. You have everything you need."

17

And on and on. I know she means well but not even Jillian, an eyewitness growing up, truly understands what I went through. She couldn't. There was no bridge between what Jillian saw our mother say and do and what I felt at the core. That's where the damage was, at the core. That's where the Treva-that-should-have-been was upended. No pep rally will convince me that everything is okay. See Mother in a different light? Jillian is crazy to even suggest this could be a good thing. I am not going.

I shift my gaze from the water to Jillian to tell her, but a realization flips my stomach. Jillian told Mother that I don't have a job. I know she did. And Mother thinks I've failed, that I'm miserable, and wants to see for herself and gloat. If I don't go, she will say it was worse than she thought, that I couldn't bear to show my face. I rock my leg as a hint of spunk returns. No way will I give her the satisfaction.

"We'll be there," I say in monotone.

Jillian flings an arm around me and squeezes. "Really?"

"Mm-hm."

She stands and outstretches her hand to pull me up. "I'm glad, Treva. I think you made the right decision. Now let me see those girls and this beautiful house you put together."

My body rises warily, not trusting what my mind has come up with.

Chapter Two

Box cutter in hand, I tear through wardrobe boxes in my walk-in closet looking for the outfit. The professional movers lifted sections of clothing at a time from the Chicago closet and placed them in cartons, and I cannot find the section I have in mind. I've blown past business suits, evening wear, outerwear, and gradations of casual wear, from athletic hoodies to summer linens, until now, at the thirteenth, I believe I've found the desired grouping. Several pieces hang on a metal bar inside the box, smashed together. I shove each aside quickly until I find the selection of choice: a Dana Buchman camp shirt—toast color, three-quarter length sleeves—and Tahari jeans. Power casual. Understated. Like I haven't thought too much about it.

I shower, dress, spread my beauty essentials across the marble vanity in the master bath, and stare intently into the mirror. First, I sweep my limp hair into a chignon. Two small pimples have nestled on the chin and right cheek, which I hide. And those eyebrows. Though I had them waxed one week ago, stray hairs dot the landscape, muddying the well-sculpted arch. I fumble through two makeup bags and a toiletry bag for the slanted tweezers, then run downstairs, find it in a side pocket of my purse, and pluck six hairs that make all the difference.

I apply tinted moisturizer, concealer, bronzing powder, clear mascara on the brows, black mascara on the lashes, eyeliner, two shadows, and a cream blush, all with an expert touch acquired from many visits to cosmetic boutiques. With a nude pencil, I line my lips and top them with lip balm and lip gloss, then stare at my fully-made-up face. Eyes full and sultry. Cheekbones high and well-defined. Nose and lips just sassy enough to be sure of their ancestry. All of it accented in the proper shades. Just right.

I round up the girls, each of whom has been cleaned, coiffed, and attired in outfits I took similar pains to find. I even took the time to redo every one of Hope's braids. Hezekiah, in the same clothes and not about to change, herds us to the car and, once the girls are in, takes my hand and pulls me aside. "Sweetheart, whenever you want to get out of there, just look at me and I'll know." I squeeze his hand and get into the car.

A few minutes later we turn into Jillian's neighborhood and, from memory, Hezekiah navigates his way through the development and pulls up to a house that looks much like the others on the street—a late '70s split-level with a brick-and-siding front exterior. He parks in front, behind a Mercedes-Benz sedan, and steals a quick glance my way.

"I saw you," I say. "Don't worry. I'll be all right."

"You're all right now, 'cause you've got me." He's smiling, of course.

Hezekiah jumps out and walks to the passenger side to help the girls and me, then holds the small of my back as we move silently up the driveway, past two minivans in the carport, to the front door, the smell of barbecue catching every step. Heavy steps. *God, I can't do this. I cannot do this.*

"Welcome, welcome," Jillian exclaims, opening the door before we ring the bell. She has changed into a cotton sundress. Clinging to a leg is three-year-old Trevor, and behind both is Cecil, who opens the door wider.

"Man, what's up? Is it true, are y'all really back?" Cecil asks, clasping hands with Hezekiah as they pull one another to a hearty hug.

Hezekiah smiles broadly. "Yeah, man, couldn't stay away forever."

My eyes cut away in disagreement.

"Treva, life must be treating you well. You're looking wonderful, as usual. Give me a hug, girl."

I use the hug to peer over Cecil's shoulder but cannot see anyone.

"Y'all come on in. The kids can't wait to see the girls," Jillian says. Every few feet another of Jillian's and Cecil's children appear until Hezekiah and I have hugged and affectionately queried all four: Trevor, five-year-old David, eight-year-old Sophia, and ten-year-old Courtney. Trevor has Cecil's pecan-colored complexion, but the girls and David are a carbon copy of Jillian, which has always struck me as curious, how Mother's genes could pass so strongly to Jillian and to three of Jillian's children, yet bypass me altogether.

"Where's Grandma?" Hope asks, and I stare down at her, perplexed, wondering from what planet we've acquired this girl. Why would she care where Grandma is? She doesn't even know her. Hope hasn't seen her grandmother since she was two, and I certainly haven't talked her up.

"In the dining room waiting for us," Jillian says. "Cecil had just put the food on the buffet."

My hand flexes nervously and Hezekiah grabs it, massaging the back with his thumb. He knows I am never comfortable around my mother. She is critical, condescending, and, more than anyone else, puts me in hyper-self-conscious mode. Add to that the upset of three years ago when I returned home for Daddy's funeral. The mean, hurtful things she said to me bore a hole into my heart. I never know what to expect when I'm around her, except this feeling of dread.

The children breathe gaiety into the group as we troop through the cozy living room and approach the dining area. There she is, Patsy Parker Campbell in full view, seated at the table's helm. She rises and stands regally in place, as if the queen in a receiving line, waiting to give her subjects the favor of a greeting.

She hasn't changed. Still sleek, with silk Georgette pants flowing smoothly from her Pilates-trimmed waist. *I look good, don't I, to be in my sixties?* I can tell she's been lifting, even if Jillian hadn't told me. Her upper arms hold the long, sheer, white linen jacket with extra poise. I saw it at Neiman's on my last fling on Michigan Avenue and liked the "stand-collar." "We no longer say 'Chinese,'" the saleswoman told me.

Patsy chose the white silk jersey tank to go underneath. I must admit the white on white looks good against the wisteria pants. I'm glad now that I didn't buy it.

Hair still layered short, flawless makeup, diamonds begging notice in the ears, on the wrist, and on two champagne-colored fingers. I unfold my own for inspection and remember, gladly, that I touched them up, then fold them back under my crossed arms. Arms that have begun to shiver every few seconds, as if reacting to intermittent gusts of cold wind. I am happy to be in the rear.

"This must be Hope," Patsy says, looking down at the eager face belonging to the arms that hug her waist.

"Yes. Hi, Grandma," Hope says, grinning.

Patsy returns the hug. "And how old are you?"

"Five...almost five and a half. I start kindergarten in two weeks."

"And I know this is Joy," Patsy says, her attention diverted to the slightly taller girl behind Hope. Joy, eight and shy with those she doesn't know well, leans a shoulder into Patsy.

"That's not a hug, is it? Give me a big hug." Patsy bends lower, embraces Joy, and strokes her hair. I feel myself tense.

"Hi, Grandma," Faith says, following a gentle tap on the back by Hezekiah's free hand.

"Faith, my, how you've grown. You're what, eleven now?"

"Twelve, actually."

"Almost a teenager, right, Faith? She can't wait." Hezekiah slips his hand from mine and slides forward. "Hello, Mother Pat. It's nice to see you," he says in a lively voice, arm around her shoulder.

"Hezekiah, always a pleasure. I saw your mother the other day. That salon of hers is always bustling. A lot of colorful people in there. I wonder why I go sometimes, but nobody does my hair better than Darlene Langston."

Hezekiah's lips dart out, back, to the side, contemplating, then return to a smile. "My mother's very talented, isn't she?"

He moves aside to make room for me, a courtesy that flips my stomach. It's time. I step toward my mother, cognizant of my girls, my nieces and nephews, and the sweet spirit that abides in my sister's home. Actually, the children are enjoying a rambunctious reunion and paying no attention to me, but I *feel* they are watching. I feel that if I say or do the wrong thing, they will know it and be negatively impacted. I can just hear my girls: *Aren't we suppose to honor our mother? Was that honoring?* Then there's Jillian busily arranging condiments, drinks, and a couple of desserts, and Hezekiah and Cecil talking off to the side. I know they're watching. I can hear them, too: *Make the right choice, Treva. Rise above, Treva. She is your mother, Treva.*

The shivers have stopped, calmed by the anger of remembrance of that last visit. I look at Patsy and lock eyes. I want her to know where I stand, to know she is not off the hook.

Patsy, impervious to judgment, returns the stare with half of the wide, engaging, deep-dimpled smile so many admire. I have never seen the dimples directly. Patsy graces me always with the dimpleless half smile.

We stand two feet and a world apart. Simultaneously, our five-foot-eight-inch bodies honor civil custom, the children, or whatever it is we are honoring, and lean in. Clothes brush, one hand pats the back. Jillian thankfully pierces the silence.

"Dinner is ready and piping hot. Cecil barbecued ribs, chicken, and hot dogs, we have lots of side dishes, and if you save room, there's a peach cobbler and a chocolate cake. The kids will eat at the kitchen table, the adults here in the dining room. Cecil, you ready to pray?"

The family links hands in a circle and Cecil prays, thanking God for the food and for our return. Jillian and I prepare seven plates and settle the kids at their table in an assortment of chairs. Famished, Hezekiah and I pile our own plates and sit down, legs touching under a lace tablecloth, Hezekiah's habit to comfort me. Jillian and Cecil sit across from us.

The Queen returns with her plate, scoots the head chair forward, and casts her hazel eyes upon Hezekiah.

"Hezekiah, your mother tells me you've got a nice position over at the University of Maryland. Tell me about it."

I breathe deeply, twice, and realize I'd been dreading the official opening remarks. *So, Treva, exactly how is it that you've moved back home and failed to tell me?* I'm relieved that Hezekiah has the floor. I hope he hogs it.

Hezekiah's eyes light up. "It's an incredible opportunity. I've been given an endowed chair in education, which is a blessing, but what I'm really excited about is the chance to direct a new center on urban education. That's one of the reasons I was willing to leave Northwestern and come back to this area. My passion is to make a difference in the lives of young African American mathematicians, people who are traditionally underserved."

"Well, that's wonderful, Hezekiah. I'm proud of you," Patsy says, and gives him a slight smile. "I know you'll do well there. I sure wish you would consider bringing your talent over to Howard, where there are a plethora of African Americans who could benefit from your expertise."

"Well, Mother Pat, Maryland is the one who made the offer. And the research done by the center will benefit African Americans nationally, we hope, not just at Maryland."

"I could set up a lunch between you and a few principals at Howard. See if they can come up with an offer for you."

"Mother Pat, I've already accepted the position at Maryland. I start on Monday."

"Well if I had known about it—" A glance my way, "—maybe I could have done something sooner. I just wish you all wouldn't favor these large white institutions over universities like Howard."

Here we go.

Patsy slices chicken from her drumstick, takes a dainty bite. "I still cannot fathom why these girls did not continue the family legacy. My parents attended Howard University and I never thought of enrolling anywhere else. Neither did Charles, rest his soul. What other institution has such an illustrious roster of black alumni? Who else has endowed black society with so many doctors, lawyers, and dentists? We expected Treva and Jillian to be third-generation Howard alums, and their children the fourth. Yet they decide to go over to Maryland. *Maryland.* If you forego the prestige of Howard, at least go to an Ivy League."

It matters not that four of us at the table are alumni of the University of Maryland. Or that we have heard this before. Or that the last time I heard it, I responded. It was three years ago at Daddy's funeral, where the social buzz around Patsy had quickly moved from the death of her husband to the presence of her daughters. Many hadn't seen us in years, some hadn't seen us at all, and Patsy, duly encouraged, shifted her mourning to Jillian and me.

"They've been such a disappointment," she said to a circle of friends gathered to the side of the pew. "Jillian squandered opportunity and Treva, well, she could have done more for herself, too. For one thing, she should have gone to Howard like I told her, but all their lives, if I said, 'left,' they went right." She looked over at us and cut her eyes back to the group and to their sympathetic nods.

I had cut my own conversation to hear that one, and when we took our seats, I leaned my head to Patsy's ear and said, "When did you ever talk to me about attending Howard?" It was a violation of my vow. I had resolved the day before to never speak to my mother again.

Patsy's head touched against mine as she replied with a tight voice, "Treva, you knew of its importance."

That was true. Patsy had always spoken of Howard's importance, but she never talked to me about going there. Only in hindsight had she decided that I should have gone. Matching her voice tone, I spoke on top of the minister who'd begun the service. "I knew of its importance to *you;* that's why I didn't go there."

Today, I don't challenge. I don't want to rock the boat that contains me and my unemployment. I am trying very hard to pretend she doesn't know.

Patsy takes another bite and raises her fork at attention beside the plate so we will know that she is not through. No one thought she was. We sit, forks clanging against earthen stoneware, finding refuge in baked beans.

"I guess they have renounced all vestiges of their upbringing," she continues. "I always imagined that if they were going to live in the area, they would live in the area, in upper Northwest where they were raised, or a location of similar stature. But first Jillian moves to Prince George's County, now Treva.

"Who, really, moves out here? No offense to your family, Hezekiah, but surely you understand the rich history of upper Northwest. These girls were raised among some of the most prominent black families in the country. They've been exposed to true culture. They don't belong here. Their father and I worked hard to give them the best and they've showed no appreciation. I don't know why they insist on living an unorthodox lifestyle."

This rant, actually, is all about Jillian. It's always about Jillian. The bit about expecting us to go to Howard was about Jillian. She expected *Jillian* to go to Howard, and did speak to her about it, all her life. When I didn't go that was fine; Jillian would go. But Jillian didn't. Now, Patsy wishes I had gone because she thinks that if I had gone, Jillian would have followed.

Patsy lives for the day when Jillian will embrace life with the flourish Patsy envisioned—the high-end, status-conscious, social whirlwind of a life of so many in Patsy's don't-call-us-we'll-call-you-if-you're-one-of-us organizations. Jillian has always refused, politely.

Jillian is very polite and respectful, which is how she has maintained a cordial relationship with Patsy despite a history of conflict. Jillian is also loving and fiercely protective, which caused much of the conflict—because she chose to love and protect me. Patsy resented that. She also resented that when Jillian and I fought, we made up, that we have a habit of sticking together, of laughing and crying together, that we attended the same *different* university together, and now, apparently, that we live in Prince George's County together.

I am suddenly amused, given that I resisted living here. In Patsy's self-centered world, Jillian and I chose this county just to spite her. I realize in this moment that she doesn't know me well at all. I love the misunderstanding, though. I backed into this one but I'll take it. I'm so tickled I think I'll make my first comment.

"Mother, Prince George's County is fine," I say good-naturedly, raising Hezekiah's eyebrows. "And it'll be like old times for Jilli and me." Patsy doesn't like that. *Jill-i-an is what we named her,* she said once.

Jillian smoothes the tablecloth with her fingers. "I love it, Mama. The kids have wide open spaces to play, the homes are very affordable, and the people are nice and, shall we say, unassuming. And since we do live here, there's no need to belabor the point, is there?" She lays her napkin on the table, rises, and checks on the children.

I am not amused anymore. Three remain with Patsy, and I've escaped pointed questions thus far. I know what's next and hope the men will run interference. *Come on, Hez, Cecil, banter the Redskins about, talk rookies, coaches, special teams. Something.*

Cecil clears his throat.

Yes.

"Hezekiah, man, have you—"

"So, Treva, where will you be working?"

Unbelievable. She snatched the floor right out from under Cecil and he's too nice to snatch it back. That my mother continues to casually eat tells me there is nothing casual about the question. She is more interested in reaction than information. She already knows.

I square my shoulders, finish the short rib I'm working on, dab the corners of my mouth, and sip lemonade as I formulate an answer in my head. I would never tell her that, despite eleven years of late nights and weekends in the office, persuasive briefs that yielded favorable court opinions, and three federal court jury trials that ended in client victories, my worth was reduced to dollars and cents. Maternity leaves for Joy and Hope pushed me deep into the billable-hours-production hole, and I had not snagged significant new business for the firm, unlike some of my male counterparts who had carved out niches in intellectual property and landed tech clients with matters that generated millions.

A vote for promotion to equity partner had been delayed for two years to give me time to increase my numbers. And I was on track in doing so. So when I informed the head litigation partner that I'd be moving, I assumed he'd arrange a transfer to the D.C. office. He did, but soon thereafter, after Hezekiah had accepted his offer, the D.C. office called that litigation partner—not me—to explain that a hiring freeze had been put into effect. There was not enough business to keep the current attorneys busy, and they did not foresee a market upturn in the near future. Had I been a top producer, I know they would have found a way to ease me in. As it was, no one fought for me; my time with the firm ended. And every other top firm I contacted sang the same hiring freeze tune.

I have no idea what I will do.

I finally meet Patsy's waiting eyes. "I'm taking a break right now to get acclimated to the area again and make sure the girls are settled in their schools; then I'll begin a search in earnest."

"If the problem is that you can't find work, I can call your father's old firm. I'm sure they would be glad to do me the favor of securing you a position there. Charles made that firm a lot of money."

So that's her angle. I had thought she'd be gloating over my current state of affairs, but I should have known her own affairs would be uppermost in her mind. *How will it look if both of my daughters are unemployed?*

"I'm fine, Mother. I'll handle this myself." I will not be beholden to her for anything.

Sophia, David, Joy, and Hope, who've been running around the house, run breathlessly into the dining room. "Can we go outside?" they ask in unison.

"*May* we," Patsy responds.

We all look at her.

"The proper wording is 'May we,'" she says.

In unison the children respond, "May we? Please?"

Cecil comes quickly out of his chair. "You can, and you may. Let's all go. We'll sit on the patio while the kids play." Hezekiah and Cecil are out the patio door in five seconds flat.

I help Jillian clear away the dishes and take in her house in the process. It remains the most homey home I've ever visited. Framed photographs hang in the living room and two stairways, chronicling various stages of the children's lives. Courtney, Sophia, and David's many arts and crafts projects and penciled drawings adorn shelves, bookcases, and the refrigerator. And because Jillian homeschools, books poke out of every conceivable crevice. An atlas of the world, an atlas of world history, an atlas of the Bible, a children's encyclopedia, a children's dictionary, a children's thesaurus, and other reference type books are perched on two kitchen shelves intended for cookbooks or decorative items. Patsy thinks Jillian has wasted her life by opting out of a career. I tend to agree, but I can't help but admire her dedication.

I don't envy her this, though. I would go crazy in Jillian's shoes.

The late-evening air is very pleasant, hardly any humidity. The children are playing tag, flying down the jumbo slide, face first sometimes, and now, playing a silly game of hide-and-seek in which the hiding places expose most of their body parts. Poor little Trevor is hiding under the tabletop beside me. I try to shield him with my legs but Joy spots him. "Found you," she says. "You can't hide under glass!" I'll give them ten minutes and get out of here.

The sliding door opens and Jillian emerges with a fresh pitcher of lemonade, pretty yellow circles floating on top. "Thanks, Jilli," I say, lifting my glass. Pouring, Jillian says, "You're welcome" in her best Mailbox imitation. She and I giggle and Patsy shakes her head, not up on *Blues Clues*. I sit back in the wooden patio chair, sip, and enjoy the laughter. I'm relaxed. Tired, but relaxed. I had thought I would unpack a few more boxes when we return home, but I'll have just enough energy to fall into bed.

Patsy is quiet, sitting upright on a chaise lounge, smiling with dimples at the revelry. The scene is reminiscent of a normal family gathering. At least, what I've seen of "normal" from Hezekiah's parents. Nothing about our family has ever been normal. But right now, in this moment, it seems normal.

Hide-and-seek ends abruptly, since David, the seeker, has abandoned the game in favor of a swing. Hope grabs another swing and Faith picks up Trevor, seats him in the last one, and pushes. Courtney and Sophia climb the rope ladder on the side of the playscape and dangle their legs over the edge of the fort. And Joy wanders over to me, clearly tired, having insisted all day that at eight years old she didn't need a nap. I scoot over to allow room for her as Patsy calls, "Joy, come over here so I can get to know you a little better."

Joy sits at the edge of the chaise lounge, feet pointed toward the fun, joining her young comrades in spirit. The pastel plaid walking shorts with a scalloped edge that look so darling on her have a stain I hope is not grass. That's what I get for trying to have her look cute.

"Look at this hair," Patsy says, fondling it. "Do you know the last time I saw you, I guess you were five, your hair fell to about here?" Patsy presses a squared fingernail a couple of inches below Joy's shoulders. "Now look at it."

I look too, despite myself, in reflex to Patsy's command as she stretches a braid down the length of Joy's back. I feel alone, helpless, wishing I had other conversation to drown out this one. Jillian has stepped back into the house and Hezekiah and Cecil are throwing a football across the yard. I look for only a second and turn away before the image crushes the heart that has begun beating wildly within me.

"Have you ever worn your hair down?"

"No."

"Oh, you should wear it down." Patsy unloosens one braid, then the other, and combs her fingers through. "See, that looks beautiful!"

I close my eyes. Tears sting them, and my skin is crawling with a prickly sensation that feels like needles. Anxiety, one doctor told me. I wish I had octopus arms to scratch every place it itches. Discreetly, I move my hands to my lower back, arms, and chest, then to my scalp. It has been awhile since it last happened, not since I last saw Patsy.

Jillian can say it's a new day all she wants to; my body doesn't agree.

I lift my eyes and find Hezekiah's. He knows it's time.

Chapter Three

Why did we have to come back?

"Mommy, I wanted to play some more. Can't we stay longer?"

I am down the driveway, past the Benz, at the Expedition's opened door. "Hope, we're leaving," I say. "Get in."

And my little medium-brown daughter hops in the vehicle, followed by Joy, my fair-skinned child with her hair *down,* and the eldest, Faith, my dark-brown firstborn.

That's what they all are for the moment. Colors. Whenever I see Patsy, I receive the same gift: her magnified lens.

Our car doors close, we roll down the road, and I am trying very hard to get her face out of my head.

Come over here, Joy.

I focus on the landscape out of my window and it doesn't help. The land is in Prince George's County, which takes me to the woman who just chastised us for living out here.

Do you ever wear your hair down?

I shift in my seat, behold my now *very* light-skinned husband, a *very* light-skinned Joy, whose hair I will re-braid the second we get home, a *very* dark Faith, and an in-between Hope. They're still colors. Didn't help. I turn back around.

See, that's beautiful.

I shut my eyes and it's worse. Patsy and Joy. Patsy and Joy. Then it changes, as I knew it would, to Patsy and Jillian. I am five years old, and

I know. I see the way Patsy fawns over Jillian, who, by the age of two, had convinced skeptics that her milky skin would not turn any darker. I can see Patsy caressing Jillian's silky hair, hair Patsy let hang down her back like a crown of glory. Patsy's glory. For this time, Patsy had done her family proud. "Now Jillian, that's a beautiful child," Patsy's mother, Vivian Parker, would say within my hearing.

I knew. Knew when Patsy didn't hug me specially. When she didn't finger my braids. When she didn't pick me up to cuddle me because I was "so cute" the way she did with Jillian. I knew the truth, that Patsy didn't think I was cute.

Patsy's friends agreed, with their sad stares. I hated when people came over, and they often did, making me uncomfortable in my own house. In they would file: "Jillian, you look so pretty today. Come here, sweetie!" Then, my five words: "Hello, Treva, how are you?" One after the other, their faces an accusation. *Do you truly belong in this family?*

I wondered myself. I didn't share the skin tone of either of my parents, certainly not the ultra-fair Patsy. But from an old family picture I found my likeness, Jupiter Campbell, a smoky man with a wide smile and jet black naturally curly hair. He was my father's grandfather who married a light woman, producing a brownish son, grandfather Harold. Harold married light, too, and bore my Daddy, Charles, a lighter brown. I was a throw back, a reversal of fortune, my coloring affected also by some "darkies" on Daddy's mother's side, as I heard Patsy and Vivian figuring one day. There were no darkies in Patsy's line, only ultra-fair.

Patsy didn't know what to do with me. I was foreign to her. The kink in my hair was foreign to her, so she styled it once a week. She brushed Jillian's incessantly.

That signified Patsy's role in my life—hardly any personal attention, which was fine if all I needed was my hair combed. But I needed eye contact, extended conversation, a seat on Patsy's lap, an advocate. When life brought the horror of adolescence, I needed Patsy to tell me it didn't matter if no one called, that I had no close friends besides Jillian, that

Jillian got invitations I didn't, that people snickered at the contrast between us. I needed Patsy to tell me it was all right because my family loved me and that was all that mattered. I needed more than Jillian's refusal to go; I wanted a gutsy declaration from Patsy that we didn't need those snobs anyway.

I should understand, Patsy would say. Not everyone gets invited. Not everyone is born with the favor of good looks. No, she would not ask any of her friends if their sons could escort me to the cotillion. No, she would not prevail upon cousin Gregory in college to take me. Would I, though, encourage Jillian to participate when her time comes? She and that Kendrick Mays would be perfect together and he's already agreed. "Oh, stop crying, Treva. Just forget it!" she said.

I tell myself that now—*just forget it*— as we wind through our neighborhood. Forget *her.*

"Mommy, when can we go to Grandma Patsy's house?" Hope says.

Poor thing. So full of life and love for people. So innocent. Didn't even realize her grandmother was too enthralled with Joy to be bothered with her. Grandma Vivian did the same on our visit three years ago, telling Hezekiah, "Hope looked a lot lighter in the baby picture you sent. I thought you had another Joy." When Grandma Vivian died the following year at 85, I did not attend the funeral. "No time soon," I say.

"Why?"

"Hope," Hezekiah says, "Mom is very tired right now. We'll talk about it another time, all right?"

For the first time we park in the garage and enter the house through the door just off the kitchen. I find it hard to get my bearings. Not even sure where to put my purse. I look around at the boxes and realize anew what has happened. We actually live here. I feel as if someone picked me up and placed me in the middle of somebody else's life. *My life is in Chicago.*

I begin thinking again about asking my firm to take me back. I could work during the week and fly back East on the weekends. I could get an apartment near O'Hare. That could work, and I would feel better, more in control. I would be where I want to be, in the job I like, in the geographic area I like, only dealing with this D.C. life a couple of days a week. I could even…. I catch myself.

I need to go to bed.

But not before I do Joy's hair.

I call Joy into my room and we sit on the bed, my back against a pillow propped against the headboard. I can almost imagine Patsy's shock when she birthed a baby that looked nothing like her because Joy, with this creamy skin, looks nothing like me. She is all Hezekiah. I worried at first how I might view such a baby. I hoped her color would-n't flash like a neon sign whenever I saw her, a taunting reminder of every negative experience I'd had with others of similar hue. That had never been the case with Jillian, and thankfully, it didn't happen with Joy.

What strikes me when I see Joy is her uncanny resemblance to the Langston clan—Hezekiah, his mother and brother, and even a couple of his aunts and cousins. They all have wide foreheads with high cheeks and a diminishing jaw-line, narrowing to a slightly pointy chin, and her resemblance to them stirs good feelings. I have nothing but fondness for Hezekiah's family. His mother, Darlene, a strong Christian woman, took me under her wing as a daughter-in-law, even though I was an unsaved woman. She loved me from the heart and prayed unceasingly for me. That's what I see when I see Joy, a wellspring of Langston spirit…until days like today intervene, and the external dwarfs the internal.

As I brush her long wavy locks, I become Patsy, she becomes Jillian. I brush faster to get it over with, find the part down the center, and throw the brush on the bed. With the comb, I define the part and smooth the crinkles, handling hair that is nothing like my own. Bouncy. Soft. The comb glides through from scalp to ends, no problem, in its natural state. Easier than Hope's and Faith's. It occurs to me often, how much easier my life would be if all three had Joy's hair. How quickly I'd get done, with no fussing and crying from Hope. I can't deny it, I'd prefer it. Like Patsy.

I twist the rubber band on the end of the second braid. "All done, Joy." When she doesn't move, I bend over her and see closed eyes. No wonder. It's almost ten o'clock and we haven't slept since the car ride last night from Chicago to Maryland, and then only intermittently. The drive finally caught up with Hezekiah. He plopped down on the bed the minute we returned from Jillian's. A bull couldn't ram him out of his sleep.

I scoot out from behind Joy, lift her in my arms, and push my tired bones down the upstairs hallway, through the library alcove, and into her bedroom. I lower her into the bed, thankful I put the bedding on before dinner. I walk through the adjoining bathroom and into Hope's room. She stirs at the sound and moves her head about the pillow, sending her thick, spongy braids flying. I run my hand down each of the seven, stretching them to the middle of her back and letting them spring back up. I used to do this to my own hair at this age, wanting it to stay down, show the length it really was. It didn't seem fair that my hair looked shorter than it was. I pull another down again, watch it spring back up, and feel a sudden lump in my throat. A sadness. I don't exactly know why. I guess I could take my pick.

I need to go to bed.

I kiss Hope's cheek and walk down the hall to Faith's bedroom, the only one fully unpacked and semi-organized. Black artwork sits on the floor below the section of wall on which she wants it hung. Black dolls line the shelves, interspersed with African-American literature and poetry. Her lavender-and-yellow flowered quilt matches the bright yellow walls which we had painted before our arrival.

Faith lay atop the covers in sweat shorts and a T-shirt, hair wrapped in a black silk scarf, body blossoming into maturity. Seems overnight my first baby has gotten breasts and a shapely bottom. No telling what the teenage years have in store for a girl who so far has sidestepped a fascination with boys and general mischief. And no telling what's in store now that her grandmother has suddenly dropped back into her life, a grandmother who will not hesitate to make known to her the pecking order of color.

I drop to Faith's bedside, drained. I look at my daughter, my mirror image, then tip my head up and glance at the array of stuffed and painted faces celebrating blackness around the room. They are all dark like Faith and me, and smiling. I bought them as an investment when Faith was young, those and the artwork and the books, all to build a positive self-image. Right now it seems a joke. Patsy could shatter it in one thoughtless encounter.

What did I expect anyway? That Faith would love being dark? She's not blind. She has to see the way strangers "oooh" and "aaah" at Joy and speed those same eyes past her. I've never asked how she feels when it happens. I'm too fearful of the answer. It would break my heart to hear of her own inner struggles and perhaps her struggles at school. I rarely even hear her talk about friends.

Hezekiah says I have a warped view, that "black is beautiful" pervaded the collective conscious decades ago, and I would know it if Patsy's bias hadn't been drummed into my soul. He is forever pointing out chocolate brown supermodels, actresses, singers, anyone in the public eye, to prove his point. But I tell him it doesn't mean they're considered equal. I understand the slogans and the politically correct perspective and the need to elevate some darker-skinned women into the upper echelons of the beautiful people. I get it. But I *live* the true perspective. I see it in people's eyes. And if by some miracle Faith hasn't yet had her rude awakening of the way the world sees her, she'll get it soon…from her own grandmother.

My head falls on the bed beside her. *It's not fair. It's just not fair.* I wish Faith hadn't taken after me. I wish I hadn't taken after Jupiter Campbell. And I wish we hadn't come back. I stayed away for a reason, for protection. I stayed where I could best pilot my life and emotions. I hate the thoughts and reflections my mother awakens within me. I hate looking this intensely at myself, and at Faith, and feeling, painfully, that I'm aligned with the strangers and Patsy.

When I find the strength to do so, I rise and make my way to bed. I know what I have to do. Keep my mother out of our lives and find a high-powered legal position. That's the only way I'll stay sane and feeling good about myself—as good as I'm able.

Chapter Four

I hang up the phone and strum my fingers restlessly on the glass-top kitchen table and then loop one hand through the handle of an olive green mug and sip my second cup of Breakfast Blend. I flip through my notes and grab the phone again.

"Brobeck & Stiles," the receptionist answers.

"Hello. May I speak with Richard Flanagan, please?"

"Mr. Flanagan is out of the office. May I put you through to his voice mail?"

"Is his secretary available?"

"I'm not certain. Who may I say is calling?"

"My name is Treva Langston."

"One moment."

The ringing sits me up straighter as I wait.

"This is Mr. Flanagan's office, Jennifer speaking."

"Hi, Jennifer, my name is Treva Langston and I'm calling because I sent a cover letter and resume to Mr. Flanagan about one month ago for a position in litigation and have not received a response. I wanted to check on the status of my application."

"Ms. Langston, Ms. Langston," the woman repeats. "The name sounds familiar...."

I perk up and pace the room. Maybe finally I'll get somewhere, at least an initial interview.

"Yes, here it is. Ms. Langston, I'm sorry. Mr. Flanagan dictated this letter to you this morning and I have it right here. Unfortunately, Brobeck & Stiles is not hiring litigators at this time. He was very impressed with your experience, but we had to let one person go just last week. He wishes you well in your pursuit."

I try not to let her hear the disappointment. "Okay, thank you very much."

I hold the phone and stare into space. This is the fifth rejection this morning from second-tier law firms that I would have never considered in law school, and didn't have to. My grades put me on the short list of every top law firm I applied to for a summer associate position. The fact that I secured a prestigious clerkship with a federal judge enhanced my credentials all the more. After graduating and clerking for two years, I had my pick of offers and went with Thompson & Klein, one of the top ten firms in the world. Now, nothing. The market has hurled me head-first into an abyss. What am I saying? Hezekiah did that.

I punch the "talk" button to call Hezekiah and update him on my journey downward. He's at work, his second week on the job, more excited and more convinced this was the right move than before he started. I couldn't be more convinced that he's crazy. We should have stayed where we both had feet firmly planted on an upward path.

Three rings and then, "You have reached the office of Hezekiah Langston...." I click off. Where is he, anyway? Probably drinking his coffee with colleagues or meeting with the dean about upcoming faculty searches or any number of things that make for an interesting life.

My eyes float around the kitchen. It is nine-thirty A.M., the day is ahead of me, and I have nothing to do. Every box has been unpacked, contents put away. Every picture hung. Every book shelved. Even the towels have the nerve to be washed. And with the girls starting school today, the quiet screams that I am the only member of the family without a life.

The day had started out promising. I accompanied Hope to her first day of kindergarten, a first for me as well since my work schedule had not allowed me to do the same for Faith or Joy. Hezekiah came too, unwilling to let go of his first-day-of-kindergarten ritual. Actually, the first day of every school year is a ritual. Hezekiah grills turkey sausages, flips wheat pancakes on the griddle, and makes a big deal about the grade each is now in. For kindergarten, Hezekiah likes to go into the classroom, take a picture of his daughter on her big day, and satisfy himself that the environment is warm and stimulating enough for his baby girl.

Hope had gone to "Meet Your Teacher" day last week, so this morning she breezed in, happily mimicked Mrs. Troyer's "Good Morning," and dashed around the room to the various learning stations with a gaggle of little people. Hezekiah and I hung around with the other parents until Mrs. Troyer gently kicked us out, then peeked in on Joy in her third grade room, and Hezekiah dropped me back home. I told him to have a great day, and meant it, because I intended to do the same. I would check on job prospects and somebody would schedule me for a lunch where I would speak persuasively about the experience and dedication I could bring to their practice. I would even settle for a thirty-minute look-see in some partner's office. I conducted those myself. If the firm wasn't actively hiring but a good resume came in, one person would screen the candidate to see if he or she was worth bringing in for a full day of interviews despite market conditions. If one firm would do that for me, I could sell myself.

I was expectant when Hezekiah left. Now—

The phone, still in my hand, rings with a loud shrill. Maybe....

"Treva Langston."

"Girl, you think you're at work or something?" Jillian says.

"I guess it's on the brain." I do not feel like talking. If I had waited a second for caller ID to kick in, I wouldn't have answered. All I want to entertain right now is a job prospect. "Aren't you supposed to be teaching?"

"P.G. may start school in August but we still start on the Tuesday after Labor Day. I'm on vacation for one more week."

A loud thud sounds in the background and crying erupts. "It doesn't sound like vacation to me."

"Aren't you in a lovely mood?"

"I'm frustrated. I've been calling about jobs and nobody's hiring. This is unreal. I've been looking for months." I glance at my notes again, ready to make the next contact. "Can I call you later?"

"Well, I did call to tell you something. You can't spare one moment?"

I keep the sigh inside. "Go ahead."

"Treva, I am so excited. For a long time now, I've been praying about bringing a small group of moms together during the day for a Bible study—"

My eyes roll of their own accord. Is this what couldn't wait? I crook the cordless in my neck and rise to find something to do, maybe water the tall plants I insisted the movers load onto the truck.

"—a time when we can support and encourage one another, pray together, the whole thing. There are lots of Bible studies at church on Sunday and on Wednesday night but nothing like this. We could really minister to each other. A few people told me months ago they would love to do it, and a little while back I met a young woman who could really benefit from it. And now you're here. It's the perfect time to start."

"You're thinking *I'll* be part of it?"

"Hoping."

No, thank you. "Jilli, I am not a stay-at-home mom. I'm an attorney who's doing everything I can to get back to working sixty-plus hours every week, very soon." I tilt the watering can to drip the last bit onto the ficus. "I'm sure your idea is a good one and if you have some ladies interested, by all means, go for it."

"Treva, I said it was for moms, during the day." Jillian is using her teacher voice, slow and measured. "They might be home all day, part of the day, or part of the week. We'll try to find a time that can accommodate everyone's schedule. Looks to me like you're the most flexible right now. If things change, fine. You won't be bound for life. And anyway, you have to say yes because I want to use your house for the first meeting. Mine is too busy."

"I don't know about all this, Jill. It's not sitting right with me. I don't know these people. I'm sure we won't have much in common—"

"Oh goodness, Treva, they're Christian moms. What more do you need to have in common? I bet you'll be surprised by what a group like this could do for you. It'll be good for all of us. Uplifting."

I sigh loudly this time at Jillian and her pie-in-the-sky ideals. Must be easy to concoct good-natured, warm and fuzzy deeds when life's been nothing but kind. Jillian and her eternal optimism grate at times, more so when it requires something of me. But I have to admit it was Jillian's optimism that provided the lone bright spot in my life growing up, especially at night when my own thoughts terrorized me. Jillian and I had separate rooms, but when Jillian was about seven, she insisted on sleeping in my double bed every night, and every night in the dark she would say, "I love you, Treva. You're my favorite sister in the whole world." My thoughts would fly away for a little while.

"All right, Jilli. I'll host the planning meeting but that's it; I'm not committing to the Bible study. And you'd better have it sooner than later because I don't plan to keep these leisure hours for long."

"I'll contact the women and find out what would be a good date and time, and I'll let you know what we come up with."

"Wonderful!"

"Bye, girl."

I dial the next firm on my list, a list that records the Washington firms to whom I have sent a resume. I exhausted the top firms and the top corporate legal departments long ago, and thought long and hard before sending out this wave. I can't see myself working in an office without messengers to file pleadings in court or an extensive law library. At Thompson & Klein, if I needed a case, I walked downstairs, pulled it off the shelf, and read it, or had someone copy it. In the off chance the case was published in a reporter we didn't have, I would send a messenger to retrieve it from elsewhere, and I'd have it within hours.

These firms likely don't have such perks. But it's easier to get a job if you have one. All I want is to get in the door, and I'll be looking to leave the minute I get there, the minute the blue-chip firms reopen theirs.

"Rhinehart, Winston & Strong."

I give my spiel. Two minutes later, I cross them off my list.

———

On the third lap across the pool, it hits me. I know what Jillian is up to. Trying to engineer my spiritual life. Jillian and I did not grow up in church, and neither of us had read the Bible by the time we entered adulthood. But Jillian became a Christian soon after she graduated from college, and she seemed to immerse herself in it immediately. All I heard was "the Bible says" whenever I talked to her. I had to tell her, just as I had had to tell Hezekiah, that I didn't want to be preached to.

When I became a Christian myself three years ago, Jillian was more excited than I was, and I'm sure she assumed that I would immerse myself in the Bible as she did. I didn't have time. I would leave for work early in the morning and return late in the evening, working even then from home. My Bible time came on Sunday mornings as I followed along with the pastor.

I didn't think much of this until a phone call from Jillian one evening a couple of years ago in which she enthused about a "thread" she'd noticed across several verses in the Old and New Testament. "That's nice" seemed an ill response, but given that I was writing a brief, I said it anyway to move us along, certain that couldn't be her reason for calling.

I learned it was when she continued, asking if I happened to have noticed it as well, as though we'd chat about it. I said, "No, I haven't." Had I read the verses? "Not really." Then the clincher: "Do you *have* a Bible you read regularly?"

"What kind of question is that?" I asked.

"What do you mean, 'What kind of question is that?'"

"Just what I said."

"It's not that complex, Treva. I'm just asking if you have a Bible that you read, your own personal Bible."

"Of course I have one."

"What kind?"

"What do you mean?"

"Study Bible, devotional Bible, life application Bible, NIV, NASB, New Living, King James...."

"I have to look."

That was all Jillian needed. My younger sister took me on as her personal project. For my birthday that year, she bought a big, black genuine leather Bible and asked from time to time if I'd had a chance to read any of it. "A little but not in depth," I would say, which was true. I had skimmed some of the notes. Then last Christmas, she gave me another Bible, a prettier one in a different translation. "You might enjoy this better," she said.

I did like the look. I like all new books, the freshness of the pages, the promise they hold. I get lost in books, even academic books. That was my favorite part of school, getting the books and leafing through. That was my strength: school. No one could take that from me. I competed head-to-head and came out on top every time. Algebra and calculus, chemistry and biology, English literature, French, it didn't matter. If I could read it, I could understand it.

The Bible is different. The day I got the one with the pretty font, pastel colors, and devotions for women, a few days before Christmas, I sat down with it, drawn to the warm layout and graphics. But as I flipped through the pages and pages and pages, I wondered what the goal was. Read the whole thing from beginning to end, over 2000 pages? Start in the middle and not have a clue what's going on? I did look at the Gospels as Jillian suggested but frankly didn't have a clue there either. Not really.

I read the words of one chapter and got a feel, but nothing of the deep meaning I supposed was there. I was staring at a mountain, without the wherewithal or the time or even the desire to climb it. And the case law I needed to digest for a brief due two days before Christmas was within reach. I closed the Bible, put it between bookends on my nightstand, and when Jillian asked if I'd had a chance to read it, I gave the same answer: "A little but not in depth."

This must be Plan C. Jillian is taking matters into her own hands.

Not that Jillian is lying. She probably did think of having a Bible study long ago, knowing her, but at this point, with me back in town, I'll bet I'm her primary motivation. I touch the pool wall as if complying with an Olympic rule, turn, and begin my last lap. Whatever. Let Jillian do her thing. Things could be worse than having a sister who wants me to read the Bible. If Jillian has time to worry about my spiritual life, so be it. I'll focus on reclaiming the part of my life that brought a measure of ascendancy and respect—the part with the elder parking attendant who always smiled with admiration and once quipped, "Not many of you in this building"; the woman at the building's gourmet coffee stand who knew I wanted a mocha with skim and whip and prepared it before I reached the front of the line; the secretary who made my work a priority and cranked out briefs, copies, tabbed binders, and Bates-stamped exhibits with speedy efficiency; and the security guards, clerks, and bailiffs at the federal court who knew me by name and extended special courtesies because they were proud of a black woman coming to sit in counsel's chair wearing a power suit and carrying a power briefcase, clicking heels with authority down the hallowed linoleum halls.

I hoist myself up and sit on the tiled edge of the pool, bones tingly from the laps, invigorated. Kicking my feet in the water, I allow myself hope. I won't be depressed about today, awful as the rejections were. It's Monday, the week's before me. By Friday I could be in a dream interview. All I need is one "yes." Why wouldn't God want to bless me with the kind of life I had before?

I head to the house to give myself time to take a shower and do my hair before I have to pick the girls up from school, more life in my step than before the swim. He'll bless me. He will. He knows my well-being depends on it.

Chapter Five

"Mommy, where did you put my overnight bag?" Faith yells down the stairs.

I walk to the foot of the stairs in the kitchen. "It's in Joy's room. All of you can put your things in one bag. You're only staying tonight." I begin clearing away the dishes from the girls' after-school snack.

"They're welcome to stay two nights, you know. I would love to have my grandbabies as long as I can," my mother-in-law, Darlene, beams.

"I know, Ma, and we appreciate you taking care of the girls but we'll pick them up tomorrow so we can get to Grace Bible Fellowship on Sunday morning. Their worship programs for kids and the youth start at nine and the girls have really enjoyed the last two Sundays."

"That's Jillian's church?"

"Mm-hmm, we're thinking about joining."

"I like their pastor. I went there a couple of times years ago when they were much smaller, over there in Landover Hills at the time. They've got a huge complex now."

"I like the pastor too. I've even thought about his sermons on the ride home, which is new for me. Our last church had an interim pastor for the longest time and I couldn't get into him. I'd either fall asleep or start planning the next week."

"You *could* come visit my church, you know."

"No offense, Ma, but we want a kids' program. Hezekiah said folk in your church want the kids to sit in the pew for two or three hours and not make a peep."

Darlene lets out a hearty laugh. "I know you're right. Long as you're plugged in somewhere good, that's all that matters." Darlene hops off the bar stool and looks around. "A week and a half ago you had boxes everywhere. It didn't take you long to get this place together. You've done a good job."

"Thanks, Ma. You know me; I can't stand clutter."

"Have you gotten used to being back yet?"

I give her a look.

"Trust me, baby, God has nothing but good planned for you."

"That's what they say."

Joy dashes into the kitchen with a big box. "Grandma, can I bring my puzzle? Mommy said to ask since it's a thousand pieces. Can we work on it together? Please?"

"Sure, sweetheart. If we don't finish, we'll just leave it till next time. I've got some books for you all at the house too."

"Joy, tell Faith and Hope to come on. Don't keep Grandma waiting all day."

Darlene waves me away. "Chile, I'm fine."

"By the way, Ma, I need to make an appointment to bring Faith by the salon for a touch-up. Might bring Hope too. She needs to have her hair relaxed."

"Don't you bring that baby. I will not do her hair, nor will I let anybody at the shop do her hair. I told you to wait until she's at least eight. Now, you could take her someplace else. I certainly can't stop you."

Darlene knows I would never take her anywhere else around here. She's one perk to being back. My mother-in-law can do hair. "But, Ma, do you realize what I go through each and every time I do that girl's hair? You never had a little girl. I should bring Hope by your house every week so you can wash and comb that thick hair and hear her scream out of control. After two weeks you'd slap some relaxer on there."

"You ain't talking about nothing I don't know. I've been doing hair for more than thirty years. I've done every type of hair of every age. And I still say, not before she's eight. Should wait longer than that to tell you the truth."

"No, ma'am. She'll be there on the *day* she turns eight."

Darlene shakes her head at me.

"Is that my favorite mother's car blocking my side of the driveway?" Hezekiah's voice bellows through the garage door as all three girls walk into the kitchen.

"Daddy!" Joy and Hope race into his arms and climb up on his waist. Faith is by his side too, deep in the bear hug. When he's able to break free, he smothers Darlene with a playful squeeze. At five-foot-two, her small frame is hidden for a moment.

"Boy, go on now," Darlene says with pride.

"Daddy, we're going to Grandma's. Look," Hope says, pointing to the big sack.

"I know," he says with a wink, curling an arm around me. "Whose idea do you think it was?"

He called this morning from work with a romance plan, glad to finally have family nearby to enlist for support. I couldn't feign enough excitement to match his. After five business days of not one phone call from one employer, I am not up for romance.

"Okay, girls." Darlene claps her hands. "Let's take this show on the road." Darlene grabs my hand and whispers, "Daughter of mine, take advantage of this time. I know you haven't been happy but this is your *husband*. Nothing and nobody but God himself is more important."

"I hear you," I say. And I do. With me, the disconnect comes in the doing.

Hezekiah dismissed me from the lower level so he could bring the food from the car and prepare the meal. He's the chef in the family, apprenticed in the school of Darlene Langston. I cook, sort of, but not nearly as well or as often. Hezekiah had dinner on the table most week-nights, which the family always ate together; that is, the four of them. I often didn't make it home in time from work. He has an endless reper-toire of menu items, some he has fixed for years, others he downloads on a whim. I don't know what he has going down there now but it sure smells good.

And I *feel* good. Fresh from a whirlpool bath with the lights out and candles blazing, falling in and out of sleep as the jets pulsated against my skin, my mind is tranquil. I didn't think about much of anything for the first time in a long time.

Now I am enjoying our bedroom, remembering why we designed windows on three walls. Streams of light pour in from the early evening sun, a beautiful gold against the bronze and black of the bedding. I am luxuriating, sitting on the bed with legs outstretched, slathering on Channel No. 19 body lotion. Then, since Hezekiah hinted I might need it, I slip into the bikini I wear only for him, and on top of that, a silk, deep red tropical print sarong skirt with matching tank. Taking Darlene's words to heart, I want to look good for my husband.

After makeup, deep red polish on my toes, sling-back sandals on my feet, and a check in the mirror, I poke my head out the door. "Can I come down now?" No response. "Hez, I said can I come down now?" Guess not. I turn to find something to fill a few more minutes as Hezekiah strolls in with a red rose and a kiss, takes my arm in his, and escorts me down the stairs.

"Did you forget we're staying in tonight?" Hezekiah says.

"No," I say, looking into his eyes.

"You made yourself up this fine just for me?"

"Don't act like it's a first."

"Second?"

I bump Hezekiah down a stair then extend my arm again.

He kisses me. "You look great, babe."

"Thank you, babe."

Hezekiah leads me to the dining room, pulls out a chair, and seats me at a table transformed by red and cream-colored roses, red and cream candles in candelabras of varying shapes and heights, and two elegant place settings side by side.

"We didn't have these candles. Where did you get these?"

"Ahhh, see, I've got a few things up my sleeve."

Hezekiah pushes my chair in and disappears. I am smiling from ear to ear. *He's the best thing that ever happened to you.* He really is, though I didn't think so in the beginning.

Hezekiah taught the small group section of Probability and Statistics while a graduate student and, as a business major, I sat in his class faithfully every week during the fall of my junior year. I had no interest in him at all, apart from what he could tell me about higher mathematics. His light skin and wavy hair were a turnoff, reminding me of the guys I knew growing up who never had more than those two words for me. Hezekiah was no different—a smile and small talk for others, a somber nod for me. Fifty minutes, three days a week, for three and a half months, and I'd be through with him.

But the day after the final exam I got a call on the hall phone of my dorm, a familiar voice I couldn't place summoning me to the lobby. I stepped from the elevator and saw him, the graduate assistant, leaning against the front desk. He didn't speak but pulled me into a quiet corner, his touch compounding my confusion.

"Treva, I don't know of any other way to say this than straight out since I'm here and potentially making a fool of myself. I've been looking at you for three months. You're beautiful, you're intelligent, and I want to get to know you. It's against policy to date a student so, to be safe, I had to bend over backward to ignore you until now. How about one meal before you go home for break? Or we could take a walk since it's kind of nice out. Whatever you say."

A meal sounded good. I was hungry, through with exams, and ready to unwind. Mostly though, I was intrigued and, of course, flattered. This man had found out where I stayed and taken action. I had had a couple of men interested in me on campus, even dated awhile, but those were acquaintances first, people who, I assumed, came to like something about my personality. I'd never been targeted or called *beautiful*. My mind flashed through weeks of class, picturing myself in the outfits I'd worn, now that I knew he'd been watching. Patsy had done one thing for me for which I was thankful— amassed tons of nice clothes. And she expected them to be worn, not for special outings but as a daily regimen. I still remember what I had on for Hezekiah's impromptu visit—a royal blue cardigan paired with a matching sleeveless turtleneck and black wool slacks. I was ready. Curiosity spoke for me: "All right. I haven't had dinner. How about What's Your Beef?"

We walked to the Student Union and into the only eating place with a wait staff. I ate there alone sometimes for lunch and had come to know Gabriella, the hostess. She showed us to a quaint table for two and jabbed me privately in the ribs, grinning her approval. Suddenly I didn't know why I was there. We were mismatched, and he wasn't my type anyway. I had trained my heart not to skip a beat for his kind, in fact, to *reject* his kind. Yet I knew others would think he was handsome. What was I doing in their seat? And why didn't he see the disparity?

"For the lady of the house, a special appetizer sure to please. Maryland crab cakes with jumbo lump crab, no filler, no shell." With tongs Hezekiah lifts a plump crab cake from an oblong serving dish and places it, sizzling, on the small plate within a plate in front of me, then puts one on his own.

I stretch my neck to peer into the serving dish. "Sir, I'll take two."

"This isn't the main meal, you know."

"I worked out today."

I savor the second addition to my plate, put the cream cloth napkin in my lap, and poise my fork.

"Father in heaven—"

I lower my head and fork quietly to the table.

"—I thank You for my wife and for this opportunity to spend time with her, loving her. Bless our time together, Lord. And please bless the food. I want it to taste real good to her. It's a special night, Lord. We thank you in Jesus' name. Amen."

That surprised me about Hezekiah that first night at What's Your Beef. We had returned from the salad buffet and he'd asked, "Do you mind if I pray?" I thought he'd shoot up a cursory prayer and be done, but he seemed to be talking to God, thanking Him for the meal and for my agreeing to come. I didn't comment. I wasn't sure what was up with him. Was it for show? Was he a nut?

I'm not quiet by nature but learned at a young age to sit back and observe. I did that at dinner, trying to find something wrong with Hezekiah. I hoped he'd be arrogant or shallow. Uninteresting. Strange in whatever way I deemed it. But he was animated, mannerly, and more open about his life than I was with mine. He was also well-read, which got me animated when I had to challenge inclusion of two books on his top-five Great Books list. And he was funny, so funny I didn't realize I'd gone from a demure chuckle to an unrestrained, belly laugh until he said, "Look at those dimples! I didn't see you smile once in class." That was our evening. Carefree and fun. Intellectually stimulating. Engaging.

But not promising.

People held no promise, save for Jillian. Education, yes. A career that told the world I was somebody, yes. Not people. Not Hezekiah. Much as I enjoyed his company, I invested no hope in it, even decided against telling Jillian about him over Christmas break, knowing she would have grown hopeful for me.

But in the spring semester he didn't go away. Every call, every visit, every chorus of laughter knocked against my inner fortress, until the weight of it broke one day before his very eyes.

"And now for the pièce de résistance," Hezekiah announces. He rounds the corner with two oversized, deep, wide-rimmed dishes piled with linguine and jumbo shrimp and sets them on the table with obvious pleasure.

"Hezekiah, I can't believe this! Crab cakes, lobster Caesar, and now this. These are my favorites!" Fresh seafood was a definite plus to being back on the coast.

"What a coincidence!" Hezekiah leans down and kisses me on the cheek. "You know I love you. Gotta hook you up sometimes." He sits down, leg grazing mine.

"Hez, this is so good," I say, mouth full, talking into the fork. Two forkfuls later, a shrimp convicts me. I devour it, sigh ruefully. "Hez, you are so good to me, you really are. And I've given you so much grief lately. I know it's not your fault things have worked out the way they have."

"Was there an apology in there somewhere?"

"I said it."

Hezekiah leans over, cups the back of his ear.

"I'm sorry, okay."

"Accepted. I don't want to dwell on it another second. I'd much rather focus on other things." Hezekiah reaches under the table, pulls my thigh closer, and kisses me. "If you hurry up and eat, I'll give you a massage in the Jacuzzi."

I give him a pout. "No seconds?"

Stuffed, Hezekiah and I lie under a canopy of stars out back on an oversized beach blanket on the grass, still eating, now fresh strawberries and New York-style cheesecake, the only thing he didn't have time to make himself. The blanket is wet from our Jacuzzi-soaked bodies; the thought didn't occur to either of us to dry off. We were lost in one another, enjoying a rhythm I hadn't allowed us to experience the entire two weeks we've been here. The dessert was my idea, as well as who should get it. My eyes didn't leave his body until he crossed the threshold to the kitchen. Hezekiah is as fit as he was when I met him.

"Your turtle cheesecake tastes better than this, babe," I say.

"You're hanging with it, though."

"Mm-hmm." I lick the last of the creamy cheesecake from my fork and smile wide. "I believe I have shown full appreciation for each and every thing you've served tonight." I plant a kiss on his lips and lay the back of my head on his chest, thinking. "Hez, being back here in Maryland, spending this night with you, I can't help but think about when we were dating on campus. Do you remember that day at the Dairy?"

Hezekiah strokes my hair. "Do I remember? I'll never forget. That day changed everything for me. You opening up like that...." I shift to see Hezekiah's face. He's deep in thought. "I knew that day I wanted to marry you," he says, and I turn again in surprise. He continues stroking me. "I did. I wanted to take you and run off to a deserted island somewhere and start your life over, build you up the right way. I was so torn spiritually...." Hezekiah sighs. "You know, those were the hardest months of my life, figuring out what to do. I loved you so much and I just couldn't leave you.... I can't deny that I did what *I* wanted to do." He stops stroking and holds me. "I'm so thankful God is merciful and forgiving. Seemed like as soon as we got married, a new fire lit within me and I got closer to God than I had been before college. He's brought us a long way."

He holds me tighter and I place my arm around his waist, closing my eyes, remembering. That day at the Dairy definitely changed the nature of our relationship.

The Dairy sold homemade ice cream on campus and Hezekiah and I walked there often that spring semester. One afternoon we sat in a booth enjoying our cones, talking about nothing in particular, when he made me anxious with a stare and said, "You are so beautiful."

Something deep inside shook. Tears moved faster than I could contain them. I tried using the cone as a shield, looking down at it, licking, but when I saw the trembling of the hand that held it I threw the cone down on the table, smearing it with double chocolate dip, and shoved my arms around myself.

Hezekiah stared differently now. "What's wrong?"

Now Jillian, that's a beautiful child.

"Why are we here, Hezekiah? Why am I here?"

His brows furrowed. "What?"

"Why do we spend all this time together? I see the way women look at you, then look at me. You could have your pick of any number of women on campus. Why aren't you with them?"

"Treva, I don't see anybody looking at us. I don't know what you're talking about, and I'm with you because I want to be, and I thought you enjoyed being around me."

"I do...."

"But...."

I talked to the air, refusing his eyes. "These last few months have taken me way past where I wanted to be. I did not want to get to the point where I looked forward to you, just you, no matter what we were doing. The sane part of me screamed it was an illusion, that at any moment I would find out you're not real. That moment just arrived. Congratulations."

He flung open his arms. "What did I do?"

"Saying I'm beautiful. Is that how you get what you want?"

"I have what I want right now, Treva, spending time with you."

I met his gaze. "Fine, if you sincerely like spending time with me, then you need to be honest. The first day you came to my dorm, you said I was beautiful. The flattery was nice, got you a date. We're beyond that now, I guess we could say we're friends. You don't need to lie to me. I don't like games."

"Treva, I'm not playing games with you." Hezekiah leaned in. "You are a *beautiful* woman. Why can't you see that?"

Treva, you weren't blessed with beauty, it's just a fact. Thank God you're smart.

Exasperated, I thrust my forearm on the table next to his. "Why can't *you* see *that?*"

Hezekiah shrugged and lifted his palms. "And?"

I rolled my eyes and looked away. "Stop pretending it doesn't matter that I'm dark."

"Your complexion is what makes you beautiful. That, your dreamy eyes, those cheekbones, and those dimples—when you choose to show them."

I scowled, plunked back in the booth, and tipped my head northward, away from Hezekiah's probing eyes. I had said too much and had not a clue what to say or do next. The gray dingy ceiling would be my focus—Hezekiah'd probably say that was beautiful too. He was either a liar or...or.... What if he did believe what he was saying? *Why* would he believe it? Why was Hezekiah so different? And he *was* different. That had been clear for some time. The praying. And the way he dated. He said good-byes in the lobby, never in my room. Never had been in my room. Never kissed me, not really, just a light peck on the mouth. I was already close to thinking he was weird. Now I had proof.

Hezekiah grabbed my hand and held it. "Tell me about you."

My stomach dropped at his words. "You already know me, Hezekiah." I pulled my hand back, embarrassed by the trembling, left my neck resting on the back of the seat cushion. Continued counting water spots on the ceiling.

"No, I don't. I know the surface you—what you like, what you're good at. I don't know *you.* I don't know anything about your life or what's in your heart, and apparently something's in there that's causing you to doubt me. We're not leaving until you tell me all about Treva Campbell. We are not leaving." He crossed his arms, sat back, and stared me down.

I sighed and cupped my face in my hands. How could I talk about things I didn't want to think about? I never *talked* about things. They happened, I shoved them down, then moved on. I had a hard enough time trying to keep a step ahead of the voices and images that comprised my life. Here he wanted me to turn around, meet them head-on. I could already feel the stress of his request gnawing at my insides. Why would I consent? Why even let him get that close?

I snuck my gaze downward to look at him and my heart leaped. He had captured it, despite my internal warnings. I didn't know where we were headed but I knew we couldn't go far if we kept on the surface. I had to allow us to go deeper. I crossed my legs, lightly scratched my scalp and arms, clasped my hands before me and looked at them. "You'll have to...." I cleared my throat and looked at him, slid my eyes back down. "You'll have to bear with me because I've never done this. I'm not even sure how to begin." A dismal laugh escaped, correcting me. "Of course I know where to begin. If you want to know about Treva Campbell, the story has to begin with Patsy Campbell."

I spoke for two hours to a silent audience, to gritted teeth, to eyes at times glazed with sadness, at times ablaze. Minutes into the telling I had somehow steeled myself and kept remarkably composed, clinical, going deep with facts and feelings, constraining emotion.

When I finished, his emotion bubbled forth. "I have never heard anything like this. Right there, in D.C.?" he said, pointing in that direction. I nodded. "Treva, I'm sorry; they're crazy! Can't you see how *wrong* they are?" I tilted my head slightly, noncommittally. Hezekiah groaned, propped his elbows on the table, and let his head fall into his hands. He rubbed his temples, lifted his head again. "I wish I could just take your mind and empty it of all that *junk* and replace it with truth. That's what it takes, God's truth."

Anxious flutters bunched. *Don't go there.*

He grabbed my hand, forced my gaze. "Treva, do you know God?"

The flutters rolled from the pit of my stomach to my chest, wild in flight. It was out. On the table. Hezekiah had dangled God's name in conversation now and then, more often than I cared to hear, but always in a fashion I could ignore. Why this? Why now? My gaze drifted downward. He had to sense my unease. *I've answered without answering: No.* He wants to hear me say it, to confirm. Then what? What will he do? How important was this question? I eased my hand away from his and rubbed the mounting chill on my arms. I hadn't thought this conversation could get any heavier or deeper, but he plunged us there with a simple yes or no query.

I exhaled, gathering myself. I'd spoken plainly about everything else, no need to pull back now. We both needed to know where the other stood on "God."

I decided to start off on as positive a note as I could. "Hezekiah, I do believe there's a God, and as I think about it, I don't know why because no one has ever told me about Him directly and I've never been to church—"

"You've *never* been to church, not even for a wedding or funeral?"

I shook my head. "But for whatever reason, I acknowledge that He's out there somewhere. It's safe to say, though, that I don't *know* Him."

A gleam entered his eye. "May I be the first to introduce you?"

I didn't say I hadn't been introduced. I've been introduced all right. Resisting the urge to shrug my indifference, I reasoned that his introduction would definitely be one I hadn't heard. It wouldn't kill me. I stilled my shoulders. "Sure, go ahead."

Hezekiah's entire being lit up. "Treva, God is...." He looked up, searching. "Man, I've never had to describe Him like this. He's *God*. He's the Creator of the Universe. Most High. He's the beginning and the end, the first and the last. He's all-powerful, all-knowing, all-wise, and yet, He's kind and loving and just and—What?"

"Nothing."

"Why did you roll your eyes?"

I sat up straighter. "You have to admit He's not that way toward everybody."

"Not what way?"

"Kind and loving and just."

Hezekiah's expression fell. "Why do you say that?"

I looked aside, then back to him, rubbing my arms again. "I told you how my mother and Grandma Vivian were. Seemed like every time they got together they were agonizing over me. Bemoaning the tragedy of it all. A glimpse of me was all it took to get them going, which was why I avoided them as much as I could. I remember when I was eight, I was looking for a book and found it in the kitchen. I dashed in and out because that's where they were, but what I heard just outside the kitchen froze me in place."

Hezekiah leaned forward, concern in his face. "What?"

"My mother said, 'You know, I've been wondering lately whether she's the one who's cursed or me.' I didn't even know what 'cursed' meant at the time but I knew it didn't sound good. I was glad Grandma Vivian asked what she meant. My mother said she was talking about the Bible, Genesis, where God cursed Ham. She said she remembered reading an article about it a long time ago, about why dark skin is a curse. Then she said, 'I'm just wondering who the curse is on. I always thought it was on the individual made dark, but now I don't know. I feel like it's on me, too, all the stuff I put up with. When will everybody stop whispering?' Grandma Vivian told her, 'Probably never. Just focus on your rainbow. That's in Genesis too. First you got the rain, then you got the rainbow—Jillian.'"

Hezekiah's jaw tightened. He rubbed his hands down his face. "Treva," he said, and I had never heard him speak with such intensity in one word. "That is *not* what the Bible says. And it's a lie that dark skin is a curse. I bet they've never even—"

My head shook with confidence. "It's not a lie, Hezekiah, no matter what the Bible says. You've never lived the life I've lived. It's certainly not a *blessing*. And for me, it was a double curse. I couldn't be dark in a family of dark individuals. I had to be the ugly duckling, the black sheep, the tragic anomaly in a world of light, thin, and straight. God dealt me the back end of life. And I decided a long time ago that I would do without Him, just as I had to do without other so-called important figures, like parents."

Hezekiah spent hours trying to refute my mindset, that day and beyond, to no avail. He so wanted me to believe, to make his decision easy. He admitted his dilemma. He grew up Christian, knowing he needed to marry a Christian woman, yet had fallen for me.

I was surprised, ditto his parents, about a year later when he proposed, but I understand now how he could make that decision. He had drifted from regular church attendance during college and graduate school, and though he studied his Bible, he had no accountability on campus. He was able to pursue our relationship unchecked. But something else informed his decision—he had made it his mission to change my life. He boldly told me so as he placed the ring on my finger. He would cause me to think differently about God and about myself; and he would lead me to Christ. These high goals were in his head when he turned his back on what he knew was right and married me.

I look at my husband now, asleep the minute he hit the bed. I wonder what length of time he anticipated for my turnaround. After all the praying he did, I'm sure he imagined that by now, fourteen years into the marriage, I'd be happily saved, loving God, and loving myself. But nothing is as romantic as we hope.

Life for me is never ideal.

I did get saved three years ago but I didn't get beamed up to heaven. I was looking for something close to that given all Hezekiah had described about new life in Christ. I had always thought that if I ever got to the point where deep in my heart I believed, the moment would be grand. It would be a *moment*. I would know a change had come. I would feel the burdens of my life lift and flap away. I would rejoice at their parting, wave wildly as they sailed into oblivion. I would feel joy and peace knock me down upon arrival, and I'd giggle as they filled me from head to toe. But in my *moment*, what I felt was sick and even more burdened over an awful exchange with my mother. Her words had been the very thing that propelled me, broken, to the feet of Christ. But because of those words, I couldn't bear the memory of that evening. I shoved it down with every other Patsy ordeal and moved on, and the salvation moment got buried with it. I couldn't even talk about it.

I'm sure that's not what Hezekiah had imagined.

I did feel differently about God, though. Like a shaft of light into a darkened cave, He was real. Not out there somewhere. Real. Around me. In me. I knew by the trembling of my soul. It had awakened. And as the days and weeks passed and I tried talking to Him, mostly in frustration, I sensed He was there, listening. I never sensed a response as Hezekiah does, but it was enough for me that He was listening because I had a lot to say. I wanted to know, if He truly hadn't cursed me as Hezekiah said, why it felt like a curse. And if He truly hadn't dealt me the back end of life, why did it feel like the back end. I wanted to know why my life had been robbed of joy, why even my salvation moment had been robbed of joy, why I had a heartless mother, why, why, why. It felt good talking to the One who understood. I didn't have to tell the story, didn't have to explain how I felt. He knew. Everything. I could cry without saying a word. He knew better than I which memory had broken through.

Those times with God were cathartic, but my sense of real victory came when I walked into the firm each day. I never got off the elevator on my office floor, though I could have used a passkey at a side entrance. I entered through the main floor with the grand staircase. A thrill shot through me every time as I inhaled power, money, and success. My back always straightened, my head lifted, my hand smoothed the suit that looked the part. I was ready for the day, mind set to dig in. I relished the hard work and the long hours that so many of my fellow associates complained about. They were stepping-stones; the harder and longer I worked, the higher I would climb.

Or so I thought.

Sighing, I hop out of bed, slip on my robe, and knot the silk belt. *Lord, I've spent a lot of time asking questions and being satisfied with no response. I don't know how You go about it but I want answers. I need answers.* I nestle my feet in furry slippers and pad down the hallway. *I need to know why, once again, I am staring at the back end. The one thing that did give me joy—my career—is gone. Why must my life be so utterly filled with disappointment? What exactly is new life in Christ and why am I not enjoying it?*

I'm stopped at the top of the stairs by the arrival of my next question. *Why am I not enjoying You?*

Walking slowly down the back stairs that lead into the kitchen, the question rattles in my mind. Was it even *my* question? I've never thought about whether I'm enjoying God. How does one *enjoy* God? My thoughts scamper immediately to Hezekiah and Jillian, who always seem enthused about their relationship with God, always pumped up about what He's teaching them, what He's done, prayers He's answered. A wave of sadness comes over me. I guess I'm on the back end of that too.

I stand in the dark with my eyes closed and hold myself at the bottom of the stairs, this new thought coursing through my being. Such an amazing thought. *Enjoying God.* I see crazy thoughts now, me dancing in the moonlight, arms raised in a waltz with a partner I can't see, swaying with the breeze, laughing, not a care in the world. Tears roll as I watch. I clutch my chest. I do want that. I want to enjoy God, not just know Him but get lost in Him. I want to feel a tight closeness. I want to love and trust Him with all that is in me. That has to be what Hezekiah imagined and prayed for me from the beginning, not a relationship but a *relationship*.

Amazing things don't happen for you, Treva.

I open my eyes with a start and flick on the lights. Moving to find a tissue, I move myself also to reality. I doubt I'll ever have a tight closeness with God, at least not on this side of heaven. There's too much in the way, too many questions He can't answer. Like, *Why would You create a child others will call ugly? How is that love?* I look up and cry aloud, "How is that love, God? How am I supposed to fully trust You, *enjoy* You, when You did that to me? *You* did that."

I look about me for the first time. Hezekiah cooked his heart out and he has the mess to prove it. Shrimp, lobster, and egg shells are scattered in a sink of dirty dishes, congealed oil in the deep fryer, a thick white ring around the inside of the pasta pot, which he didn't bother to soak, spices without lids, and spills on the counter and floor, from what I can see at first glance. Hezekiah told me we'd tackle it in the morning but a midnight clean will do me good.

I need to linger in this romantic evening Hezekiah fashioned for me, be happy in the little things. I don't know why he ever imagined the moon for me. Not for me. It wasn't meant for me.

Chapter Six

"Treva...Treva." Hezekiah shakes my arm and I turn toward his voice, eyes clamped shut. "Your mother's on the phone."

"What time is it?" I ask, yawning.

"Ten o'clock."

"What?" I bolt up in bed, wild-eyed, inserting myself into the morning. "Why didn't you wake me up?"

"I *am* waking you up."

"I mean earlier. I hate sleeping this late. I *never* sleep this late." I cannot believe I stayed up until.... When did I go to bed? Washing dishes inspired dusting the display shelves in the kitchen, which required moving every item off the shelf. And since I had rag in hand, I dusted the living room furniture too, then the entire downstairs, including the curio cabinet and each item inside. Of course, dusting produced a grubby floor, so I swept, canvassed around for something else to do, glimpsed an alarming hour on the clock—around four—and forced myself to bed.

"Do you want to talk to her?"

Of course not. I sigh loudly and rub my eyes as they roll. I need more awake time before dealing with Patsy. I am curious though. Neither of us has called the other in more than three years. "What does she want?"

"She didn't say."

I purse my lips. "All right," I say, easing out of bed as Hezekiah leaves the room. Clearing my throat of sleep, I reach over, pick up the bedroom cordless from the nightstand, and press the button. "Hello."

"Treva, did you get my message last night?"

"No."

"I called at eight-thirty and left a message."

Jacuzzi hour. "I haven't had a chance to check. We were busy last night."

"Well, I thought you might like to know that I've arranged for you to interview with Brooks Donnelly." I fly out of bed and press the phone closer to my ear. "I understand you've been amassing rejections and I took it upon myself to call Theodore Dutton. He's on the executive committee there; your father mentored him when Theodore was just a first-year associate. Wonderful fellow. He will see you Monday morning at nine o'clock. Also, he said to fax your resume. He'll be there all weekend."

"Am I meeting with him alone or with others as well?" While I am exploding with enthusiasm, I sound sedate. I know I said I didn't want to be beholden to her, but that was when I had a modicum of hope that I could find something on my own. Pride has been cast to the wind.

"He didn't say."

"Well. I appreciate this. You certainly didn't have to do it."

"Apparently I did. You seem to have hit rock bottom. When you need help you should humble yourself and ask."

Elation flows too wildly within me to retort. That's Patsy's way, with me at least—offer help in one breath, slay you for needing it in the next. We both know she isn't offering assistance out of the goodness of her heart anyway. She needs at least one of her daughters on an upwardly mobile path. She'd be mortified if the only report she could give of Jillian and me is that we are both jobless and living in Prince George's County. That just wouldn't do. "Like I said, I appreciate it."

"You must let me know what happens."

Only if the news is favorable. "Okay."

"Girl, if you don't sit still, you're going to get it."

Hope's back is arched, bottom out of the chair, comb dangling from a tangled mass. "Mommy, it hurts! I don't like this!"

"Sit down. Now."

"No, Mommy. It hurts when you use the comb."

"How else will we get the tangles out? If I don't comb it, it'll get worse. Is that what you want?"

"Yes."

"Hope Renee, if you make me late...." Hand to Hope's shoulder, I forcibly seat her. Taking a section of hair, I begin detangling, a journey that will take me from the scalp to the middle of her back. One inch later, she howls again and grabs my hand.

"Stop! It hurts!"

This is ridiculous. I have less than thirty minutes to finish Hope's hair so she can get to school and I can get downtown. I am not even dressed. And the little time we have is being wasted with these antics. I haven't done one braid.

Hezekiah should have known better, letting the girls get in the pool last evening. It was incredibly warm and I had dashed to the grocery store to satisfy everyone's taste for strawberry ice cream. When I returned, all four of them were frolicking in the pool with their heads *under* the water. I could have screamed.

Well, I did.

"Who's going to wash and comb these heads tonight?" I yelled across the water. "I need to prepare for my interview."

"Oh, Mom!" they said collectively, including Hezekiah, who added, "It'll be too cold to get in the pool before you know it. We want to enjoy it as long as we can."

Thankfully, Faith has learned to wash, blow dry, and style her own hair. I washed the other two and thought I could quickly style Joy's, sit Hope in front of videos, and work away. But when Joy's was done, Hope had fallen asleep, and I knew better than to tug and pull on her head while she slept—one tug too many and I'd arouse a bear. Hope is sweet as can be in every instance but two—when she's awakened and when she's getting her hair done. I combined both once, never since.

"Ouch! You're *hurting* me. Don't use the comb. Please!"

"Mommy," Joy says, peeping her head in the bedroom door, "Daddy said he'll be ready to take us in fifteen minutes."

Great. *Lord, why, why, why? Why do we have to go through this every time? Why can't it be easier? Did you have to make her hair this hard to comb? Please let me get this over with and get out of here.*

I had the same thought as a little girl each time my mother sat me down to do my hair. It wasn't fair. Jillian's head didn't jerk violently at hair-combing time. No screaming. No crying. And hers didn't take forever to do. I would sit in that torture chair for hours it seemed, while Jillian went about her business. I remember the day I realized that hair was part of the curse too.

Hope's entire face is lined with desperation, her eyebrows curved downward in fury. "Are we almost done?"

I stare into the tightly coiled mountain on her head. "Yes," I say. With deft hands, I draw all the hair to the crown, brush the front, back, and sides, wrap a thick scrunchie around it, and let it flop every which way. So what if tangles abound underneath. I've had it.

If I could roll down the window and shout "Hallelujah" without drawing attention to myself, I would do it. I would yell away the frustration and declare a turnaround. Hey, why not. I push the button and watch the window disappear. "This is it!" I say at the top of my lungs. "This is the day things change!"

I am so excited I don't care about the stop-and-go traffic. I like it, actually. I like being behind the wheel in early morning with a purpose to the day, headed downtown. I am in my element. Back in the groove. If things go as expected, I will sit in this gridlock each and every morning and not complain, thankful I am not sitting at home. I promise.

I rest my head on the leather cushion and tap my fingers on the armrest to the rosy beat in my spirit. *God, I just know this is my blessing. You made me wait, Lord, but that's all right. I appreciate it that much more. And You did it through my mother! You do work in mysterious ways.*

My fingers shift from tapping to snapping and a song leaps to mind, one perfect for my mood. When traffic stalls again, I flip open the armrest, rifle through CDs, and draw out Maurette Brown Clark, my dorm mate at Maryland. Sliding it in, I raise my hand at the first line: *I can feel the breaking of day....* I shout "Amen" and bob my head when Maurette sings, *My blessing's got to be on the way.*

Minutes later, on New York Avenue, the beat within stops and I decrease the volume of the CD, overcome. I knew where I was going but until I got to this point, I hadn't thought about the space I'd have to travel through. Emotional space.

Approaching the North Capitol intersection, I stare safely ahead until, almost through, my eyes dart right, drawing a mental map to my child-hood home, where Patsy resides still. Such a beautiful place, tucked inside the tranquility of Rock Creek Park. I had a favorite window, in Daddy's upstairs study, from which I could see nothing but treetop clus-ters and chirping birds. I would sit in there with a book when I could, when Daddy wasn't working, and read or stare out. Taking flight.

When last I was there, three years ago, that study was the scene of our ugly confrontation.

Forcing my thoughts from that end of the District, I snatch a sheet of paper from the passenger seat and confirm Brooks Donnell... *the* then check the dashboard clock. Eight-thir... town in good time, just a few mo...

music back up and watch the landscape brighten before my eyes, from McDonald's cups and paper bags kicked street side to pristine landmarks I came to appreciate only after moving away.

Turning on Pennsylvania, I spy the building at a distance, white and imposing. Brooks Donnelly occupies the entire fourteen floors, the result of a recent strategic move from Connecticut Avenue. I read about it last year in *The American Lawyer,* how they negotiated a favorable lease in a tenants' market during a real estate slump and revamped their staid image with the help of a trendy design firm. *The American Lawyer* crossed my desk every month at my old firm and I always took time to flip through it, imagining myself among the profiles of lawyers who had accomplished some feat worthy of ink. The women, always perched on the edge of an oversized, gleaming desk, legs crossed and arms folded, had brokered a multimillion-dollar deal or won a sophisticated court case. I saw myself mailing a copy to Patsy with a sticky note on my featured page and a scribbled victory message: "See, I made it despite you."

I spot the side street I need, whip right, and pull into the parking garage, heart thumping. *Oh, let this be a daily routine.* Will I come to know this parking attendant too? Will I get my own parking spot? For now, I ease my SUV into a visitor space, grab my briefcase, and head to the elevator, checking the time again. Eight-fifty. Perfect.

In the building lobby a young, portly security guard eyes me. "Can I help you?" he says, lips barely parting.

I hear Patsy's voice in my head—*"may," not "can."* "Yes. I have an appointment with Theodore Dutton. Treva Langston."

The man lifts a phone, repeats my name, and nods me over to the bank of elevators, mumbling, "Main reception is on '2.'"

I wonder if I'll have the pleasure of his daily acquaintance. "Thanks. Have a great day," I say cheerfully.

The elevator bolts to the second floor and as the doors part, I try not ~~rk~~. Warm, natural rays pour from the top floor by a giant light pipe ~~central atrium. To my left, a plasma screen television streams headlines from CNN in closed caption. And to the far left gleams a glass-walled law library. I head right, to the reception desk, itself something to behold. The woman behind it seems a mere appendage to her surroundings: a convex station with a thick slab top of marble, front panels cloaked in toffee leather, and a hefty stainless steel base. Behind her looms a high, concave granite wall with Brooks Donnelly emblazoned in classy lettering. I thought my old office's design was impressive. Now it seems dark and stodgy.

"Good morning, Ms. Langston. One moment, please," the receptionist says, then lowers her voice to answer an incoming call with headphones. She is a middle-aged woman with a severe bun and kind eyes, fingers flying across a computer keyboard set beneath a pane of glass in her desktop. Done with the message, she looks up. "Thank you for waiting, Ms. Langston. Mr. Dutton will be right with you. Would you like coffee, tea, water? We have soda too."

I would love a cup of coffee. I had time for one cup before I left the house and two is my norm. But I can just see myself crossing legs in agony, dying to go to the bathroom but afraid to stop the flow of the interview. "No, thank you."

The receptionist gestures behind the marbled petition. "Please have a seat and make yourself comfortable."

As I walk away, I take in more of the surroundings, fluffing the back of my hair, which Darlene squeezed me in to do at the end of her day Saturday. I wish now that I had asked for directions to the restroom to freshen my makeup and double-check my appearance. I button my black suit jacket and consider the effect, then unbutton it again to show my silk blouse.

Leather sofas and upholstered chairs of unusual custom design are clustered in various seating arrangements. I choose the cluster closest to the lobby corridor. Not a minute later, I hear a quick stride across the lobby, and a man appears before me. I jump up and level my belongings on my shoulder.

"Treva, Theodore Dutton, it's nice to meet you," he says with a firm shake. He is somewhat tall and slender, wearing crisply tailored navy slacks and suspenders, no jacket. I had pictured someone with graying hair but his is jet black all over. Probably a rinse.

"Mr. Dutton, nice to meet you as well. Thank you for agreeing to see me."

"My pleasure. When Patsy told me your situation, I wanted to see what, if anything, we could do. And you must call me Theodore."

I shudder at what "situation" Patsy may have told him, not wanting to look desperate. But who am I kidding? I am desperate. And whatever Patsy said, it worked, because I'm here. I smile and say, "Thank you, Theodore."

"Tell you what," Theodore says, motioning me forward, "let me show you around the place. We've had quite a few changes since your father was here." Then, over his shoulder, "Quite shocking, Charles's passing."

Theodore strides to a conference room a stone's throw from the lobby and I follow behind. "Yes, unbelievable the way it happened."

My father died working. A woman pushing a vacuum into his office found him slumped over the desk and called the ambulance. He'd had a heart attack and was pronounced dead at the hospital.

That it happened, given my father's apparent good health, shocked me, but not where it happened. Daddy lived at work. As a child, I knew he'd be gone before breakfast and home well after dinner. When he did get home, he'd eat and continue working into the night, stopping at our bedtime for quick conversation: How's school? Working hard? Everything fine?

He didn't break for weekends, often working until late afternoon, part of that time spent with clients on the golf course in nice weather. Patsy made sure he carved out Friday or Saturday nights, sometimes both, for entertaining. If he needed his tux, she had it cleaned and hung on the closet door, next to her fresh Saks garment bag. They were both very comfortable in their social circle. Daddy wasn't the back-slapping, gregarious type but could work a crowd with his quiet charm and instant name recall, and, as I learned later, much of his legal business was cultivated at these gatherings. But even so, he didn't live for them, not like Patsy.

I liked Sunday evenings when we'd sit in the dining room, all four of us, and Daddy would quiz Jillian and me on current events, ask what books we'd read, and delve more deeply into our studies. He was a serious man, but his presence was calming and dominant. When he was home and really *present,* Patsy softened. So it seemed anyway. She showed more patience with me and treated Jillian and me more evenly, never allowing Daddy to hear her sharp tongue. If only he had been around more.

"He certainly is missed," Theodore says, standing in the center of the two-story conference room. He gestures proudly. "This renovation was near to my heart. I helmed the committee that worked with the general contractor and the interior design firm. We had definite goals in mind for the image we wanted this office to project, and I believe we achieved it. This is the largest of our conferencing facilities. Accommodates more than one hundred people." Theodore gleefully pushes a button and panels spring open. "Plasma screens for conferences, built-in ceiling-mounted projectors, and those walls convert to frosted glass for privacy."

He shows me the moot courtroom, the library, artwork throughout, a café with stunning views of the city, and his favorite, the cappuccino bar. We sit now in his corner office, with me engaged happily in a recitation of my litigation experience and its benefit to Brooks Donnelly's practice.

"Treva I'm very impressed, frankly would have expected no less from Charles's daughter." Theodore clasps his hands in front of him. "As you may know, Treva, the legal community is in the midst of a hiccup. Happens every so often, and we're certainly not panicking. Yet, in these times the executive committee favors austerity in hiring."

God, no. Don't let him close the door. Please.

"That said," Theodore continues, standing to his feet, "I will go to bat for you, Treva, and not just because of Charles. You would be an asset here, and I believe the head of litigation would agree. This is what I'll do. The executive committee is meeting on Friday. Once I secure approval for a litigation hire, we'll bring you in to meet the litigation partners. I think they'd love to have you on board."

Beaming, I stand and shake Theodore's outstretched hand. "Theodore, I appreciate your support. Having met you and heard so much from you about the firm, I'm even more enthusiastic about this opportunity."

I stop by the cappuccino bar on the way out and get a cup of coffee, wave good-bye to the receptionist as I hop on the elevator, and chirp "Have a nice day" to the grumpy building attendant. This place is feeling like home already.

Chapter Seven

"Shoot." The doorbell is ringing and I still have a million things to do. I dash the sugar into its bowl, pour half-and-half into the creamer, peek in the oven, and whirl around frantically to see what else I can do in the space of five seconds.

Ding-dong-dong-ding.

"One minute!"

Please be Jillian. I hasten to the door and open it, sighing relief. "Girl, you've got me hopping this morning. It's almost ten o'clock and I still haven't gotten everything ready," I say, hustling back to the kitchen.

"What 'everything?'" Jillian calls after me. "Treva, I hope you didn't think you had to...Girrrrl!" Jillian's eyes catch the center island. "Look at these flowers! They're beautiful," she says, sniffing red, purple, and yellow petals. "And fresh fruit? Is this a crystal bowl?" Jillian gazes beyond the island. "And what are the place settings for?"

"The quiche."

"Are you serious? For us? I would have been thrilled just to see fresh coffee brewing. If I had known you were laying out a feast I would have come by even earlier to help. You know you didn't have to do all this."

"True. I also didn't have to play hostess to this thing," I say, sliding a bubbly quiche lorraine out of the oven, "but once I agreed, you know I'd never let it be said that I didn't do it up right."

"These women aren't like that, Treva."

"Mm-hmm." They're probably *just* like that. Critical. Judgmental. People get on my nerves. "Anyway, I didn't do as much as it seems. Darlene made the quiche and coffee cake last night and brought them over early this morning for me to warm."

Jillian chuckles. "Oh, don't worry. I wasn't confused. The day you whip up a quiche will be an awesome day indeed."

I laugh with her. "So is the number the same? Four are coming?"

Jillian drops her purse and tote bag by a seat at the table. "Right. Four. I had asked three others but for one reason or another they backed out." Jillian shrugs. "It's fine. This is the group God intended."

I set the quiche on a square black trivet in the center of the rectangular glass top, silent. I told Jillian not to plan on my presence in the group. Today is strictly a favor. After this I'm done. She can occupy herself with contrary notions all she wants, and she'll only be disappointed. "Who's taking care of your kids?"

Jillian washes her hands and brings the coffee mugs from the counter to the table for me. "Mrs. Banks, the woman next door. We've known her for eight years now and she's such a blessing. She's agreed to come over every Friday morning while I go to Bible study. Plus, she's a retired teacher and said she could help the kids with their schoolwork."

"You've gotten to know your neighbors pretty well, haven't you?"

"I try to get out and walk," Jillian says, pouring piping hot coffee into the carafe. "I need the exercise and I meet a lot of people that way. That's how I met Monique, who's coming today. She lives around the corner and sometimes she walks with me in the evenings now."

The doorbell sounds.

"Is it ten o'clock already?" I snatch a wet cloth and start wiping the counters in vigorous circular motions.

"Five till. I'll get it."

I whisk crumbs into my hand and dump them into the sink, grab six dessert plates from the cabinet and put them beside the coffee cake, then grab the orange juice out of the refrigerator to pour—

"Treva, it's so good to see you!"

I stop, weighty jug dangling in hand. *I know it's not....* I turn. It is. Perky Carmen, strolling into my subdued earth-tone kitchen, smiling bright. Same Keds, with jean capris this time, hair down in a bouncy bob. "How are you, Carmen?" I say. She crosses the kitchen floor, and when it's clear she's going to hug me, I tense a bit. I'm not a hugger, not with people I don't know well, which means I rarely hug anyone outside of family. I fill the decanter with orange juice as she hugs my neck, my head leaned in toward her. "I'm great," she says.

"Treva, I forgot to tell you Carmen was coming," Jillian announces. "I couldn't believe it when she told me you two had met. I met Carmen at Grace Bible Fellowship a couple of years ago and we became fast friends."

"Jillian told me you've been coming to GBF. With all the people, I haven't seen you," Carmen says. "Oh, and I'm so sorry we haven't gotten together yet. I'll have to get your number before I leave."

I smile nicely and busy myself with the last-minute touches.

"Malcolm must be with your mother," Jillian says.

"He is, and you know this is Stacy's third week of kindergarten. She's so excited she doesn't know what to do. She was disappointed, though, when she and Hope were put in different classrooms."

I nod my head. "Hope was disappointed too." I neglect to add that Hope has been bugging me to get together with Stacy. I've been putting her off because it'll mean interaction with Carmen.

"I am so excited about this Bible study," Carmen says, perching herself on a bar stool. "I was thinking about it all week. It's going to be so awesome getting together with other women like this."

Jillian leans over the counter. "I know. I think it'll be awesome too."

I smile again, remembering my hostess role.

At the doorbell's ring, Jillian leaves and returns escorting two more women into the kitchen. I hate that time got away from me. I styled my hair and applied my makeup but hadn't yet dabbed on lip gloss. And I had decided to change from these linen pants to a V-neck sleeveless dress, thinking the others might be well-dressed, but I never made it upstairs. I scan the women. All are wearing blue jeans. Goodness, they all have on tennis shoes, too. I can live with my appearance.

"Treva, Carmen, let me introduce you," Jillian is saying, gathering us together. "This is Monique Wright, my neighbor, and Willow Fusell, who went to Maryland with me, after you left, Treva. And this," Jillian says, rocking a little one in her arms, "is Willow's very new baby, Zoe."

"Hold up," Monique says, pointing at Willow. "'Asked and Answered,' right? Willow. Yeah," she says, nodding at her discovery. "That *is* you. This is wild."

It sure is Willow, sickening-beautiful in a pair of faded Levi's, nary a hint of makeup, hair blow-dried stick straight, hitting her shoulder blades with perfect evenness all the way across. Younger than I am and already made a name for herself defending the wife of a Washington Wizards' basketball player who'd been arrested for murdering him. The wife hired Willow because they'd been childhood friends, but the press said she should have retained a more seasoned defense attorney. Willow had just left the D.C. public defender's office and joined a noted criminal defense firm, but she hadn't had any experience with high profile cases. The trial, broadcast on Court TV, proved the press wrong. In the end, they were praising Willow for her courtroom presence and for refuting police evidence that the husband had been asleep when his wife shot him. The jury believed it was self-defense and the wife went free. In no time, Willow was the new hip panelist on the popular nightly show, "Asked and Answered," spouting legal expertise on the latest publicized trials.

I feel myself shrivel before her. The successful career. The prominence. The pretty brown face worthy of bright lights and close-ups. I lower my eyes, panged anew over my bottomed-out existence.

"Girl, please," Willow says, waving away Monique's stare. "It's not a big deal. Believe me, there's more to life than being on television." Her hands clasp tightly together suddenly and she bows her head. "But thank You, God, for one viewer." Laughter spills out of her.

"Thank Him for two," Carmen says. "I try not to miss it."

"Same here," pipes in Jillian.

My stomach tightens when I keep silent, too morose to add a "Me too," knowing I even tape it on occasion.

"Seriously?" Willow says. "That's so cool! Thank you for the encouragement." Her eyes peruse the kitchen. "This is a fantastic house, Treva. Thanks for hosting us."

Great. Thoughtful, too. "Thanks, and you're welcome," I say.

"It's definitely a nice house," Monique adds, moving to inspect the copper-accented backsplash. "I was wondering, what do y'all do?"

"Excuse me?" My thoughts snap from Willow's charmed life versus my depressing one to the question I must not have heard right.

Monique leans over the counter to finish her inspection and turns around. "I mean, y'all got this mansion and all, I was wondering what you and your husband do."

My attention turns fully to Monique and her shoulder length curly-straight hair, her light, light skin, her sculpted red nails with a black design I can't make out on the tips, and her size 12 Hilfigers on a five-four frame. Nosy, uncouth self. Has she ever been taught protocol and proper decorum? Now I'm forced to either tell her to mind her business, nicely, or tell her what she wants to know, and given Willow's presence, I'd rather do the former. In fact it would be easier. But the please-be-gracious-and-go-with-the-flow look from Jillian is squeezing me the other way. I take in a breath and try my best to clear my face of irritation.

"Monique, this is nowhere near a mansion but to answer your question, I'm an attorney and my husband's a professor."

Monique takes this in, or it could be that she's taking *me* in since she's looking me up and down with a slow nod and nervy green eyes. She looks away without comment.

"I didn't know you were an attorney, Treva," Willow says.

I knew it. Here it comes.

Willow smiles. "Where do you work?"

I could strangle Monique. "Before we moved here, I was a litigation associate with Thompson & Klein for a number of years in Chicago—"

"You go, girl!" Willow says.

"—and right now I'm waiting to hear from Brooks Donnelly."

"That's a great firm as well," Willow says. "So why—"

The doorbell sounds and I cheer inside, not wanting her to ask why I'm not with Thompson & Klein's D.C. office. I step quickly away. "I'll get it this time."

"Why don't we take a seat at the beautiful table my sister prepared," Jillian says. I hear Carmen gushing over the spread as the group moves in that direction.

A heavy sigh escapes as I walk to the door. *Lord, why did I agree to this? I'm ready for them to leave already. Why am I even home right now? Please, Lord, let me hear from Theodore Dutton today.*

It's Friday, exactly one week from the day Brooks Donnelly's executive committee was supposed to have met. I hung by the phone all day last Friday, certain Theodore would call to schedule my return visit. Now I'm trying desperately not to fret. Meetings get pushed back. People leave town. Anything could be happening.

I open the door for the last expected lady. "Hi...um...Are you...here for the Bible study meeting?"

"Yes." The young woman's eyes move between the doormat and me. Her arms are folded around a Bible resting on an ample chest, much of it revealed in the black halter. Thin braids frame her cinnamon-colored face and drape her shoulders and waist, running past the touch of beige fabric that hugs her tiny hips. Spindly legs stand atop chunky platform shoes. She looks all of nineteen or twenty. Her slight voice adds, "I'm sorry I'm late."

"No, it's, it's okay. Come in."

I lead the woman into the kitchen and Jillian and Carmen jump up from the table. "Asia, you made it!" they say, hugging her close. Jillian introduces Asia to everyone and they take a seat.

"Shall we pray and get started?" Jillian says. Monique's and my eyes dart to Asia, who's head is already bowed. "Dear Lord," Jillian begins, "I have prayed for this day and I am so thankful to see it, to see moms from different walks of life come together to study Your Word—"

Moms? I sneak another curious peek at Asia.

"—I pray, Lord, that You would anoint our fellowship, lead us as we plan our study, and in all things, be glorified. Thank You for the host and for this wonderful meal. We ask that You bless it for the nourishment of our bodies, in Jesus' name. Amen."

The women look tentatively at me and I tell them to please help themselves. "That's all I needed to hear," Willow says, lifting a section of quiche from the ceramic dish. "I'm letting it be known right now that I'm having two pieces if there's enough, so if any of you want to call me greedy you can. I *love* quiche." She smiles and tickles Zoe's chin in the car seat beside her. "And I'm nursing so I have an excuse."

A faint smile sneaks up on the inside. I think I could like Willow if she weren't so perfect.

"This is delicious," Carmen says, eyes twinkling. "Everything, even the fruit. The strawberries and cantaloupe are so sweet."

"I'm glad you like it," I say.

"This is the best quiche I believe I've ever had," Willow says. "Is this homemade?"

I nod my head and ignore Jillian's eyes. It *is* homemade.

"Treva?" Asia says. "May I have a piece of coffee cake?"

"Sure," I say, passing the serving dish toward her, thoughts active. *Why in the world is this polite girl at a Bible study dressed like she's headed to a hip-hop video shoot?*

"From talking to each of you individually," Jillian says, lowering her fork, "it sounds like ten o'clock Friday mornings is a good time. Is that right?"

Everyone nods but me.

"Okay, let's plan on that," Jillian says.

"Jillian," Monique says, "where are we going to meet every week?"

"That's one of the things I wanted us to talk about," Jillian says.

"I think we should take turns," Monique says. "I might not have a mansion but I'm willing to host too."

My eyes narrow on Monique as she slides the quiche into her mouth and sucks down my orange juice.

"That's great, Monique," Jillian says. "Carmen and Willow said they're willing to host as well. You all know my kids are at home during the day so my house wouldn't work. But I think this will do just fine. We'll rotate among the four."

The *three*. I wonder why Asia's home wasn't included as a possibility.

Jillian reaches into a tote bag beside her chair and produces several books. "These are the Bible studies I told you all about. They're published by Line Upon Line Ministries and they lead you through an in-depth study of Scripture. We'll get the most out of this if we do our homework every week. That way, when we come together, we can discuss it and watch the teaching DVD. All we need to decide now is which book of the Bible we want to do so we can place an order. They've got a study on almost every one." Jillian passes out copies of the ministry's catalog.

"How about starting at the beginning, in Genesis?" Willow says, head buried in the catalog.

Monique sighs, pinching off a piece of coffee cake with her fingers and popping it in her mouth. "We've heard those stories since we were in pigtails in Sunday school. Can we do something different?"

"I hope we'll be going a bit deeper than we did as children," Willow says.

"Ooh, this sounds really good," Carmen says, turning the page of her catalog to face us. "They've got a study on Daniel."

"See, that's what I'm saying," Monique says "How many times do you need to hear about Daniel in the lions' den or Shadrach, Meschach and Abednego in the fiery furnace? I could tell you what happened if you want to know."

Willow lets loose a deep chuckle. "So you're a real trip, huh?" she says.

What was your first clue?

"I'm just saying, we already know Daniel," Monique says, shrugging her shoulders, pinching off more cake.

Carmen smiles. "Well, Monique, do you know the time period in Israel's history in which that book took place, why those four youths happened to be in Babylon, what God was revealing through Nebuchadnezzar's dreams and Daniel's visions, and what it means for the future of this world?"

My eyebrows raise at Carmen, head tilts to Monique.

"Why don't you write the study for us, since you know everything?" Monique's eyes lock with Carmen's.

Carmen smiles still, and it appears totally genuine. "All I know is there's a lot I *don't* know, Monique. That's why we're coming together, to learn."

"So what do you want to study, Miss Thing?" Willow says to Monique, a chuckle still in her voice.

Monique keeps her eyes fixed in front of her. "I don't know. I don't even know why I'm here."

Well, glad we have something in common.

Monique picks at the edge of her catalog. "I just came because Jillian invited me, and she's so nice and everything, and I wasn't doing much else since I don't work on Fridays. But I told her it probably wouldn't work for me. I don't get along real well with women and I say what's on my mind which gets me into trouble, so...."

Willow lifts a fussy Zoe from the car seat and lays her on her shoulder, patting her back. "Honey, I'll meet you where you're at because I speak my mind, too. Honesty goes a long way. If we can have that, we'll be all right."

Jillian grabs the back of Monique's hand and squeezes it. "Remember what we talked about, Monique. It doesn't matter how things have always been. It doesn't mean they'll stay that way, not with God in the mix. I've been praying a long time for Him to move in a special way with this group—and I'm just going to believe He'll do it, for each of us."

"Whoo!" Carmen yelps with a shoulder wiggle. "I'm even more excited now. And, Monique, we've all got *stuff*. That's what makes a group like this come alive. We can keep it inside or we can let it out and help one another. I say let it out, and your personality may be just what we need to get us there."

Monique's head nods slightly. She picks up her catalog for the first time and starts reading.

"So," Jillian says, "Genesis and Daniel are on the table and I'd be up for either one. I'll throw out another suggestion. The book of John."

"Really, Jillian?" Willow says. "I'm not trying to sound like Monique," she smiles Monique's way, "but at least three Bible studies I've been in over the years have done that book."

"Okay, you all," Jillian says in the affected teacher voice, "I know we can come to some agreement on what to study. Whatever it is, we can't go wrong."

"What about Ephesians?"

Catalogs bow as everyone looks in Asia's direction.

Asia has her Bible open with the booklet on top of it. "It says here that Ephesians teaches believers who they are and what they have in Christ. And look at this quote: 'It will change your life.' That's what I want. I want to know who I am in God's eyes. I want to know what being a believer is all about. And I definitely want some changes in my life."

My stomach drops and a shiver runs through me. I'd been thumbing through the catalog inattentively, but now I sit up and quietly turn to the Ephesians page.

"Praise God!" Jillian says. "Oh, Asia, we all need to know who we are."

"And who we're not," Willow says. "Ephesians is an awesome book, and it's been a long time since I've studied that one. I say we go for it."

"Ephesians has my vote," says Carmen.

The table turns to Monique.

"What? I'm down with it." Monique laughs. "I'm sure y'all do need to know who you are."

"She's baaack," Willow says.

"Treva?" Carmen says. "Is Ephesians all right with you?"

I look up from the page and at the women, desire swelling within me to do it. Wasn't I just pleading with God last week for answers? Isn't this what I wanted, to know what life in Christ is about? Wasn't I looking for a change? Maybe this study is just what I need.

Maybe. Partly. I don't know. It might not answer anything for me. It definitely wouldn't answer my deepest questions. And if things work out as Theodore predicted, I won't be available soon anyway. According to him, it's as good as done.

I tell them, "You know, I had already told Jillian I didn't think the study would work with my schedule. My commitment was really just to host this planning session. I'm sure you all will enjoy it, though. It sounds great." I lift cold coffee to my lips and gulp it down. Is this a *sadness* I'm feeling?

"Aww," Carmen says. "I thought you were doing it with us."

Jillian stares.

"I know," Willow says. "And I was just sitting here feeling like God had brought together the very six people He wanted for this group. It was just...I don't know...a feeling."

"Are you serious?" Jillian says. "I had the same feeling, that this was the group God intended. I told Treva before you all got here."

Willow cocks her head and pouts. "You're *sure* you can't do it? Is it because you think you'll be starting soon at Brooks Donnelly?"

Why is she questioning me? "That's part of it, yes."

"'Cause you could always start the study and if you have to bow out later, you bow out. Just take it one week at a time. I bet you'd still get something out of it. But I have to admit I'm being selfish. I was looking forward to getting to know Jillian's sister."

"I appreciate that, and I understand what you mean about taking it one week at a time, but...I think I'll just pass."

Jillian looks down at the papers in front of her. "Okay, well, let's talk about ordering the materials."

I excuse myself, head to the bathroom just off the kitchen, and park by the sink, staring at the light wood grain of the floor. This is ridiculous. Why do I feel like crying? What is *wrong* with me? I wish they would just leave. I want to own my own thoughts, not have Jillian's and Willow's buzzing around in my head. The world won't screech to a halt if there are five in the group instead of six, and I'm tired of hearing God's name invoked where I'm concerned. "Maryland is where God wants us." "This is the group God intended." "God brought six together." Everybody's a soothsayer. I wish Dutton would call right now and put Jillian and Willow out of business. I would love to announce that they were wrong, that God had nothing to do with their "feeling" about the group because God intended all along that I be occupied in a white building downtown at 10:00 A.M. on Friday mornings. And if things go the way *I* feel they will, that's where I'll be next Friday.

With the back of my hand, I sweep a lone tear off my cheek. I'll go back in and start clearing away the dishes. A few more minutes and cursory good-byes, and I'll be through with them. I'll be fine, as soon as they leave.

Chapter Eight

"Is it ready, Daddy?" Joy asks, sliding across the kitchen floor in her socks.

"Almost, Scootaboo." Hezekiah pours the last of the batter onto the griddle and lifts bacon from the skillet. "Got your words ready?"

"Yep."

Hope, entering just behind Joy, enthuses, "Me, too! You'll never, ever be able to spell mine, Daddy!"

"Think you'll stump me, huh? We'll just see about that."

I raise my head at the interruption, *The Washington Post* clutched in hand, then return to my article. Brooks Donnelly is embroiled in an international patent infringement dispute involving two powerhouse pharmaceutical companies. The article details the ramifications for the consumer; I want to know how to reference it intelligently when I meet with the litigation group.

Hope bounces over and tosses her face before mine. "Mommy, are you going to work?"

I grimace inside at the reminder, slightly lowering the paper. "No, sweetheart."

"Then why are you dressed up?"

"These are just slacks and a blouse."

"And heels, Mommy."

"I know, but I'm not going to work."

"Are you going *anywhere?*" Hope says.

I look back at the newspaper. "No plans yet."

"Good." She hugs me. "We can do fun stuff."

Fun stuff? I'm not in the mood for fun stuff. This is the first month of Saturday mornings I've spent at home in years and I'm about out of my mind. I was supposed to be in the office by eight, making great strides with the research or writing project at hand since the phone wouldn't ring and other weekly interruptions would have vanished. Saturdays were the best days in the office, productive days. Of course, then I didn't have time for fun stuff but it's not my nature anyway. I'm not into *fun*. Hope should know that by now. I'm not the one who jumps and rolls on the bed or dodges the ball or runs around the house playing tag. That's not my world. In my world, something else is always beckoning, something I need to be doing to further my career, or now, to resuscitate it. In this Brooks Donnelly waiting mode, I'm just trying to maintain my sanity. Fun would only irritate me.

"Breakfast is served," Hezekiah announces. "Wash up and get your plates."

"We already washed up, Daddy," both girls say, rushing to the food.

"You did not," Faith says, coming into the kitchen.

"We did. You didn't see us," Joy says.

"You two never wash up. Let me see if I smell soap." Faith grabs Joy's hand and Joy pulls it back.

"Told you," Faith says, grabbing a plate.

"Bleh!" Joy blurts, the lovely sound she makes when sticking out her tongue.

I sigh loudly, lifting my head. "Cut it. I can't even concentrate here. If Joy and Hope want to eat with filthy hands, it won't kill them."

"But Daddy said—" Faith says.

"I said cut it, Faith."

Hezekiah gives me an eye outside the view of the girls. I lower mine.

"Okay, Daddy, ready for my first one?" Hope asks, adjusting her little body in the kitchen table chair with her food.

"Ready," Hezekiah says, tucking whole wheat pancakes into his mouth.

Hope grins. "Hippopotamus."

"That's too easy," Joy says.

"Is not."

"Don't forget," Hezekiah says, "you have to say what it means. I don't have to spell it if you can't tell me what it means."

Hope wrinkles her brow. "It's an animal, Daddy."

"And what do we do if the word is an animal?"

"Tell something about the animal," Joy and Faith say.

"Oh, that's right," Hope says. "It…lives in water?"

"Okay, that's good, baby girl. Now," Hezekiah says slowly. "Let's see…h-i-p-p-o-p-o-t-a-m-u-s."

Hope throws her head back dramatically. "Ugh."

"My turn," Joy says, mouth full. She grabs her piece of paper off the table and looks at it.

Hezekiah touches my knee and says, "Aren't you going to eat, hon?"

I glance up briefly. "I will, when I'm finished reading the article." If I ever finish it. Now that the troops have descended on the kitchen, I certainly can't digest it. I'm having to read every other sentence twice and may as well have skipped the last couple of paragraphs on the foreign litigation. My mind couldn't focus at all. I'd rather steal away to a quiet place to fully grasp it all, but Hezekiah might balk, and I don't want to hear it. *Why not eat with the family? You're home; why not be present?* That's what he said last week, same time, when I spent Saturday morning in the office reading from a pile of published cases litigated by Brooks Donnelly that I had found online and printed. I rolled my eyes at him.

He should know better than anyone how I'm wired, how much I need to keep my hands stirring the pot.

"I'm waiting, Joy," Hezekiah says.

"I know, I wrote down five words and I'm trying to figure out which one is the hardest." Joy beams, a single front tooth missing. "Okay, Mediterranean."

Hezekiah stares blankly at her.

"There's no definition, Daddy. It's a sea."

"Since you say there's no definition, give me two countries that border the Mediterranean," Hezekiah says.

Joy draws a map in the air for guidance, then points up. "Italy and Greece."

"Good job! But I'm sorry to have to tell you this," Hezekiah says. "M-e-d-i-t-e-r-r-a-n-e-a-n."

Joy groans.

"Looks like no one will stump me today."

"I will," Faith says, whipping out her list. "Perspicacious: shrewd or discerning."

"Good word, Faith...but not good enough. P-e-r-s-p-i-c-a-t-i-o-u-s."

"Wrong," Faith sings with delight.

"That *is* right."

"Wrong, babe," I say, rising, folding the paper. I lay it on the corner of the counter; I'll read it again after breakfast. The food suddenly smells good and I stack three pancakes on a plate and drizzle syrup on top.

"I suppose you know the *correct* spelling, Mrs. Langston?" Hezekiah says.

"Sure do. P-e-r-s-p-i-c-a-c-i-o-u-s."

Faith leans in toward me as I sit, a glint in her eye. "Bet you won't get my next one."

"Bring it on, baby girl," I say, sliding an unconcerned fork into my mouth.

"Onomatopoeia: when a word is named for the sound it makes."

"O-n-o-m-a-t-o-p-o-e-i-a."

"That's right, Mom!" Faith stands to high-five me across the table.

"Mommy, if *you* played, we'd never win," Hope says.

Hezekiah frowns at her. "I beg your pardon."

I chuckle. "You all didn't know I was the spelling champion in school, did you?"

Faith gives me a curious look. "Mom, where did you go to school? I know Daddy grew up in Largo and went to Largo High. In fact, we drove by and went inside the other day. But I don't know where you went. And did you live in the District the whole time you were growing up or did you live somewhere else at some point?"

I give the information requested and as they move on in conversation, I lag behind, unsettled, swimming in the exchange. Was I not sharing basic information, as if with a new acquaintance, and not my oldest daughter of almost thirteen years?

The scraping of a chair against the tile jars me from my thoughts. "What are we doing today?" Joy asks, getting up for seconds.

Hezekiah looks at me, then at the girls. "I don't know. What would you all like to do?"

"Something fun," Hope says awkwardly, head bobbing back and forth with a piece of bacon dangling from her mouth.

"Hope, stop playing with your food and eat it," I say.

She smashes the entire piece in her mouth and says, "Can we? Can we do something fun?"

"Sure. What do you have in mind?" Hezekiah asks.

"It's warm; we could go swimming out back," Hope says.

"Hey, we haven't been to Six Flags yet, and it's not even far from us," Faith says.

"Yeah, and they have a water park too," Joy says.

Hope jumps up and flings her arms around Hezekiah's neck. "Ooh, can we? Can we, Daddy?"

"Sounds like an awesome plan to me," Hezekiah says, always up for theme parks, water parks, carnivals, fairs, anyplace he can be a big kid. "Let's do it. I had wanted to go while it was still warm. Today's perfect."

I'm ahead of them, rapidly formulating a response.

"Mommy, are you coming?" Joy asks.

I just don't know which one to use. I hate crowds, and a Saturday amusement park crowd is the worst kind. I hate the whole idea of water parks, sloshing around in what has surely been contaminated by the hundreds of people who sloshed there an hour before, some of whom haven't bathed, probably the very ones passing rude discharges into the water. *"I've got work to do"* has lost its punch now that I have no fixed deadlines, but it's true. I do have work. I could be notified today of a Monday morning interview at Brooks Donnelly and I haven't gotten through that pile of published decisions. I've got to prepare. *"I don't feel like it"* sounds terribly grouchy in light of their exuberance, but it rings with the most truth.

I look into waiting faces. "I'm really not feeling too well."

Hezekiah's gaze falls to the table.

"What's wrong, Mommy?" Joy asks.

"I'm just...feeling a general malaise." Of the soul. "I think I'll sit this one out. I know you all will have a great time, though."

"What's 'malaise,' Mommy?" Hope asks.

"It's when you feel a little icky inside," Hezekiah says, rising and grabbing Hope from the table, lifting her into the air.

"Whoa!"

"I want a turn!" Joy says, jumping up.

Hope's legs fly as he swings her around, then Joy. Winded, he sets Joy down and says, "All right, let's get ready. How about we go to the amusement park first, get on as many of the scariest rides as we can, then go over to the water park?"

"Yeah!" the girls say, scrambling up the stairs.

I lift appreciative eyes to Hezekiah for easing me out of that moment, but I'm guilted by what I see in his. A faint sadness, covered by a weak smile. I know he wanted me to go. A nudge flits through my stomach. I should change my mind. We'll be gone only a few hours.

In the hot sun. Long lines. Get home tired and drained. Day shot. As it is, my evening will be spent washing and combing hair. Day *and* evening shot.

It's just an amusement park. Not like I'm missing high school graduation.

I watch Hezekiah walk over, bend, and kiss me on the forehead. "Hope you feel better," he says.

He takes the steps one at a time, no spring.

My eyes follow him until he's halfway up, then I stand, pour another cup of coffee, grab the newspaper article, and walk with both to the office.

Chapter Nine

The garage door closes behind me and my eyes zoom immediately to the upright handset on the desk area in the kitchen. No blinking light. No messages. I walk to the desk, plop my purse down, toss the keys in the side pocket, and bow my head, hands clasped over my nose. I don't know why I do this to myself. On the ride home, after dropping the girls off at school, I saw Theodore Dutton drinking his morning cappuccino, handling his administrative tasks first thing, one of which would include me. Whatever the holdup had been, it had finally cleared. He could make the call. I saw myself listening to his invitation to meet the litigation team *today*, darting up the stairs, slipping into the navy blue single-breasted suit that's facing outward on a hook in my closet, and heading downtown. My heart raced during the entire drive, leaped as I slid the key into the lock. I just knew good news awaited.

I lower my hands and look at the phone again. Nothing.

Now what?

I stare absentmindedly around the kitchen. It's Thursday already, another week drawing to a close, almost two weeks since I should have heard from Dutton. It's getting harder to fill the minutes and hours of waiting, of expectancy, of ever-mounting depression. I wouldn't dare go anywhere. I'm tied to the phone. Heart skips whenever it rings. And when it doesn't. It skips when my old office sails through my mind, or just about any aspect of firm life. It skips a couple of beats when I think it all might be gone forever.

I release a long sigh and rest my eyes on the morning paper atop the counter. I'll start my day there, with a second cup of coffee, then do what I always do—head to the computer to read the umpteen windows I've left open, all related to Brooks Donnelly. My online searches have moved beyond cases litigated by the D.C. office to cases litigated firm wide, and articles written by or about the firm's attorneys. By the time I sit down with these people, I might be more of an expert on Brooks Donnelly's global affairs than they are.

I dump into the sink the old coffee grounds from the pot Hezekiah and I shared earlier this morning and measure out more, pour in water, and push to brew. The aroma floats straightway throughout the kitchen and enlivens me somewhat as I flip through the paper and pull out the business section, pitching it onto the table. I stand waiting for the carafe to fill, leafing through yesterday's mail, and I see them—big block letters peeking up at me from under the pile. I pull the binder out and face the words head-on. "Ephesians: an In-depth Bible Study." And under them, in smaller but still prominent type, that promise: "It Will Change Your Life."

Jillian rang my doorbell late in the day Monday, car running in the drive. "In case you change your mind," she said, and passed the binder into my hand. She smiled, her eyes dancing mischievously, and jumped back into the car. I stood in the doorway feeling as if something beyond what was happening was happening. I had said no and felt good about it once the women left. By Monday it was a thing of the past. Why was it in my hand? Why were my insides fluttering?

I shook my head and closed the door. Jillian, that was why. No need to think deeply about it. She just couldn't leave it alone. I flung the binder on the desk, sure again of my decision. Sure as well, since it was Monday, that I'd be employed by the end of the week, closing the subject for good.

Here it is again in my hand. I guess it comes with a flutter. I flick through the endless sheets of notes and questions and white space meant for my answers and toss the binder back onto the pile, turning to pour my coffee. I'm glad I said no. It's way too much. By the look of it, one assignment could take hours, the first hour just plodding through the introduction and instructions.

I take a careful sip of hot java as I ease into my seat. Unfolding the business news with a snap, I scan the headlines, cross my legs, flip to page two, uncross, cross the other way, skim page three, bend over slightly...*How do I stop this stupid fluttering?* A million butterflies must have been loosed to twitter and dip and execute flying free falls from my rib cage to the pit of my stomach, all to make me uneasy or drive me batty, or both. I know it's about that study and I just don't get it. I do *not* have to do it. I don't *want* to do it. "Leave me alone!"

Stunned, I cut my eyes aside. Did I just yell out, in my kitchen, here by myself? Who am I talking to?

Clarity descends instantaneously, and my eyes cut upward this time. *Okay, Lord, I did say I wanted answers but is this what You do? You send butterflies? Are You trying to tell me to do the study? Because it just won't work, Lord. For one thing, it starts tomorrow. Do You know how much work I'd have to do between now and then? A whole week's worth would take the entire day. Plus, what if Theodore Dutton calls this afternoon or tomorrow morning, or even next week—please don't let it be next week, Lord—but what then? What's the point of starting if I'll have to quit so soon? Plus, plus, Lord, those women. You know I can't be around them. Carmen is too happy, Willow's too together, Asia—she obviously has issues—and Monique, Lord, I'd end up choking her. I don't like being around people anyway. You know that. I've been disappointed too many times, and a small group setting like this is a recipe for disaster.*

I'm not doing this study, Lord. It's just not...worth it.

I stare into the coffee, stirred by my own thought. *It's not worth it.* I guess I've stumbled to the heart of the matter: I don't believe the study will do what it promises. I don't believe it will change my life.

The butterflies still, my entire being seems to still, as I sense the heart of the matter unfolding further.

You don't believe the Bible can change your life.

I fall back in my chair, eyes wide, dumbfounded. What is God telling me? *Is this God?* It sounds like my voice, in my head, but these are not my thoughts. It has never even occurred to me to ask the question, yet here's the answer—no, the charge—staring me in the face. I turn it over in my head. *Do I believe the Bible can change my life?* I know I *believe*. I'm a *believer.* I believe Jesus died for me and rose again. Believing is how I was saved. But this strikes me as a different "believe." Sounds like the question is whether I think the Bible can do what I thought my salvation moment would do—take this life of mine that's been plagued from day one, give it wings, and send it flying off to cloud nine. No. I know better now than to believe that. If I did I would read it, daily perhaps, like Hezekiah, Jillian, and even Faith. Faith said she doesn't even want to ride the bus to school because it goes hither and yon before it reaches the building, a waste of time she says, time she'd rather spend in her Bible in the mornings.

Maybe I'm afraid to believe again for big changes, afraid of what will happen *after* I believe. I would open those pages, longing to know God better. Longing to discover what I've been missing in this new life in Christ. Longing to finally meet that joy unspeakable and peace that passes understanding that I thought would embrace me long before. Longing to find what God thinks of me. Me. I would need to see *me* on the page, to know that He really does consider me special, that I'm not just a blip on His universal screen. I'd long for all of these things, only to grow more disillusioned. I wouldn't get the kind of insights about God and self that Jillian gets; I wouldn't come away, as Hezekiah does, riding high on the mercy, love, or grace that jumped from the pages into his heart. Like everything else, I'd come up short.

The fear steps boldly from the shadows of my mind to plain view. I see it. I even feel it now, a foreboding, warning me away from extravagant hope. *Don't do it, Treva. Don't look for cloud nine. That kind of hope isn't for you, not in this life. It's the hand you were dealt, the cross you must bear.*

Your blessings will come later, in glory. If you hope for more now, and He fails you, you'll be totally devastated.

Sadness grips me and my head falls into my hands. *Well, thanks, God. I was fine when I wasn't thinking about the Bible. I would have been better off reading my newspaper. I prayed for answers, not a painstaking view of the problem. Not a close-up of my fears. Why did You bring me down this road? So I could be depressed about my working life and my spiritual life? So I could meditate more precisely on my woes? What am I supposed to do now?*

I get an answer, and it sits me up straight.

Believe.

My heart beats faster and I look around the room, uncertain still about this two-way communication deal. *Did You just tell me to believe, Lord? Because a few minutes ago You told me I don't believe. If I don't believe one minute, how can I believe the next? I can't just do it. It's not something I can turn off and on, Lord.*

I sit for a moment, waiting for God to explain Himself. What I really want is for His voice to fill the room, to be sure He's speaking to me, to know exactly what He's saying. But there's nothing, only the last little word ringing in my ears. *Believe.* Still, I can tell that one word is at work already inside of me. My back straightens and my heart is thumping wildly, ready to respond. I push back in my chair, pondering "believe" as my feet carry me up the stairs, commanding my next move. I know where I'm going and what I have to do—but that's just it. It seems I *have* to do it, like it or not. Everything in me is rushing to do it, declaring a mutiny and throwing my mind with its fears overboard.

From among the other books between bookends on my nightstand, my hand lifts the second Bible Jillian gave me and in moments I'm in the kitchen again, at the table, with the Bible and that fat binder somehow before me. The flutters don't awaken this time. Probably moved on to torment somebody else. Their job here is done. All is quiet and peaceful on the inside, all but my mind of course. It's flailing in the deep, grasping for that sermon about Peter, who, if memory serves, was not shoved overboard but went willingly. What did Jesus do when he was going under? Didn't He help Peter back into the boat?

He said, "You of little faith, why did you doubt?"

I stare curiously at the ceiling, wondering if I remembered or if God remembered it for me. Silenced, I sigh as my hand flips the binder open. I'm sure of one thing. This study *will* change my life and either send me soaring or drown me in despair.

I turn to Week One and read a bolded section of words at the top of the page. "The most important part of each study session is prayer," it says. "This is God's Word, and the goal is not to determine what it means to *you*. The goal is to determine what it means. Pray that God's Spirit will guide you into all truth, and that you will gain insight with understanding." I drink in the words, surprisingly awed. Closing my eyes, I pray the model prayer exactly.

My brows knit at what follows in the notes. Why did I not realize that Ephesians were people, people living in a city called Ephesus, and that Ephesus is in modern-day Turkey? And why did I not know that this book is actually a letter written to them by the apostle Paul? I pause for a moment, that small discovery jelling in my mind, then begin flipping through the New Testament. So Romans is a letter written to believers in Rome, First and Second Corinthians are letters to believers in Corinth, Galatians to believers in Galatia, Philippians to believers in Philippi, and so on. Duh! Am I a complete dunce? What did I think they were? I shake my head at myself. I didn't think anything, didn't think about them at all. *Treva, you've got to be the only believer in the whole world who didn't know this.*

Next it says to do a background study on the apostle Paul, and I find myself turning right away to the verses given in Acts and Galatians because I don't know much about him either, other than what his title conveys, and that he's mentioned a lot in church. I also read verses in Acts about Ephesus and how the people there worshiped the goddess Artemis. The notes add more to the history of this city, including the prostitution, magic, and sorcery that pervaded the place, to give us a flavor of what the believers were dealing with, and why certain truths needed to be addressed in the letter written to them.

Done with the background, my heart leaps a bit as I turn to Ephesians, ready to begin. I position the Bible in front of me just so, angle my writing paper to the side of it, pen on top. Binder on the other side. Ready.

Wait. I turn back to the instructions in the binder to remind myself what I'm supposed to be looking for as I read. I scan with my finger—who, what, when, where, why, and how, comparisons and contrasts, causes and effects, lists, places, time indicators…. Okay. We're also supposed to mark key words in the text using colored pencils. This, it says, will magnify essential truths, especially when the key words are repeated throughout a chapter or entire book.

Jillian does this, but she was always into highlighters and such. She marked up so many lines in her schoolbooks I didn't know how she could decipher what was important from what wasn't. I never needed that kind of visual prop. And from the sample sheet provided in these instructions, it looks way too complicated. Some words are colored over, some have pictures drawn over them, squiggly lines, arrows. I won't bother. The fact that I'm doing the study at all is more than enough for me.

I take a breath. Okay. I wonder if I should say the prayer again, now that I'm starting the actual book. I flip back in the notes to remember it and bow my head as I recite it. Okay. Chapter one.

Verse one, so far so good—Paul, an apostle, to the saints at Ephesus. Hey, I actually get that. Verse two, "Grace to you and peace from God our Father and the Lord Jesus Christ." Straightforward greeting. No problem. I continue into the body of the letter. Hmmm…Not sure I understand this part…I kind of understand this sentence…I really don't understand this one…Coffee's cold…I don't even know what this word means…Phone!

I jump up and view the caller ID. "Unknown," just as calls made from my former firm use to say. I know it's Theodore Dutton. I clear my throat and grab it. "Hello."

"Mrs. Langston?"

His assistant. "Yes?"

"We understand you've just moved to the area and we'd like to welcome you and let you know that we've got great deals right now on long-distance phone service—"

I slam the phone down, a second later feeling a touch of remorse, but only a touch. They shouldn't be pestering folk anyway.

Situated again, I gaze at the page, not sure where I left off, words running together in a jumble as my mind romps once more with Brooks Donnelly. The words had started running together anyway, words I'd have no trouble absorbing in a legal context—intention, administration, inheritance, purpose, pledge—but in a spiritual context, I'm struggling, feeling like an unseasoned grammar student. I know I could look up explanations in the commentaries Hezekiah has amassed, but the notes caution against this. Initially, we're to spend time reading and observing the text, patiently, prayerfully, noting the things we've been told to look for. "This will heighten the joy of discovery," it claims. "You'll be surprised at what the Spirit of God will lead you to understand." All I've discovered thus far is how clueless I am.

May as well start over, and slow down. And try harder to focus. After I warm up my coffee.

I get up, warm the coffee, and hold the mug to my lips as I take in the verses once more. After a few, I narrow my eyes and look more closely. I get excited when I see a pattern. By verse ten, I'm changing my mind, eager to test the theory. I jump up and walk over to the cabinet where the girls keep their art supplies and pull out a container of colored pencils. Yellow seems fitting so I take it, run my eyes back up to verse three, and color "in Christ." I go through the chapter and color every "in

Christ" and "in Him," and one "through Jesus Christ." It pops. I like it. And its begging to be made into one of those lists the notes talk about.

I look over what I've colored in, title my page, and make my list, underlining the key words. I notice my hand trembling as I write.

What Believers Have in Christ:

1) blessed with every spiritual blessing in the heavenly places *in Christ*

2) He chose us *in Him* before the foundation of the world

3) He predestined us to adoption as sons *through Jesus Christ*

4) *in Him* we have redemption through His blood

5) *in Him* also we have obtained an inheritance

6) sealed *in Him* with the Holy Spirit of promise

I stare long at this list, trying to get under it, trying to step into it. *I've* been blessed by God, chosen by God, predestined by God, adopted by God, redeemed by God, given an inheritance by God, and sealed by His Spirit. *Me.* Am I not seeing *me* on the page as I had hoped? In the far reaches of my being screams an awareness that I should be running around the house, shouting hallelujah, stomping every care and fear I've ever known deep into the earth because it says here that *God* has done these things for *me.*

But I stare, sinking instead of rising because the words are still there, on the page, not in my being where I need them. How do I get them there? It would certainly help if I understood exactly what they mean for my life.

As I ponder this, I'm reminded that the group meets tomorrow to discuss these very verses, to listen to teaching on these very verses.

And I remind my reminder that I have nowhere near committed to actually attending the group.

I get a feeling of control with that, and throw my leg up over the side of the boat, fighting to hoist myself back in, back in control. I heard them say the next meeting would be at Monique's. That's the last place I plan to go tomorrow.

Chapter Ten

The chirping startles me and my eyes leave the road for a second to find it. When traffic slows, I slam hard on the brake, return my gaze to where it ought to be, and use a hand to grope around in my purse for the cell phone that's never in its cell phone pocket. I hardly ever get a call on it now. I'd forgotten I even turned it on.

I flip it open, quickly see who it is, and my posture corrects itself immediately. I don't have to guess how she got the number. "Hello."

"Treva, I'm glad I caught you," Patsy says.

"Mother, I'm driving, and I prefer not to talk—"

"This will only take a minute," she says. "I expected you to call me after your visit to Brooks Donnelly. Do you have a start date?"

My eyes flit across the fleeing landscape, rolling so hard they hurt. I can't stand her snippy tone or the reminder of what I don't have. "Not yet. The process is still ongoing."

"Process?" Patsy spits. "I arranged for you to meet with the chair of the executive committee of that firm, the firm for which your father made millions. You should have bypassed the *process.*"

This had not occurred to me. I had been happy just to be *in* a process, not concerned with bypassing one. Patsy has a point, a troubling one. Was this unusual, given the circumstances? Was there something about me or my experience that gave Theodore pause? I thought my time with him had gone well; he seemed delighted with me. But something very well might be wrong. That man had to have enough clout to bring me on board forthwith. Even if he did need committee approval, it wouldn't take two weeks. I faint inside as the little hope I had seeps out of my being.

"Treva, did you hear me? What are you doing?"

"I'm *driving*." I can feel stress rising like spurs on my back, doubly nerve-racking since I can't drive, talk, and scratch. "Mother, I really have to go. The connection is not very good anyway. I will let you know when I know something."

"Yes, call as soon as you hear."

I close the phone, toss it in the passenger seat, turn into my neighborhood with the security gate that's never secure, make it to my garage, and sit. I can't do this. I can't walk through that door, see a phone with no blinking light, see a full day with no agenda, see a life with no life. I rest my forehead on the steering wheel and close my eyes. Moments later my head springs up. Is my phone ringing?

I snatch the key from the ignition, pull on the door handle which won't budge, jab the unlock button and yank on it again, fumble with my house key in the lock as I count the rings, and lose a mule as I stumble over Hezekiah's tennis shoe at the door and rush across the room to make the save. I punch the button quickly and speak, a calm professional tone belying the scramble.

"Hey, did Mama call you?"

Closing my eyes, I take two good seconds now to catch my breath. "I can't believe this."

"What?"

"I just broke my neck to get to this phone."

"For me? Thanks!"

"Jillian, I am not at all in a joking mood. And yes, Mother called, and I'm not in the mood to talk about her either."

"Good, we're on the same page then, because I didn't call to joke or talk about Mama. I called to see if you're coming to Monique's."

I eye the phone suspiciously, wondering if Jillian was camped outside my kitchen window yesterday, watching me. "Why would I be coming to Monique's?"

"I just hoped…you know…maybe you had gone ahead and started the study." A pause. "Did you?"

I want so badly to lie. I hate to have her think her ploy at the door worked. Collapsing in a chair at the table, I say, "I did some of Week One but I didn't get a lot out of it."

"That first chapter is jam-packed, isn't it? I had to make a list to help me understand what was there."

"Really?" I say, eyeing the patio door now, tempted to investigate how easy it would be to unlock the front gate and make one's way around to the back. "I actually ended up making a list, too." To her gasp of enthusiasm, I add, "But I can't say it helped much."

"Treva, I'm telling you, you'll be blessed if you come. I've got the facilitator's guide and the DVD and I previewed the lesson last night. Dr. Mason Lyles does the teaching himself. He founded Line Upon Line Ministries as an outgrowth of his church, to teach people how to study the Bible and live in the light of what they learn. Girl, he tells it like it is. He doesn't even have an audience before him, but all he apparently needs is the Word to charge him up. That man stays on fire.

"Anyway, Dr. Lyles breaks down chapter one in such a way that you get this glorious view of what God has done for you. Then, without snatching your pedestal out from under you, he lets you know in that Dr. Lyles' way—Buuut, it's not really about you. It's about God, and His glory. And he breaks that down, too. Girl, it's awesome. I hadn't even noticed how many times the chapter said it was all for God's glory until Dr. Lyles brought it out.

"But Treva, on top of all that, before we even get to the DVD, there's a special lesson we're supposed to do in the group. And that's going to be awesome too. You've got to come."

Of course the butterflies are back, not as wild, but active enough to do a couple of free falls in favor of going. I had already thought about it, right after I dropped off the girls and again as I sat in the garage. Just the bare thought that I could go. I didn't mind the thought because I didn't have to do anything with it. I didn't have Monique's address and certainly wouldn't call Jillian to get it.

But now she's made the call, forcing me to deal with that bare thought that I could go. I glance around at what I would do if I were to stay home—read the newspaper and read articles online while waiting for the phone to ring. Jillian's invitation sounds a bit more inviting, for today, as a way to kill time.

I look down at myself. What should I wear?

"Jillian, I've got about an hour to think about it. Why don't you give me the address just in case?"

I drive slowly past Jillian's house, round the bend, and find Monique's, parking just across the street. It has a red brick and beige aluminum front, like Jillian's. The lawn, neatly cut, is a crazy quilt of small brown patches. A beige Toyota Camry sits atop the driveway, a Mercedes SUV behind it.

I let the engine purr a moment, wondering if anyone has seen me from the window, the fact that I'm here a sudden mystery. What was I thinking? I was crazy to leave home when Theodore might call. What if he wants me to come into the office today? What if he leaves a message and departs for the weekend? I would lose it if I have to endure another weekend of not knowing simply because I missed the timing of his call. I'll ask Jillian for the notes.

I shift the car into drive and hear, "Hey, Neighbor! You came!"

Carmen rolls past, window down, smiling, and parks in front of me. Jumping out, she walks to my side of the car and leans over. "If I had known you were coming, we could have carpooled."

Right.

I grit my teeth and smile, hard as it is, throwing the car back into park. "Hi, Carmen." No use trying to leave now. "Let me get my things."

"It's a beautiful day, isn't it?" she says, her eyes to the heavens as I step out.

"Mm-hmm," I say.

Carmen stretches out an arm to hug me and then chats about nothing all the way to the door. When our host opens it, she crosses the threshold first, saying, "Hey, Monique. It's so good to see you again." A hug follows, Carmen's doing, making my hello awkward. Well, more awkward. It was already awkward because I was reminded when Monique opened the door that I really don't like her. I'm sure it has something to do with the fact that she started off on the wrong foot two minutes inside my house, only to prove herself consistent as the morning progressed, but it's not just that. It's those eyes, those green pools that flashed all kinds of attitude. It's the way she tossed that sandy brown hair. The way she held her jaw, as if she'd suffer the world if she had to but only on her terms. Watching her now, though, she seems cheery enough. Maybe my house was a fluke. Maybe she's not the major put off she seemed to be.

Carmen moves inside and I step closer to Monique, possessing neither a hug nor a statement that it's good to see her again. I do realize that I'm entering the woman's home and need to be polite and respectful, so my jaws deliver a smile and I lift my eyes—only to find in hers, if I'm not mistaken, a change of expression. They're a little less bright than with Carmen, and her smile has lost its teeth. I wonder for a moment if she read my mind, knew I didn't like her, and responded in kind. But she couldn't have. For all she knew, I had a hug for her as well. And if I did, I would keep it at this point. The lack of love apparently flows both ways. I hold her gaze and say, "Hi, Monique. Thanks for having us."

"No problem," she says, smile all but gone. "I'm surprised to see you. I guess you changed your mind."

I answer in the affirmative as I enter, wanting to say I've changed it again. I stare straight ahead, feeling strange and not expecting to. I knew I would feel ambivalent about being here, within myself, given all that's going on with me, but to be hit with discomfort from outside, from Monique.... I find this bizarre since I know why she rubbed me the wrong way at our first meeting but I can't think of a single thing I did to her. I even answered her tactless question when I would have preferred to impart something altogether different. Wasn't Carmen the one who set her straight? Why did she get a warm reception?

Old places and people forge together quickly in my mind, people like Monique, sandy-haired and green-eyed. People from whom I encountered this vibe regularly. But those people had money and position. Those people would look down on Monique, who seems to have nothing they value. Who is she to treat me as coolly as they did?

I finger the shoulder strap of my Louis Vuitton tote, my eyes vaguely aware of my mushroom-colored linen top and gauchos, and the three-inch cork-wedged sandals, all of which I thought for some time about and selected after a few try-ons, a bleakness reverberating inside. Monique apparently didn't even care that she slid into the same jeans she had on last week—something I could never do. But why should she care? Her place was bestowed at birth, as soon as she opened those green eyes.

"Everybody's downstairs in the family room," Monique says, closing the door.

"Monique, your house is so nice," Carmen says, looking into the living room on our left, a vision of black leather, platinum, and chrome.

"It's all right," Monique says, turning her nose up at her own walls and ceiling. "I keep telling Sean he needs to push for those promotions so we can move up out of here. I'm trying to get to one of those neighborhoods where y'all live. But, girl, he's not aggressive enough. I told him I'd go to work full time myself but he doesn't want me to. He likes me to be home when Jamal and Taj get out of school, which is cool. I like being here when they get home too. But every time I drive through those neighborhoods and look at the model homes, it kills me to come back to this ol' place."

Carmen touches her shoulder. "Monique, seriously, it's a very nice house, and I love what you've done with it."

She glances around at the furniture and shrugs. "Thanks, and I know I shouldn't complain. To be honest, it's more than I ever had."

I follow behind as Monique leads us down to the family room, which is actually two rooms, the one off to our right obviously dedicated to her boys. A huge racing track covers the back half of the room, accommodated by vinyl flooring, a table covered in Legos sits to one side with several works in progress, trucks, fire engines, helicopters, army men, and who knows what else are scattered throughout, and most prominent are two chairs in front of a television with Play Station controls. We keep straight ahead into an area that is quite a contrast from upstairs. This is lived in, cushiony, gently worn.

Willow jumps up from the sofa when she sees me, Zoe in her arms. "I didn't know you were coming!" she says, hugging me.

Jillian hugs me too, a tight hug without words. I know she's glad to see me.

I say hello to Asia, who's legs are covered this time—painted over it seems—in denim. I'll be curious to see her stand. Her breasts are somewhat contained in a leather tank top. She's traded the platform shoes for knee-high black heeled boots, which have got to be sweltering in this September heat, and her hair—rather, somebody's hair—is freed from braids and hanging down her back. Skipping the refreshments on a side table—Krispy Kremes and a red drink that's probably Kool-Aid—I sink into a seat next to Jillian, my insides sighing. I should have had a third cup of coffee before I left.

Jillian comes forward on the loveseat. "Ladies, I'm so glad we could all make it here for our second meeting. What an awesome lesson we have this week. I can't wait to get to it. But first, any prayer requests?"

Willow raises her hand. "I do." She gently tucks a sleeping Zoe into her car seat. "We said last week that everything that's said in the group remains confidential, right? 'Cause I don't normally tell my business in a group setting, but I really would like prayer power on this." Willow stops and sighs. "Zoe will be three months old in a couple of weeks, which means the end of my maternity leave. I had no idea I would feel this way but I don't want to go back to the firm."

I stare at Willow in disbelief.

"I want to be home with her, to see every new thing she does, but Damien is against it. He doesn't want me to give up my salary. We had it out last night. It wasn't the first time, and it probably won't be the last. I told him if I quit today there was nothing he could do about it." Willow stops. "I guess I need prayer for my attitude too, huh?"

Jillian chuckles. "And we'd better pray for Damien's strength because I know how you get, and he might be tempted to knock you upside the head."

"Who's side are you on?" Willow says, hand to her hip in mock displeasure.

"Girl, you know I love you," Jillian says. "And I'm with you on the goal, but we have to make sure you don't tear the house down to get it."

I half hear them chatter on, thinking I might raise my hand and ask for prayer to have Willow's problem. I can't believe I have to listen to how badly she wants to leave a well-paying, well-respected job. I can't even delight in the fact that there would be a great position open in the marketplace. My background is civil law, not criminal law.

"Any more prayer requests?" Jillian is saying.

Now I really should raise my hand. I did like Willow's phrase—prayer power. I could use some of that myself, group prayer on the Brooks Donnelly situation. But there would be too many questions, especially from Willow. And I have no desire to tell the tale of how Treva became the jobless wonder, from pinnacle to pit in a single bound. Actually, confidential or not, I don't want them knowing much of anything about me. I'm here by the skin of my teeth, don't plan to come again, and won't pretend that some sort of bond could arise between us.

I'm not one to share my business anyway. At work it amazed me when my colleagues would stand around in coffee klatch conversations and divulge problems with spouses, problems with children, and problems with in-laws. To show team spirit, I drank coffee with them on occasion and shared a problem or two with a remodeling contractor or one of the girls' teachers. But anything beyond that I considered private. That wall I erected a long time ago between people and me has stood firm. If I don't expect much from them, I have no cause to be disappointed.

With a "let's pray," Jillian bows her head and the rest of us follow suit. "Father, You are indeed awesome to gather this group of ladies around Your Word. I thank You for the book of Ephesians and for its power to change our lives. I pray, Lord, that You would give us insight and understanding regarding what we've read this week. I pray that You would anoint our fellowship and cause us to truly bond with one another—"

If I say "Amen," am I agreeing with that request?

"—Lord, we lift Willow up to You and her desire to be at home with the baby You've blessed them with. May Your will be done. I pray that Willow would not cause strife in her home over this but that she would patiently look to You, knowing that You do all things well."

Jillian looks up to encourage others to join in. A few seconds pass and Carmen adds, "And, Lord, You know all of the unstated needs of the women here. I pray that You would meet us in a special way."

When no one else speaks up, Jillian closes the prayer and smiles. "Okay," she says, "I told you all I was looking forward to today's lesson. When I got the study materials this week and looked through the facilitator's guide, I loved how it expanded the theme of chapter one of Ephesians. If you did your homework—" Jillian looks around the room and smiles, "—then you know the focus is on all the glorious things God has done for us as believers. But before we get into that, we're supposed to look first at another chapter that talks about us from God's perspective. Psalm 139."

"All right, now," Willow says. "That's my psalm."

"Must be for you, Asia," Carmen says. "You said you wanted to know who God says you are."

Asia has already begun turning the pages in her Bible. I'm right behind her, wondering what's there.

"That's why I got excited," Jillian says. "It's like Dr. Lyles knew exactly what we needed. Will somebody read it out loud for us?"

"I will," Asia says, and I find myself listening, not for the words of the psalm but for whether the girl has mastered phonics. "O Lord, You have searched me and You know me. You know when I sit and when I rise; You perceive my thoughts from afar."

Curiosity satisfied, I sink into the psalm, eyes closed.

"You discern my going out and my lying down; You are familiar with all my ways. Before a word is on my tongue you know it completely O Lord...."

"Mmm," Willow says. "That's what I'm talking about. Right there. Can you believe that?"

I shake my head, mostly to myself. It really is hard to grasp.

"Such knowledge is too wonderful for me, too lofty for me to attain...."

I open my eyes to see if that is really in the psalm.

"For You created my inmost being; You knit me together in my mother's womb. I praise You because I am fearfully and wonderfully made; Your words are wonderful, I know that full well. My frame was not hidden from You when I was made in the secret place. When I was woven together in the depths of the earth, Your eyes saw my unformed body. All the days ordained for me were written in Your book before one of them came to be...."

Asia is stopped by quiet tears. I was stopped before that, at the part about being knit together in Patsy's womb, trying to picture it as a divine event. It's not that I didn't know that God is the author of life, but hearing it this way makes it clearer, drives home His culpability. Why would God choose *her* womb to knit me in? And how, with such a creative hand, did He come up with me?

I glance around the room and see evidence of what else He is able to do. Every face is lighter. Monique and Jillian He made extra light, fine-featured, straight-haired, and light-eyed. He gave Asia light brown eyes and flawless skin. He gave Willow an electric smile, a model's jawbone, doe-like eyes, thick, gorgeous hair, *and* a perfectly proportioned tall body. And to Carmen He gave a girl-next-door beauty and a counte-nance that reflects always, even if annoyingly, that everything is perfect in her world.

Each of them can look in the mirror and see that she is fearfully and wonderfully made. I guess I'm supposed to believe it by faith. I wonder, once again, why I am here, why I am again the odd one, just as I was growing up, and why God sees fit to bless everyone disproportionately better than I am blessed.

I close my Bible before Asia is finished, and Jillian flashes me a puzzled look. I study my nails.

Asia reads the last line of the psalm and the women go on and on about God and the miracle of the womb. I tire quickly of these praises that wouldn't be praises if God hadn't stamped "beautiful" all over them. If I hear one more comment about how awesome it is to be knit by Him....

"The thing is," Monique says, "the psalm lets me know, 'Hey, you're all that because God is the one who put you together.'"

There it is.

And here I go.

"I'm pretty sure you thought you were 'all that' anyway, didn't you, Monique?" I cringe as my words hit the air, unable to believe I actually said it. All eyes are plastered on me.

"What did you say, Treva?" Monique says. She tosses her hair. The green pools flash. I'm not turning back.

"I'm just saying, I bet you didn't need the psalm to tell you that. The way you carry yourself, seems like you already knew you were 'all that.'"

"Well, I could say the same for you. I'm not the one with the law degree, the mansion, the BMW, and the high-end wardrobe. Yeah, I might not be able to afford it but I know what you're wearing. And no, I don't walk around thinking I'm 'all that.'"

Monique flings her locks behind her ear again, ticking me off further. *I don't walk around thinking I'm all that.* Liar.

"O-kay," Jillian says. "Let's turn to chapter one of Ephesians. Sounds like it's a good time to explore those spiritual blessings."

When Jillian looks at me, I roll my eyes at her. *"Awesome lesson."* I shouldn't have listened to her this morning. I want to go home, wait to hear from Theodore Dutton.

I'm not sure what the spiritual blessings entail, but I know for sure I'll feel better when I have a tangible blessing.

Chapter Eleven

I can see the red light blinking the moment I open the garage door and step into the kitchen. I snatch up the phone and dial into voice mail, breathless.

"Treva, it's Theodore Dutton. Please give me a call at your earliest convenience."

I throw down my tote bag and dial the number to Brooks Donnelly. He called! Nervous energy propels me from one end of the kitchen to the other.

The receptionist puts me through and in a flash he is on the line.

"Theodore Dutton."

"Hi Theodore, this is Treva Campbell Langston, returning your phone call."

"Yes, Treva, thank you."

I cannot read his voice.

"I had told you that I would seek approval for a litigation hire at the next executive committee meeting but we had several emergency agenda items and could not address it until this morning."

Not a problem.

Theodore chuckles slightly. "Most of the committee members are old codgers like me and knew Charles very well. They were thrilled that you've shown an interest in working for us."

Great.

"The committee thought your credentials were impeccable, and your experience in litigation is impressive. You've done quite well. The committee was also of a mind to overlook the current market condition. Brooks Donnelly's financial position will not undergo strain with the addition of an upper-level associate. Now, there is a final matter," he says.

I stop moving and listen extra hard.

Theodore clears his throat. "The D.C. office of Thompson & Klein did not extend an offer for you to join their litigation practice. You were very frank about the reason and the committee is not concerned, as Thompson & Klein apparently was, with your numbers or with the amount of business you've developed. We have no problem giving you time to develop business as you hone your legal skills. What *is* of concern is the lack of an offer from them. Our incoming attorneys are highly sought after, the cream of the crop, if you will. We hire the best. The committee frowns upon hiring anyone who has been turned down by a competitor. Indeed, when Charles served on this committee, he was adamant that each applicant had to have at least one additional offer from an equally prestigious firm. My advice to you, Treva, is to secure such an offer, at which time bringing you on board will be no problem."

I remain fixed in my spot, processing the rejection then teleporting myself to a meeting of this committee at which I inform them that they are all a bunch of pompous jerks who have ruined my life—after which, I plead for reconsideration.

Maybe I should plead with my old firm, just for the offer, promising I wouldn't actually accept.

I thank Theodore for his time, punch the "off" button, then the "talk" button, dial, and wait.

"Hezekiah Langston."

"I didn't get the job."

"Oh, sweetheart, what happened?"

"I don't feel like talking about it. Bottom line, I didn't get it. My career is over. I need you to pick the girls up from school."

"But I have a meeting—"

"I don't care what you have to do; just pick them up!"

I slam the phone into its cradle and squeeze my twitching arms as my eyes dart about the kitchen, looking for who knows what. An idea, maybe. A solution. Medicine, for nervous breakdowns.

The phone rings, I see it's Hezekiah, and I bound the spiral steps up to the second floor, to our room, and shut the door. I can't deal with him or the girls. I don't want to deal with myself. Don't want to analyze the situation or plot my next move, worry, cry, or get drastic. I don't want to shiver either but my arms keep pulsating to their own panic-beat. I just need to shut down. Just shut down.

<hr>

"Mommy, Mommy."

Something is wrong. It's the middle of the night; somebody's in trouble.

"Mommy, I have something to show you. Open the door."

"Me, too!"

My eyes pop open and I shoot up in bed. A hint of sun is seeping through the window coverings and I have no idea how morning came and why I am still in my gauchos. I turn my head to view the time. Four o'clock P.M.

I remember it's the same day, fall back on the bed, and fight for the sweet refuge of slumber.

The door handle shakes. "Mommy! Why is the door locked? Open up!"

If these girls do not get away from that door, I might lose my mind. I don't want to hear about their school day, cannot stomach their joyful noises, don't want anything demanded of me.

"Girls, I don't feel well," I mumble.

"But I just want to show you a painting I did today," Hope says.

"And I want to show you my spelling test, Mom," Joy says. "I got every word right."

I really don't care, and I am without my usual wherewithal to pretend I care. This second I am reminded—and I don't know why the thought is flooding my mind, but it is and it's true—I did not even want to have more children.

Faith was enough, and even she was ill-timed. I didn't want to have a child until well into my thirties, after I had made partner. But she surprised us, coming into the world just a short while after I graduated from law school, during the first year of my judicial clerkship. In the short run, it wasn't too great a problem. I had her in late November, and the period between Thanksgiving and Christmas turned out to be relatively quiet at the court. When I returned in January, the work was just picking up again. Jillian, who had just graduated from college, was staying with us for a time and helped care for Faith. It worked out quite well.

Not so with Joy and Hope. We had moved to Chicago by then, and Hezekiah and I had gone back and forth for almost four years over whether to have another baby. He wanted a house full. I was fine with one. I was a young associate working long hours, trying hard to prove that I could do as good a job as the men. They had wives at home during the day to care for their children and could work into the night if need be, which was hard for the working mom-attorneys to match. But I did my best. We had a nanny come to the home part of the day during Faith's toddler years and Hezekiah relieved her in the afternoons, an arrangement that allowed me to give myself to the practice. More children would only complicate matters.

But Hezekiah insisted we have at least one more, and I finally agreed that a sibling would be nice for Faith. And nice for me, when the new baby was old enough to keep Faith company.

Of course Joy was born during my busiest time ever at the firm. Many of us in litigation were embroiled in a publicized patent dispute in federal court in San Francisco and I was given the responsibility of handling the damages phase of the case. The team traveled to and from the West Coast for court hearings and depositions but, near the end of my pregnancy, the team traveled without me. I immediately felt the impact of not being there. The partner-in-charge handed off important assignments to others to whom he could turn and say, "Run with this." When I went on maternity leave, I tried to stay in the loop. But when I returned to work six weeks later, the team was in San Francisco, and on my desk was a file for a small contract dispute in local state court.

Two years later I was sitting in our office's main conference room with a software client who had been sued by a large software company. At the table were several senior partners from business, intellectual property, and litigation, and several associates dying to work on the case. I very reluctantly excused myself, scurried to the ladies' room, and came quickly out of my suit jacket. I was heated, rapidly becoming weak, and angry with myself for eating the tuna salad sandwich that the messengers had obviously allowed to sit too long before the meeting.

I soon learned what I really was. Pregnant. Pregnant despite the pill and my declaration after Joy that we were definitely done.

No big software case for Treva. By the time the case started heating up, I was showing and, attorneys being attorneys, no one said my pregnancy had anything to do with my inability to work on this case that would require extensive travel, commitment, and zero time off. I was simply given other work.

It wasn't until the year I was up for promotion to partner that I was shown, quietly by a female partner, a printout of my "numbers." I wouldn't make it, she said, because of the dips in productivity. Because of two maternity leaves. Because of Joy and Hope.

Had I made partner, a transfer to the D.C. office would not have been an issue. I'd be at work right now, not trying to ride out a panic attack under a fortress of quilted silk pillows, with Joy and Hope hastening the destruction of my last nerve.

"I know how to pick the lock," Joy tells Hope, and their footsteps patter away, sure to return.

Where is Hezekiah? He should know I'm not in the mood for this. Why isn't he interceding?

Sometimes I wonder why I got married. I really do. I'm probably the type who should have stayed single. Do what I want, when I want, in the city I want.

Where is this coming from?

Something jiggles in the door handle and the girls jostle with one another for the right to break in.

"Girls, get away from there," Hezekiah yells from somewhere.

About time.

"But, Daddy, I wanted to show Mommy," Hope says, rattling her paper.

"You'll have to show her later. She's resting."

The disturbance moves away from the door and I am upset because I'm wide awake now and suddenly contending with another little girl, leaping with pointed toe across a hardwood floor. Leaping. Twirling. Giggling. I sit up in bed again, wondering what to do with her, how to get rid of her.

I really might be going crazy. Is this how it begins? Does the mind start running its own course, downloading this thought and that until you're in a corner with your arms tied to your sides?

Leaping. Twirling. Giggling.

I force myself out of bed and walk into the bathroom, pulling the double doors behind me. I set seven rosemary lavender candles ablaze all around the room, close the blinds, and sit lotus-style on the lushly carpeted floor, inhaling calm. Rest. Tranquility. I've never done this before but I saw it on *Oprah* or somewhere in the last couple of weeks and it's worth trying. I need to calm my nerves.

"I'm a world renowned ballerina! I have lots of fans. I'll grace my fans with a double encore."

Okay. Not working.

I jump up and shove the little girl aside with deep knee bends and side bends. I spread my feet apart and stretch my fingertips to the floor. The pull invigorates me and I stretch ten more times and start jogging in place, pleased with my cardiovascular offensive. I wonder if Oprah has tried this strategy. I should write and share.

I jog hard in my pants and jersey top until winded and turn on the shower, peel off my clothes, and stand where pulsating water from four shower heads can pummel my skin. Reclining on the shower seat, I work a rose and lavender sea salt scrub over my legs. The scent, the flickering candlelight, and the steady patter of the water do their job. My mind is still. Relaxed. The ballerina girl is gone.

But the moment I close my eyes, the scene fills my mind.

"Treva, I'm telling you this because I'm your mother and you need to hear the truth. Stop all this fantasizing about being a ballerina. Not just anybody can be a ballerina. They'd never put you on stage; you're too dark. Be realistic about your goals."

Her eyes bear into me a few minutes more as she leaves, then turns the corner. My toes point anyway, legs take to the air…and quickly go limp. It's gone. The dream is gone. My chest hurts badly from the sobs gathering there and grief thrusts me to the floor, racking my entire body. *Why does she have to be so mean? Why does she hate me?*

I haven't remembered that day in a long time but I guess it remembered me, came to torment me. "Be realistic about your goals." That's what I did, amazingly. At ten years old, I adjusted and got new dreams. Realistic dreams. Law, business, medicine, and a Ph.D. became my options, each with its own appeal. Eventually law edged ahead. Trial law. Asserting myself, persuading, and arguing struck a chord, as did the prospect of another kind of stage, the courtroom. I didn't know much about it but I knew I could talk and people would watch and listen. And if I did well enough, I would be more than "just anybody."

I turn off the shower, blow out the candles, slip into my nightclothes, and get back in bed, my mind shifting its own gears.

You failed at the realistic goal, too, Treva…and the main goal. You'll never be a partner, a judge, well renowned in your field. You'll never be "somebody."

Chapter Twelve

It is five in the morning on Saturday, the day after my life ended.

Sounds melodramatic, I know, but in this moment, at this kitchen table, with a robe on and no plans for the day, the month, or the rest of the year, no timelines or deadlines, no office, secretary, or business cards that tell the truth, that's how I reckon it. My life has ended.

The only fitting thing to do in such a state is sleep. And I would like to, but I slept from six in the evening until eleven, when I unlocked the door for Hezekiah, and then from eleven until five in the morning, when my body seemed to say, "Enough already." My eyes popped open and I lay there with chapter two of Ephesians in my head. Not the verses, of course, but the push to get up and read it. I could see the vision: me, here at the table, Bible open, colored pencils sharpened, mind focused.

Jillian would say it's the best thing to do in a time like this, to get into the Word. All I know is the Word shooed me out of bed and got me downstairs to this table, and all I've done so far is remember why the first half of yesterday was almost as rotten as the second. I knew it wouldn't work. Not me with a group of women, up close and personal, and especially not women who are so…so…pretty. Prior to yesterday, I hadn't even focused on the fact that they were all alike, so to speak. All I could see at first was the glare of their individual selves, the unique and peculiar qualities that made them separate and distinct from one another. Now I see them clearly as separate and distinct *from me*.

Sighing, I rest my head on the back of the chair. I don't need this. Being back and seeing my mother were enough to reawaken old internal battles. That group only intensifies the struggle. I hope God and Jillian are satisfied that I gave it a try because I will not meet week after week with women who magnify me to me, making me acutely self-conscious. I'm done.

I look down and Ephesians Two stares up at me. I haven't read a word yet and since I just quit the group, I wonder whether to continue with it. I wonder, too, what Hezekiah cooked last night since hunger pains are shouting that I missed lunch and dinner. I get up to look in the refrigerator and almost jump out of my skin at the sound of the phone ringing. *Who in the world....*

"Hello."

"Good morning," Jillian says in chipper fashion.

"What are you doing calling so early?"

"I tried calling you yesterday afternoon and no one answered. Then I called in the evening and Hezekiah said you were asleep, which totally shocked me, so I'm calling now."

"Because you thought the crack of dawn would be the ideal time?"

"You've always been an early riser."

I head to the refrigerator again, open it, and stare inside. "Not anymore."

"Aren't you up?"

"Not because I wanted to be."

"What is going on with you, Treva? That's why I called yesterday. It was clear you did not want to be at that Bible study, and your comments to Monique—"

"I don't even know why you included Monique," I say, lifting a plastic container to see what's inside. "She's full of herself and she talks too much. And I've been meaning to bring up Asia. Jillian, what is the deal with her? You have got to talk to her about leaving the house in those clothes. It seems like you two have a good relationship and she respects you. I think—"

"Treva, I want to talk about you. What is going on with *you?*"

I shelve the container of green beans and lift a casserole lid. "Nothing." *Could I eat potatoes au gratin this time of morning?*

"That's not true."

"I mean it, nothing. Absolutely nothing. That job I really wanted, at the firm where Daddy worked? I didn't get it."

"Okay...."

The casserole lid clings when I put it back in place. "See, I knew you wouldn't understand."

"I just said, 'Okay.' I was waiting for you to finish."

"No, you weren't. That was the 'okay' that means, 'So, what's the problem?' Because you don't understand. And, really, how could you? You've never worked."

"What?"

"I'm just saying, Jillian...."

"Anyway, when did you find out you didn't get the job?"

"When I got home from Monique's house."

"So, what was going on with you *at* Monique's house?"

"Same thing. Fed up over the job situation. Plus, the group is just...." I shrug my shoulders.

"Just what?"

I take my head out of the refrigerator and let it close as I mull over my answer. I don't openly discuss color issues with Jillian. She knows, of course, that our mother and grandmother treated us differently because of our skin. She knows she was treated better, by them and by our peers, and she was there the times I was mocked, called "ugly," and put through various other ordeals. She's cried with me on more occasions than I can recall. But I never discussed how I felt. There was strength in staying quiet. I could pretend I'd gotten over it when the tears dried, that their words hadn't become my words. And my thoughts. I would bury my head in a textbook, crank out the As, and keep moving. Jillian always said that I would make it to the moon if I made it a goal and that I was unflappable. Jillian, the cheerleader. She even told me I was beautiful.

She was the first to say it. When I was fifteen and she was twelve, and the family was spending time at Highland Beach, and the girls as well as the boys would come calling for Jillian every day, I remember her telling me, "I don't like these people. They act like you're not here. Have they ever looked at you, really *looked* at you. You're beautiful. I hope you know that. You do know that, don't you?"

I smiled faintly and returned to my novel, thankful for her kindness, broken up inside because they did act like I wasn't there and, no, they never really looked at me, and, no, I didn't know I was beautiful and the words of my sympathetic little sister had no power to convince me otherwise.

But I never told her that. Talking about it would have catapulted me to another level of anguish, as it did with Hezekiah at the Dairy.

I tell her now, "I'm just not a group person."

"I know, but we've only had two meetings and we're still getting to know each other. I think God is going to do great things with this group."

"I'm sure you do."

"And don't you think the DVD lesson was awesome?"

I have to admit it was. The DVD was the only thing that lifted my mood at the meeting. "I did learn a lot from it, so maybe I'll just continue with the study on my own and order the DVD for myself. You and I can even talk about it each week. We could have our own Bible study." I smile inside at the compromise I've hit upon. Jillian can be happy that I'm doing the study and I can be happy that I'm out of the group.

"Well, we'll see."

We'll see? What's that supposed to mean? Is she saying "We'll see" about us having our own discussions about Ephesians? I can't imagine that she'd refuse that. She must be doing her soothsayer bit again. She "sees" things turning out differently. I'll be right there in the group because that's what God intended. I wonder how I appear in the vision. It's authentic only if I'm holding a clump of sandy brown hair, having snapped after seeing Monique toss it for the fiftieth time.

I finish the call and sit down with a bowl of cereal, turning my attention finally to the lesson. After reading the day's instructions and praying the model prayer, I begin reading chapter two, looking for key words and phrases to mark.

"And you were dead in your trespasses and sins, in which you formerly walked according to the course of this world, according to the prince of the power of the air, of the spirit that is now working in the sons of disobedience. Among them we too all lived in the lusts of our flesh, indulging the desires of the flesh and of the mind, and were by nature children of wrath, even as the rest. But God, being rich in mercy, because of His great love with which He loved us, even when we were dead in our transgressions, made us alive together with Christ (by grace you have been saved), and raised us up with Him and seated us with Him in the heavenly places, in Christ Jesus. For by grace you have been saved through faith; and that not of yourselves, it is the gift of God; not as a result of works, that no one should boast."

I stop midway through the chapter to examine what I've read. With a black pencil, I draw a pitchfork over "prince" and "spirit" as directed. Dr. Lyles wants us to mark every reference to the devil, and he listed all of the synonyms used for him. The point is to become aware of what the Bible says about the devil, his activity in the world, his authority over unbelievers, and his attacks against believers—but I don't much like the point. I've never wanted to hear about "the enemy," as Hezekiah calls him. The subject gives me the shivers. The way I see it, thinking about him only invites trouble. I'd rather expend my energy elsewhere.

Continuing, I spot the word "formerly" twice, then scan the second half of the chapter and find two more. I color them with a turquoise pencil. Formerly walked according to the world and the devil; formerly lived in the lusts of our flesh and were children of wrath; formerly separate from Christ; and formerly far off from God. I draw a line down the center of a piece of paper and write the "formerly's" on the left side, with the heading, "Before Salvation."

Crunching on granola cereal, I head the right side of the paper, "After Salvation," and start hunting for something to list under it. My spoon quickly lowers itself as I read verses five and six. God made us alive, raised us, and seated us in the heavenly places, in Christ Jesus. *In the heavenly places.* Didn't I see that in chapter one? I flip back and find the phrase mentioned twice. Fishing through my colored pencils, metallic gold seems perfect. I color in the three phrases and meditate on what they're telling me: I'm blessed with every spiritual blessing "in the heavenly places." God raised Jesus from the dead and seated Him at His right hand "in the heavenly places," and is this right? God raised *me* up with Jesus and seated me *with Him* "in the heavenly places."

My heart and mind begin racing. I need to get this. I *know* I need to get this.

I push back in my chair and open the kitchen door that leads to the patio, shutting it behind me. The sun has blossomed on the morning, affirming its promise, telling me it's a new day, beckoning me to a new outlook. I pull my coral silk robe closed as I breathe the crisp air, looking skyward with wonder, these truths rolling about in my head. *God saved me, made me alive, raised me, and seated me in the heavenly places.*

But what does it mean to be seated in heavenly places? It seems so extraordinary, so out of this world, so away from the cares of this world. And if I understand correctly, it happened the moment God saved me. It's the moment I had been looking for. I really was beamed up to heaven. In a way. But what kind of way? I'm certainly still here, certainly situated in the same cares. Does this become real after I die? Or is some aspect of it true now? Should I feel like I'm in a different place, a better place? Right now?

I walk slowly around the pool in my slippers, thinking. Is this what new life in Christ is about? I can see how awesome it would be to live life from above, to feel like I'm on top of the world, nothing plaguing me, nothing bringing me down, nothing making me feel inferior. How *could* I feel inferior? How *could* I be depressed? *I'm seated in heavenly places.* My heart is exploding with such hope that it might lift me bodily from the earth and power me to the heavens. It's ready to soar, and so am I. I can feel the tears pushing up, longing to roll with rejoicing. And that word brings me to a standstill: believe. *Believe.* The vision returns—me laughing and dancing, arms raised with my partner, a heavenly waltz under the stars.

But sadly, the questions return, too, the ones I can't answer. How can I be seated in heavenly places, in the place of blessing, when I can't get a job? When I have the same mother and memories to contend with? When I have the same skin, with the same need for a relaxer every six weeks? *I've been meaning to ask You about that, Lord. Why is it that most women on earth have straight hair, while a small segment of us are left to figure out what to do with this hair. It seems so unfair. If we want any kind of freedom, we have to cut it off and go natural, which You know I'm not willing to do, which means I'm a slave to the chemical. Which means, among a zillion other things, that I can't swim unless I have two hours to wash, condition, blow dry, and style afterwards. Which means I can't swim as much as I'd like.*

Maybe You can tell me, because I need to know. What is heavenly about being a dark-skinned woman with kinky hair and a tanked career? And why, once again, can I not enjoy the application of a fabulous Bible verse to my own life?

I wait a moment, the sound of joyful birds twittering on tree limbs. But not the voice I need to hear. No answer. Not that I expected one.

I guess, for me, "heavenly places" is after-I-die real.

The gleaming sun, a bother now, drives me back indoors. No one has awakened yet, a welcome relief. I don't want to deal with them today either. I'm going back to bed.

Chapter Thirteen

The deep, orchestral sound of the doorbell reverberates throughout the house, but I keep surfing. I've been clicking through listing after listing for an hour, almost hypnotically, and no doorbell is going to disturb me. I decided this morning that I wouldn't stay in bed or in my robe. I would get dressed, come into this office, and find a job in cyberspace. I haven't found anything of remote interest yet, but I'm determined to sit here until I glimpse a ray of hope. I'm not expecting anyone anyway and the car is tucked in the garage. They'll go away eventually.

The doorbell sounds a second time. A third. And a fourth. I rise grudgingly, hand glued to the mouse, and finish scrolling down the page. Leaving the office, I huff to the door to tell whoever that I don't want any, after which I'll complain again to security about leaving that gate open.

I flip the lock and yank open the door. "What are you doing here?"

"Good morning to you too." Darlene smiles. "I knew you were home. Do you plan on stepping aside so I can come in?"

"Of course, Ma."

"I wasn't so sure. You didn't return my phone calls," Darlene responds, walking past me toward the kitchen with a covered platter.

I trudge behind her. "I know Hez told you to call me. I could tell by your tone in the messages."

"And?"

"Ma, I know your heart is in the right place but I wasn't in the mood for a pep talk. Still not."

Darlene turns to face me. "What are you in the mood for? Sittin' around the house moping? You didn't even come to the barbecue yesterday after church. The weather was perfect and I fixed your favorites."

I won't mention that I didn't go to church either. "I know. I can't believe Hezekiah didn't make me a plate."

Darlene opens the refrigerator and arranges a spot for the large oval dish. "He did, but I guess he forgot it. I saw it in some foil on the kitchen counter. So I made you a bigger one. I've got some macaroni and cheese in there, some Langston ribs and chicken, and a few other goodies. One has banana in it."

My stomach gurgles in response. After that bowl of cereal Saturday I didn't eat much the rest of the day, and yesterday only nibbled here and there. "Thank you, Ma. I can feel my appetite coming back."

"I'd like to know where it went. And why." Darlene hefts her purse onto the granite top, puts a foot on the bottom rail of the bar stool, and lifts herself into the chair. "And I'd like to know why you've been laying up in bed all depressed-like. I 'bout fell off my seat when Hope told me you stayed in your robe all day Saturday."

"I'm sure Hez told you I didn't get the position I really wanted. It was the only opportunity I had left to work at a top-tier firm."

"And by the way you've been acting, you must feel like the world has ended."

"Not the world, just my life."

"Treva, I know you're disappointed and it hurts my heart to see you so sad. But, honey, don't get confused. It's just a job," she says, with her knack for making a no-nonsense statement sound sweet. "What aspect of God made Him unable to get you that position?"

I look at her blankly.

"Right. Nothing. The earth is His and its fullness. If He wanted you to have the job, you would have it. Or any of the other ones you applied for. Looks to me like He closed the door, sweetheart."

"What do you mean, 'He closed the door'?"

"He does that. First of all, it's part of His shaping and molding of us. He wants to know if you'll rise above, whether you'll still be thankful."

"Thankful for what?"

Darlene shakes her head. "Didn't you tell me you were studying Ephesians?"

"Just started, really."

"Well, then you had to see tons to be thankful for. I mean that book just fires out the gate with one thing after another that God has done for you. Shoot, just three years ago you were dead and didn't know it. Headed straight for hell. Remember I told you?"

"Which time?" I say wryly.

"But God, being rich in mercy, because of His great love with which He loved you—" Darlene lets out a hallelujah laugh. "Whoo, didn't know I knew that by heart, did you? Girl, God is something else. He had mercy on you. He saved you. Raised you to new life. You are blessed. You don't need to be walking around here *de*jected and *re*jected. 'Be thankful in all things,' He says, Treva. Why? Because He loves you and He knows what's best for you."

I glance downward, questioning.

"Well, let me get out of here. I told Russell I'd be right back. He's always wanting to work on that yard. I told him it'd be nice to rest for once on my day off." Darlene chuckles and eases off the stool.

"Wait, what's the rest?" I say, moving from my ho-hum lean over the counter.

"Rest of what?"

"You were talking about why God closes a door and you said, 'First of all...' Is there a second part?" If Darlene has answers as to why God would do this, I want to hear them. If this is some sort of test, I'd like to know what I need to do to pass it to get God to reopen that door. I've already written a note to self to try to be thankful.

"Oh, chile, I know for sure I'm getting old. I did have more I wanted to say."

Darlene opts for a lower kitchen chair this time, one at the table, and I join her.

"See, it's how He guides us. He'll close *this* door in order to move us toward *this* one," she says, motioning with her hands. "Sometimes He just wants to open your eyes to what's already there. You may not be working downtown but it doesn't mean life is over. Just the opposite. He has other things for you to do. God always has a plan for you, Treva."

I nod my head at this promising news. God has a plan for me, one I haven't thought of. He probably wants me to think outside the box. I'll bet there are all kinds of legal positions I haven't considered. "So how do I find out what He has for me?"

"Pray, and read the Word. There's much in the Bible about what God would have you do. I can give you three passages to look at off the top of my head. As a young wife and mother I meditated on these all the time: Proverbs 14:1, Deuteronomy 6:5-7, and Titus 2:3-5, all about home and family."

I stare at her blankly again as she jots these verses down on a notepad nearby and hands them to me. "Let me ask you this, Treva," she says, eyes soft yet earnest. "I know you've always had career goals. What about home? Do you have goals for your home and your family? Dreams? Things you pray toward?"

"Mm-hmm," I say, trying to sound convincing.

"Good, 'cause there's nothing more important than your role as wife and mother. You're the heartbeat of the home. The manager. Teacher. Nurturer. Prayer warrior. God wants to do so much through you in your home, work that sails on into eternity, but it's not easy. That proverb I gave you says, 'The wise woman builds her house, but the foolish one tears it down with her own hands.' And I'll tell you who helps us tear it down—the enemy. Ooh, girl, don't get me started." Darlene picks up a bill and fans herself. "He is always trying to seduce women away from the building process. Did you get to that part in Ephesians yet about how the devil has the world under his influence?"

"I just read it Saturday."

"So you know I'm right—"

I'm not even following.

"—The enemy has women thinking they're not about anything unless they get out of the house and throw themselves into a career. How you gonna build if you're never home? He wants us to think there's nothing praiseworthy about taking care of a home and raising kids. Wants us to run ourselves ragged 'til the only thing we have energy left to do in the home is tear it down. We start snapping at the kids and sucking our teeth when they call us, no energy left to be a helpmeet to our husband, to show him some love.

"There's nothing glamorous about our job description but, honey, the rewards are phenomenal, both here and when we get our crowns." Darlene stabs her finger into the table. "Right here is where God wants to raise up the next generation for the kingdom. You think the enemy wants that? We're in warfare, Treva. And we get the victory when we press in and make the main thing the main thing."

My heart is thumping with all this talk about the devil. Warfare? What is that about? I have a million questions but one has bolted to the top of the list. "So are you saying I shouldn't work?"

"Treva, you know I worked when Hezekiah and Isaiah were growing up. To me, the question is not always 'whether,' but 'how.' I remember when I started doing hair, everybody told me the only way to make money was to take appointments early and stay late. I would have never seen my boys. I wanted to have breakfast with them, be there when they got home. I heard all kinds of stuff about their day and was able to address it, just by being there when it was still fresh in their minds. I came into the shop at nine and left at three. And guess what? Didn't work Saturdays, either. Guess what else? I think God sent every black stay-at-home mom in the metro area to that shop, plus working moms who found time to get away during the day. Maybe I *would* have made more money if I would have done it the other way, but it would have cost me in the end."

"But you can't do that in litigation," I argue. "You can't just work from nine to three."

"I'm saying, make home a priority and let God order everything after that. You don't have to be figuring and conjecturing. Just acknowledge Him; He'll direct your path."

My head falls into my hands, hurting. This is way too much information, advice—*whatever*. Did I even ask for all of this? I should have let her go when she got up the first time. She must think I'm not "making the main thing the main thing." This is crazy. I'm supposed to acknowledge God about...what? Being at home? I'm already home. That's all I am is "home." If I'm doing warfare by being here then I guess my guns are blazing.

Darlene hops up, thankfully, and slides the strap of her purse onto her shoulder. "All right, I'm leaving for real this time."

I follow and wonder why it is so obvious now that my home is not in order. Darlene is walking on a filthy floor, and it takes many days for dirt to show up on these earth-colored tiles, past countertops cluttered with junk mail, bills, newspapers, other papers, magazines, an empty milk carton, an empty strawberry carton with strawberry juice glistening beside it, and a sink I won't describe. And I hope she doesn't suddenly have to go to the bathroom.

She heads for the door and starts her little self down the walkway to where she's parked her car at the top of the semicircle. "And I'll tell you a secret," Darlene says over her shoulder. "That Bible study group you're in is an answer to prayer. It'll change you in ways you can't imagine. And it's good to have the fellowship of other believers."

Well, that's nice. I already quit.

"And, sweetheart, while you're home, enjoy those babies. You have time to just enjoy those babies."

I watch Darlene until she drives away and then push the door to a close. My feet carry me back to the office, where my hand jiggles the mouse to reactivate the screen I'd been viewing. I click "next page" and watch the job listings unfurl.

Chapter Fourteen

"I'm not going!" I announce it loudly to squash all objection. It's 9:30 A.M. on Friday, half an hour before the Bible study, and I've gone back and forth inside myself since I woke up. My position is clear: I've quit the group. But something keeps tugging at my resolve, disturbing it. I've reasoned that I haven't quit the study and that I actually completed the homework for the week. Ten minutes ago I even called the 800 number and ordered the teaching DVD, thinking that would bring peace. Still, an unction inside is saying, *Go.*

I won't. My voice is louder, and I'm looking forward to my day. I'll pop by the interior designer's shop and peruse fabric for window treatments. Then I'll drive down to Wisconsin Avenue and spend leisurely time in Saks and Louis Vuitton. I deplore the loss of my six-figure salary, but I'm thankful for the significant increase the University of Maryland offered Hezekiah to get him there. Thankful, too, that Hezekiah hasn't put me on a budget yet, because I've had my eye on a new Louis for some time. And since I'll be in the Chevy Chase area, I think I'll ride through the neighborhood of houses to dream about what might have been.

The shrill ring of the bedroom phone jars me from my plans. I walk to the nightstand and answer.

"Treva, I'm glad I caught you."

Automatic eye roll. It must be the syrupy voice, and the incessant smile; I can see it through the phone. Nobody could actually be this happy. "Hi, Carmen. What can I do for you?"

"You're probably about to walk out the door to get to the study but I'm wondering if you could do me a huge favor. Asia needs a ride to Willow's house and I told her I'd pick her up, but I don't want to go by myself. Could you ride with me?"

"Well, I.... Why can't you go by yourself?"

"Umm, it's just because...I mean, it's not dangerous or anything, I don't think. I just would feel comfortable if I had someone with me."

My curiosity soars. I wondered where Asia lived, and how she lived. The girl is a mystery. Quiet and respectful in demeanor, whorish in appearance. I don't blame Carmen for not wanting to drive to her home alone. No telling where it is. P.G. has some areas I wouldn't want to be caught alone in.

I stare into space, weighing my distaste for the group against this intriguing opportunity. I don't normally have an interest in people's lives, but I've never met anyone like Asia. Maybe we'll go inside, get some insight into her home life. I do wonder what makes her tick.

"Okay, I'll ride with you."

"Thanks, Treva. I'll be there in a couple of minutes."

———

Carmen motors her beige Honda Odyssey around my drive and I jump in. Through small talk I learn that she and her husband, Karl, met and married in Raleigh, North Carolina, that he's an anesthesiologist, and that she was a registered nurse before she had Stacy and quit.

I give the bare-bones version of my life, and just when I'm certain she'll probe for more, she doesn't. Instead, she's rolling down her window and turning into Asia's neighborhood, a fabulous neighborhood a mere seven minutes away. Ours has a gate with a passkey. This one has a live guard.

Why did Carmen need help coming here?

We gain clearance and cruise past a man-made lake with a wooden bridge. Mothers and toddlers are leaning over it, feeding the fish and ducks. Normal-looking people are working in their yards or walking their dogs. I cannot find a fit between Asia and this neighborhood. Her age alone sets her apart from them. They look to be in their 40s and 50s; Asia is nineteen. Is she married to a much older man?

Carmen makes a couple of turns and pulls up the drive of a stunning home, behind the Mercedes SUV I saw at Monique's house, which immediately makes me wonder why Asia couldn't drive it today.

"Oh, good, she's outside," Carmen says, mostly to herself. "We'll be fine."

I want more, of course, but don't ask.

Asia is standing out front in another short, short skirt that has the nerve to be low-waisted. Under it, and I wish I hadn't noticed, the top edge of a thong peeps out. It's a little late in the season for bare arms but Asia has them, her breasts poking out like torpedoes in a tight knit top. She is holding a baby and scurries to the car to ask if I can hold him, which I do. Then she runs and gets a car seat, deftly hooks it up in the back of the van, and says, "I'm sorry. I couldn't take DeRon to my mother's today. He's a little more active than Willow's baby. I hope the group doesn't mind."

"Only if you won't let us hold him," Carmen says.

"And thanks for picking us up. My husband just, well, he didn't want me to drive the car today. Sometimes he trips a little, wants to let me know who's in control."

Asia and DeRon settle in, Carmen drives off, and I'm steamed. I didn't get to go inside to see how she lives. Didn't get to see the husband, nor a picture of the husband, and he seems like a piece of work. Nothing, except the neighborhood, which is an interesting fact but only adds to the mystery.

I definitely gave more than I got in this bargain. We're on our way now to the Bible study.

Chapter Fifteen

Asia prattles and coos with DeRon in the back row of seats of the Odyssey while I admonish myself. It's awful of me to be amazed, but I am amazed that Asia's mothering is so natural and loving. She's enjoying her baby, peek-a-booing until he squeals and singing dippy nursery rhymes.

It's so foreign to what I expected, though I don't know exactly what I expected. Detachment? Disinterest? A level of devotion akin to her skirt length?

"You like being a mom, don't you, Asia?" Carmen asks, peering quickly into the rearview mirror.

"Mm-hmm," Asia responds softly. "It's the best part of my life."

Asia's words turn my head. I study her as she kisses DeRon's button nose and consumes herself in his world. Overcome, I turn my gaze to the road and a slight sting shuts my eyes. It's foreign all right. Foreign to me, as a child and as a mother.

Much of our short drive is along a main corridor from which several luxury home communities branch. Willow lives in one of the oldest of these communities, built in the early '80s. Carmen turns into York Estates and heads up a winding road that twists and forks so often that I'm sure I could not find my way out. At the next bend, Jillian's van comes into view. Carmen parks the Odyssey behind it.

The stately home, white bricked and shrouded by trees, occupies a vast corner lot. Carmen, Asia, DeRon, and I ascend a pebbled walkway and Carmen rings the doorbell.

Sparkling eyes, a wide smile, and a bright yellow and powder blue sweat suit greet us. "Good morning! And how are youuu?" Willow sings to DeRon, tickling his chin. "Hey, Monique!"

I turn to see Monique coming up behind us, clad today in black crop pants and a short-sleeved, button-down, pink denim shirt.

"Hey, Willow. Hey, everybody," Monique says. "I couldn't wait to see this house. I knew it would be something, tucked all back here in the woods."

I make the effort to control my eyes, open my mouth, and speak to Monique, turning my head back quickly.

"Come in, you all," Willow says. "Let me show you to the family room. DeRon can crawl and do whatever his heart desires. We're baby-proofed. Help yourself to coffee and juice. I have assorted bagels and cream cheese too."

We step into a sun-drenched space with a two-story center foyer that separates the formal living and dining rooms, both of which have wide entryways and appear ample in themselves. We walk through the foyer, down a hallway, and into a kitchen that flows into the spacious family room. Blue and gold ties the two rooms together, woven together in a beautiful fabric on the bar stools at the center island and on the sofa and loveseat. A sunroom sits beyond the family room, anchoring that end of the house, with a stone floor-to-ceiling fireplace as its centerpiece. Jillian rises from the floor when she sees me and gives me an elbow. "Thought you weren't coming," she whispers.

"Long story," I say.

"Where's Zoe?" Carmen asks.

"Taking her morning nap." Willow's eyes brighten and tear up at the same time. "I don't know if I can wait until we officially get started. I have to tell you all thank you again for praying for me last week...." Willow lets the tears roll.

Jillian goes to her side and puts an arm around her.

"It's just so amazing," Willow says. "God is amazing. Last night I was giving Zoe her bath and Damien came in and stood by the door, just folded his arms and stood there. I said, 'What?' and he said, 'Nothing,' so I kept doing what I was doing. I wrapped her in a towel and carried her to her room, put her pajamas on, and nursed her in the rocking chair. Y'all, Damien sat beside the rocking chair, still watching.

"After I put Zoe to bed, Damien said he knew how much I wanted to leave the firm and that he had been blowing me off because he couldn't believe I would do that. He said he hadn't even bothered to pray about it because it made no sense to give up that kind of money. But he said that at work yesterday he couldn't get it off his mind, and when he came home, he just wanted to watch me, that he had never really *watched* me with the baby. Then he said, 'I don't know how we're gonna swing it but, baby, go ahead and leave. I can see why you want to be with her.' Y'all *know* that was God!"

"Oh, my goodness, not even a week later!" Jillian exclaims, throwing her arms up in praise.

"Willow, He is able!" Carmen says, hugging her.

Asia hugs her too. "I'm happy for you."

Monique says, "I guess I'll hug you but I'm having a hard time feelin' this one. All that work you did to get where you are. What if you can't go back? What if you have to move from this house? I'm dying to get a house over this way and you're probably headed my way."

"Oh, Monique," Willow says, hugging her, "you are something else, girl."

Monique adds, "But God did answer that prayer, huh?"

I feel the need to say something so I try out a couple of comments in my mind. "I'm happy for you too" doesn't work because I'm not. I don't know how I feel about the fact that she's leaving her law career to stay at home. I can't help but compare her situation to mine, her joy to my frustration. I suppose I'm jealous—she has her heart's desire, I don't. This is just great. Maybe that's what I'll say—"That's great, Willow." But I'd have to smile to make it sound genuine and I don't feel like smiling.

One thing is certain. She'll come down a peg, from star attorney to mom. That's probably more than a peg. Despite how we got there, we'll be on the same plane. Won't have to see her on television spouting legalese, on top of her game, reminding me that I've been sidelined. Or will I?

"So, Willow, you're giving up 'Asked and Answered' too?" I ask.

"Actually, no. It takes very little of my time, and it'll be a fun way to continue to dabble in the law."

Just great.

"Willow's testimony is right on time," Jillian announces. "That's how we're going to start our discussion today, with testimonies. Because Ephesians Two talks about the goodness of God in salvation, we're supposed to share how God saved us. And based on what you all have shared with me, we're all believers, so this should be a great time of praise. Let's go ahead and pray and get started."

Anxiety shoots down my spine. I don't want to think about how I was saved, let alone share it.

Everyone sits and quiets down, save DeRon, and Jillian prays, then asks who would like to go first.

"I'll go," Monique volunteers, tossing that hair. "Mine is short and sweet. I grew up in Suitland, and every Sunday and Wednesday night my grandmother dragged my two brothers and me to church. I sang in the children's choir, the young adults' choir, all that. Always got in trouble for talking and chewing gum. I never stopped going, even when I graduated from high school and started working. It's always been a part of me. Since I got married, though, I've been going to Sean's church, which is very different from the one I grew up in—a little more teachey.

Sometimes that man goes way over my head, but I still go. Couldn't imagine doing anything else on Sunday morning. That's really it."

Jillian scoots forward in her chair. "So when did you commit your life to Jesus. When did He become your Lord and Savior?"

Monique tucks her hair behind her ear. "I'm not totally sure what you mean."

With a tender voice, Jillian asks, "Monique, did you do the lesson this week?"

"I started it...but I didn't get very far."

"Okay, let's see...do you understand the gospel message? Has anyone ever explained it to you?"

"Somebody had to, all these years I've been in church. But...I don't know. I know Jesus died on the cross and rose again. I know that." Monique's voice trails off.

"Yes, and that's central to the gospel. The teaching video is going to cover this, but I feel like the Spirit is moving and we ought to talk about it now." Jillian lifts her Bible from her lap and moves to a floor seat next to Monique. "I'm going to assume no knowledge on your part, Monique, to make sure you understand, because it's so important," Jillian says, in full teacher mode.

Monique nods her head, looking down.

Jillian continues. "All of us have sinned and fall short of the glory of God. This first verse in chapter two tells us that every single one of us walked under the power of Satan. He was our father."

"But I'm a child of God," Monique says, flashing her eyes at Jillian.

"If you're saved," Jillian says carefully. "In the book of John, Jesus said you're either a child of the devil or a child of God, and you become a child of God when you believe on the name of Jesus."

Jillian drapes an arm over Monique's shoulder and pulls her in close. "Before we believe, we're dead, Monique. Dead in sin. That's what this chapter is about. We're without God and without hope in the world."

"So you're saying dead...what, spiritually?" Monique's voice is bare.

"Exactly, Monique," Jillian says. "You talked about those Sunday school stories so I know you remember Adam and Eve. Remember God said they would die if they ate the forbidden fruit?"

"Yeah."

"But they didn't drop dead right when they sinned, did they?"

"I used to wonder about that," she confessed.

"They still died, though. They died spiritually, which meant they were separated from God, and they eventually died physically. Same with us. We're dead spiritually, separated from God. And if we go to our death that way, we'll spend eternity away from him in hell."

Monique draws her knees in, wraps her arms around them, and tucks her head between them. Carmen's head is bowed in her hand. Willow's arms are folded, eyes closed. Asia is holding DeRon. I'm afraid to move. I might ruin the moment.

"So...," Monique tries, her voice a quiver. Head still down, she clears her throat. "So, what do I have to do to be saved?"

Jillian answers, "Repent of your sins and believe. Believe that Jesus was raised from the dead. Believe that He is the way, the truth, and the life, and that no man comes to the Father but through Him. Believe that He is your salvation. Make Him the Lord of your life."

Monique swipes her hand through her hair twice and I wonder now if it's an anxious gesture because, at the third time, she leaves her hand there at the crown and her body droops with the first audible sob. I thought she'd been crying before but her face was hidden. Now, every couple of seconds, her body droops down with a soft sob, hand still at the crown.

"I'm sorry y'all," she manages. "I'm trying to stop crying but I can't. I never cry."

"Monique, God loves you. He's drawing you to Himself, right through this study. He's opening your eyes. The enemy had you in his church trick bag, thinking membership saved you. Girl, only the blood can do that," Jillian says softly.

Carmen starts singing softly, as if on cue, with a startlingly beautiful voice. "What can wash away my sin?"

Jillian and Willow respond in song, "Nothing but the blood of Jesus."

"What can make me whole again?" Carmen sings.

"Nothing but the blood of Jesus."

The three of them chorus, tears matching Monique's, "Oh precious is the flow, that makes me white as snow, no other fount I know. Nothing but the blood of Jesus."

"Hallelujah!" Willow lets out in a praise-moan. She stands, arms outstretched. "Hallelujah, Lord God! *You* have the victory. The enemy is defeated!"

"Forgive me, Jesus," Monique says, shaking. "Forgive me. I want You to be Lord and Savior of my life."

Willow pulls Monique to her feet and embraces her, saying, "Praise God! Praise God!" Carmen and Jillian encircle Monique too. Asia sits with a sleepy DeRon, her right hand half raised in praise as she rocks with her eyes closed. I wish I could hold the baby. I need an excuse for not rising to join the circle. I can't even will myself to rise. I don't feel a part of that circle. So I close my eyes too, as if entranced in my own praise moment.

After they talk and pray with Monique for a while, Monique shakes off her tears with a raspy chuckle. "I am so embarrassed. I had the nerve to volunteer to go first."

They hug her again and Jillian says, "God knows how you talk, girl. He said, 'Go on, I've got something for you.'"

Monique laughs and swipes more tears.

"See, now you'll do your homework, won't you?" Carmen says.

Monique flops down on the sofa. "Definitely. This is wild. I never would have thought…." Monique covers her face and shakes her head. "Y'all go on. I want to hear *your* stories."

"I'll go," Willow says, lowering herself to the carpeted floor. "Mine will *really* be short and sweet," she says, tossing a smile at Monique. "I grew up in the church, in Baltimore County. And my mother says when I was four, she was reading a children's book to me about Jesus and I told her I loved Jesus and wanted to live with Him forever. She says I prayed with her right then, asking Jesus into my heart. I don't remember that part but I do remember always talking to God and having a heart for Him. Didn't always do right, now," Willow chuckles. "Jillian could attest to that. But I've always loved God. I would be nothing without Him."

"My parents didn't go to church but my grandmother did," Carmen says, nestled back on the sofa. "And she would pick me up and take me to her country church house. It was a respite for me. It really was." Carmen drifts into silent reflection. "Anyway, only a handful of us kids were in the Sunday school, and we would sit on this old tore-up couch in a small room of the church building and Sister Reynolds would talk to us about God. When I was twelve, it all came together in my heart. I remember crying, just like Monique, and Sister Reynolds kept me after class, didn't even care if we were late for the morning worship service, and led me to the Lord. God saved me…in more ways than one." Carmen sinks back into her thoughts.

"Well, Carmen and Jillian know my testimony," Asia says, stroking DeRon's tuft of hair. His little body is laid across her lap and thus across the entire length of her skirt, leaving long bare legs showing forth.

I liven up, all ears.

"One Sunday morning about three months ago I was driving down 193, me and DeRon, and I was upset, going nowhere in particular. I saw Grace Bible Fellowship. I don't know how many times I had seen it before, had to be hundreds, but this time it was bigger. I passed it and kept looking behind me until I just turned the car around and entered the parking lot." Asia's head lowers. "I didn't know what I was going to do. All these people were doing what they normally did, parking and walking into the building. Here I was, not at all dressed for church—"

Really?

"—and didn't know if I was late, early, or what. I just knew I had to go in. I took DeRon and walked in and felt like walking right back out because of the way people were looking at me. I wanted to cry, and then this smiling face marched up to me. It was Carmen." Asia turns toward Carmen.

"She asked me my name and took me to a women's Bible study that she was on her way to. When we got there, she introduced me to Jillian. After the Bible study we talked and talked. And they listened to me. I think that's the first time anybody really listened to me. Carmen and Jillian walked me to my car and we ended up in the car for almost an hour. They told me about Jesus and about salvation."

Asia looks over at Monique. "I cried, too, and I immediately knew God must have driven my car to that church. He saw my pain. It wasn't hard at all for me to give my life to Him."

I keep watching Asia, waiting, hoping she'll peel back more layers, but she's apparently done.

Jillian looks at me, her expression questioning whether I will go next. Mine answers: "No."

"My turn, I guess," Jillian says. "Our parents didn't go to church, grandparents either. They didn't see the point. So I never stepped foot in a church. After I graduated from Maryland, I didn't know what I wanted to do with my life yet, but I knew I didn't want to go back home. Treva and Hezekiah were married by then and Treva was pregnant, getting ready to start a clerkship."

Tell the story without telling all my business.

"I stayed with them for about a year and helped out with Faith when she was born. I got to know Hezekiah's mom, Darlene, while I was there.

And if you know Darlene, you're going to know *something* about the Lord, whether you want to or not. I *love* Darlene. She led me to Jesus and became my spiritual mother. Treva's too, eventually."

All eyes fall upon me. And we sit. And sit.

"Treva, you ready?" Jillian asks.

"I need to talk to you a minute," I say, gathering the straps of my tote.

Jillian and I walk to the foyer.

"Jillian, you know I have no intention of going back to that night," I say, fishing through my purse for car keys. "I can't believe I'm here. I'm leaving."

"Why?"

"Jillian, you very well know why."

"Honestly, I don't."

I look up from my purse and into her eyes. "Why would I want to remember that night?"

"For the same reasons I talked about with Monique. Because that's when God saved you. It's a testimony."

"I understand all that, but that's not the only thing that happened that night. Why would I talk about that, Jillian?"

I finally dig out the keys and remember. No SUV. Sighing, I say, "I forgot I rode over here with Carmen. Can I use your van to get home? And you can ride with Carmen back to my house when this is over."

Jillian holds my gaze for a moment. "I could, but Treva, you don't have to run all the time. Mama doesn't have power over you, and neither do those memories." She grabs my hand when I avert my eyes and waits until I look at her again. "The only power they have is the power you give them, and running gives them power," she says. "Just talk about it for once. Allow God to minister to you. He works through people, Treva. That's what a group like this is for, to help you. I know it's difficult but—"

"No, you don't know, Jilli," I say in a hushed, biting tone, stepping closer. "It's easy for you to say 'stop running' and 'just talk about it.' You don't *have* any bad memories. You let *me* handle this the best way *I* know how."

"The best way *you* know how doesn't make it the best way." Jillian matches my tone, taking me off guard. "I've watched you, Treva, for years. *Your* way isn't working. Jesus has set you free and you're not walking in it." Jillian's voice is rising. "You can't even testify about *how* He set you free because you're still living in the horror of that night rather than the glory. I was there. I saw what God did. He turned evil into good. And by now you should be able to shout it from the rooftops."

Jillian raises a shaking finger and points it at me. "And don't you tell me I don't have bad memories," she says, voice asunder in tears. "Every time Mama acted ugly with you, *I* hurt. I hurt for you. *And* I hurt for Mama. You don't think our lives *affected* me!"

Willow walks up, and behind her everyone else, including toddling DeRon. "What's wrong?" Willow asks, taking my hand.

I snatch it away and hold my arms. "Nothing." Then, "I just need a ride home."

"I can run you home," Carmen says.

"Thanks, Carmen," I say, moving toward the door.

"No problem. Let me get my purse."

Carmen walks back to the family room and Willow says, "Treva, I hate that you have to go. Really, is something wrong? Is there anything I can do?"

"You know what, Willow?" I say, throwing my hands up and turning toward her. "You can get me a job because I didn't get the one at Brooks Donnelly. You can also move me back to the Midwest. Oh, and erase my bad memories—although my sister here thinks I should chat about them, just tell women I don't know all about my life so we can sing Kumbaya or something."

Carmen returns, keys jingling.

"Wait, Carmen," Willow says, hand flattened in the air. "Treva, I don't think you should leave. You don't have to tell us anything if you don't want to. I understand where you're coming from."

"That's the thing. I don't think you do understand. How could you? You're Willow Fusell. What *hasn't* gone well for you? You're 'black America's darling.' Isn't that what *Essence* said in that article? 'The perfect combination of beauty and brains?' Come on. You couldn't possibly understand anything about me. You have your nice little life. Your nice little story about coming to the Lord. Your nice testimony of how God answered your prayer in record time. Well, I never had a nice little life." *Don't you cry, Treva. Don't you break down.* "I don't have a sweet story about coming to the Lord. And I sure don't get my prayers answered."

I turn and reach for the door handle and Willow reaches for my rigid body. I tense further as her hand gently pulls my shoulder, attempting to turn me around. I resist, needing desperately to get out of here. I would walk home if I had to.

Willow comes closer, keeps her left hand on my shoulder, and begins kneading my back with the other. The sensation causes a slight tremor to coarse through my body. I close my eyes, trying to stay in control.

Still kneading, Willow begins praying, "Oh, God, this is my sister in Christ and she's hurting." Those words alone cause my head to fall and tears to spill from my eyes. "But, Lord, nothing is too difficult for You," Willow says. "You are able to heal her. You are all-powerful. Let her know that. Let her experience that. Show Yourself strong in her life, for You are stronger than her past, stronger than anything that raises itself against the truth." Willow prays soothingly and every word seems to relax a muscle. "And, Father, may Treva know Your love for her, Your deep, earth-shattering, bondage-breaking love for *her*. Cause her to know that Your love is shed abroad in *us* and that we are willing to stand with her and *will* stand with her. We praise You, Lord, for what You are doing right now in her life. I see You, Father. I see You working. We pray all these things in Jesus' name."

Willow tugs on my shoulder again, and this time I turn around. My head finds her neck. A low wail escapes my mouth. *I'm losing it, in front of everybody.* My upper torso quivers as I strive to contain my sobs, but they're striving too, for freedom. I smell Jillian's perfume hugging my side and hear Carmen at my other side, praying softly. Behind her Monique touches my shoulder and directs, "Let it out, Treva." I hear babbling by my ear too, and know Asia and DeRon are there.

I keep my head planted forever it seems, and they all huddle with me in the forever. When finally I lift my mascara, liner, foundation and blush-stained face, I know what I have to do.

Chapter Sixteen

The mini congregation has assembled again in Willow's family room, waiting. I said I would share my salvation experience but I haven't yet said a word. They assured me that they weren't in a hurry.

Zoe has awakened and Willow is nursing her in a corner of the sofa. Asia is crawling behind DeRon on the floor, embarrassingly so given her conspicuous thong. Jillian, Carmen, and Monique sit cross-legged in their seats, legs bobbing in time with one another.

I'm sitting at the other end of the sofa, grappling with my decision to open up. Weary now, I'm thinking it was rash, emotional, and unwise. Do I really want to share this with them? I haven't talked about that night since it happened. What sense does it make to tell people I barely know?

But I keep hearing Willow call me "sister." "Sister in Christ." In my mind I can picture the yellow down the page of my Bible, telling me all I have "in Christ" and "in Him," including blessings. Is this one of my them? A sisterhood? Odd. Asia? My sister? And now Monique?

A series of thoughts awaken within me. Were Jillian and Willow right? *Did* God put this strange group of women together? And if He did, does that mean He maneuvered to get me here? Does He go that far? A line from Willow's prayer runs through my head—*"I see You working."* God actually moved Carmen to call me about riding with her? He knew I would jump at the chance to find out more about Asia! I would laugh if I had it in me right now. He sure knew I wouldn't have come otherwise. The quiet promptings I'd been feeling all morning weren't moving me, though if I'd had a heart to listen, I guess I would have known that was God too.

If He did all of that to get me here, I have no doubt it was primarily for this moment, so that I could tell this story. As anxious as I am, the thought of God behind all of this gives me strength. *Lord, You've got to help me through this.*

I will myself to the edge of the sofa, exhaling audibly. The bobbing legs still. Willow lifts her head with a reassuring smile. Asia takes a seat on the family room fireplace at full attention.

"When my father died three years ago," I start, the floor my focus, "I knew I had to go home, but I knew it wouldn't be easy. See...." *Do I tell this?* "My mother...never...well, she never liked me. I was too dark. She never treated me as her daughter. She fed me and clothed me and made sure I had a bed to sleep in, but there was no love. After I left for college, we rarely communicated. Over the years we exchanged Christmas cards, birthday cards, she would send gifts for the girls. That was it. I hadn't been to that house in ten years. But when Daddy died, my first thought was of how to get home. Death does that, I guess. Takes you home."

I lift my eyes and theirs reassure me to continue.

"So we left Chicago and drove out here. Got in town the night before the funeral, picked up Darlene, and headed to the house." I give a life-less chuckle. "Darlene and my mother, now that's interesting. They met in Judge Crawford's chambers, where Hezekiah and I got married, which is another story. Anyway, at dinner afterwards, Darlene tells my mother her hair would look much more stylish if she wore it a different way, and she proceeded to describe the style. I was thinking, 'Uh-oh,' but my mother actually listened and made an appointment to see Darlene the following week. Been going ever since. They have a weird tolerance for one another.

"Well, we got to the house and I saw my mother looking mournful and withdrawn and I realized she's always that way, at least where I'm concerned. Always somber, grieving the very fact of my existence. I grew up watching her do a constant Jekyll and Hyde—she'd be gloomy and short with me, bubbly and talkative with Jillian. So this time the only difference in her behavior was that everybody got to see her grieve. And tote a glass of white wine, something she also didn't normally do in the open.

"Jillian and her family were there, too, and she and I slipped away to Daddy's study. That was his favorite place—mine, too— and we wanted to remember him there. When we walked in, we saw copies of the funeral program on the desk and we read it. Jillian immediately called for Mother to come upstairs."

I pause to gather myself, mortified that my arms have begun shaking. My fingers move to the inside corners of my eyes, squeezing tears. Willow slides with the baby to my end of the sofa and puts an arm around my shoulder.

"Take your time, Treva," she says. "We're here to help you deal with it."

I wait a few more seconds, then recount the scene as it unfolds in my mind.

"Mama," Jillian said, "the program says 'Tribute to Dad' and has my name beside it. Treva's the oldest. She should have that honor."

"Clearly I felt *you* should have the honor. The programs are already printed, Jillian."

"You should have asked me first, Mama. It's not right. If you won't let Treva do it, then nobody will. We can just cross it off the program."

"You will not embarrass me that way, Jillian. Of course you will do it."

"No. I won't."

Patsy grabbed the programs and slung them across the room, creating a paper whirl. "I have had it with this stick-together routine. Jillian, your entire life you have refused to ascend to your rightful place. You just don't get it. It's not about who's the oldest. You're the ideal, you're the chosen one. You're the one who was blessed with ideal skin, hair, and eyes. You're the one people gravitate toward. You're the one for whom doors have always opened. But you won't walk through them! And for what?"

Patsy jerked her head toward me. "What on earth did I do to deserve you? If there is a God, why would He inflict such a punishment on me?"

She stormed out of the room.

A shooting pain traveled down my left arm and into my thumb and fingers as I sank calmly to the floor.

"Oh, Treva," Jillian cried, stooping over me, "Mama is not in her right mind. She's grieving, she's been drinking, she's—"

"Jillian, she's right," I muttered, flexing my fingers and wrist to discard the pain. Another gripped my chest and tossed me forward. I cupped my mouth as it sprang open in a dry heave.

Jillian slumped to her knees. "Right about what, Treva? That's foolish."

I wrapped my arms around my waist, doubled over. "I never belonged. I think it may have been some kind of punishment like she said. For her and me."

Jillian jumped up and ran out, returning with Darlene, who sat before me on the floor and lifted my head with a finger. "Baby, Jillian told me what Patsy said and it's a lie. Don't you believe no lie like that, straight from the devil himself. You weren't a punishment. You were a blessing. Children are a blessing from the Lord."

Her words caused the pain to shoot through my arm again. I rubbed it and dropped my head.

"Do you hear me, Treva? God didn't make any mistakes. He placed you in this family on purpose, for a reason."

"It really doesn't matter, does it?" I said. "Whatever the reason, we know the result. My own mother hates me. She truly hates me. I always knew it…." My voice choked with tears. "But I tried to pretend I was misreading her. Then I acted like I didn't care. But she's my mother! How can I not care?"

Darlene placed both hands on my upper arms. "You're wrong, Treva. We don't know the result. We see today's result, and, honey, the day's not over. What Satan meant for evil, God can turn around for good. God can take your ripped up soul and heal it."

I swiped my nose with the back of my hand and Jillian passed me a tissue. "Is this the part where you tell me how Jesus died on the cross for me? Between you, Hezekiah, and Jillian, I know it by heart."

"Yes, you do. But do you *believe* He died for you? Could Jesus really love old dark, ugly Treva, who's not good enough for her own mother? Why would He love you? You're nobody."

I clutched my shirt at the chest and moaned.

"That's what you think, isn't it? That you're ugly? That you're not good enough? Not even for God."

I moaned louder and Jillian quietly closed the door.

"Baby, if you were the only person on God's green earth, Jesus would have died for you. You!" Darlene said, shaking me lightly. She shifted to the floor space beside me, draped an arm around me, and joined my tearful sway from left to right. "And like I always said—you act like you don't want to believe it—but when Hezekiah brought you home the first time, I said to myself, 'I'll be darned if that's not one of the prettiest girls I've ever seen in my life.' You're beautiful, Treva. And I'm not even talking only-in-God's-eyes beautiful. You are a beautiful woman. You've just been caught in all this fake, the-lighter-the-better mess that God ain't got no parts of. He wants to deliver you out of this lie and bring you to the truth. Honey, God's got better for you; He's got a higher realm, a heavenly realm."

I stop talking and reflect on what Darlene said. "Heavenly realm." *Heavenly places.* I had no clue what she was talking about or that it came from the Bible. If only I understood it.

"After Darlene said those things, everything just clicked, everything she, Hezekiah, and Jillian had been saying over the years. I knew then and there that I needed to be saved and *wanted* to be saved. Darlene talked and prayed with me up there for over an hour."

"Oh, Treva, I can't believe all of that," Carmen says. "So what happened with your mother?"

"I had nothing else to say to her. Well, one thing, at the funeral, but nothing more. She apologized to Jillian later and said she may have had too much to drink. But she apologized only because she hates to have Jillian upset with her. She never said a word about it to me. I didn't talk to Patsy for three years, not until I moved back here."

"What happened then?" Willow says.

"Not a lot, actually. Surprisingly. She hasn't changed, though, and I'm staying as far away from her as I can."

Carmen shakes her head. "Treva, I am blown away. I've heard stories that it used to be that way but I had no idea...."

"I don't get it," Willow says, scooting up on the sofa while stroking Zoe on her lap. "I don't see how she could still be perpetuating that kind of color prejudice. What world is she living in? Darker skin has been universally acknowledged as beautiful, finally, in every type of medium. Treva, *you're* beautiful. I'm with Darlene. When I walked into your house, I admit my first thought was surprise because you looked so different than Jillian, but my immediate next thought was, *That's a pretty woman.*"

"I thought the same thing when I saw her," Carmen says. "I had seen her husband first and, like you, I thought, *Hmm,* because I wasn't expecting the contrasting tones—it's weird to even admit that we do notice color, isn't it—but right after that, I thought, *Here she is moving in, should be looking a mess, and she looks great.*"

I look down, remembering that day, and how badly I felt I looked.

"I'm glad you all are telling her this," Jillian says, "because she never believed me when I would tell her. And, Willow, you asked how my mother could still perpetuate that prejudice in today's world. You can't rationalize prejudice. It's what she grew up with, it's what she believes. The shame is that she got Treva to believe it as well."

"But praise God, Treva, for where He's brought you," Willow says. "I know it was painful for you to share this, but thankfully it's in the past, where it ought to be. These last three years must have been awesome for you in terms of growing in the Word and being able to strip away those lies." When I stare straight ahead, Willow says, "You no longer believe those lies...do you?"

I try to shake my head no, because it's the right answer, but all my head does is fall, with the tears.

Willow jumps up with Zoe, puts her in the bouncy seat, and returns to the sofa, taking my hands. "Treva, I said God was working in my prayer earlier but I'm beginning to understand even better now. If you're still struggling with this, then you need to know He wants to lift you up out of it. Don't you see it?" Willow tugs at my hands. "The things you've had to deal with, we're covering right here in this Bible study. It's no wonder the enemy didn't want you to take part—and I see now that that's all it was. When you said you weren't going to do the study, that was *his* plan, not God's—"

My stomach drops. It's one thing to acknowledge that God wanted me here, quite another to acknowledge that someone else, besides me, didn't. This is the second time this week someone has referred to "the enemy," Darlene being the first, and both times have been unnerving. Can he really influence my thinking?

"—So here you are, not at home but right in my house," Willow is saying. "Why? Because greater is He who is in you than he who is in the world. God wants to bless you. Look what we've learned in just two weeks, and these are only a couple of examples but we could talk about it all day. Your mother said Jillian was the chosen one, but we read that *you* were chosen *by God* before the foundation of the world—"

"Amen," Jillian says.

"—And the whole 'looks' thing. We read Psalm 139! Look at God! How much plainer can He say it? We're *all* fearfully and wonderfully made, not a select few."

"I hear you, Willow, but I had a hard time with that," I admit quietly. "All I could see was how all of *you* were fearfully and wonderfully made."

"Since we're being real, I had a hard time with that too," Monique says.

"With what?" I say, turning toward Monique.

"With the thought of being fearfully and wonderfully made."

"I thought you said the psalm let you know you were 'all that.'"

"I know. I was trying to convince myself," Monique says.

I furrow my brow at her and cock my head. "So why did *you* have a hard time with that?"

"It's a long story, and I shouldn't have interrupted. I guess I just wanted you to know that, you know, that you weren't alone."

Monique's tone is soft and my eyes linger on her a moment. "I don't mind the interruption, and I'd like to hear the story, if you're willing to share it," I say, surprising myself.

Monique exhales. "I don't think I've ever gone this deep in one day." She looks upward as if contemplating where to start. She clasps her hands and tucks them between her legs. "Okay. My mother never married but she lived with this one man, Derek, for a long time, and that's who she had my two brothers by. After they broke up, she hooked up with this white man for a little while and got pregnant with me, by mistake—she told me that." Monique pauses, hanging her head for a moment. Looking up, she continues, "People in the neighborhood called me 'white girl' and 'mongrel' and every other name they could think of. I stayed to myself because of the way they treated me, but then they said I thought I was too good for them. I don't know how many fights I got into because of somebody pushing me, saying, 'She thinks she's cute.' The funny part is that I didn't think I was cute. I hated the way I looked because *they* hated the way I looked. And I hated that I couldn't get my hair in the styles the other girls wore."

Monique swipes through her hair. This time it doesn't bother me.

"I just wanted to be black. Just straight up black. Even now as an adult I just want to blend in. I get so tired of people asking me, 'What are you?' I get so tired of having to explain. Sometimes I just want to say, 'You know what? I'm what came out in the wash. I'm the "oops" that happened when my mother had a fling with a white man I never knew.' When we read that psalm, I wanted so badly to believe that God had knitted me together on purpose. But how could He have been in a *fling?* How could He have been in a *mistake?*"

Monique covers her face and I'm compelled to hug her, but my mind keeps me planted. I would feel awkward given the tension from the last meeting, and the things I said. But she did reach out to me in the foyer, and just now. And I may be the only one in the room who understands how she feels. I lean forward and push up out of my chair. When I touch her shoulder, she looks up, startled, and Jillian moves over so I can sit between them on the love seat. My arm curves around Monique's neck and our heads huddle together as we weep openly.

After a few moments Monique lifts her head, saying, "Treva, I really didn't like you." Brushing tears from her face, she continues, "I thought you were stuck-up. I know, I'm the last person who should think that about somebody. But you looked stunning to me, and I thought you knew it, too, because of the way you carry yourself. Plus you're a lawyer and everything, and I never did all that great in school and didn't even go to college. Then I heard your story. I'm sorry, Treva," Monique says, hugging me again.

"Monique, I'm sorry, too, because I didn't like you either." We both laugh softly. "You have the look that everybody praised growing up. And I automatically categorized you."

"I told you," Jillian says. When I throw her a puzzled look, she says, "I told you God had plans for this group. Didn't I?"

I roll my red eyes playfully.

Carmen stands and looks around at everyone. "Ladies, can we pray? I'm so full right now with everything Monique and Treva have said that I'll burst if we don't do *something* for them."

"Definitely," Willow says, hopping up. "And, Monique, I was sitting here thinking about what you said, and I want to tell you that God *is* in the flings and the mistakes. He's God. He's the author of every human life, and He took great care in making you exactly how He wanted to make you, for His glory. Sometimes I think He delights in shaping people from different races, making it difficult for the masses to separate themselves according to this color and that color. I think He kind of smiles when folk can't figure it out; He's like, 'Yeah, that's what I intended.'

"And the next time somebody asks you, 'What are you?' you think about this day, your new birthday, and you tell them, 'I'm a child of God.' That's all they need to know, girl."

Monique smiles. "I like that."

"Willow, you're on a roll," Jillian says, walking to her side.

"And I'm not finished," Willow says, motioning for the rest of us to join them in the circle. She chuckles. "You know how I get, Jillian, when a fire is lit under me. Treva, I was thinking more about your situation. We should pray for your relationship with your mother. You need grace to deal with her, because what if God doesn't want you to stay as far away from her as you can? What if He wants to use you in her life?"

Her words coil around one another and form a tight knot in the pit of my stomach. The look I give Willow is enough of a response.

"I've been praying a long time for God to work a miracle in that situation," Jillian says. "All things are possible, right? I would love to have this group pray about that. And hey, after we pray maybe we can actually get to the Bible study and watch the DVD. If everybody still has time."

A chorus of agreement rises and we grab hands in the circle and pray. When I hear my name mentioned in conjunction with my mother, I stack my own silent prayer on top of it. *Lord, I know they mean well but they don't understand. My prayer is the same as the one I prayed the night we arrived, that even though we're in close proximity again, You would erect a barrier between Patsy and me to prevent her from affecting our lives in the least way. Lord, if there are any miracles to be had, I'm praying that You would entirely remove Patsy from my life and every bad memory she created.*

Chapter Seventeen

Carmen drops me off at home after four hours at Willow's. I'm drained but feeling good. I feel good about the lesson, about the group, and surprisingly good about opening up. I would not have guessed that those women would shower me with such love and caring, or that it was in us to act as silly as we did when Monique broke out with her own rendition of "I Will Survive" at the door. I don't know how those words came to her, but they were right on time.

She told me, "Girl, we need to sing this when that old monkey gets on our back." Then she took my hand and goaded me into a disco two-step, needing to sing the words only once before everybody caught on: "I will survive. I will survive. Oh, as long as I know the God of love I know I'll be all right. Jesus died so I could live, all my sins He did forgive; I will survive, I will survive...."

Willow grabbed Carmen, Jillian grabbed Asia, and we twirled one another around that foyer, singing loud, and then Willow charged us, "Tell that enemy, 'So now go, walk out the door, just turn around now, you're not welcome anymore, Jesus died so I could live. All my sins He did forgive; I will survive, I will survive. Hey, hey!'"

I don't think I've laughed that hard in my life. The memory's got me chuckling still and snapping my fingers as hunger sends me straight to the kitchen to fix a late lunch. I open the refrigerator and fill my hands with honey turkey from the deli, Swiss cheese, lettuce, a tomato, and Dijon mustard, and the phone begins to ring. Dumping everything on the counter, I dash to answer it. At my hurried "Hello," I hear, "Treva, have you not gotten my messages?"

The voice is unmistakable but I question my ears still. What timing that my mother should call now after the morning I've had. "Yes, I got your messages," I say. "I didn't feel like talking about it just yet."

"Well, you knew I expected an update. I assume you heard from Theodore Dutton?"

"He called, yes." I place two slices of whole wheat bread on my plate and begin spreading the Dijon in nice smooth strokes, perfectly, right up to the crust.

"Treva, I will not pull teeth here. What did he say?"

"Oh, they didn't offer me the position," I say, nodding to "I Will Survive" while positioning my turkey just so on the bread.

"And why not? How dare he do this after all Charles did for him."

I lay a crisp piece of romaine and a slice of tomato on top of the turkey as I tell her in very abbreviated form what Theodore told me. Then I take a bite.

"And he said that was Charles's policy? I don't know, maybe it was. It seems to me the requirement is easily satisfied. Call your old firm and explain the circumstances—that you need an offer but only for the purpose of securing another one. They should be willing to do that much for you."

"They said, 'no,'" I say, irritated that our thinking is so aligned. Monday morning I called my former litigation supervisor and brought him up-to-date on my dismal job search, ending with Brooks Donnelly and a pitch that he arrange for the D.C. litigation head to offer me a position on paper only. He refused, citing ethical considerations. I hadn't shared the attempt with anyone until now.

"It appears your options have dwindled to nothing then. As I understand it, Brooks Donnelly was your last shot at a blue-chip firm."

I allow the last bite I've taken to clear my throat, determined to keep my mood. "Blue-chip firms are not the only option. There are other firms."

"No, there aren't. None worth mentioning, but you know that as well as I. What in heaven's name do you plan to make of your life now? Sterling credentials were your equalizer."

My stomach twists and the sandwich falls from my hand to the plate. "My what?"

"It's no secret, Treva. I've never had to spell it out this plainly because you've always excelled. You've always known that you *needed* to excel. For you, anything less than a Brooks Donnelly constitutes disaster."

"In whose eyes?"

"In the eyes of people who matter," Patsy snaps. "And in my eyes. Yours, too. You would never be satisfied at one of those 50-attorney firms with tacky décor and low-budget coffee. And why should you? You were on your way, Treva, associated with one of the top firms in the world. Frankly, your career has been the one thing you've given me to speak proudly of. I saw you becoming a federal judge one day, something I always wanted for Charles."

I should be angry that she just told me that I'm not good enough. I should be angry that she used a tone as nice and natural as any motherly wisdom, as if there's anything natural about a mother telling her daughter she doesn't measure up. And I should *really* be angry that she presumes to speak for me, as if we have an open agreement that I don't measure up. But none of these things are new. She's done this one way or another my entire life.

What I'm angry about is that I'm tempted to be halfway happy. My mother praised my accomplishments for once. She actually envisioned something great for me. She spoke proudly of *me?* I should know. That was the whole point of her help with Brooks Donnelly. That's the reason for these calls. She wants me back where I was, in a place that kept her head high, a place she could be proud to tell her bridge club members about. I should know Patsy well enough to know that if she had a daughter who graduated at the top of her law school class, clerked for a federal judge, and worked for Thompson & Klein, she would crow about it. But to hear her *say* it.... I hate that it causes a stir in my belly. I hate that I long to hear more. What *exactly* did she say in her proud moment? Who was present? What was the response? Was it one occasion or several? I hate that I want to linger with her words and enjoy them. Because I can't. They're not present, they're past. I *was* on my way. She *was* proud of me.

Her words for me now: "Your life is a disaster."

I shove my plate and it slides the width of the counter, tottering against the backsplash. *Why does she always get to me?* I rub the prickly places on my arms, remembering how hard it was to deal with the ghost of Patsy when I was away and estranged. Now I've got Patsy live, fresh angst for my already overburdened soul.

Thank You, Lord, for confirmation. Thank You for letting me know that I was right. I cannot experience this woman for more than two minutes. And I'm thankful as well, Lord, that now that this Brooks Donnelly matter is concluded, we'll have no cause for contact.

"I will survive" sounds in my head. Only if I'm far from her.

"...and Heddy Truesdale's daughter, Genevieve, remember her?" Patsy says, oblivious to my mental absence. "She's president of that cable television network, the financial one...I can't remember the name of it. She graduated from Howard, of course, then got her MBA from Harvard, and now look at her. That Heddy can't stop talking about her. And Cecelia Knight, I know you remember her, always the life of the party. Jillian could have been, too, if she had had a mind to. Anyway, Cecelia is now a partner on Wall Street, at Gibson, Rowe. Her mother says she's on track to be managing partner one day. Oh, and—"

"Mother, I've got to go pick up the girls," I say. Or vomit. Either is preferable.

"I just wanted to let you know how well these girls who grew up with you are doing. Treva, you have got to work diligently to get back on course. I honestly don't know what you can do at this point. Maybe you could pray for a miracle, since I hear you're into religion now. What a travesty if neither of my daughters distinguishes herself. You were close, Treva. Don't give up. You know you won't be satisfied with less than the best."

Again she speaks for me. Again she's right.

Chapter Eighteen

"Daddy!"

My stomach lurches as I check the time on my computer screen. It's 6:07 P.M.

"Where's Mommy?" I hear him say.

"In the office," the two youngest proclaim.

I'm in trouble. I know it, I know it, I know it. The house is a wreck, I haven't cooked, and Hezekiah clanged enough pots extra loudly last night to let me know he wasn't in love with the current arrangement. I did feel a tinge of guilt when he rolled up his sleeves and whipped up pork chops smothered with gravy on the fly, but it proved a point. Why shouldn't he be the one to cook since he does it so well?

It's not that I refuse to cook. I've done meals since we moved here, easy meals like tacos and spaghetti. But that was before. In the last week and a half, since the rejection from Theodore Dutton, Hezekiah has entered an aroma-free house. Every evening I've felt a prod to get up and prepare *something* before he got home but I've simply been stuck, unable to do anything but sit at this computer and look at job listing after job listing, then wonder why I'm looking at job listing after job listing since I haven't found a promising one yet. Then I scan various legal news sites and wonder why I'm depressing myself by scanning various legal news sites. But it's more depressing to walk away. Scrolling through these pages keeps my mind immersed, steadfast on the goal.

Do you have goals for your home and family?

Shut up, Darlene.

My head collapses on the desk. I'm more than stuck. I'm paralyzed. Petrified. What if God has permanently shut the door on my legal career? What if all I have to look forward to is the ever-present intolerable need to dust and figure out what's for dinner?

"Treva," I hear my husband say, and I know that I was right about being in trouble. No "Hey, Babe." No immediate kiss. "Are you sick or something?"

"No," my muffled voice says.

"Then what are you doing?"

I lift my head to a screen covered with fast-moving geometric designs and quickly shake the mouse. "I was reading the decision issued by the Supreme Court on copyright infringement." Sounds important enough.

"Did you expect me to cook again tonight?"

I twist my neck and run my eyes down my husband's university threads—cuffed, British tan trousers, white button-down polo shirt, Cole Haan loafers. He looks dapper, and greatly perturbed. "I… thought…maybe."

"Treva, look, I don't mind cooking, you know that. I used to come home from work almost every night from Northwestern and cook and didn't complain. But if I'm working all day, and you're home all day, can a brother get a hot meal prepared? Is it too much to ask? And how about helping the girls with their homework?"

"They didn't tell me they needed help," I say, swiveling in my chair to face him.

"That's because you said you didn't want to be disturbed while you were in the office. Soon as I got in the door they bombarded me with it."

I sigh. "If I was still working at Thompson & Klein I wouldn't even be home yet. It's really not a big deal that I'm trying to get some work done in the office."

"Treva…." Hezekiah bites his lips. "Does it matter to you at all that I'm hungry, and the girls too?"

I come lazily out of my seat. "Do you want to call the Chinese place and have the food delivered?"

"Do *I* want to call?" Hezekiah looks at me as if I've grown a tail and then walks out.

I am not sure whether that means he's going to call or that I should call.

I am not sure why my guilt is suddenly morphing into anger. I knew I should have fixed dinner. I knew Hezekiah would be annoyed. But now *I'm* annoyed that he expressed it. He knows what I've been going through with this unemployment. He should be patient and thank God when I do find the wherewithal to rustle something up in that kitchen.

"I'm hungry." What am I, a short-order cook? Is this my lot in life, waiting for my husband to come home from a satisfying day at work so I can serve up a June Cleaver smile and a hot plate? He gets treated like a king and I get what?

My purse waves at me from the credenza, the keys curl their fingers. I come, scoop them up, and step softly out of the office. Voices rise from the kitchen as I scurry down the hall, dash through the living room, open and lightly close the French doors that lead to the loggia. Over the patio, out the gate, and into the side door of the garage, I suspect Hezekiah hears the car starting and the garage door lifting.

And if he didn't do it yet, I suspect he knows he'd better make that call for Chinese.

I have no idea where I'm going and no idea what I'm accomplishing. As I speed north on I-95, I am overwhelmed by the very real possibility that I am going crazy.

Wasn't I feeling better when I left Willow's on Friday, just four days ago? Hadn't their prayers and support boosted me to a flow of laughter and chatter, to dancing even, to a peaceful place that held me and whispered, "You don't have to go back"?

But I did have to go back—back home. It screams failure. Every moment of the day reminds me that I'm not where I ought to be. There's no peace there, only anxiety, and I'm suffocating. No fulfillment. No excitement. No intellectual stimulation. No pay. And loads of expectation. If it weren't for the Internet, I'd be crawling up a wall.

As the highway splits and I-95 veers right toward Baltimore, I keep left on I-495 and eventually take the Rockville Pike exit to North Bethesda. As I move through the stop lights I see a P.F. Chang's I didn't know was there and whip right. Hezekiah loves this restaurant, as do I. His home-delivered Chinese meal won't be half as good as mine.

When I turn the engine off and grab my purse, I see my Bible as well, still in the car since Sunday service, reminding me that I'm two days late in starting this week's homework. I reach for it on impulse and frown. *Why would I take that inside?* On a normal day I wouldn't read the Bible in a restaurant, and certainly not now when I'm staging a mini-revolt. Who takes a hose to the bonfire?

I jump out and walk toward the restaurant, my pace slowing midway in the parking lot as I look back at the car, then continue toward the host who has the door opened for me to enter. Breezing in under his arm, I hear myself say, "One moment. I forgot something."

As my feet scurry back to the car, it's clear that for now the clash is not between Hezekiah and me but between me and the tiny part of me that's revolting against my revolt. I feel it, a single flutter of resistance, a mere lightweight really—if it weren't moving muscles to action. I won't worry, though, about being torn, not when I've got the biggest piece, with adrenaline tied to it. I'm pumped. I'm going to enjoy myself. This is *my* night. "Nothing wrong with that, is there?" I ask the Bible tucked under my arm as I stroll back to the door. It bobs along in silence. My fire can blaze on as long as the hose is turned off.

The Tuesday night crowd is light and I'm led right away to a booth. With dim lighting. Too dim to read. *So there.*

The server asks what I would like to drink and, since I know what I want, I order the appetizer and entrée as well.

Surveying my surroundings, my lips curve to a smile. This is wonderful. Just what I needed. An impromptu break. A bit of rebellion to spice up my life. I wonder what they're thinking at home.

I wonder what would happen if I never returned home.

I remember an article about a woman who did that. Upped and left. Had spent fifteen years at home all day tending to a husband and four kids and got bored. Had an affair with the UPS man and packed up while the kids were at school.

After a couple of months of this, I'm getting a glimpse of her frustration. I don't need the affair; I'd be fine by myself. I could stay on the computer all day if I want and not worry about who needs to eat. And who needs homework done. And clothes washed. And socks darned, which I don't do and don't know how to do, but I bet Darlene would tell me I need to learn. I bet that woman in the article darned socks. Probably pushed her over the edge.

A gentleman places a Coke with lemon on a square coaster—my indulgence of empty calories—and behind him, a woman presents a lovely extravagance of crab wontons and sets it before me. I sip and feast until more than half the food is gone, then push the plate aside to save myself for the main course.

My eyes skip from patron to patron, to the various servers shouldering food, none of which appear to be mine, to the Bible on the seat beside me, to the woman seated alone at a table reading a novel—I wonder if she snuck out on her family too—back to the Bible.

A yawn seeps out and I know why. That fried mass of crab and cream cheese is settling, bringing down my rebellion high. I sip the Coke to recharge and wave down another gentleman for a refill. I haven't seen my personal server since I placed the order.

I drum my fingers on the table, looking aimlessly around, covering a yawn again. This is terrible. I'm not supposed to get sleepy, or bored. If

I had planned this right I would have brought a novel myself, except I don't read novels anymore. Never have time. *Hmph.* What am I saying? I've got lots of it.

My eyes fall on the Bible again and my pulse quickens at the sudden remembrance of Dr. Lyles's DVD lesson Friday, which we finally got to after my testimony. To my delight at first, he focused on the new believer. As if reading my mind, he answered many of the burning questions I had about "heavenly places" and new life in Christ. He confirmed that believers dwell in a different place. "As different as death and life," he said. "Literally." He got an animated gleam in his eyes and stepped from behind the podium and into a spirited stride across the floor, saying, "Remember what Jesus said when He raised Lazarus from the dead? 'Unbind him, and let him go.' That's what happened when you were saved. You were raised from death to life, transferred from Satan's domain to God's kingdom, out of darkness to the marvelous light. You were lifted to a heavenly place."

That part of Dr. Lyles's message was encouraging, but then he addressed my next question, and his answer didn't cheer me. He said, "But somebody is saying, 'Why don't I *feel* like I'm in a heavenly place?' Can I tell you straight? 'Cause you're confused, still thinking like the world, trying to bring the world to heavenly places. Heavenly places—excuse my French—ain't got nothing to do with the world. It's not heavenly because life is easy and everything is flowing like you want it to. It's not heavenly because it's Christmas every day and you get all the goodies you want. It's heavenly because it's the place where God dwells; it's heavenly because it's holy; it's heavenly because God equips you with everything you need to be victorious in the world *even if* things aren't flowing like you want them to and *even if* you don't get all the goodies you want. Beloved, it's heavenly because, finally, your eyes are opened to truth and you begin to understand the will of God for your life."

It was the "will of God" part that flipped my stomach, specifically, the fact that He *has* a will for my life. Dr. Lyles whipped out his Amplified Bible from behind the podium, saying Ephesians 2:10 sounded so good in that translation that he had to read it. The substance of it was seared into my brain. It said we are God's workmanship, recreated in Christ Jesus to do the good works that God planned for us beforehand, that we should walk in them. And this was the part that got me at the end of the verse:

"living the good life which He prearranged and made ready for us to live."

Dr. Lyles pumped his fist as he read that last line, then strode to the camera. "Now tell me that doesn't get you excited!" he said. "Before the foundation of the world, God planned good works for you to do. He planned the paths you would take. You thought you knew what you were doing and where you were going and then, Wham! He saved you, He raised you, He seated you, and He said, 'I prearranged a life for you, a *good* life.' Beloved, there's nothing better than being in God's will. If you're a new believer, not sure yet what God's will is for your life, seek Him and stay in this Book. He'll show you."

I remember thinking afterward that I must not be in another kingdom but on another planet. I was supposed to be excited that God had prearranged my life? *Rearranged* was more fitting. And why would I dare seek to know His will? I had the sick feeling He was already showing me—"Thou shalt sit at home and stare at the wall." The good life? I didn't think it would be Christmas every day but I didn't think I'd be mourning every day either.

Squeezing lemon into my new Coke, I hear Darlene's voice floating in, mixing with Dr. Lyles's. *"God wants to do so much through you in your home, work that sails on into eternity...."*

My brain starts formulating questions I don't even care about, wondering if the work Darlene referred to falls under the "good works" Ephesians refers to. Out of curiosity, my fingers tip open the front Bible cover. It's still there, the note Darlene wrote during her visit. I was so vexed when she left I almost threw it away but couldn't bring myself to do it. I do love Darlene. She's the only true mother figure I've ever had. So I buried it with old bulletins from church instead.

I tilt it upward and take a look. Deuteronomy 6:5-7, Proverbs 14:1, and Titus 2:3-5. "All about home and family," Darlene said. I close my eyes and hold my forehead, feeling the evening turn, that tiny part of me gaining strength. I pop my eyes open and search the faces of the scurrying servers, trying to find mine, trying to move my thoughts from the direction they're creeping. I'm not going there tonight. The whole point was to get away from home and family, not read verses about them.

I tuck the note back inside the Bible. My food has to arrive shortly. I'll read the verses another day. *I promise.*

"Ma'am," my server says, walking up from behind. I think it's my server. Been so long since I've seen her. "I'm very sorry. The cook made a mistake with your order and I had to send it back. He prepared orange peel chicken but you had ordered the shrimp."

"The chicken is fine," I say.

"I'm sorry, Ma'am. I already sent it back. Rest assured, though, that I've talked to the manager and your meal will be on the house."

"Do you know how long it will be?"

"About another ten to fifteen minutes. I'm sorry."

I sigh so loudly she turns back around briefly before heading to the kitchen, or wherever she hides herself. *All right, Lord. You've done it again. You've gotten my attention. But I'm only reading one of these passages, and I'm picking which one.* I lift the Bible onto the table and consult the table of contents, opting for Titus. The Old Testament is more burdensome I've heard. I'll take the grace side of things. Flipping past Ephesians, I eventually spot it. Good, it's short.

> *"Older women likewise are to be reverent in their behavior, not malicious gossips nor enslaved to much wine, teaching what is good, so that they may encourage the young women to love their husbands, to love their children, to be sensible, pure, workers at home, kind, being subject to their own husbands, that the word of God not be dishonored"*

I spend a few moments deducing the obvious, that Darlene is the older woman and I the younger, because based on the first reading I'm in no hurry to move to a focus of what this younger woman is to do. I should have picked the proverb. It occurs to me that Darlene already told me what it says and it's a lot easier to swallow than this one. What was I thinking? I'm tempted to close the Book altogether but the adrenalin seems to have switched sides, quickening the beat of my heart, spurring me to continue, to even make a list. I reach into my purse for a pen and piece of paper and read the passage again. On the back of an envelope I write down what's expected of me and examine it.

Love my husband.

Love my children.

Be sensible.

Be pure.

Be a worker at home.

Be kind.

Be subject to my husband.

My eyes brighten as my server heads this direction with a delicious-looking entrée, but she continues past me. My head falls in my hand, the list filling my vision, its demands squeezing my brain. Why does more than half of it revolve around *them?* It's just as Darlene said, all about home and family, all about home and family taking command of my existence. Just the one line—worker at home—sends a chill through my bones. This is what I feared. This is why I ran. It's right here in black and white, the "good" life that was prearranged for me. God has shut the door on my legal career. He wants me to be June Cleaver.

I reassess my revolt. I'm not clashing with Hezekiah or a tiny part of myself. It's God. Again.

Lord, I may as well say it because You can read my mind. I don't like the idea of subjecting myself to Hezekiah and I don't like the thought of being a "worker at home." It's just not me, Lord. I have ambitions and dreams. I'm not saying home and family aren't important, Lord, I'm just saying it's depressing to be there all day. I mean, it's fine for someone like Jillian, that's her gift, but mine is...is...bigger than that. Sort of.

And it's not that I don't love Hezekiah and the girls. I do love them, Lord. Why did You have to put that on the list anyway? It's so obvious.

Asia pops to mind, and the conviction I felt in the car. I picture DeRon at school age, hunched over the table doing homework, Asia hanging right with him, hot pants and all.

Maybe Asia never had big dreams.

Suddenly, one word rises from the list and tightens my stomach. *Love.* That word was highlighted in the homework last week for chapter two. I turn back to Ephesians and there it is. *But God, being rich in mercy, because of His great **love** with which He **loved** us...* I wish I had my pencil cup. I'm itching to draw little pink hearts over both "loves."

In chapters three and four I find four more. But it's the beginning of chapter five that grabs me. *Therefore be imitators of God, as beloved children; and walk in **love,** just as Christ also **loved** you, and gave Himself up for us....*

"Sorry again for the wait," my server says. She sets the plate to the right of my Bible and I leave it there, unable to eat, my mind too busy making connections. Jesus loved me so much that He gave Himself up for me. God loved me with such a great love that He saved me. And I'm supposed to imitate God. Imitate His love.

Lord, is this why Titus 2 says to love my husband and children? Are You talking about with Your love? That kind of love laid down its life. What are You saying, Lord?

After ten o'clock I ease into a quiet house that is completely darkened on the first floor. I turn on the kitchen light and gasp at the sparkle. The table and countertops have been de-cluttered, the sink cleared, the floor spotless. I expected a conflict when I walked through the door and instead got...relief. This kitchen had been hanging over my head for days and the burden has just vanished. Was Hezekiah doing me a favor? Is he saying he realizes the stress I've been under and how difficult it's been for me to function around here? Is this a peace offering? Maybe it was a good thing I left, if it changed his tune.

I take a couple of steps and stop. I could be all wrong. Hezekiah could have gotten so aggravated that he had to do something with it until I returned. He tends to busy his hands when he's in a bad mood, and a mop would be an excellent way to act out frustration.

I slowly ascend up the back stairs, hoping Hezekiah has fallen asleep. The bedroom door is closed and I lower the handle gently. As it moves I grimace at the bright light that greets me, and the voices. Hezekiah is in the recliner watching ESPN. He cuts his eyes over at me, then back to the television. A peace offering, it was not.

I head to the bathroom and close the door. It reopens immediately, causing me to jump. Hezekiah is in my face, expressionless. I move to step around him; he pulls my arm back.

"About to leave again?" he says.

"Hezekiah, I just needed a little time to myself."

"Time to yourself? Treva, you have the whole day to yourself. Then, soon as I get home, you run out? Is it that you needed time away from me?"

"No. Maybe. Well, it wasn't you; it was what you were saying."

"That I wanted dinner?"

"Hezekiah, lower your voice."

"Nah, I'm trying to understand this. First you say you left to have time to yourself. Now it's because I wanted dinner?"

"I just can't handle all these expectations on me right now. I'm trying to cope with being unemployed, trying to figure out my life. If I cook, I cook. I don't need you telling me I have to cook."

Hezekiah glares down at me for long, uncomfortable seconds. "What is it *exactly* that you can't handle right now, Treva? Your family?"

I stare at the floor, mulling all I could say. Looking up finally, I tell him, "I just want things the way they used to be."

Hezekiah folds his arms. "I've got a news flash for you, Treva. The way things used to be wasn't all that great either."

My brows turn up at him.

"I know you're surprised. Things were great for you, right? As long as you were on partnership track, billing hours, eyes on the prize, life was wonderful. But what about our family life? How often did you make it home for dinner? How many times did I cover for you with the girls because you couldn't go someplace with us? When was the last time you joined us for a movie? Did you ever go sledding or ride on the Ferris wheel at Navy Pier? What about a parent-teacher conference?"

"Hezekiah, you know what it takes to make partner. I *had* to work long hours."

"No, Treva, you didn't. You didn't have to be the first one in the office and the last one to leave. You didn't have to bring work home *every* night and bill eight hours *every* Saturday."

The home and family theme of Titus 2 steals into my mind. I push it back out. "Well, if you had a problem with it, you should have said something."

"I did, in more ways than one. You just weren't trying to hear it. There was no point getting in your face and arguing about it all the time because it wouldn't have made any difference. Instead of arguing, I spent a lot of time praying, praying for a change and praying that I could be patient with you in the meantime."

I fold my own arms now. "So I guess you're glad I can't find a job."

"You know me better than that, Treva. I would never be happy about something like that. I did hope that in this period while you were looking, we could enjoy some much-needed family time. But nothing has changed—just Treva doing her thing and the rest of us doing ours. Your stunt tonight made that real clear. Here I was, having to cover for you again. 'Mommy had to run out and take care of something.' I found out something while you were gone. I think I've about run out of patience."

Hezekiah shakes his head, staring past me. "I think you'd be coping a lot better if you had lost us and kept the job." His eyes lock with mine now and he waits.

This is the part where I assure him of the absurdity of that notion. *"You all are infinitely more important than that job."* But I won't do it. First of all, this discussion has left me in an uncharitable mood, and second, I can't truthfully say that they are infinitely more important than my career. They're both important. In fact, I had a vision for my career long before I had a vision for my family.

Actually, I never had a vision for my family. I never even had romantic notions of what my wedding would one day look like, certainly had none of what family life would look like. Hezekiah and I just happened to fall in love and marriage became the next logical step.

I didn't think much about a family even after that, other than the fact that I didn't want to start one until years later, after I'd been promoted to partner. I knew those initial years at the firm would be intense, and that I'd need to go above and beyond to make it. But unfortunately Faith came quickly, and then the other two. Was I supposed to shift my drive into neutral? Alter my goals? I never considered giving Thompson & Klein less than my best. Hezekiah was in a flexible profession that allowed him to spend the bulk of the before-and after-school time at home with the girls. It only made sense that he be the one to do it. And with his personality, he was perfectly suited to do it.

I, however, am not. Work suits me. Being at home feels suffocating. Right now, marriage and motherhood feel like straitjackets. Without them, I could be free, doing as I please, working in Chicago. That's why I chafe at Titus 2. If it aims to pare down my existence to nothing but wife and mother, I have no desire to attain to it. I do want my marriage and my family, but I don't want to be swallowed up in them. I want *my* life, the one I originally envisioned, then I'll be able to deal with *our* life. Like it used to be.

Hezekiah gave up waiting for my assurance moments ago. He's gone. When I go to bed he doesn't turn toward me or hold me.

It's just as well. I didn't feel like being bothered anyway.

Chapter Nineteen

The sound of running water rattles my sleep and I lift my head at the intrusion, trying to figure out what is going on. My heavy lids tell me it's the middle of the night but the clock says 7:00 A.M. I close my eyes again and roll over, not sure which to believe, and my insides suddenly flutter, remembering last night.

Now, I've got marital issues to contend with on top of everything else. If I were smart, I would march into that bathroom and tell my husband that stress got the best of me and there is no way I would be coping better if I had lost my family instead of my job. Better yet, I should sashay in there in this lavender silk chemise nightgown and bring him back to bed. He'd be so shocked I believe all would be forgiven.

But, surprise, surprise, I'm in the mood for neither. I'll do well if I can smile and say "Good morning." Knowing Hezekiah, he'll accept that little white flag and smooth over the bump I created. "Joy cometh in the morning," he likes to say. No matter what transpires the night before, he somehow shakes it off by dawn. *Lord, let it be so.*

I slide out of bed, open the double doors, and catch his eyes in the mirror. I smile. Not a big one, but a real one. I inhale slightly and say, "Good morning." He shuts off the water and puts his razor away, turns and comes toward me. My muscles relax, anticipating—needing—our morning hug.

"Morning," he says, and continues past me.

I wait for more but I can tell he's in his closet so I move to the sink and slowly begin brushing my teeth. I never brush my teeth first. I go to the bathroom and jump in the shower but I figure he'll have to come back in here for something and I want to be in his line of sight, see if he'll ignore me or talk.

I finish brushing without a peep from Hezekiah and decide to shower quickly. The girls need to be prodded along for school and there will be time to catch Hezekiah downstairs at breakfast. With every passing minute, my need to see him increases. I need to hear him say something more. Something, period.

I grab the first sweat suit I see hanging in my closet, poke my head through the top while looking for my tennis shoes, almost trip over myself as I rush my legs into the pants, and scurry down the hall. The coffee smells wonderful. Maybe we'll have time to enjoy a cup together.

I scamper down the back stairs and see no one at the table, and no one in the kitchen. My heart skips and I open the door to the garage. Hezekiah's car is gone. Did he have an early meeting?

The phone rings and I spring to it. *I'm sorry, Sweetheart,* he'll say. *I should have said good-bye.*

My eyes scan the orange numbers in the handset and fall. It's Jillian.

"Hey, Jill," I say.

"What's wrong?"

"I don't have time to get into it," I say. "I have to get the girls to school. Can I call you back?"

"I'm just calling to see what time you want us to come over tonight."

"Tonight?"

"Dinner, remember?"

"Oh." I do remember. I invited Jillian as we were leaving Willow's house last Friday, when I was in a fairly good mood, which mood has long since passed. If it were anyone else I would reschedule, but Jillian takes me as I am and the invitation was long overdue. I only hope

Hezekiah will be back to his normal self by evening. "I did forget but how's six?"

"That'll work. Can I bring anything?"

"The meat and two side dishes," I say, walking through the house and motioning for the girls to get in the car.

Jillian laughs. "I know you're serious too. Girl, don't go out of your way for us. Just do what you always do—get carryout."

"I just might. I'll see you later."

Armed with a reason, I call Hezekiah on his cell, rolling my eyes when voice mail kicks in. I leave a message that we're having dinner guests and instruct him to call me back, sounding urgent, though I have nothing else to say. I'll think of something before he calls.

I drop off the girls and head home, contemplating my day. With company coming I need to clean bathrooms, dust, and vacuum, and figure out what's for dinner. I sigh in annoyance. Prior to Jillian's call, I had nothing planned for today but I sure don't want to fill it this way.

And yet the house does need cleaning, guests or no guests. And after last night, I definitely needed a dinner plan, that is, if I care at all about my marriage. And given my heart's reaction to Hezekiah's coolness this morning, I must.

At a green light I hang a U-turn, following a sudden unction to drive to the grocery store. I won't do carryout. I'll surprise Hezekiah with a good home-cooked meal. In the parking lot I call Darlene, who gives me the recipe, ingredients, and you-can-do-it speech I need. Returning home, I put the groceries away and feel the pull of the computer. Someone may have posted the perfect job this morning, and I've got to read the legal news.

On my way to the office I stop in the powder room and I'm horrified. I knew it needed attention but when did it come to this? Gingerly I lift the toilet seat and wince. With one male in the house, how do we reach this level of disgust under here? I groan loudly, knowing all kinds of filth await me throughout the house. Might as well get this over with. I gather the cleaning supplies, glove my hands, and get to work.

Three hours later, I quit. I am tired and sweaty and bothered that my time has been sucked up by an endeavor that reverts in less than a week. I snatch off my gloves and toss them on the marble top. What am I doing in *my* bathroom anyway? Nobody in Jillian's family will be anywhere near here, and my mission is not to clean for clean's sake. That's for another day, and another person. My next mission will be to find a reputable cleaning service like we had in Chicago.

I leave the bucket and the caddy with sponges and cleaning liquids in the middle of the floor, unwilling to suffer them another moment, and take to the stairs. I sense emotional revival as I round the bend to the office, anxious to plop in my leather chair and start the addictive work of scrolling through sites. There is always one more to check out. Hope is one click away.

I flick on the lights, push the power button on the computer, settle in my chair, and the doorbell scoops me right back up. Probably UPS. When I didn't make it to the Louis Vuitton store, I ordered my bag online.

Glancing through the narrow window beside the door, I spy Carmen out there and move immediately out of view. I'm not presentable. My hair was thrown hastily into a ponytail for cleaning and once again I am wearing a *sweat* suit. I've a mind to leave her standing there, whether she saw me or not. I like Carmen well enough now, but she's got to learn. This willy-nilly stopping-by stuff has got to stop.

I give a start when she rings the doorbell again, feeling her eyes bearing down on me through the wood. All right. Maybe it'll be quick. I open up and plant myself in the doorway. "Hi, Carmen, what can I do for you?"

"Do you have a moment?" she asks, a bit sadly.

I'm obligated now to enter her world, ask what's wrong, listen, and in so doing, use up more minutes of this ever-dwindling day. It's past noon already, and as it stands, I may not have time to hit all of my legal news sites. Soon I'll need to get in that kitchen and study the directions Darlene gave me for the spinach lasagna I plan to tackle. This is just not a good time.

"It's not a good time, is it?" Carmen asks.

I have an out but what good is it, with Carmen sounding so pitiful? "Oh, it's…I can take a minute," I say. I lead us to the living room rather than the kitchen, where I'd have to offer her a drink, prolonging her stay.

I sit on the sofa and watch Carmen unzip and ease off her jacket.

"It's getting chilly out there, isn't it?" she says.

"Mm-hmm," I say. "So what's going on, Carmen? Is something wrong?" Carmen gazes into her clasped hands and sighs. "Treva, I debated about whether to come over here, but…I couldn't get you off of my mind."

"What do you mean?"

"Your situation."

"What situation?"

"I mean, what you told us about your mother, it broke my heart. God's given me a real burden for you. I've been praying every day, and I wanted to know how you were doing."

Frowning slightly, I say, "Carmen, I'm fine. I don't dwell on that. It just came up because of the focus of the lesson that day."

"Still…I just feel like…growing up with a mother who feels that way about you, it has to affect your life in a lot of ways. *Infect* might be a better word. I had to let you know that if you ever want to talk, you shouldn't hesitate to call."

I am wholly uncomfortable with Carmen contemplating my life. If she wants to pray for me, hallelujah. But don't *think* about me and how my past might be affecting my present. I'm not a mental case; I don't need a shade-tree psychologist. And what is this about God burdening her? Why do I feel as if God has given her a window into my life, perhaps a window I myself haven't seen through?

I push back in my seat and cross my legs. "How old are you, Carmen, if you don't mind my asking?"

"Twenty-eight."

"It's sweet of you to be concerned but, Carmen, I'm ten years older than you. I've done a lot of living and a lot of learning about how to deal with life. You don't have to worry about me."

Carmen stares long, then looks down. The girl could at least pretend to believe me. Why do I feel that God is downloading my personal business to her right now? I'm waiting for her to say, "Treva, you don't have to lie. I know you ran out on your family last night. You've alienated your husband. Your life stinks. Just talk to me."

When she looks up I smile, hoping to recharge the Carmen that got on my nerves, the peppy one. I'm more comfortable with her.

"I'll let you go," Carmen says, rising. "You're coming Friday, right?"

"I'll be there," I say.

"Okay, I'll see you."

"Oh, Carmen," I say as she opens the door, not willing to let her go, not like this, "thanks again for picking Hope up on Saturday and taking her to the park with Stacy. She couldn't stop talking about it."

"You're welcome," she says, and closes the door behind her.

The béchamel did it. I had beautifully minced my shallots and crushed my garlic cloves through a nifty new press I bought at the grocery store to make the white sauce. I'd set the timer on the microwave to cook the flour for exactly one and a half minutes. Milk, bay leaves, nutmeg, salt, and pepper had been whisked gradually into the pan and reduced to a low simmer for ten minutes. I had no problem tending it occasionally as I blanched, shocked, drained, and wrapped the spinach in a clean kitchen towel. But when I turned my back for a moment to wring the towel in the sink, which became its own absorbing exercise since green water never did cease to drip, I smelled it, very faintly, and abandoned the green ball. The sauce, a fraction of its former self, no longer swirled.

I should have chosen the no-fuss version Darlene offered, but no, I had to aim for the one with a hundred steps. Darlene had fixed this one for Hezekiah and me the week we moved here and we raved about it. I wanted mine to inspire the same response, not necessarily from Jillian and Cecil but from Hezekiah. If he sees me trying, that will likely be enough to snap him back to his old self. But I want more. If I'm putting this much effort into it, I want him raving.

I had planned to have the lasagna layered before picking up the girls from school. Now, because I had to redo the béchamel, it's six o'clock and I'm just lining the bottom of the baking dish. Jillian and family are promptly ringing the doorbell.

"Jillian, I am so sorry. It'll be another forty-five minutes before we eat," I say.

She walks in with the children trailing behind her. "No problem. Cecil had to work late anyway. He's meeting me here."

"Good, Hezekiah had to work a little late too," I.tell her, hiding my disappointment over the way in which I acquired this news. Hezekiah never called back. Late afternoon, his secretary called to tell me he'd been in meeting after meeting but had gotten my message and would be home at about six-thirty. He has never been too busy to call me himself. I had wanted to talk to him to know where we stand. I didn't want to find out in front of Jillian and Cecil.

The kids dash off to play and Jillian sits at the center island, watching as I spread the spinach mixture over the noodles. "Okay, I'm impressed," she says.

"Don't be, until you see how it tastes."

"You've got a point," Jillian says, chuckling, "but I'm still impressed to see you laboring. So what was wrong with you when I called this morning?" Jillian asks. "You sounded down."

"Hezekiah and I had gotten into a little spat last night. Then he hardly said a word to me this morning and left early."

"Hezekiah?"

"I know. He was hurt. I kind of ran out on him last night, and when he told me I'd probably be coping better if I had lost my family and kept my job, I didn't respond."

"Treva!"

"I know," I say again. "Jilli, I love my family, don't get me wrong. I just need more." The rubber spatula slows as I add, "Do you feel like your life is on hold? Like, there's so much more you could be doing?"

"Than what?" Jillian swigs a bottle of water.

"You know, than teaching your kids arithmetic and grammar."

"But it's more than academics, Treva. We go for a walk and look at the cloud formations and talk about the first verse of Psalm 19: 'The heavens declare the glory of God; the skies proclaim the work of His hands.' David will print the verse, Sophia and Courtney will write it in cursive. We talk about 'heavens' and 'skies' being synonyms, nouns, and subjects in these clauses; I ask for another synonym for 'declare' and 'proclaim,' and we discuss their function as simple predicates. Sophia and Courtney identify the direct objects and prepositional phrases, and then they diagram the verse. We keep going like that through the entire psalm and at the end, they have it memorized.

"There's nothing like teaching my children about God and His Word. No, I don't see my life as 'on hold.' I feel like I'm living the abundant life Jesus talked about."

I put the dish into the oven and sit on a bar stool next to Jillian. "But being with your kids all day, that doesn't get on your nerves? How do you do it?"

"Of course they get on my nerves sometimes," Jillian says. "God is how I do it. All that fruit of the Spirit we're supposed to be walking in— I get ample opportunity to develop it each and every day. Some days I feel like God keeps me under His thumb, chastising me for what I said and how I said it."

I show my surprise. "You seem like you never have any challenges, like everything's always easy for you."

"That's because you never ask," Jillian says quietly.

The comment packs a punch. "What?"

Jillian looks directly at me. "You *never* ask how I'm doing. I've been homeschooling for five years and this is the first time you've asked me about it. I'm frustrated sometimes, disappointed, whatever, and there have been days I've called you to vent about it but we never get to it. Your issues always take precedence." Jillian speaks matter-of-factly, worsening the sting.

"Jillian, you know if you needed to talk to me about something you could've just said it. I can't believe you're saying that." I am truly shocked.

"Treva, honestly, it's been this way for years. Half the time you don't even call me back. There are many things you don't know simply because you didn't call back. You're consumed in your own world."

"Jilli—"

"Mommy, can we go to the brunch, can we go to the brunch?"

I hear the voice before I see the body. This is not the time. I want to explore this with Jillian but Hope skips into the kitchen with Faith close behind.

"It does sound nice, Ma," Faith says. "Think we can go?"

"You got your invitation, right?" Jillian asks.

"What are you all talking about?" I ask. "We haven't gotten any invitation."

"Ours came a couple of days ago," Jillian says.

"Well, maybe we're not getting one, whatever it is, unless it came today. I haven't checked the mailbox yet."

"I'll get it, Mommy." Hope runs out.

Faith continues, "It's an invitation to a brunch with Grandma Patsy. Courtney was telling us about it. She said they go every year and they get to dress up."

"Oh," I say. "No, you won't be going."

"But you haven't even seen the invitation," Faith responds.

"Don't have to see it."

Faith stares at me incredulously.

Hope plops the mail on the counter, gives Faith her personally addressed envelope, and tears into her own. I take it from her.

"I thought you didn't want to see it," Faith says.

I ignore her and read the elegant raised lettering. "'The Washington, D.C. chapter of Alliances, Inc. cordially invites you to the annual Tea and Roses Brunch honoring our distinguished grandmothers for faithful service to family and community." I rummage the pile. "Did my invitation get lost?"

"Only granddaughters are invited," Jillian says.

I wonder why Patsy even sent my girls an invitation. Probably wanted Joy there and knew she would only get her in a package deal. Or Jillian told her to send it. "So why do you let Courtney and Sophia go? You never liked these kinds of events growing up."

"It means a lot to Mama, helps keep the peace. And they do enjoy themselves."

Hezekiah opens the garage door and Faith and Hope run to welcome him. I wait hopefully.

"Daddy, look. Look what we got," Hope says, thrusting the invitation into Hezekiah's hand.

"You all go entertain your cousins," I say. "You only have a few more minutes before dinner's ready. Daddy and I will talk about the invitation later."

"Aww, Mom," Hope says.

"Go on, now," I insist, noticing the hello hug Hezekiah is giving Jillian. Not knowing whether he'll give me one, and not willing to risk embarrassment, I open the oven door to check the lasagna.

"That smells delicious," Hezekiah says, approaching from behind. "Did Ma bring it over?"

"No, I made it," I say, turning to face him.

"Really?"

"Yes. I wanted to surprise you."

"You definitely did that," he says, his eyes bearing into mine, with what feeling I cannot discern. I anxiously await his next move.

"Mommy, did you talk about it yet?" Hope inquires from around the corner.

"No, Hope. We'll call you when dinner is ready." Frustration leaps from my voice. The moment is ruined.

"So what is this?" Hezekiah says, glancing at the invitation Hope gave him.

I lean my back on the center island and cross my arms. "One of Mother's events, a brunch. All three of them got an invitation, but they won't be going," I say, ignoring my promise to discuss it.

"Why not?" Hezekiah says, his brown eyes showing immediate dissent.

"Because I don't want my children around those people, and one in particular."

"Treva, first of all, your mother is in a special class by herself. Not all of those women are like that."

"How would you know?"

He takes a step closer to me. "My mother does hair, remember? She's met lots of women who belong to the same organizations as Patsy and she said they're wonderful people."

"Well, that's not my experience." I step around him to the refrigerator, open it, and take out the salad I've already prepared.

Hezekiah follows me with his eyes. "Treva, you're going back twenty to thirty years or more. And even then it probably wasn't as bad as you thought. Probably just a few who shared your mother's...inclinations."

"Why are you defending these people against me?" I say, staring into the romaine lettuce, biting back tears.

"I'm not defending anybody, Treva. I'm just looking at the situation for what it is." He turns to Jillian. "So what do they do at this brunch?"

Jillian explains.

"Treva," Hezekiah says, "the girls never see their Grandma Patsy. They don't know her at all. And I'm sure you'll never take them to her house. This brunch sounds like a nice way for them to come together. When is it?"

"In less than two weeks, the last Saturday in October," Jillian replies.

"Oh, that's homecoming weekend. Perfect. I have that education reception, remember? We had already said we were going to get my mother to watch the girls."

"Right, *your* mother," I say.

"Treva, I'm not afraid of them spending a couple of hours with Patsy. She's not out to get them. It's a brunch for goodness' sake."

I shake my head. "She doesn't have to be out to get them. It's just who she is. I told you about our phone call on Friday. She hasn't changed; that woman will say anything. One wrong comment from her and Faith is ruined."

"I don't believe that." Hezekiah squares his stance. "First of all, Faith is not that fragile. Have you ever listened to that girl? Second, Patsy is not that powerful. Even if she *were* plotting and planning our children's destruction, it wouldn't prosper. God is our protection. We don't need to hide our children from their grandmother. Let 'em have a good time. They should go."

Being subject to their own husbands.

Ugh! Why is that popping into my head?

The timer dings and I ease a hot and bubbly lasagna out of the oven. It looks delicious. As if on cue, Cecil arrives and moments later we are seated in our formal dining room. I did nothing to pretty the table. The silk flower arrangement, which I had had specially designed in Chicago, looks ordinary and drab. I should have lit the candles as I'd planned, but once the brunch invitation surfaced, I lost focus of the evening.

I watch Hezekiah as he lifts his fork. "This is really good," he says. "*Really* good."

I would find joy in his praise if he would look at me, compliment the chef personally. He's sitting beside me but our legs are not touching. His body is angled away from me, slightly, but to me, obviously. I doubt Cecil detects that anything is wrong. Hezekiah is his normal effervescent self. But I'm greatly noticing that his conversation is inclusive of the guests and our children only.

Tears rush to my eyes and I bat them back, not even sure which thing has caused this surge of emotion. Probably all of tonight rolled up into a neat little ghastly ball. I haven't forgotten the sting I felt when Jillian said I never ask how she's doing, nor the sting of knowing that she associates being at home with abundant life, while, for me, it's been more akin to life being snuffed out. Is something wrong with her…or with me? And of course there's Hezekiah choosing to treat me indifferently. Why? Why can't he give me grace as always, use his humor to move us past this?

And Patsy, who deals in death and destruction. I don't care what Hezekiah says, those girls are better off without a relationship with her. How could I send them to an event with her without my oversight and protection? If she destroys Faith's spirit, there is no telling what I would do.

Chapter Twenty

"'Now to Him who is able to do exceeding abundantly, beyond all that we ask or think, according to the power that works within us, to Him be the glory in the church and in Christ Jesus to all generations forever and ever. Amen.'

"This is Paul's marvelous doxology," Dr. Lyles says. He's handsomely suited in a navy blue that slims his obvious middle pudge. It's hard to tell on screen, but he's probably no more than six feet, a warm-brown-toned, dignified looking man with gray-peppered, receding hair and crows' feet that tickle the corners of his eyes when he smiles. At the moment he is standing behind the glass podium with reading glasses tucked past those graying temples. Soon he'll lay them down again and resume his passionate pace across the studio floor.

As much as I recoiled at the end of his message last week, I can't help but like Dr. Lyles. That fatherly twinkle in his eye sneaks into the heart, and that gentle smile coats the medicine he spoons down the throat, making you feel as if he's giving it only because he thinks it's good for you.

I'm not bracing myself for any medicine today, though. I'm moving forward on Carmen's love seat in eager anticipation. This is the segment of the teaching I've been waiting for. When I finally got around to doing the homework, I couldn't believe chapter three was the "exceeding abundantly" chapter. I didn't even know "exceeding abundantly" was in Ephesians, and when I saw it, excitement raced through me. The verse said He could do more than I ask or think, and knowing all that I'd been asking and thinking, I could hardly contain myself trying to imagine how He might top it.

I decided I had been too hasty, thinking the door had been closed for good. Why would God do that? It would make no sense in light of this verse; He would be doing *less* than I ask or think. No, I had to be in some kind of holding pattern. Maybe God wanted to show me that my priorities were out of whack. And for the sake of argument, I conceded they were. Right then I vowed to cook more, make sure the house stays clean, be kind and whatever else was on that Titus list. Promotion would come.

I look down at my Bible and take it in again. God is able. Able to do exceeding abundantly. Able to snap His fingers and call forth a high-powered legal position handmade for me. One better than my old job and better than Brooks Donnelly.

I chuckle to myself when I look over at Monique and see her with a pen and paper at the ready. Probably thinking about God being able to get her that exceeding abundant house she desperately wants.

"How many of you have heard this verse quoted?" Dr. Lyles is saying, divesting himself of the glasses.

We all show agreement, save Asia.

"I know 'bout every hand went up. People love to quote this verse. You get goose bumps when you read it, don't you? Makes you all tingly thinking about this exceeding abundant God who can get you that Benz you've always wanted, or the million-dollar house, or that dream job."

Monique and I shift in our seats.

"Ever read it in context? Trick question, 'cause I know you did your homework, right? And if you did your homework, what you saw was a series of things that had to happen *in* you before God could do exceeding abundant things *through* you. That's right, I didn't say *for* you, I said *through* you."

Puzzled, I look down at my Bible again. What "series of things" is he talking about?

"Yes, God does want to do things *for* you and it's simply His nature to give good gifts to His children, but God is not nearly as concerned with your getting that Benz or that high-falutin' job as you think He is. This verse doesn't make Him a genie in a bottle—snap your fingers and there He is, ready to grant your every wish. I'm sorry to be the one but I'm gonna have to burst your bubble." Dr. Lyles walks up to the camera, half covers his mouth, and whispers loudly, "It's not about you."

Backing up, he raises his arms and points upward with both index fingers. "It's all about Him. All the rest of it is nice but compared to Christ, Paul said 'count it all dung.'"

"Aaamen. Tell it, Dr. Lyles," Willow says, switching to a seat closer to the television. Dr. Lyles looks at the camera in a close-up shot and nods his head as if he heard her.

"God wants to do exceeding abundantly all right. He wants to do exceeding abundant things *through* you to bring about His will on earth. He wants to touch that co-worker through you, that neighbor, that checker at the market you see every week. More than anything, though, God wants to work through you in your home."

Give me a break. Not home again. Hezekiah is distant still and I haven't come up with any words yet to draw him closer. I can't tell him what he wants to hear: my career is not as important as my family. I'm not going to lie to make him feel better.

Dr. Lyles makes his way to the stool. "If you've studied Deuteronomy with me, you know about God's will for the family. I stayed in chapter six, verses five through seven so long y'all thought I'd lost my mind. I know you did—"

I flip to the front of my Bible and snatch Darlene's note out, checking the Deuteronomy verses. Same ones.

"—But I had to stay in that chapter because it's so important. God's plan is for the parents to teach the children. Teach them what? His Word. How? What did He say? Diligently. When? When you sit, when you walk by the way, when you lie down, and when you rise up. You've got it. All the time, as a way of life. This is one of those good works I spoke of last week. This is when you can get really excited, run up and down the street, and shout 'Hallelujah'—when you see God do beyond all that you ask or think with your children, giving them a heart to know Him and follow after Him."

Dr. Lyles shoots off the stool. "But guess what? You can't do Deuteronomy 6 unless *you* know the Word. You can't see God do exceeding abundantly unless *you're* where you need to be. 'According to the power that works within us.' Isn't that what it says?

"That's why these verses right before the exceeding abundant verse are a prayer, that Christ would dwell in your hearts. *Dwell*. Not just be *in* your heart but fully abiding, totally consuming your life, which happens as all the stuff that's got nothing to do with God is pushed out. When Jesus consumes your life, you'll come to know, really know, His love— the breadth and length and height and depth. And oh, beloved, that's the key. When His love fills your being, it's not about you anymore. *Then* God can do exceeding abundantly in your life and through your life." Dr. Lyles fades and the television screen turns blue.

Willow stands and clicks off the set. "Thank God for Dr. Lyles," she says. "I had been struggling this past week, you all. My mother-in-law came by for the express purpose of talking me out of leaving the firm. She said my feelings about it are clouded because I'm postpartum, and if I were thinking clearly, I would know I've worked too hard to throw it all away. She said it wasn't healthy to revolve my life around the baby, that there was nothing wrong with living for myself too, keeping my mind engaged, doing something I enjoy. I couldn't stop thinking about what she said. I kept wondering, 'Is that what I'm doing, revolving my life around Zoe? Is it unhealthy?'"

"That doesn't sound like you, Willow," Carmen says, refilling our water glasses and offering what remains of the delicious breakfast pastries she provided. "I can't believe you were second-guessing yourself about something like that. How could it be unhealthy to be with Zoe?"

"I know, that's why it was bothering me. I usually *wouldn't* question myself about something I feel deeply about. But that seed got planted and I couldn't shake it. I'll tell you what, though—I'm thinking clearly now. When Dr. Lyles started talking about Deuteronomy 6, I was straight. If I'm working those crazy hours, how would I teach Zoe when I rise up, when I walk along the way, and when I sit down? I'd be doing good just to see her first thing in the morning and at night before bed." Willow crosses her legs, shaking her head, spunk increasing with conviction. "No, my life isn't revolving around Zoe, it's revolving around Christ. I'm supposed to die to self, not live for self, okay? Like the world revolves around that job. Like my life won't matter if I'm not a partner. The devil is a liar. Ooh, that Dr. Lyles encouraged me beyond belief."

While everyone joins in, adding comment after comment, I stare off in the distance. I certainly can't say that Dr. Lyles encouraged me; he managed to whip out that medicine again, and the aftertaste is bitter. I don't know what to hope for now, what to think, pray, or do. And all this talk about Jesus totally consuming my life is scary. What does that *look* like? Being filled with His love sounds nice and dreamy but after that mini study session at the restaurant I know we're not talking nice and dreamy; we're talking sacrifice and surrender. Willow said it—*dying*. How is that encouraging?

"Willow, you should have called me when you were dealing with that," Jillian says. "I'm an old pro. For years, my mother's been giving me that same talk your mother-in-law gave you. In her mind, I've totally wasted my life. She's always pining away about my unfulfilled potential. But that's the world's way. You're not a success unless you've busted through somebody's glass ceiling."

"What's wrong with defining success that way?" I ask, jarred from my thoughts. "I would love to be the first black woman on the Supreme Court, or some other significant first."

"Nothing's wrong with the desire if God put it there," Jillian says. "But, Treva, we both know why that would be 'success' to you. I've told you for years you don't have to prove anything to Mama. She's in darkness; don't let her drive your life. You'll both end up in a ditch."

Bristling, I cross my legs. "I'm not trying to prove anything to Mother. I have my own dreams."

"Treva," Willow steps in, "you asked what's wrong with defining success that way. It's just another one of those things that we have to renew our minds about. The world has a lot to say about a lot of things, but when the Word says differently, that's what we listen to. The world has all kinds of definitions for it, but in God's eyes you're a success only if you're in His will."

June Cleaver's irritating smile dances through my mind. "I've been thinking about 'God's will' since Dr. Lyles's message last week. How do I *know* His will exactly? I admit I haven't read much of the Bible but it can't possibly cover everything. Look at my situation." I hesitate for a moment, unsure about sharing my plight, but my desire to gain insight is greater. "I haven't been able to find a legal position and, speaking of mothers-in-law, mine says God may have closed the door. Well, how do I know that? Am I supposed to just stop looking? How would I know it's truly closed if I stop looking? What if it's closed for just a season? And what if I happen to find one? Does that mean it's His will?

"And here's another thing. I was reading the verses about women in Titus 2 last week. Okay, so I could say God's will is for me to be a 'worker at home.' But what does that mean? Is it my main job? Does it mean that *when* I'm home I make sure my house is in order? See? It's not all spelled out. How am I supposed to figure out all of this? It's totally confusing to me."

"Have you asked?" Willow says.

"Asked what?"

"Asked for His will."

My eyebrows furrow and I lift the glass to my lips. "I don't understand the question." I take a drink of water, not sure I want to understand.

Willow leans forward in her seat. "I'm saying, have you prayed, 'Lord, all I want is Your will. Show me what that is. Have Your way.'"

My stomach does a leap and twirl. "No. I'm not brave enough for that kind of prayer," I admit. "I can't even truthfully say that all I want is God's will. What if He does want me to do nothing but keep house. Or worse. What if He wants me to homeschool like Jillian and never get a break from my kids?"

Jillian opens her mouth to respond as Asia says, "I'm thinking I'd like to home-school."

Incredulous, I look over at her. It was enough of a stretch picturing Asia helping with homework. I won't even tax my brain to come up with an image of her choosing curriculum and fashioning a course of study, not while she's sitting over there in a long jean dress that would be darling were it not for the several slits that extend from ankle to upper thigh, as if she dipped it in a shredder.

"I've been looking into it already," she says. "I didn't know so many African Americans in P.G. County were doing it."

"Yeah, I've been meaning to talk to you about it, Jillian," Monique says. "Taj's teacher has been tripping, trying to put him in a remedial math group when all he needs is for her to slow down and explain it better. I told my husband I'd teach him myself before I let that label be put on him."

"We definitely need to talk," Jillian says. "That's why a lot of people start home-schooling, because they realize we do have options. And, Asia, you're right. It's really growing in this area. We've got a large group just in our weekly co-op. I can get you some information. There's even a day at the park on—"

"Okay y'all," Willow says, "we're on a bit of a tangent here. Sister Treva has an issue on the table."

"I'm sorry, Treva," Monique says.

"It was my fault. Sorry for interrupting," Asia says.

"Don't apologize," I tell them. "I should be thanking you. I was in no hurry to go where Willow was leading me."

Willow kneels in front of me and takes my hands. "All the paths of the Lord are loving-kindness and truth to those who belong to Him. There's no need to fear His will for you, Treva. If you like, I'll pray with you."

I toy with different versions of "no" but they each stick to the roof of my mouth. Why did she have to ask outright? I can't very well say no, out loud, to God's will. I give her a weak nod and she squeezes my hands.

"Father in heaven, we praise You because You do all things well. We acknowledge You as the Most High God who rules over the affairs of mankind. You do according to Your will in heaven and on earth. You are sovereign, Lord. And, Father, I thank You for Your daughter, Treva. I thank You that You have an awesome plan for her life. I pray that You would give her a strong understanding of that fact and that You would help her to cast down any wrong imaginations to the contrary.

"Lord, right now I ask You to help Treva to lay down her will on Your altar. Take it, Lord, and exchange it for Your will for her life. I know, Lord, that what looks to her like a dead end is nothing but a pathway to Your glory. As Dr. Lyles said, it's all about You, Lord. Be exalted in her life. And when You're doing exceeding abundant things through her, we'll be careful to give You the glory, Lord. In Jesus' name, Amen."

Chapter Twenty-One

"Ma, thank you for coming in early for us." I give Darlene a hug as I enter the salon.

"I don't mind coming in at seven if you don't. My Saturdays get booked quickly but I don't schedule anyone before nine," Darlene says.

"Well, I appreciate it. We just got an invitation this week for a brunch with my mother and you know I couldn't let her go like this." I run my fingers through Faith's hair. "She's got a lot of new growth. I should have gotten her in here long before now."

"I heard about this brunch. When is it again?" Darlene squeezes her granddaughter hello.

"Next Saturday," I say. "How'd you hear about it?"

"Faith told me. Come on over here and get up in the chair, baby."

"When did you talk to Faith?" I ask, eyeing my daughter.

"Faith is my e-mail buddy. You didn't know that? I e-mail all my granddaughters, but Faith is the one who writes the most."

"I didn't even know you used the computer, Ma."

"Learn something new every day, don't you?" she chuckles.

"Guess I do." I sit in the styling chair next to Faith and turn it in their direction, gazing around the cozy shop. The walls, a warm mauve, display artwork of black women with various hair styles, and there's one of three girls with braids playing patty-cake. Olive green contrasts nicely with the mauve in the area rugs in the waiting area, in the flecks that run across the cream-colored linoleum, and in the collection of ceramic pots that house her luscious plants. She has four stylist stations, and three chairs each for shampooing and drying. I don't know if she's ever had more than two women working for her at one time, though. She says if she has two who show up on time and do a professional job, she's a happy woman.

Darlene takes her products from a cabinet, sets them on a tray, and begins basing Faith's scalp. "I hear you're going shopping for her dress today too."

"It may take more than today. We've got to find the right dress. I don't even know what twelve-year-olds wear these days to an event like this."

"Thirteen," Faith says, head leaning to one side.

"Not yet. You've got three more weeks."

"Speaking of which," Darlene says, "I hear there's going to be a party."

"Finally," Faith says. "We never get to have birthday parties."

For good reason: they're too much work. "I wouldn't call it a *party.* It's a celebration of a major milestone in your life with a few family members."

"And friends," Faith says.

"Faith, you just moved here," I answer. "You can't possibly know anyone well enough to invite to a family get-together."

"Mom, I *do* have friends," Faith says. "Amber, Kelly, and Jamila. We sit together every day at lunch."

"I've never heard you talk about them," I confess, slightly embarrassed.

"When do we talk, Mom?"

The question causes me to stagger inside. "Faith, we do talk, you know that."

"No, we don't, Mom."

I gulp back tears, stricken silent. How could Faith say that, and in front of her grandmother?

Darlene busies herself with applying relaxer to Faith's roots and I pull my Bible out of the tote bag to seek refuge from the burdensome silence. My hand trembles. My eyes dart around the page, looking for answers. When *do* I talk to Faith, or Joy, or Hope? I respond to them. I tell them what to do. But talk just to talk?

My mind flashes to the twenty-minute drive this morning to Darlene's Silver Spring salon. I spent the time thinking. About my life. What had come of it. Where it's headed. That's what I do. Think. Dream. And when I could, I worked. I don't recall a single word I said to Faith after, "Time to go."

I turn my chair slowly away and brush an eyelid with the back of a finger. Faith stated it so naturally. That's the life she lives—her mother doesn't talk to her. Would she say the same about Hezekiah?

I know the answer. Hezekiah is the one who eats breakfast with them. He's the one who gets the 4-1-1 about the school day while he cooks dinner. He's the one they gather around.

Hezekiah's voice sounds in my head—*You're in your own little world.* Jillian's—*Your issues always take precedence.* Dr. Lyles—*It's not about you.* Why is this hitting me so hard? When Hezekiah told me earlier this week, in effect, that I'd been falling short at home, I let it roll off my back. I knew I'd missed out on a lot of things like dinners around the table, but I also knew Hezekiah had taken up the slack. The girls had a parent at home, their needs were taken care of, they were well-adjusted, healthy, and happy.

But that one comment from Faith has blown my presuppositions. Maybe they needed more. Maybe they needed their mother.

My face contorts as emotion overwhelms it. I have just enough composure to place my Bible in the bag and hasten to the restroom. I close the door, lock it, and flop myself over the square-rimmed sink, heart caving, filled with questions I've never asked myself or thought about. They tumble forth with the tears. How could I? How could I have called this love? How could I have thought it was sufficient? It isn't love, getting frustrated when the girls show me a drawing while I'm trying to read a legal opinion or sucking my teeth when "Mom" sounds in the house or half-listening when Hope and Joy bombard me with "Guess what's?"

Ugly truth fills me. The edgy remarks, the "you're interrupting me" sighs, the plain lack of joy in motherhood grieves me.

O God, I haven't been the mother You would have me to be. I haven't loved my children, not with Your kind of love, not with a selfless love. Acknowledging it in my heart deepens the hurt. *And the way I've treated Hezekiah.... O Lord, forgive me. Forgive me.*

I fold toilet tissue and blow my nose, swiping my cheeks with the back of both hands. *But, Lord, as bad as I feel, I don't know what to do. I know I need to change. I do. But how? I have no idea where to begin.*

It comes to me instantly, simply, standing me erect.

I wait out the end of the tears then splash my face with water and dab it dry with tissue. My makeup needs freshening but my purse is by the chair and I'm too preoccupied to care. I walk out as Darlene positions Faith under the dryer, thankful for a few minutes to talk freely with my mother-in-law. Returning to my chair, I say almost breathlessly, "Ma, can we talk? So many things are clicking for me."

"Sounds like I'd better sit down." Darlene plunks herself in the seat Faith occupied and says, "What is it, baby?"

"I'm not even sure where to start." I bite my lip. "Okay. You know we're doing Ephesians, right?"

"Right."

"And as soon as I read that I was blessed in heavenly places and seated in heavenly places, I got excited."

"Would have been crazy if you didn't."

"But when I read the Titus 2 verses you gave me, I didn't get as excited. Well, I didn't get excited at all."

"Mmm," she says, but lets me continue.

"But now I know why. Listen to what Dr. Lyles said yesterday on the DVD."

"You know, I heard a tape of his not too long ago. That man is teaching the straight word. He said something about—"

"Okay, Ma," I say, "I'll forget my train of thought. It's just coming together for me and I don't want to lose it."

"Go on, chile."

"Dr. Lyles said that we love to think about what God can do *for* us, when we ought to be thinking about what He wants to do *through* us, especially in our families."

"So true."

"That was me. I got excited about heavenly places because it's what God has done *for* me. Titus 2 is what God wants to do *through* me, in my home, and I resented it. I didn't want my existence to revolve around home and family. I didn't like my life being tied to Hezekiah's, my fortunes vanishing because *he* got a job someplace else. And I blamed the girls for my lack of work. If I hadn't had maternity leaves, if I had been able to bill more hours and not feel the pressure of getting home, I would have been a partner by now, I could have transferred to the D.C. office." I sigh heavily. "But, Ma, Faith shined a floodlight on my soul. In five seconds all of that turned rotten inside."

"Out of the mouth of babes," Darlene adds softly.

I nod and reflect on that a moment, bowing my head slightly as I continue. "In the bathroom, I was thinking about how far I am from where I need to be and how I don't know what to do to get from here to there. But then it came to me. I'm exactly where I need to be. Someone prayed for me yesterday, that I would want to lay down my will, and here I am. I'm not crazy about the way God answered, but He did answer. For the first time I know I need to change."

Darlene grabs my hand across the space between us. "Yes, He did answer, baby. And it's a blessing. He showed you, *you*. It hurts but it's for the good. He's bringing you higher."

"That's the other thing that came to me," I say. "*He's* doing it. He brought me to a place where I wanted to change, so He'll take me to where I need to be. He'll help me appreciate being a wife and mother. He'll help me love Hezekiah and the girls the way I should." I look into Darlene's eyes. "Won't He?"

"That's what Dr. Lyles was saying, sweetheart. That's the exceeding abundant God we serve. He is able to do the work in you so that through you He'll get the glory."

The dryer clicks off and Darlene rises to rinse out the conditioner. I reopen my Bible before she leads Faith back to the chair, not ready to make eye contact. I keep my eyes plastered to the page, to two blurry words, praying as Darlene styles Faith's hair. *What's the next step, Lord? I need the very next step. Please lead me.*

As we leave the salon, a deep breath with a full release of air ushers in my new mindset. "How about breakfast?" I say, pushing the remote to unlock the car doors.

"Really?" Faith says.

"Sure, it's nine o'clock. Aren't you hungry?"

"Starving."

Faith hops in the passenger side and I back out, praying again. "Faith?"

"Yes."

"You were right. We don't talk, not like we should. And it's my fault."

Faith makes a full body turn toward me.

I continue, "I want you to know that I'm praying for God to help me to be a better mother to you, and I hope you can forgive me."

Faith turns and looks out of her window, the sheen of her new do glistening in the light. Darlene gave her wispy bangs and cut the rest evenly, just off the shoulders. She looks lovely, no matter what Patsy and her friends will think.

"Of course I forgive you, Mom," she says, turning back. "That's what Jesus would do."

With admiration, I ask, "When did you grow up?"

"I told you I'm thirteen." Faith laughs at herself and I smile.

Faith and I arrive home after a successful outing in which we chatted more about Amber, Kelly, and Jamila, and found a dress that we both considered perfect for the occasion. Thanks to Faith, the conversation was not hard to maintain. I learned that once engaged, she becomes a little motormouth. More than once she surprised me with her wisdom, wisdom I thought beyond her years. I was saddened that I hadn't known this about her, and that I hadn't played a part in cultivating it.

"Thanks, Mom. This was an awesome morning," Faith says.

"Really?" I say, genuinely surprised by her assessment.

"Yeah, I had fun."

"Hey, Dooby-Doo. Don't you look cute," Hezekiah says, playing with Faith's bangs, a baseball cap perched on his head and a light jacket slung over his arm.

"Thanks, Dad," Faith says, running upstairs with her dress.

Hezekiah grabs his keys from the desk. "I'm going to watch the game with Dad."

"What game?" I say. He didn't even greet me.

"The *game,* USC vs. UCLA."

For a second, I'm glad. I had agonized over what to say to Hezekiah. I know I need to ask his forgiveness as well, but it won't be as easy as with Faith. He wants a pledge of total commitment, a statement that my career has suddenly plummeted in importance and my family is all that matters. I'm not there yet, not in all honesty. So what *do* I say? This is what got me in trouble Tuesday night, and I still don't have a response. Hezekiah's leaving gives me more time.

That's all the positive spin I can put on his departure, though. He's leaving to get away from me. Watching a football game with his father shouldn't raise a red flag but it does. This is not my Hezekiah. On Saturdays, Hezekiah wants to know what we can do together, as a family. If he watches a football game, he watches at home, and only if nothing else is going on. My Hezekiah kisses me, humors me, speaks lovingly to me. But since Tuesday night he has been a new man, indifferent and short on words.

"When will you be back?" I ask, moving slowly toward him as he moves to the door.

"After the game."

"I'm saying, when do you think that'll be? *Right* after the game or will you hang out for a while over there?"

"I don't know, Treva. We'll see," he says, shutting the door.

I stand there as a figure of stone, not bothering to wipe the tears that spring to my eyes. I want my Hezekiah back. *Lord, what do I do? What do I say to him? Please show me.*

———————

Peeking out of the window, I check the darkened street. Hezekiah should be here any moment according to Darlene. She left here twenty minutes ago and arrived home just as he was pulling out of her driveway. "The timing is great," she said, so excited she called from her cell phone inside the car. "I'm praying for you, baby," she said. "I just know God is in this."

If He isn't, I don't know what I'll do. I'm hoping I truly heard from Him. I feel that I did. When I asked Him what I should do, an idea popped into my head, and it was certainly nothing I would have come up with on my own. But it's kind of crazy. Would God give me a crazy idea?

I cast a glance at everything once more and check the window again. Headlights beam onto the driveway and my stomach lurches. *Oh, God. What if Hezekiah does not respond favorably to this?*

I push a button on the remote and music pipes through ceiling speakers throughout the lower level. I take my place and wait.

The door to the garage opens and closes but I don't hear any footsteps. Hezekiah is taking it in. "Treva?" he says.

I wait quietly.

Hezekiah's shoes move tentatively through the kitchen, his way lighted by a sea of candles.

"Treva," he says again.

When he reaches the foyer I slowly descend the spiral staircase in my satin wedding dress. White tea lights flicker on both ends of each stair, making my entrance grand. Hezekiah sees me and mutters, "Oh, my Lord."

He walks to the staircase and takes my hand as I make my way to the bottom. "Treva, I...What...I...." He stops and tries again. "You look stunning. What's going on?"

I stare into his eyes and announce, "Today, Hezekiah Langston, is our wedding day. I am redoing my vows."

"I don't understand," he says.

"You will," I tell him, smiling.

"How did you do all of this? You look...stunning," he repeats.

He lifts my white-gloved hand and turns me around. I gladly oblige, the dress more beautiful and special to me now than the day I first wore it fourteen years ago. We didn't have a big wedding, which didn't matter to me at all. I could count on one hand the people I wanted there, and Hezekiah knew that the church he had grown up in would not be an option. His pastor would not marry believers with unbelievers, and Hezekiah didn't want to face the questions that would come if he tried to find a way around that policy. He had no excuses; I was not willing at that time to even visit the church. So instead of a church wedding, I asked Judge Crawford, the judge for whom I clerked, to perform the ceremony in his chambers during my third year of law school. Though I had not started clerking for him, I had already been hired and had gotten to know him through occasional lunches he scheduled with his current clerks and upcoming clerks who lived in the area. Only Jillian and both sets of parents would be present. It seemed silly to wear a traditional wedding dress in such a setting so Jillian and I searched bridal shops for something elegant yet less than formal.

When Jillian saw this dress, she gasped, "Oh Treva, this is it!"

"But it's floor length," I said.

"But look at it, Treva. It's gorgeous. It's you. You know how you like a little something different." Jillian held the dress aloft. "Look at this."

Jillian fingered the section of the dress that made it distinct. The gown was sleeveless with lingerie straps and a sweetheart neckline accented with crystal beading. But the attraction was absolutely its bottom half. It gathered at the side seam with satin covered buttons and from there, the dress featured an asymmetrical wrap over a satin inset. When Jillian showed me the back with a dramatic V-shaped neckline, I was sold.

I was ecstatic when it slid onto my body today with the same ease. The bridal shoes were too small, though, since my feet grew a half size after my pregnancies. Hidden underneath are a pair of beige pumps. And the simple headpiece I wore at the wedding was lopsided and wrinkled, but at its best it would not have compared to Darlene's touch. When I called to tell her what I had planned, she asked how I would wear my hair. She offered to help, stopping by a florist shop on the way. I had no idea how she was styling my hair, but when I looked into the mirror, it was swept beautifully atop my head with white petal adornments and single ringlets tumbling past my ears.

"I am woefully underdressed," Hezekiah says, eyeing his blue jeans and polo shirt. "Do I need to change? Where are we going?"

"To the backyard," I say. "You don't need to change a thing."

"Where are the girls?"

"Jillian and Cecil came to get them."

Hezekiah shakes his head. "I can't believe this."

Together, hands intertwined, we blow out all of the candles and I lead him through the loggia, down a cobblestone path to the left, to a grand gazebo that the landscape artist insisted would provide a "darling" respite from the sun and stress of life. I assumed I would be working then and told him, "Darling or not, what's the purpose of paying for a structure we won't have time to enjoy? If I do get time to dawdle in the backyard, it'll be in the pool in summer." Hezekiah claimed it as a place where he could meditate and pray, and where we could have a romantic breakfast or two in nice weather. I wonder if God knew it would be used for this purpose tonight. It's perfect.

I stop a moment. *Of course He knew.*

God must have arranged for this balmy evening too. Last night the temperature was chilly but now I am quite comfortable in bare arms. Cecil lit the two tiki torches for me and they stand now, like blazing sentries, awaiting our arrival. We take our place between them, just outside the entrance to the iron gazebo. Hezekiah waits for whatever I have planned.

In an instant the fairy tale beauty of the night fades and I remember why we are here. I gaze at the ground as tears choke the words I practiced all afternoon. Hezekiah embraces me and I cry more, thankful for his tenderness, thankful to have my husband's arms around me again.

Gathering myself, I say, "Hezekiah, you know that when we got married, I was not a Christian. I loved you in my own way but I didn't have the power to love you the way…well, the way you should have been loved. And when I became a Christian three years ago, I don't think I acted any differently at all in terms of the love I showed you. Not until the last couple of months. And then I only got worse."

I stop and sigh and wonder if it's gotten colder because chill bumps are raising on my arms.

"But, Hezekiah, something else has been happening these last couple of months. I've been reading the Bible and learning more about God. Hezekiah, I didn't know that God had something to say about marriage. I didn't know He had something to say to wives and mothers. I didn't know I was so far from...from...."

"It's okay, sweetheart," Hezekiah says, stroking my back.

"No, it's not okay. That's just it. That's why we're here. It is not okay," I say, letting a fresh wave of tears pass. I force the words out. "Hezekiah, I have not been the wife that I should have been." Confessing it plainly gives me strength. "I have not loved you selflessly, I have not submitted myself to you, I have not respected you, and I have not given our home a place of priority. Frankly, listening to myself, I don't know why you've stayed with me."

"Treva, you know that's not an option for me. Till death do us part."

"But I haven't given you that same commitment, not from the heart. I couldn't answer you Tuesday night because I honestly couldn't say what my level of commitment was. And at first I didn't know what to say today because I still didn't feel I could give the right answer. But then I realized I could just tell you the truth, that I'm not where I need to be, but for the first time, I want to be. Sort of."

Hezekiah lets out a deep chuckle. "Sort of, huh?"

"I told you I was being truthful," I say, glad for the light moment. "What I mean is that God is doing something inside of me that's giving me a desire to be where He wants me to be, but it's all in process. It's unnerving because I don't know what it entails or where God will lead but I do know that I need to follow. So...."

I squeeze both of his hands and look directly into his eyes, heart pounding. "Hezekiah Langston, I pledge to be the wife that God calls me to be. I pledge to love you with God's love, to respect you, to submit to you as unto the Lord, and to build our home rather than tear it town. I make this pledge by faith, depending on the strength and grace of God to work in and through me. Oh, and till death do us part."

"Treva Langston, I pledge—"

"But I didn't expect you to—"

"Shh," Hezekiah says, pressing a finger softly to my lips. "I pledge to love you as Christ loved the church and gave Himself up for her. I pledge to dwell with you with understanding, to honor you, and to submit myself to Jesus, who is the head of our home. He will never leave us nor forsake us, and I will never leave you."

Hezekiah's arms engulf my waist and the small space between us closes as he kisses his bride. It ignites a rush within me of promise and newness, of hope and life, so much so that it scares me. Should I *be* optimistic? What if I fail? What if I'm Treva-as-usual next week, not caring an iota about dinner and feeling suffocated by my family?

I cut short the kiss and tilt my head back. "Hezekiah, what if I *can't* change? I'm almost forty. I've been career-minded since I was ten. I had to be. That's the only way I could—" A flash of fear consumes me now. What path have I placed myself on? I knew where the other was leading, to higher elevation, to a pronouncement that I'm somebody. This path...I don't see it taking me there. What am I doing?

"You said it yourself, sweetheart. By faith," he says, grazing my lips. "If you ask me, God is already handling things. Look what you've done today. Is this normal?"

I stare upward playfully, as if contemplating. "You mean I'm not typically garbed in wedding attire?"

Hezekiah smiles. "Sweetheart, God is doing beyond what we could ask or think, just as I prayed."

My eyes grow wide. "You prayed that? When?"

"All the time. You're a handful, girl."

I roll my eyes, knowing he's right.

"But you're *my* handful," he says, resuming the kiss, working it slowly, teasingly. "I'm thinking," he says, managing to keep our lips locked, "that the problem is not that I'm underdressed, but that you are overdressed."

"Oh, really?"

"How long will the girls be gone?"

"All night."

"This evening gets better and better," he says, scooping me into his arms.

"Hezekiah, you're going to drop me," I protest.

"I've got you, Mrs. Langston. I'm never letting you go."

Chapter Twenty-Two

Monday morning, 5:10 A.M., I hop out of bed, energized. Not since my working days have I welcomed the predawn hour with gusto. I was motivated then to rise extra early, beat the traffic into downtown Chicago, and bill two good hours before the workday bustle filled the halls. Face-time was motivation in itself, since the head litigation partner shared the first pot of coffee with me.

Lately, though, I had been sleeping as long as I could, allowing just enough time to shower, dress, and make sure the girls moved speedily through their cereal. I knew it was an outgrowth of a depressed state but I didn't fight it. No point in greeting dawn for a lackluster day.

But this morning is different. Life is different. I want to get going first thing, start my homework early Monday for once, make breakfast for the family, greet them leisurely rather than bark orders for them to hurry along. This weekend opened up something new in me. It feels strange, as if I don't quite know myself. I'm ready to test the waters, see what I'm like.

I quietly slip into blue Nike shorts, a matching sports bra, a T-shirt, and walking shoes, and take the back stairway into the kitchen. At this hour I'll have time for a power walk on the treadmill after I study. I measure out water and coffee grounds and push the button to brew, pull the Bible and study binder off of the bookshelf, and my jumbo cup of colored pencils out of the cabinet above the desk. After using the girls' pencils for a couple of weeks, I bought my own set of fifty Crayolas.

I turn to Week 5 and scan the assignment for day one. "Read Ephesians, chapter four, straight through, remembering to look for the 5 W's and an H. Then read it again, marking key words and phrases with your colored pencils."

Hands cupping a toasty mug, I sip and read. Halfway through the chapter I'm marveling at what I see, a summation of my weekend in spiritual prose. I read it again and again, each time gaining a little more understanding of what happened.

"...that, in reference to your former manner of life, you lay aside the old self, which is being corrupted in accordance with the lusts of deceit, and that you be renewed in the spirit of your mind, and put on the new self, which in the likeness of God has been created in righteousness and holiness of the truth."

I grab a pen and write the directives in my binder.

Lay aside the old self.
Be renewed in the spirit of your mind.
Put on the new self.

I mull them over, skip a line, and write again.

Lay aside the old wife and mother.
Be renewed in the spirit of your mind.
Put on the new wife and mother.

That's what I did! That's exactly what God led me to do. How awesome that this would be in the homework today. I continue reading, and the very last verse in the chapter holds me.

And be kind to one another, tender-hearted, forgiving each other, just as God in Christ also has forgiven you.

My heart melts as Faith and Hezekiah come to mind, and their willingness to forgive despite years of putting up with my "old self." And God. What a blessing to be reminded that He set the standard by forgiving us first. *Thank You, Lord, for waking me up early and blessing me with Your Word. You know it's not always easy for me to understand these verses, Lord. And sometimes I understand them but can't receive them. Sometimes I don't want to receive them…just being honest, Lord. So I'm happy this morning to read verses that are timely and encouraging. It's nice to get a boost now and then and—*

My mind moves me out of prayer, nudging me with one word from that last verse—*forgiving*. My insides tighten, sensing the reason, and I come quickly out of my chair. Time to exercise. I don't want any stress this morning. I'm determined to stay upbeat.

I poke my head into Hope's room and catch her sitting on her yellow and pink flowered quilt, reading.

Startled, she says, "Did you call me, Mommy? Because I didn't hear you."

"No, I was making sure you were up but I see you're dressed already. You must have risen early."

"I did, Mommy, and I washed my face and brushed my teeth and I put my clothes on, and since I still had a lot of time, I decided to read."

"That's great, sweetie," I say, noting that she's gotten better about pairing together matching clothes. I continue down the hall and then go back up to her doorway. "Know what? Let's do your hair."

Her mood flips as she inches back on the bed. "Nooo, you don't need to comb my hair today. See?" Hope flattens the flyaway hairs back in place with her hand. "That's what *you* do. It's fine. Plus we don't have time; I'll be late for school."

"You just said yourself we have a lot of time."

"Mommy, no, please!"

"It'll be all right," I say, dashing into the girls' bathroom to get what I need.

Hope pouts as I climb on the bed and nestle behind her. I open the canvas bag of hair supplies and unwind the scrunchie from Hope's hair. "What are you reading?"

"*Were* reading? I can't read when you're yanking my head down."

"Okay, what *were* you reading?"

"Frog and Toad."

"When did you get that?"

"I got it from the library last week." Hope tosses her neck back with a puzzled look. "Remember I told you in the car on the way home from school last week?"

"Oh."

I look around Hope's room as I finger through the bigger tangles. She has arranged her books on two long shelves, stuffed animals on another, and various homemade and school-made objects on the bottom. It's very well-organized. I wonder if she did it alone and how long it has been this way, but no way will I ask. What if it's been weeks?

I come into my daughters' rooms every evening but with purpose. To kiss them and say good night, and it's too dark at that time to check things out. I never come to hang out with them or to explore their interests or to do what I am doing now. If I need them, I call them. This is a nice change of pace.

"Mommy, what are you doing?" Hope shrinks and flinches under the comb.

"I'm parting."

"Why?"

"I'm trying a new style."

Dramatic sigh. "*Why?*"

"It'll be cute, just watch."

I part the hair slowly across the top of Hope's head from ear to ear, then make six parts from the forehead to the crown. In no time, the rhythm returns and I have beautiful cornrows in the front, secured with a red barrette that Hope herself fished out of the bag to match her red shirt. Amazingly, she relaxed and couldn't wait to see the finished product.

"Mommy, I didn't know you could do this."

"I used to practice on your Aunt Jillian."

"Tanya at school wears her hair in cornrows. I can't wait for her to see me."

When I finish the back, I turn her toward me and kiss her forehead. "You look so cute," I say. "Now let's go eat." I watch as Hope walks through the bathroom and primps in the mirror. "Thanks, Mom," she yells.

In the kitchen, Joy and Faith are standing by the stove, perplexed. "Who is this for, the Bible study people?" they're asking Hezekiah as I walk in.

"I don't think so. It's Monday," Hezekiah says.

"It's for you all," I say, hands on my hips, smiling.

"Why?" the girls ask.

"Just because."

"Wow, thanks." The girls put homemade waffles and fat slices of bacon on their plates and carry them, and their bowls of strawberries, to the table, ogling Hope's hair as she proudly strolls in.

Hezekiah spreads whipped butter on his stack and warms his syrup in the microwave. "What's Jillian's favorite cake?" he asks.

"Favorite cake? Why are you asking that?"

"Isn't she the one who got you into this Bible study?"

"She's definitely the one."

"Then she deserves much love cause I'm getting a lot of return on this investment. Wedding on Saturday, hot breakfast on Monday?" Hezekiah walks over and pulls me close with one arm. "Thank you, sweetheart," he says with a kiss.

I press into his chest, inhaling his natural scent, then close my eyes for a brief second and inhale our marriage. I lift my chin and kiss him again.

"Mom, isn't it time to send out invitations for the birthday party, or get-together, or whatever?" Faith says.

I carry my own full plate to the table, famished after my workout. "It's two weeks from this Saturday so it's certainly time. We can work on the guest list when you get home."

"That's easy," Faith says. "Aunt Jillian, Uncle Cecil, Courtney, Sophia, David, and Trevor, Uncle Isaiah—"

"Have you talked to him?" I ask Hezekiah.

"A couple of times. You know Isaiah. Always got this thing and that thing going on. He's rarely at home. I told him it didn't make any sense that we hadn't hooked up yet, but I think he's dodging me. He thinks I'll preach at him. Hasn't even returned my last few phone calls."

Isaiah, four years older than Hezekiah, bounces from venture to venture. Since dropping out of Maryland over twenty years ago, he hasn't held a job for more than a year. He prefers, as he puts it, entrepreneurship, and involves himself in all sorts of schemes legal and questionable. Those and his women keep him quite busy. It breaks Darlene's heart but she prays strongly for him nonetheless. Hezekiah is hoping to make a positive difference in his life now that he's back.

"—Grandma Darlene, Grandpa Russell, Grandma Patsy—"

I thrust myself back in the chair, causing a horrible screech on the floor, something I've told the kids not to do. "Time to go, you guys," I say, walking a half-eaten plate to the sink.

The girls swallow their last bites and run to get their backpacks. I stand at the sink, caving under the weight thrust upon the morning, wishing again that we had never moved back to D.C. so that there would never be an expectation that Patsy would ever be included in any facet of our lives. It was so easy in Chicago. How do I keep the boundaries fixed here?

Hezekiah walks up beside me, his frame touching mine. "You okay, hon?"

I shift toward him. "No. I'm trying to figure out how to keep my mother away from this birthday celebration. That's too much interaction.

The brunch this Saturday, and two weeks later, a party? At *our* house? That will not be happening."

Hezekiah leans against the counter and sighs. "You knew it was coming. There's no way we can keep your mother off the guest list."

I had hoped Hezekiah would partner with me in this. Hearing his position, I move away, grabbing my purse from the desk and lifting the keys from the side pocket. "Maybe not off the guest list, but I can keep her out of my house, even if I have to forget to put her invitation in the mail."

"Treva, this is going to come up at Thanksgiving, at Christmas, and on every other special day. You're going to have to deal with your mother. How does God get the glory if you're avoiding her all the time?"

I hear the girls arguing over who has the right to take the Uno cards to school to play during lunch, an exchange I would normally resolve by taking the cards myself and leaving them here, but I let them have at it, taking the couple of minutes to rally Hezekiah to my cause. "Hezekiah, do you realize she has never even apologized for her behavior the night before the funeral? Think about the things she said to me. Think about the way she's treated me my entire life. I don't *like* her, and I don't want to be around her. I might have to endure her from time to time, but it won't be in my home."

Hezekiah nods his head downward, but it's not a nod of assent. He shares my frustration, it says, but not my conclusion. When he moves toward me and begins massaging my shoulders, I know I won't like what he's about to say. "Baby, I know this is hard. I know it is. Your mother ain't right, plain and simple. But remember what you told me on Saturday, all the new things you were learning because of the Bible study? Remember you said you were changing? You had to know God wasn't going to stop with me and the girls."

I sigh. "Hez, what is your point?"

"God cares about your relationship with your mother. Believe it or not, He cares about your mother. I don't know if you think about this but you're far better off than Patsy, Treva. You have eternal life and all the blessings that go with it. She has nothing. She's dead and doesn't know it." Hezekiah stops massaging and holds my shoulders. "You might be the one to lead her to life."

My head snaps up at him. "Hezekiah, I can't believe you said that with a straight face. My mother wouldn't listen to anything I had to say, especially about spiritual matters. Anyway, Jillian has tried."

"Oh, and one person sharing the gospel with you was enough?"

"I'll bet Darlene has tried, too, and others we don't know about. God can put plenty of people in her path."

"What if He wants you?"

"He wouldn't. Now can we get back to the party?"

"Ask Him."

"Ask Him what?"

"If He wants to use you in Patsy's life. Maybe He wants her at the party."

Use me in Patsy's life? The thought dives into my being and conjures a slew of others, frightening and fragmented thoughts about God, Patsy, and me and the verses I read this morning. Didn't Willow say something like this too? I wave the back of my hand, walk to the doorway of the kitchen, and call, "Girls, come on. We should've been in the car by now."

Hezekiah looks after me with lifted eyebrow as I make my way across the kitchen, muscles tighter than before the massage. "You gonna ask?" he says.

"Have a blessed day, Hez."

I snap the little pair of jeans in the air, straightening the dryer's rumples, and fold them in two crisp tilts of the wrist. I grab another and add them to the pile in short order. I have freed two full laundry baskets in fifteen minutes and am well on my way with the third, my speed spurred by Hezekiah's off-the-wall assertions. What was he thinking? A guest list, that's all we were discussing. Reasonable minds would agree that if a grandmother has a bias against the color of her granddaughter, said grandmother should stay her behind home when such time comes to celebrate that granddaughter's birth. Period. Is this a complicated issue? I answer with the snatch of a shirt from the basket.

Reasonable minds would agree also that I, the spurned daughter, object of lifelong bias of said women, should not have to deal with her on special days. We have never spent a special day with her before and do not have to start now. Thanksgiving we will go to Darlene's, Christmas will be dinner at home, and months will pass before the next holiday or event threatens to close the distance between us. Hope and Joy have spring birthdays but an intimate family dinner will suffice; Patsy can send her usual Hallmark. Once every blue moon if Hezekiah feels the girls need to see their Grandma Patsy, fine. He can take them, for a supervised visit.

I walk my piles from the second-floor laundry room to the girls' rooms and tuck them neatly in drawers. This is their job, the folding and the putting away, but when I returned from dropping them off to school, vexation moved me aimlessly about the house. I had to put my hands to something; the laundry obliged with an eager stand at attention.

I smile now, surprising myself, as Joy's size 9 labels stare up at me. When did that girl get so big? For that matter, what am I doing with an almost teenager?

I see it clearly. The season has wings and a purpose and an end. The season God wants me to pay attention to, embrace, and enjoy. The season of motherhood.

I smooth Joy's bedcovers and fluff her decorative pillows, positioning them neatly, and in a sudden reflex torpedo them both across the room as thoughts of Patsy bubble and knot my stomach, preventing me from thinking long about anything else, not even things I am finally delighting in, like the size of my child's clothes.

Finishing the laundry task I look for another. When the waffle iron, skillet, and breakfast dishes are washed, dried, and put away, I stand in the middle of the kitchen contemplating my next undertaking, feeling pulled to the office, which I'm resisting (I'm fasting from the computer for one week) and to the Bible to continue study of chapter four, which I'm also resisting.

Those verses continued swirling after I left Hezekiah this morning, a sure part of what vexed me. They were the same words I had read and embraced this morning but they were no longer clothed in encouragement and comfort. They had widened and deepened, bent on stretching me with them in the process.

A crumb on the counter gives me an excuse to wipe down the entire surface, clean the inside of the microwave, and wrestle with the stubborn stains on the stovetop. Thirty minutes later I find myself standing in the middle of the kitchen again, wrestling, with myself, remembering the prayer to lay down my will in exchange for His. *Fine. I'll go to the table.*

I read the chapter again, review my notes, uncap my pen, and do as I am clearly bidden. Slowly crossing out "wife and mother" on my paper, I write one word in their place, a wider and deeper word, and consider it.

Lay aside the old Treva.
Be renewed in the spirit of your mind.
Put on the new Treva.

God wants more than the wife Treva and the mother Treva. He wants the insecure Treva. The fearful Treva. The striving Treva. The Treva who doesn't like her mother. The Treva who doesn't like herself.

He wants *Treva.*

And that's not all He wants.

I allow my eyes to travel down the page to the rest of the words that turned on me. *And be kind to one another, tender-hearted, forgiving each other, just as God in Christ also has forgiven you.*

I fall back in the seat and drape my head over the top of the chair, content to let the blood rush since it's about to pop anyway. I don't understand why God is doing this to me. The burdens will never end. Didn't I just take life-changing, extraordinary-for-me steps on Saturday? Can I get more than two days into this new mindset of hearth and home before God loads another new thing—a gargantuan thing—on my shoulders? Can I feel better about me before I'm bombarded with demands concerning the one who ruined me? *Because that's what You're doing God—You're expecting me to forgive my mother even though she hasn't acknowledged guilt about anything. It's not fair, Lord. I just want to live my life without a single thought of her.*

Ask Him. Ask Him if He wants to use you in Patsy's life.

I lift my head, shaking it. If I ask, He might do beyond what I ask, and who knows what that would look like. I don't want to be used in Patsy's life. I want no part of her.

Chapter Twenty-Three

"Jillian, I've got a quick question for you," I say, keeping my brisk clip on the treadmill.

"Okay, long as it's quick," Jillian says.

"Do you have a set day of the week that you clean the house?"

"It's not written in stone but usually on Saturdays. We try to maintain during the week, though, so it won't get out of control. Why? Didn't you call that woman Willow recommended?"

"I've left her two messages and she hasn't called me back. That irritates me to no end. Be about your business, you know? Anyway, I had to go ahead and clean the house myself yesterday and you won't believe this but I used the time to start memorizing Ephesians."

"What?"

"Remember that book you gave me?"

"That was at least two years ago."

"I know, and to be honest I hadn't thought about it. But a couple of days ago I was looking at the bookshelf and that book jumped out at me. Jilli, I read the entire book that day."

Jillian gasps. "Look at God, Treva. That book is life-changing; at least it was for me. Can you believe how many books of the Bible that woman has memorized? She inspired me to go for it."

"So what have you memorized?" I ask, my interest causing me to pick up my pace.

"First John, Philippians, and since this study started, I've been working on Ephesians too."

My mouth drops. "You are kidding me!"

"Nope. Life-changing, girl."

"Well, *you* just inspired me. I might be able to really do this. I've learned the first five verses so far. Only, what, one hundred fifty to go?" I laugh at the ridiculous sound of it.

"You can do it, Treva. I am so proud of you! Now what does this have to do with your question about cleaning?"

"You know how the author says she learns her verses while she's doing mindless tasks around the house or driving places? Well, I could see how that would work because while I was vacuuming I just said them over and over and they stuck. So now I'm thinking I might just clean my own house because I think it'll help with the verses. I can kill two birds with one stone."

"Maybe that's why the woman didn't call you back. God had another plan."

I smile. "I hadn't even thought about that, Jillian. That's awesome, isn't it? Oh, let me ask you this—"

"'Quick question' you said, Treva. We're in the middle of school. I'll have to call you back at break time."

"I'm sorry, Jillian. I didn't even look at the time. Why did you answer the phone? I thought you ignore it when you're in school."

"I saw that it was you."

Jillian's thoughtfulness triggers regret within. Despite her time crunch, I have to voice it. "Jillian, I haven't told you yet that those things you said to me at my house went deep. I'm sorry for not being more attentive to your needs over the years. I really am."

"Apology accepted. I appreciate it."

Unable to resist, I say, "So, you said there are things I don't know because I didn't call you back. What exactly—" Another call beeps in and

I don't recognize the number. I ask Jillian to hold in case it's a business call for Hezekiah.

"Hello," I say.

"Hey, woman, how's life treating you?"

"Isaiah?"

"The one and only."

I shake my head. "Hold on a moment."

Reluctantly, I click back to Jillian to let her go. "Jill, it's Isaiah and I know you have to go anyway."

"Isaiah? What in the world is he up to now?"

"Girl, I don't know. Listen, I want to continue our conversation later. You won't be able to accuse me of being inattentive on this one."

Jillian hesitates. "Well, we'll see—about picking up that subject I mean. I'll talk to you later."

My brows knit at Jillian's words and I pause before clicking back to Isaiah. Forced to shrug it off, I push the button. "So you're finally in touch again, huh?"

"Aw, it's not like that, is it? I haven't been out of pocket that long. Y'all only been here a few weeks, right?" Music is blasting in the background and Isaiah seems to be carrying on another conversation with two or three more people.

"I know you're not at a club at ten in the morning, are you?" I say, tipping my water bottle up to my lips while balancing the phone and my body on the treadmill.

"Nah, nah. We're out here taking care of business. So, everything all right? How's my little brother, the professor? He at home?"

"No, he's at work."

"And the girls, how are they doing? I bet they're real big now. I saw their pictures over at the house."

Wonder when that was, probably years ago. "They're fine; everybody's fine. How about you? How's life?"

"You know me, everything is everything. I'm working on the real deal right now. Matter of fact, I'll be rolling out that way around about six. Will little brother be home by then?"

"He should be, yes."

"Cool. Y'all gonna have some peck for a brother?"

I chuckle. "We'll feed you, Isaiah. I look forward to seeing you."

"You too, sweetheart."

I hang up the phone, chuckling still to myself. He is something else. Slowing my speed for a cooldown, I place a call to Hezekiah, who is surprised and pleased that Isaiah is coming, and to Darlene, who, along with her husband, would love to snatch some time with her elusive son. Her joy is heard through the phone as she accepts the dinner invitation without a moment's thought. When she asks what she can bring, I valiantly and foolishly say, "Nothing." I will attempt my first home-cooked meal for my mother-in-law.

At four-thirty, I transfer the pieces of chicken from their spicy barbecue marinade to a large baking pan, skin side up, and place them in the preheated convection oven.

"Mommy, it's still not coming out right!" Joy pouts. "The numbers on the left side don't match the numbers on the right. This is stupid!"

I eye the rapidly melting butter, remembering my timing has to be precise. I have flour, mustard, nutmeg, salt, and pepper ready to go. Sighing, I say, "I don't see why they're trying to teach you multiplication equations so early anyway, making *me* work harder."

"So I don't have to do it, Mommy?"

I add the flour and friends and stir carefully over low medium heat. "Yes, you have to do it. Did you follow the steps like I told you?"

"Mm-hmm. It says 'y x 2 = 5 + 3.' So I put 'y x 2 = 9.' But I can't figure out 'y' because every number I multiply by 2 is supposed to be even. Isn't that what you said?"

I cut the fire to the pan a bit and pour in the two-percent milk and the condensed milk, slowly. "Girl, what is five plus three?"

Joy looks upward and giggles. "Eight."

Hope, having dumped the contents of her backpack onto the kitchen table, produces a sheet of paper. "Mommy, this is for you," she says, shoving it before my eyes.

I glance at it and avert my eyes back to the pan. "Read it for me, Hopey. I've got to keep my eyes on this and stir."

"Dear Parents, I am truly enjoying your kindergarteners this year. We have been learning many new and exciting things and it is such a joy to work with them. We do have a need that I am hoping you can—

"What's this word, Mommy?" Hope asks, thrusting it again before me.

"Accommodate."

"—accommodate. Not enough parents signed up to help in the room this year. We are in need of at least two more who can commit to one day a month. I am sure you will find, as I do, that working with these little people is indeed rewarding. Yours Truly, Mrs. Troyer.

"Can you do it, Mommy? Pleeeeease."

"Me?"

"Yes!"

I am thankful to be facing the stove so my eyes can freely express how I feel. *Me,* a room mother? Tending to all those snot-nosed kids? Helping out with arts and crafts? I hate arts and crafts. This was never an option with Faith and Joy. Notes such as these got routinely tossed. But now that I'm home, what excuse can I give?

"Hope, Mrs. Troyer needs a commitment for the year and I haven't totally given up my job search. I wouldn't feel comfortable giving that kind of commitment."

"Do you have a job *now*, Mommy?" The girl sounds like her Aunt Jillian.

I shake the cheddar and mozzarella cheese into the mix and stir until gooey. "No."

Hope hugs the back of my legs and grins. "Good. Then you can do it!"

Love your children. I shoot back within, *What does that verse have to do with being a room mother?* I groan and immediately feel bad when Hope's arms fall from my legs. "Okay, I'll tell Mrs. Troyer I can do it, for *now*."

"Yeah!"

I mix the cheese sauce with my drained macaroni and smile. Looks like it's turning out okay. I've never made my favorite side dish but I wanted to try. Hezekiah will fall out when he sees this.

After I slide the macaroni and cheese next to the chicken in the oven, I say, "Okay, you all need to clean up this table. It's a mess."

"Why?" Joy asks, drawing now in a sketch book. "We're not eating in here."

"Because Uncle Isaiah and your grandparents are coming and the house should look nice."

"Who *is* Uncle Isaiah anyway?" Joy asks.

"Daddy's brother," Faith says.

"You've never met him, Joy," I say.

"You say I did, but I don't remember," Faith says, eating an apple at the table.

"I know. You were too young. It's been about ten years since we've seen him."

At this, loud voices penetrate the garage door and it swings open. "Look what the cat dragged in," Hezekiah says, beaming from ear to ear with one arm locked around Isaiah's neck.

"Hey, hey, hey," Isaiah says, coming toward us. Then stopping, arms folded, he says with a grin, "Look at y'all, the picture-perfect family. Y'all could be the Huxtables or something."

My mind travels immediately to Claire Huxtable, the *practicing* attorney. "Isaiah, it's good to see you," I say, walking into his opened arms. He's aged a bit, eyes a little drawn, but otherwise the same, still a carbon copy of Hezekiah, minus an inch of height and the muscular frame.

He hugs me tightly then takes my arms and steps back. "Sister Treva, you know you're fine, girl." Turning to Hezekiah, he says, "Boy, what did you do to deserve a woman like this? I have yet to find me one—beauty *and* brains."

"All right, you can unhand my woman now. I know what I've got. You can believe that," Hezekiah says, winking at me.

I move the girls in Isaiah's direction and Hezekiah introduces them.

"Y'all don't have to be scared. Come here and give your uncle a hug." Isaiah bends down and gives each a sweet embrace. "I know y'all don't know me but we're gonna make up for that. Now that you're back, your Uncle Isaiah'll do all kinds of things with you."

Hezekiah lifts his brow. "Don't make my daughters a promise you can't keep," he says, without a hint of playfulness.

"I'm good, I'm good," Isaiah says, taking in his surroundings for the first time. "Life's been treating you well, Bro', real well."

At the doorbell's ring, Isaiah gives a puzzled look.

"Mom and Pop," Hezekiah says. "They can't wait to see you."

Isaiah's eyes fall, then glance sideways at Hezekiah. "What kind of mood do you think they'll be in?"

Hezekiah shrugs. "I don't know, man. What kind of mood have you put them in?"

Isaiah doesn't respond as Hope leads us to the door and opens it, springing into Darlene's arms.

Behind her, Joy says, "Hi, Grandma! Hi, Grandpa!"

Russell and Darlene come into the foyer and revolve their world first around the girls.

Faith hugs them and, smiling, says, "Look at Papa Russ. What are you doing with that cool hat?"

"What else would I wear?" Russell says, tipping his leather cap to her. "And I hear you're trying to become a teenager, little Miss. I haven't given my permission for that yet."

"Are you coming to my party?" Faith asks.

"All I need is an invite," Russell says.

"You got it," Faith says, lifting her hand.

Russell slaps it and it's sealed.

Faith turns. "Will you come, Uncle Isaiah?"

"Wouldn't miss it, baby."

Hezekiah gives him an eye as we move forward to kiss Darlene and Russell and take their jackets. Isaiah hangs in the rear of the foyer, hands in his pockets.

"You need some kind of an invitation too?" Russell says, his tone equally loving and gruff. "Come on over here, son, and give us a hug."

Isaiah moves at once, head slightly bowed. "I didn't know Pop, whether...."

Isaiah's words melt into his father's embrace. Russell finishes them, pulling back to meet his gaze. "You didn't know how we would act since you haven't called or come by in far too long. I think it's a downright shame but your mother gave me a good talking to before we came. I'm not gonna fool with you about it. Shame for a son to treat his mama like that, though."

Isaiah leans to the side to find his mother behind Russell. "I'm sorry, Mama," he says, moving toward her. "I'll do better."

Darlene grabs his hands and her mother's heart swings them. "No promises, Isaiah. I'm just going to enjoy the time God gives me with you today." Isaiah bends and kisses her cheek and they hug warmly.

Heartened, Isaiah whirls from her, saying, "I forgot! I brought something for the girls."

He heads back to the kitchen and we all follow behind. Darlene says, "Something sure smells good." I shoot her an anxious look and she smiles, saying, "It'll be fine."

Isaiah fishes through an athletic bag he brought with him and produces three CDs, handing one each to the girls. "Autographed copies," he says, his hands finding his hips as he waits for praise.

"Oh, that's Eloquence," Faith says. "Everybody's talking about him. Do you have any Israel and New Breed?"

Isaiah gives her a look that says he doesn't know what that is, let alone have it.

Joy says, "Is Eloquence the one who says, 'If she's a skeez'a, then we'z a, going to the sheets'a—'"

Darlene scrunches up her face. "What kind of mess is that?"

Hezekiah promptly collects each one from the girls and cuts an eye at Isaiah, who's digging in his bag for something else.

"How do you know the lyrics, Joy?" I ask.

She lifts her little shoulders in a shrug. "People sing it on the playground."

Isaiah pulls black T-shirts out, saying, "I've got these for y'all too." He unfolds one and a young man fills the front, his head cocked to the side, arms folded with the top hand pointing like a gun. His pants sag to his thighs and he is wearing the same T-shirt of himself.

"We'll pass, man," Hezekiah says, with an expression that says Isaiah should know better. "We're not into all that."

Darlene squints her eyes. "Let me see that," she says, extending her hand. When Isaiah passes her one, she says, "I know that's not little Ned." Bringing it closer, she says, "It's *got* to be him. Look at that face." She hands it to Russell.

"That's him," Russell says, dropping the shirt back into Isaiah's hand. "I wonder what happened."

"Who's little Ned?" Isaiah asks.

"He lived in the neighborhood for a while," Darlene says, "after you two were grown and gone. His mother worked for the phone company, worked real hard to get a house for her son and give him a decent living. Ned was a nice little fellow. Polite, I remember. They lived there for about four years and then moved away. He was about thirteen then. That was the last I heard of them."

"Well, he's the man now," Isaiah says, putting back the shirts. "And he's not 'Ned' anymore. 'Eloquence' has been number one on the charts for four straight weeks. He's my boss."

"You're working for this kid?" Russell says.

"He's not a kid, Pop."

"He must be 20 or 21 now," Darlene says.

"So, am I hearing this right?" Faith says. "You *know* him?"

Isaiah's ego swells. "Yeah, know him well. I'm getting ready to head to his crib when I leave here. We've been working some long hours."

"What do you do for him?" Darlene asks.

"Street promotion. I'm also working on the upcoming road tour. It's gonna be hyped. He's opening for La-Dee-Da and there's this intro where—"

Russell's sigh turns every head. "Isaiah, this is ridiculous. Haven't you had enough of dibbling and dabbling in every fly-by-night—"

"Pop, this is the legit deal. Eloquence is blowing up. And he has a real business plan. He wants a clothing line, and one day a restaurant."

Darlene covers Russell's hand with hers and holds it. Russell sucks his teeth and mumbles, "Mm-hmm."

"O-kay," I say, walking through the tension, "it's a good time for everybody to head to the dining room table. Hezekiah, can you help them get situated?"

"What can I do, baby?" Darlene asks, rolling up her sleeves.

"Have a seat in the dining room," I say, smiling at her. "You're not working tonight."

Hezekiah pushes her lovingly toward the table and she elbows him, chuckling.

When we are all seated and eating, we get past the music drama and my own personal drama of the collard greens not having near the flavor and texture of Darlene's, which I was able to get past only because nobody commented and Hezekiah's one comment between forkfuls was that he needed to slow down. We settle into easy banter about grades, favorite school subjects, gardening, sports, and people we know in common when Isaiah says casually, "So you're still a big-time lawyer, right, Treva?"

The question heads straight to my gut and churns it. Hezekiah's leg knocks mine to remind me that he's there. "I'm not practicing at the moment," I say.

"But she's still 'big-time,'" Hezekiah says, sailing an arm around my shoulder. "She's a Langston, isn't she?"

"I know that's right," Isaiah says.

Darlene eyes me to see how I'm doing as the conversation moves on. I lower mine from hers and stab a macaroni, then another, and another, place them in my mouth, and do it again, thinking that even Isaiah has a job and a passion, wondering what I will do if "big-time lawyer" is permanently shorn from my identity. Who will I be? Will I matter?

Chapter Twenty-Four

The next morning I'm preparing for another gathering. It's my turn again to host the group, our fifth meeting, and I can't wait for them to get here. Can't wait to tell them what has happened since our last meeting when Willow prayed for God's will for me.

This time I decided against a meal since we won't be in the kitchen. I liked Willow's choice of assorted bagels and made it my own, with fresh-brewed coffee, juices, and bottled water. I arrange them all on wicker trays with napkins, glasses, mugs, and condiments, and place the trays on the wooden coffee table. I then tuck fresh cut flowers into three slender blown glass vases, add water, and set them on the trays.

Taking in the room, I smile at the attitude I caught when Hezekiah told me a month ago that we needed to put furniture buying on hold. My three-ring-binder had been nicely arrayed with glossy brochures and fabric possibilities for this front living area. After much deliberation, I had settled on the exact pieces I wanted—an elegant white leather sofa and love seat with two chairs, all with carved feet of mahogany wood that would capture the eye as one walked through the door. The end tables had their own page, with the handsome lamps that would occupy them on the page following. I had a coffee table, sofa table, two original works of art, and an antique Persian Bakhtiari rug.

But when I sat down with Hezekiah and the tabulated cost, he said such extravagance on one salary, so soon after the move, wouldn't be wise. "Maybe one day," he said, "but I honestly don't see a problem with what we have."

As I stand here now, I don't either. In fact, I prefer it. As I had planned for the living room, I assumed it would be a space no one would use, as in Chicago. My selections were beautiful and showy, but not cozy and welcoming. The sofa and love seat, with their tight cushions and tall side arms, may have sufficed for a formal tea but not the make-yourself-at-home, stretch-out-if-you'd-like type of gathering the group has evolved into. This furniture, owing to whatever mood and prevailing style seized me at the time, is perfect. I can't believe we never put this sectional to use. It has a sleek sophisticated profile, but when I tried it out this morning, the deep cushions and plush pillows cradled me so nicely I had to fight to get back up. While the ladies could have settled comfortably in the family room, it has "kids" stamped all over it by the DVDs, puzzles, and board games stacked everywhere. This room allows us to put our feet up in womanly surroundings.

The doorbell rings and it's Jillian, pretty in a pair of jeans and a black top, no makeup but beautiful, as usual. "Going casual today?" she asks with an approving glance.

"I wear jeans too," I say, shuttling back to the kitchen to see if I've forgotten anything. I knew Jillian would comment. I've been dressy casual at every meeting thus far, but today I felt I could opt for comfort rather than how the others would view me.

"You look cute. It shows off your figure."

"Thank you, Sis," I say. "You know, I didn't get a chance to call you back yesterday because Isaiah, Darlene, and Russell came over for dinner and I spent the afternoon getting ready. I'm sorry. I haven't forgotten."

"Don't even worry about it," Jillian says, waving her hand. "How was dinner?"

I lead her to the living room as I put cream for the coffee on the table. "Fine, I'll tell you about it later." I turn to her. "But before everybody gets here, I wanted to nail down the plans for tomorrow."

"Oh, I'm coming to get the girls at 10:00 and I'll drop them all off at the hotel."

"Are you bringing them back or is Mother?"

"You know I'm bringing them back, girl."

"Just making sure," I say. "I wish you could stay at the brunch and monitor things."

"Don't be nervous about it, Treva. I think it'll be fine."

The doorbell rings again and everyone strolls in at once. As always, I pay particular attention to Asia.

"Hi, Treva. Thanks for having us over again," she says, with the same small voice she had that first day I met her. The last two meetings have deepened my curiosity of her. I've seen a special sweetness, not just with her son but with all of us as we've grown more familiar. She doesn't talk much, but when she does, her words are uplifting. I can't deny, though, that the clothes continue to mystify me. I so want to pull her aside and ask what possessed her to pull on a lace camisole and low-rise jeans that reveal the top of her lace panties.

"All right, ladies, let's get settled," Jillian says. "As always, we'll open in prayer. But we've sent up so many petitions, that if someone has a testimony about answered prayer, we should start there first."

My hand shoots up and they exaggerate their shock.

"What?" Willow says. "*Treva's* volunteering to go first? This must be good."

"Y'all, it is," I say, inching forward on the sofa. I tell them first, in quick storytelling fashion, the background of my walking out on Hezekiah and the girls at dinnertime and how he reacted, then what happened at the salon, and how the rest of that Saturday unfolded. Then I take a breath and sit back, crossing my legs and smoothing my jeans. "Let's just say the mood at the end of the day was far different than what it was at the start."

"Whoo!" Willow shouts, pumping her fist. "You go, girl! Treva! Treva! Treva!"

Willow stands and each one follows suit, chanting in rhythm. I bow my head, hiding my face with my hand, blushing beyond belief.

When the chanting dies, Monique steps to me and raises her hand for a high-five. I slap it hard. "Girl, God snatched you back from crazy. You know you had no business trippin' on a good man. From what you just said about him, he is golden."

"I always tell her he's the best thing that ever happened to her," Jillian says. "And you all should have seen her on Saturday. She was gorgeous."

"Treva, I'm so proud of you!" Willow says, hugging my neck. "God told you to do something and you did it. You know? Why can't saved folk do more of that? Why does God have to bend us over and jack our arm up behind our back before we cry 'Uncle'? Just do it. God said it before Nike did. Amen?" Willow cracks up at herself.

"Amen," Carmen says, giving me a big hug.

I look down. "Well, don't applaud me too much. When I got to this week's homework I knew God was speaking to me about forgiveness and I sure ignored Him."

"Uh-oh," Monique says. "I bet I know who God was dealing with you about. That's a hard one right there."

"Tell me about it," I mumble.

"That's a perfect transition to today's lesson," Jillian says, her words lowering everyone to their seats. After we pray, she continues, "Dr. Lyles's opening exercise pertains to the very thing Treva mentioned. He wants those who are willing to share a difficult experience in which they chose to forgive. And then he wants us to pray for anyone who's having a difficult time right now in the area of forgiveness."

Silence descends upon the room and my stomach gurgles, causing my eyes to sneak a peek at the bagels. I know this is a reflective moment and I shouldn't interrupt everybody's inward searching to get one, but since I'm not searching—as I've already relegated myself to the second group needing prayer—I angle my legs toward the table and wait to make my move.

"I figured this might be the focal point of the lesson today—" Carmen says.

I slide my wheat bagel off the tray. Won't bother to spread any cream cheese.

"—so I prayed about whether to share this. I feel like God wants me to."

All eyes stand at attention.

"I was abused as a child," Carmen says, seemingly oblivious to our wild-eyed expressions of shock. It looks as if even Jillian didn't know.

Carmen continues, folding and unfolding a tissue in her lap that she retrieved from her purse. "My father abused me sexually, mentally, and, of course, emotionally, from the time I was six until I was ten. After that, just mentally and emotionally. I found out later that he stopped the sexual part because my mother finally threatened to leave if he didn't. I discovered she knew all along, and I thought she did because she would leave the house just before every incident. My two brothers and sister were younger, so I don't think they ever knew what was going on."

"But...But your mother lives with you," Jillian says. "How...?"

Carmen nods her head slightly. "It was a long process. My father put me out when I was sixteen and I stayed with my Sunday school teacher, the one who led me to Christ. I had never known such peace or had such sweet sleep. I had always slept in fear because every night he went out to drink and I didn't know what he might do when he came home. Then I didn't know what he might do with my little sister, so I was always waking in the night to see if she was okay. I thought I might kill him if he touched her." Carmen breaks for the first time and we all dash to the overstuffed chair in which she's sitting, positioning ourselves where we can, a couple of us on the ottoman, a couple settling for the floor space beside her.

"Anyway, you asked about my mother. I didn't have much contact with either of my parents after I left. I'd only call to ask about my siblings, and if he answered, I'd hang up. While I was in college, he developed cancer of the lungs and it spread to his mouth. His life devolved to a horrible existence where he had to drink his food from a straw and could barely talk. I refused to go see him. One day I got a call that he'd shot himself."

A collective gasp causes us to find one another, to look into each pair of eyes to verify that we are hearing the same awful story.

"My mother and father never had much. She cleaned people's houses and he rarely worked. Whatever money he got, he spent on liquor. After he died, I was able to send money to help because I was out of college by then. When my brothers and sister left home—they all went to college on scholarship, praise God—I knew my mother needed to get out of the squalor she was living in but I couldn't even think about her living with us—couldn't even look at her— until I got the bitterness out of my heart. I fasted for three days. The first day I vomited with every remembrance that came forth. By the second day they were dry heaves because I had nothing left in my stomach. On the third day there was a change. Instead of seeing *us*, I saw him, sick with his jaws sunken, even though I never saw him during that time. Then I saw him with a shotgun to his head and nothing to live for. I saw his weakness and his sin sickness. He became small in my sight, utterly small. Pitiful. When God allowed me to see my father like that, it broke his hold on me. Those were the best three days of my life. They were freedom for me.

"After that, it was easier to forgive my mother. She was weak too. I was able to see her as a sinner headed for hell rather than my mother who had betrayed her inherent vow to protect me. She's been living with Karl and me for four years." Carmen looks up. "And she's saved now."

As I struggle with the enormity of what Carmen has shared, the depth of depravity that must overtake an incestuous father's soul, the depth of dread that overtakes a little girl's soul, a little girl whose girlhood is no more and whose father is just a monster, I find that I'm struggling most with reconciling the Carmen I thought I knew with the Carmen who has just been revealed. I look into her eyes, guilt-ridden, and interrupt the tearful exchanges she is having with others.

"Carmen," I say, "how is it that you're able to be so nice? So encouraging, so…" I decide to use my word. "Peppy?"

Carmen presses her lips into a thin smile and dabs her eyes. "It started as a way to survive. If I could only be a good daughter—'What do you need, Daddy? Can I get you some iced tea? Are we playing too loudly? We'll be quiet, Daddy.' Anything to please him. I became a horrible people-pleaser after that, always looking out for everybody else, to the detriment of myself and what I knew was right. If a man wanted me, who was I to tell him 'No'? What would he do if I told him 'No'? After God helped me to forgive, He showed me who *He* intended me to be. I saw that what I actually had were the gifts of mercy and encouragement."

I nod my head, understanding more than I would like, that I despised the gifts God had placed in her.

"Jillian?" Asia says. "Jillian?"

I rise to my knees to see over the chair to where Jillian is sitting on the floor. Her knees are propped up before her, head buried. Now I hear them. Silent sobs.

I immediately go to her, knowing my sister. If she were crying solely because of Carmen, she'd be talking to Carmen, not enfolded in herself. Asia must have sensed it too. We arrive at Jillian's side simultaneously, while Monique and Willow continue to minister to Carmen, who's actually ministering to them.

"Jillian?" Asia says again.

Concerned, I lift her shoulders but her head remains tucked. She uses her weight to push back down.

"Jillian, what's wrong? Is it Carmen," I say, hoping despite reason that it is. Jillian is quick to cry with someone else, for their troubles, but hardly ever for herself. Hardly ever has a need to.

When we fail to get a response, Carmen slides off the side of the chair and onto the floor, draping an additional arm over Jillian. When Jillian hears the silence all about her, she lifts her head and rolls her eyes in embarrassment over the scene.

"Carmen, I'm sorry. I did not mean to steal your moment," Jillian says, laying the side of her head on a knee.

"You're not stealing anything. And anyway, I was telling what happened as a testimony of how God helped me overcome and forgive. I wasn't in crisis mode, not like…you seem to be. What is it?"

Jillian stares at the floor, then rises and begins pacing the living room slowly, shaking her head. "It came to my mind yesterday when I was talking to Treva but I didn't get distraught about it. Not this time. I didn't even think long about it. I knew I wasn't going to *talk* about it because I had forgiven my mother and I didn't want to dredge it up again."

I stand and hold myself, wondering what's going to come out of her mouth.

"And I knew what the lesson would be about today. Of course I did. I'm the facilitator!" Jillian stops moving, shuts her eyes, and takes a breath. Opening them, she says, "Yet it didn't even cross my mind that God would have me bring it up in the group. I guess He knew *He* would bring it up, by flooding it into my soul. I don't understand it. Why now?"

"Jillian, if you don't want to talk about it you don't have to," I say, pulling her to a seat beside me on the sofa. I have never been in a position of comforting Jillian, of having to be there for her. It feels strange.

"No, I don't want to talk about it, but I feel I have to. God must have a purpose behind this and I need to see it through."

I hold her hand while my own trembles.

Jillian sighs and it travels through her body. She opens her mouth and nothing comes out. Finally, "When I was a sophomore at Maryland I went to a Que party one weekend and met this guy from Howard. We danced most of the night and exchanged numbers but I didn't think much of it. I was surprised when he called, and more surprised that we talked until two in the morning. We had a lot in common and he blew away all the preconceived notions I had about Ques." Jillian smiles vaguely. "He was soft-spoken and thoughtful and really wanted to get to know me. I hated when guys fawned over me and said I was 'beautiful' and I could tell all they wanted was to conquer me. He wasn't like that." Jillian grows quiet and I squeeze her hand.

"For weeks we talked on the phone," she continues, "and almost forgot what the other looked like. Neither one of us had a car but we started talking about ways we might get together. One day he said he had a friend who could drop him on campus in the evening for a couple of hours and my dorm seemed the logical place. I was so glad to see him and we did a lot of talking in the lobby but then he came up to my room. I got pregnant from that one time."

I knew where she was headed but I couldn't bear for her to get there. I always thought Jillian was a virgin when she married Cecil, not because she had claimed it. I just thought it. I thought I would know if she weren't.

"I told him and he was supportive. He really was. He said we were in this together and that he would be there for me no matter what. He continued to call and everything. But I still felt alone. I couldn't talk to Treva because she was in her first year of law school and always busy, always in class or the library or with Hezekiah and I did not want to burden her."

My eyes, already red from the tears of Carmen's story, are burning, along with my broken heart. Jillian won't say it to them but she already said it to me. She called, probably more than once, and I didn't call her back. I wasn't there for her.

"So a girl should be able to call her mother in times like this, right? Heaven help me, that's what I did. Called my good old mother who doted over me my entire life. Called and told her I was pregnant and lonely and didn't know what to do, and could I come home and just get my mind together. Her first comment? 'Who is he?' When she found out he went to Howard, she sighed, in relief! and asked for his family name. Not recognizing it, she said, 'Describe him.'"

Jillian bursts into tears and I with her, knowing again where she is going.

"He had a dark complexion," Jillian says finally, "so my mother said, 'Jillian, you know your father and I have dreams for your future. There is so much promise for your life. It just wouldn't do to encumber it with this...fellow's child. It would be best for all concerned to quietly dispose of the problem.'

"And I did it, not for her reasons, but because I knew that if she felt that way I would get no help or support in any other course of action. There was only so much he could do. I was left without options. I told him my decision and he said he understood."

Jillian rises and begins pacing again. "But the thing is, I've dealt with this before God. I couldn't stand my mother for what she did, but in time I did forgive her. When I graduated and moved in with Treva and came to know the Lord, that was one of the first things God convicted me about, my feelings toward her. I can't say I'm close to my mother now but we do have a decent relationship. So why did God hit me with this so hard, like I had unresolved issues with her?"

"When God hit you with it," Willow says, "what image was it? Was it of your mother?"

Jillian stops and thinks. "No."

"What was it?" Willow asks, serious in her concern.

"It was an image of me."

"Okay...."

"On the table."

"Oh, sweetheart."

"Killing my baby." Jillian covers her mouth and says softly, "I killed my baby." Then louder, "*I killed my baby.* I always blamed her but she wasn't in that room with me. She didn't make the appointment. I didn't...I didn't have to do it. I did what was easy.... I killed my own child."

I rush to embrace my sister with everything I have, our bodies sobbing upon one another. Her head rests on my neck and I rub her back, whispering, "Jillian, I'm so sorry. I'm so sorry I wasn't there for you." She clutches my waist and I am struck once again with viewing someone differently, this time my sister, whom I'm supposed to know well, who I thought never had a real problem. *What world have I been living in?*

It's confirmed once again. My own.

"Jillian?"

We both turn to Asia, who has come up beside us.

"I was thinking that maybe God wants you to forgive yourself. He wouldn't bring it up to condemn you, would He?"

Hope lights dimly on Jillian's face. "I think first He wanted me to acknowledge responsibility." Jillian lowers her head and lifts it again. "But you're right, Asia. I know He wouldn't condemn me, I know that deep down somewhere. What I don't know is how to ask forgiveness for something like this. How do I even fix my mind to ask God to wipe away a murder?"

"You do it the same way you ask forgiveness for everything else," Willow says, springing from her seat to join us. "Honey, God is faithful. If we confess our sins, He is faithful and righteous to forgive us and to cleanse us from all unrighteousness. You know it; I've heard you quote it. Don't let the devil get you to thinking you've gone beyond God's reach. His mercy never comes up short. It's abundant and new every morning." Willow shakes Jillian's arm. "Now is the time to operate on what you know, all those verses you memorize. Tell me what you know."

"That I killed my baby."

Willow glares at her. "You know that's not what I meant. What else do you know?"

"That I'm…I'm so sorry," Jillian says, not bothering to wipe her tears. I wipe them for her with the tissues Monique ran to get.

"What else?"

"I know God loves me?"

Willow tips Jillian's face up with her finger. "Take the question mark out and say it again."

Jillian looks aside. "I know God loves me."

"And?"

"And He forgives and wipes our sins away as far as the East is from the West."

Willow nods and a smile eases onto her face. "When will He leave you or forsake you?"

Looking directly at Willow now, Jillian says, "Never."

"What can separate you from His love?"

"Nothing."

"Can sin?"

"No."

"Can the sin of abortion?"

Jillian brings the tissue to her nose and blows it. "I guess not."

"'No,' Jillian."

"No."

"'For I am convinced that neither death, nor life, nor angels, nor principalities, nor things present, nor things to come, nor powers, nor height, nor depth, nor any other created thing, shall be able to separate us from the love of God, which is in Christ Jesus our Lord.' Remember you had me memorize those verses from Romans 8 when *I* was struggling with a sin from the past?"

Jillian smiles slightly but lovingly at Willow. "I remember."

"I've got one last question," Willow says. "Do *some* things work together for good to those who love God, to those who are the called according to His purpose?"

"All things," Jillian says with certainty.

"You got it, sister. Walk in what you know. The devil ain't defeating nobody up in here, not on my watch."

"Amen," Monique says. "I'm just so full right now with everything that's been said. I want to help y'all, you know? I just don't know what to do, or what I even *can* do."

"We could pray," Asia says. "Isn't that what Dr. Lyles said? To pray for anyone who's having trouble in the area of forgiveness?"

"He sure did," Carmen says, putting an arm around Asia. "Let's pray for Jillian to be able to truly and completely forgive herself, and for Treva to be able to forgive her mother. Who else can we pray for?"

Monique shares an issue she has with her brother who borrowed a large sum of money two years ago, promising to quickly repay. We all take a seat on the floor and grab hands, each taking a turn lifting up the others in prayer.

Chapter Twenty-Five

"Come on, girls, you've got to hurry up," I yell up the stairs.

Faith makes her entrance first, and when I see her I'm relieved that I still like the dress. I had so many in my head after three malls and a bevy of boutiques last Saturday that I had forgotten the details that drew us to this one. Early this morning I questioned whether it was right. It is. I walk to her, admiring the dress afresh as it hangs perfectly on her budding frame.

Faith looks past me, scanning the kitchen. "But Aunt Jillian's not here yet."

"Daddy and I are taking you now, and we've got to pick up your cousins, too, so we have to get moving."

"Why are you two taking us?"

I sigh inside with thoughts of my sister. *Life is so complicated.* To Faith, it's just a matter of a chauffeur. "Your Aunt Jillian needs some time to herself and this is a good way to give it to her. Turn around and let me look at you."

Yes. This was a good choice, and not because we rejected everything else, which we did. Everything was too grown-up or too babyish, too flower girlish or too promish. The tulle was hideous—in a ballet it would have been hideous. The satin, chiffon, and organza were over the top, more suited to an evening, though I couldn't imagine what kind of evening. I wasn't even sure what I was looking for but I knew I wasn't seeing it. When a saleswoman who seemed reasonable said she had *the* dress and produced one with a black velvet bodice over a rose taffeta skirt and a humongous rose attached at the waist and hem, I lost all hope. There was no way my daughter would show up looking like a clown, or in anything that would draw unnecessary attention to herself. She had to have an understated elegance about her, a dress that said she wasn't trying too hard, that this was just who she was.

We finally found it. Walked into a boutique in Chevy Chase and she and I both saw it and reacted immediately. It was an A-line, black, long-sleeved, lush velvet dress with black satin trim at the neckline and hem of the sleeves, mid-calf in length. As a reward, I guess, for us looking so hard and long, the shop even sold a small velvet purse with a slender strap and darling patent leather shoes with a black satin accent.

"You look lovely, sweetheart," I say.

"Thanks, Mom," Faith says, clicking about in the heels, for no reason I'm sure other than to hear them click.

"Joy! Hope! Hurry up. I want to get a picture," I say, throwing lip gloss and other select items into a smaller purse and grabbing the camera.

"Coming," they say, bounding down together in dresses that were much easier to choose because of their ages. Theirs are velvet, too, but Hope's is burgundy with a pull-through ribbon at the neckline and Joy's is navy with a ribbon trim at the waist.

Hezekiah gives a low whistle as he comes down behind them. "You three are going to be the belles of the ball."

Joy giggles. "It's not a ball, Daddy, it's a brunch."

"Ball, brunch. Whatever it is, I'm just glad only girls and old ladies will be there. I'd have to sneak in carrying my whip if boys had been invited."

"Oh, Daddy," Faith says, smiling.

I gather them for a picture by the fireplace in the living room. They look beautiful in the rich colors and bouncing curls their Grandma Darlene gave them this morning. Their other grandmother had been in the salon yesterday, I was told, getting styled for the brunch. Darlene asked how I was feeling about the event and I surprised her when I said I wasn't anxious, but that's where I was when I awoke this morning, a surprise to myself. I was thinking about Jillian and about Carmen, and all the talk of forgiveness—especially of parents. How could my heart not be swayed? I suppose the prayer power was impacting me as well. It seemed a decent thing suddenly that my mother had invited the girls, that she hadn't excluded them. And the girls were bubbling over with excitement. I decided to hope for the best.

"Hez, take a picture of me with the girls," I say, handing him the digital.

I plop on the sofa and the girls cuddle around me.

"Say cheese," Hezekiah says.

"Cheeeese," we say, breaking up with laughter when the flash goes off.

"Let's see it," Faith says, peering at the back of the camera. We join her and my heart swells when I see the perfect shot of Faith, Joy, and Hope smiling with their mom.

"All right," Hezekiah says. "Let's get out of here. I don't want to be too late for the education reception."

In the car I call Jillian to let her know we're on our way.

"Treva, I wish I hadn't listened to you," she says. "It's really silly of me to stay home. I could have taken them."

"Didn't you tell me this morning that you needed some extra quiet time with God?" I keep my voice beneath the sound of the praise music in the car and my mind aware that Hezekiah might be able to hear me anyway. I wouldn't want to reveal anything of what she revealed to us yesterday.

"Well, I did, but it didn't have to be today. I had committed to taking the girls, and I feel bad that you and Hezekiah have to run all the way downtown before you go over to Maryland."

"We don't mind taking the girls," I say, and Hezekiah gives me a look. I punch his arm, for listening and for the look. "This is your time. David has a soccer game so Cecil and the boys are out of the house, and the girls are about to leave. When do you get this kind of opportunity?"

"Never," Jillian admits.

"Take it; make the most of it."

We talk until Hezekiah and I are almost to the house. Jillian opens the door as we turn into the driveway and my eyes remain on her as she ushers Courtney and Sophia to the car. My younger sister. My sister in need of comfort, guidance, encouragement, and tending like everyone else. Like me. Why did I think I alone of the two of us was needy? Why did I think beauty made her immune?

While the girls arrange who will sit next to whom, I jump out and hug Jillian, longer than normal I suppose, as she taps my shoulder and points me to Hezekiah, who's baring his watch in the window.

I move away from her and emotion flings me back for one more hug. Teary, I say, "I love you, Jillian. You're my favorite sister in the whole world."

She weeps in my arms, and neither time nor a brunch nor a reception will part us. I stroke her hair and rub her back and allow her pain to emanate through us both. I want to bear it with her as she has born mine for so, so long.

When finally I return to the car, Hezekiah says, "Is something wrong with Jillian?"

I stare at her through water-filled eyes as we back out and Jillian walks to the house. "Yes, but God is with her. And so am I."

About the only thing that could steer my thoughts from Jillian right now is Patsy's world, and it happens in an instant as we negotiate the traffic around the Hilton Washington Hotel. It's busy today with, I'm sure, every manner of meeting and event, but I easily spot those heading to the brunch. Stately women of means, furred and finely coiffed, move with purpose toward the entrance, many alongside girls of varying ages in finery of their own—dressy dresses that extend beneath light coats, some beneath their…fur? I do a double take. *Is that girl wearing a real…?* I shake my head at myself. Of course it's real.

I continue gazing as Hezekiah hangs a couple of illegal U-turns, fighting for parking. Some of the girls' dresses are fancy, of the satin and taffeta variety, even floor length, the kind we had rejected as too much. My stomach churns. What if the majority of girls are dressed this way? What if Faith is out of place? What if she *feels* out of place, which is much worse than being so. I turn to look at her, see if she's seeing what I'm seeing and feeling what I'm feeling but she's talking to Courtney, uninterested in the scene.

As Hezekiah maneuvers around double-parked cars and jerks to a stop to await a car's exit from a spot—an illegal spot—I squint at a fair-skinned woman coming our direction, her hand clasping her mink to a closed position, though it's a lovely fifty-five degrees. In a moment I recall her name, Bernice Young, an associate of my mother's from way back, who told me once when I was thirteen that I had pretty teeth and smiled as if she'd done me a service. I smiled back and then, deciding I would feel better, widened it until my cheek and neck muscles tightened. She ignored me altogether after that, the only real service she could have done me.

I avoid her gaze while sneaking a peek to see who she's with. Must be Victoria's daughter. Looks just like her with those almond-shaped eyes, straight brown hair down her back, and, of course, the fair skin like Bernice. Victoria, my high school classmate, found me visible and familiar around test or essay paper time but otherwise nonexistent. I smiled at her, too, told her yes, I understood the material and absolutely I could explain it, but no, I wouldn't.

"Treva!" Patsy said the second time I did this. "Your behavior toward Victoria is rude and unnecessary. If you're able to help her, then give her the help she needs."

Responding with my favorite answer to Patsy, the one that gave me power and wholesale satisfaction, I said, "No."

Patsy told me Victoria has a University of Chicago MBA and is on the fast track in upper management at a cosmetics company. Maybe I helped her after all, forced her to buckle down and study.

"Okay, babe, I'll walk the girls to where they need to go. Will you be all right here?"

"As long as the police don't stop by," I say, giving Hezekiah the eye.

"What? You didn't think I would pay those outrageous parking fees for ten minutes of time, did you?"

Giving another look I turn and watch the girls step out. "You all have a good time, okay?" I say.

They give excited good-byes and troop out of view.

Two more girls walk past in floor-length dresses but it's not the dresses my eyes are drawn to this time; it's their faces. Their light faces. All of them have been light brown to light, as I think about it. No one near as dark as Faith. What if this is truly representative of the brunch? What if the entire room is shades lighter than Faith? Now, not only do I fear that she'll feel out of place, in more ways than one, but that she'll be made to feel out of place. What if her sisters and cousins get attention but she doesn't? What if no one even speaks to her?

I open the door, needing to do something, to jump out, find, and rescue my daughter and take her home. She can't handle this environment; she's never had to. I should have tried harder to explain the dynamics to Hezekiah so he could understand why she couldn't go. I should have painted a clearer picture of my own experiences, of the awful pain associated with being different and feeling ugly.

The door ajar, my hand on the handle, feeling utterly helpless, I slam it back shut. It's too late. She's dressed, she's here, she's happy. *Hope for the best, Treva. Hope for the best.*

The College of Education reception, a guaranteed bore, might be the temporary mental and emotional respite I need. I've never been to a reception here, never met these people, but I attended enough gatherings at Northwestern to fashion my own conclusion that education professors are a unique and committed breed that predictably, when horded together, will speak ever and always about all things academic. Hezekiah never denied this, simply accused law firm affairs of the same exclusivity, which I never denied, only countering that legalese is inherently more interesting than edu-speak. Today though, talk of scholarly publications, refereed journals, research grant opportunities, and the latest curriculum fads might be the anesthetic I need to deaden my increasing anxiety over what might be happening with Faith.

With effort we find parking on this bustling homecoming weekend and make our way to Benjamin, the one building that appears to have remained untouched by construction. The changes on campus are tremendous, from the totally revamped Student Union, which Hezekiah just walked me through, to the football stadium that now sits much farther skyward, to the newly built basketball arena located on the other side of campus from old Cole Field House, where Hezekiah and I used to watch the games.

Hezekiah takes my hand as we enter a spacious reception area teeming with people and leads me straight to a gentleman holding court with a small audience near a table of hors d'oeuvres. When an opening permits, Hezekiah introduces me to Dean Stanik, who switches his wine glass to the left hand to shake, then to two professors and two graduate students, all of whom do the switch and shake.

By the last introduction, a semicircle has formed with me as the focal point. I had forgotten this part, the query of the new professor's wife. *Is she reasonably intelligent? What exactly does she do for a living?* At Northwestern people had come to know me, and the only questions they asked were ones I didn't mind answering, ones centered around my life at the firm. It's been years since I've done a meet-and-greet without the proud association of a well-known law firm to prop me up.

Smacked with realization, three minutes inside the door, that this place will not be a respite but anxiety of a different stripe, I muster a weak smile and shift my weight from one high-heeled boot to the other, waiting for the first inquisitor, which in a show of deference by the others, will be the Dean.

"Treva, we couldn't have been happier when Hezekiah agreed to join us," Dean Stanik says, a deep-voiced man of medium height and build, his sport coat a relic of days past. "He's a wonderful addition to the department, keeps me on my toes," he says, half-chuckling, referring, I know, to Hezekiah's persistence in getting every cent for urban education research that the dean promised to provide. "And he tells me you're an attorney, correct?"

"Yes, I am."

"And…you enjoy it, I presume?"

"Yes. I do." *Does it matter that we're in present tense?*

"So, are you with a firm, a corporation…?" one of the graduate students asks, a young nondescript woman who didn't care enough about the reception to wear anything better than the faded jeans she wears to class. That she would be the one to aggravate my sore spot is, well, I'm thinking I could kill her.

"I'm not practicing at the moment," I say, and look away.

"Oh," she says. "So, you're…at home?"

I look back, giving no thought to the propriety of my expression. "Yes."

"Oh." Her short neck bobs as if she understands. Probably thinks I'm home by choice. Thinks I'm crazy for sitting on my degree when I could be out conquering the world as she will be in a couple of years.

Hezekiah, knowing I'm ready to move on, says words of parting and we walk a few feet to the cheese, crackers, and fruit. Picking up a plate, I say, "If we had two cars, I'd be on my way home. I'm just not in the mood, not today." Hearing no response, I turn to see my husband striding across the floor toward a gentleman making similar strides toward him. When they reach one another, I hear Hezekiah bellowing, "Long time no see, man." They do the hearty shake, talk for a moment, then Hezekiah points my way and the guy motions toward his woman. He waves her over and the three of them talk, then make their way to me. I had been hoping to get my plate and sit down, preferably in somebody's classroom.

"Treva, you remember Doug Lofton, don't you?" When I cock my head, he says, "Remember? We were in the Ph.D. program together?"

I say hello and shake his hand as I study his face. "You do look a little familiar," I say. "Definitely remember the name, though. Hezekiah was glad he had you with him."

"I felt the same," Doug says. "Those were some days, man, I tell you." Doug's face turns sour. "Remember Professor Brodis?"

"Man...," Hezekiah says, cutting his eyes. "Gave us the blues, didn't she?"

"That woman did everything she could to make our stay here as difficult as possible," Doug says. "Then got upset when we didn't want to work on her grant anymore."

"I know! And told everybody we'd never get far in the academy."

"Now look," Doug says. "I'm at Columbia, doing okay for myself—"

Hezekiah laughs. "'Okay?' Treva, Doug was just published in *Teacher's College Record.*"

I smile, assuming this is a good thing, and Doug grins, confirming it.

Doug continues, "—So, I'm doing okay, you're back here where we started, as a full professor directing a center, and she just retired, never did get promoted to full professor. Wild, isn't it?" Doug shakes his head, and suddenly remembers who's just behind him. He brings her fully into view. "I'm sorry, Treva, I didn't introduce my wife. Carla, this is Treva, Treva, Carla."

Carla extends her hand, gives me a firm shake. She's taller and lighter than I, though dark by Patsy's reckoning, her hair grazing the bottom of her ears. "How are you, Treva?" she says. "We have similar taste."

We both laugh, eyeing the other's straight-leg pants and matching thin quilted leather jacket, hers chocolate, mine black.

"I hear you two just moved here from Chicago," she says.

"Yes, we did. I miss it," I say.

"So, what do you do?" Carla asks.

Is this the only conversation starter known to man? "I'm an attorney."

"Really? So am I," she says. "Where did you practice in Chicago?"

Love the question. "Thompson & Klein."

"Excellent firm. I really wanted to work there coming out of law school but they dinged me, didn't even give me an initial interview."

I place her immediately in the lower tier of her class at a mediocre law school, the tragic student who was still looking for a job upon graduation. I hate to ask where she ended up but it would seem the natural next question. At least I won't feel bad this time. The fact that I was Thompson & Klein material should stand me head and shoulders above this woman, even in current unemployment. "Oh," I say sympathetically, "where did you end up going?"

"Brooks Donnelly, New York. I just made partner this year," she says. "I'm so excited."

Hezekiah saves me from what could have lapsed into an embarrassing silence. "Treva's father worked there for a number of years," he says. "In the D.C. office."

"What's his name?" Carla asks. "You know there are only so many of us."

"Charles Campbell," he says. "He died three years ago."

"Charles Campbell! He was head of the business group. I met him when he came to the New York office a few years ago. He was a powerful man in the firm." Carla meets my gaze. "So, what are you doing now? Did you go with Thompson & Klein's D.C. office or Brooks Donnelly?"

I feel an overwhelming, unmistakable prod to tell her I'm home, without the least tinge of regret, and why. If only it were possible. "Well," I say, "it became obvious to me that…well, that God would have me be at home right now, so that's what I'm doing."

Doug elbows his wife. "See," he says to her. "I was trying to get Carla to do that a couple of years ago when we had our baby but she wasn't hearing it."

"Girl, more power to you," Carla says, head shaking, "but I would go crazy at home."

I find myself wishing Willow were here, another attorney, one Carla would probably recognize and respect, who would gush about leaving her job and who would testify that, yes, God would give her the power, all the power she needs to do what she needs to do. I could hear Willow now. "*Go crazy? Girl, not if you have the mind of Christ!*"

But I'm not Willow. I tell Carla, "I hear you," and spend the rest of the reception in a funk, looking for a dry education confab but not finding one anywhere, only wives who keep making a beeline to me because I don't want them to, attorney wives and doctor wives and business wives who all must find their careers fulfilling since they discuss them ad nauseam. Me? I discuss nothing. What would I discuss? That I learned to make macaroni and cheese? That I signed up to be a room mother? I wonder if God enjoys putting me in these situations where I am the absolute oddball.

And I wonder if this is meant to be amusing, that the second I find joy in Hezekiah's pronouncement that it's time to go, is the very second I'm reminded of where we're going. To pick up the girls. To find out what happened with Faith.

Chapter Twenty-Six

I see Faith now, coming toward the car, chatting, smiling. Happy. I throw open the door as she approaches and ask, "How was it?"

"Mommy, we had so much fun," Hope says. "Look, we have gift baskets."

My eyes pass over it quickly and follow Faith as she steps in the car. "Faith? How was it, sweetie?"

"We had a good time, Mom," Faith says. "The program was really nice. They talked about the importance of grandmothers in our lives and—"

"That part was boring," Sophia says. "The fun part was when the granddaughters had to huddle together and come up with reasons why they love their grandmother, and then the oldest got to go up on stage and talk on the microphone—" Sophia's eyes grew wide at the microphone aspect. "—and tell everybody the reasons."

"And we won," Hope says.

"What do you mean, 'won?'" I say, my torso turned to the back as Hezekiah pulls off.

"Hope, we didn't *win*," Joy says.

"Uh-huh," Hope says.

"Mom," Faith says, "Hope's talking about the special gift bag we got because we had the most granddaughters in attendance, but the part about the reasons, there was no winner. Everybody got something for that."

"So...the oldest getting up in front of everybody, did they do that in years past?" I say, wondering why Jillian hadn't told us to expect this.

"No, this was the first time," Courtney says.

"How did that go, Faith?" I ask, cautiously.

"Fine," she says.

"People clapped for her because she spoke the best," Courtney says.

"They clapped for everybody," Faith says.

"Not like they clapped for you," Courtney says. "Aunt Treva, you know how Faith never says, 'Um' and all that like most people do. She just sounded better. Plus, she didn't even read from the paper we wrote. She just looked at the crowd and said it."

"Faith, that's fantastic," I say, wishing these girls had a videotape. As much as I want to rejoice at this, it's hard to trust a young person's perspective.

"So what did you say, baby girl?" Hezekiah asks proudly.

That was my next question, as I was wondering how Faith's speech could have been impressive since she couldn't have had much to say at all. I'm surprised they could come up with anything for that list.

Faith sits up straighter and smiles. "We love our Grandma Patsy because she always remembers our birthdays by sending nice cards and beautiful clothes. We love her because she gives us big hugs when she sees us and because she invited us to this special brunch—"

"The brunch part was mine, Mommy. I said to put that down."

"Very good, Hope," I say.

Faith continues, "—and we love her because she's the mother of our moms."

"Great job, you all, for putting that list together," Hezekiah says, and I ditto his remarks, because it surely was.

"Aunt Treva," Sophia says, "we played a networking game too."

"What's that?" I say.

"We had to break up and go to a different table and get to know another girl, then everybody had to tell the people at the table what they learned about the person."

"And you liked that?"

"Yes," they chorus.

"Were the other girls friendly?" My eyes again rest primarily on Faith.

"Yes," they chorus again.

"One girl I talked to couldn't believe I lived in Chicago," Faith says, "because she had seen pictures of the tall buildings. She wanted to know all about it."

I listen as they each tell of the conversations they had with the other girls, conversations that seem normal and pleasant. I lean back in my seat, head half turned, comfortable, very comfortable with what I'm hearing.

Hezekiah lays his hand on my knee and says softly, "I told you they'd have a great time, babe. This was good for the family. We're coming together."

I nod slowly, agreeing that they seem to have had a good time, but not willing to engage any forward notions of family time with Patsy. If Faith emerged from this one unscathed, glory to God. I don't need to test His faithfulness with another until the next blue moon.

Without a "Faith" tragedy to tend to, I get the urge, as we drop off Sophia and Courtney, to stay and hang out with Jillian. We haven't spent time together, just she and I, since I've been back, which means it's been years—probably not since she lived with us when Faith was a baby. Given her emotional state there couldn't be a better day, and when I propose it at the door, her eyes light up in agreement.

Hezekiah and the girls go home and Cecil pops popcorn for his tired kids as they all prepare to relax and watch a movie. Jillian and I jump in her car before we're sure where we're going and soon decide to make the forty-minute drive to Baltimore Harbor. On the way I fill her in on the report of the brunch, then ask her as simply as I'm able how she's doing.

Jillian sees my watery eyes and reaches for my hand, grabbing it tight. "I'll tell you something about the God we serve," she says, her lips curving surprisingly into a smile. "I knew He forgives. Of course He forgives, right? But, Treva, the *way* He forgives, the *way* He makes His thoughts our thoughts. Oh, girl." Jillian eases her hand from mine and lifts it in the air, staring at the BWI Parkway, muttering, "Thank You, Jesus, thank You, Jesus."

I try to be patient and wait, eager for her to finish.

Jillian's hand comes down to the armrest and she glances at me, shaking her head in amazement. "Treva, I wish I could explain it. I wish I could explain how He entered my world as I lay on my face before Him, how He dropped into my spirit a remembrance of the baby that David and Bathsheba had, the one that died, and David said he would go to him, one day he would go to him." Jillian glances at me again with tears of joy. "Not only does God forgive me, Treva, but one day I will go to my baby. I will see him or her. That day years ago, that awful day in that dank, God-forsaken room, that wasn't the end. Treva, it wasn't the end. I *love* life in Christ. Girl, God is *awesome*."

Jillian's hand shoots up again as she revels in the high to which God has lifted her. I shake my head in amazement myself, wondering what it must be like to have God drop into your spirit illumination from the Word so powerful that misery has to flee. Jillian pushes the CD player's power button and Fred Hammond blares through the speakers. She pushes the forward button five times to get to the song she wants, then presses down for most of the song, releasing her finger in time to hear the voices vamp, "Thank You, Jesus, thank You, Jesus, thank You, thank You, Jesus, thank You, Jesus, thank You. I wanna say, 'Thank You.'"

We sing with them, rewinding all the way to the harbor, over and over, caught up in praise, tears flying, arms waving, heads bobbing, bodies swaying, a forget-your-cares, God-is-all-that-matters experience I have never had before. When Jillian pays, parks on an open lot, and turns off the engine, we sit. Just sit. And I'm sure I am changed somehow. I have to be. God was bigger than He's ever been to me, all consuming. I don't ever want to step out of this space.

"Father God," Jillian says, clutching my hand, "we magnify Your name, for You are the Most High God, from everlasting to everlasting You are God, and yet You are mindful of us broken, sinful, imperfect humans. Thank You, Lord, for pouring out Your mercy and Your grace. Thank You for my sister spending this time with me. I pray that Your glory would continue to envelop us, and that we would keep our focus on You, knowing that when we do that, You keep us in perfect peace. In Jesus' name, Amen."

Jillian and I stroll the harbor and pick a seafood restaurant, pleased that it's early enough so that we can be seated right away for dinner. We talk mostly of our husbands and kids, and while the outing was conceived originally for Jillian's sake, I'm finding myself benefiting in more ways than one. Right now, hearing Jillian's heart for her home, the funk that descended on me at the reception, that made the world of work swell and glow once more in my eyes, seems another world away.

After dinner we walk off our cheesecake with another stroll, but as the wind begins to whip off of the water, furling and unfurling the flags in frenzied gusts, our pace quickens us to the car and Jillian drives me home. My step is light when Hezekiah opens the front door moments before I reach it.

"What's wrong?" I say, slowing up. "Were you waiting for me?"

"My mother called about a half an hour ago and said she wants you to call her."

"Okay," I say, not seeing the need for this news to hit me at the door.

"She sounded concerned about something but when I asked her if everything was all right, all she said was, 'I should talk to Treva.'"

My brow furrows. "I'll call her right now then."

As we walk inside, I ask, "Where are the girls?"

"Faith is reading in her room. Joy and Hope are watching the end of a movie in the family room."

I lift the handset in the kitchen and dial Darlene's number. "Ma, it's me," I say when she answers.

"Treva, have you talked to Faith?" Darlene says.

I hesitate. "Well, I just got home but what do you mean? When?"

"Since the brunch?"

"Yes, in the car." My heart quickens. "Why?"

"So she told you what Patsy said to her?"

"No." The hand holding the phone begins to flinch. "You talked to Faith?" I say, needing the background before the blow.

"She e-mailed me. I had told her to tell me about the brunch, and especially whether Patsy made any comments about skin color."

"You *told* her that?"

"Of course, didn't you?"

"No, I...I never thought to be that open about it." Hezekiah questions me with his eyes and I raise a finger, inhaling strength. "So what did she say?"

"Well," Darlene says, sighing deeply, "this is what Faith said happened. Apparently there was some time during the brunch when the girls moved to different tables?"

"They told us that, yes."

"Well, one time some girls went to their table and one of them asked Faith whether Joy was really her sister. When Faith said, 'Yes,' the girl said, 'How can you be sisters? You're too dark.'" Darlene sighs again. "When those girls left, Patsy told Faith, 'People said the same thing to your mother about her and Jillian. Bothered her to no end.' Then she asked Faith if she gets A's in school. When Faith said she did, Patsy said, 'That's good because you're not as pretty as Joy, and I'm your grandmother so I have to be honest. Pretty people get the privileges in life. You'll have to work harder but you can do it, just like your mother did.'"

"Ma, I have to call you back," I say. I toss the phone to its cradle, hear it miss, and bound up the stairs.

Hezekiah follows. "Treva, what happened?"

I cannot take one second to explain. I have to see my daughter. I barge into Faith's room and she's reading a novel, lying on her back on the bed, legs kicked up in the air.

When she sees us, her legs fall and her body shoots upright. "Is something wrong?"

"Faith, why didn't you tell us what Grandma Patsy said to you?"

"One of you needs to tell me what's going on," Hezekiah says. "Now."

"Tell your father what you told Grandma Darlene."

Faith shares the story in the same manner she shared the others in the car.

"Why didn't you tell us this, Faith?" Hezekiah says.

Faith shrugs. "I don't know. I guess I didn't want to talk about it in the car. I didn't want to make Grandma Patsy look bad in front of the others."

I look at Hezekiah, my hand covering my mouth, the vilest things poised at its door. "Faith," I say, my hands now cupping my face, "my concern is not whether Grandma Patsy looks bad, but with how she made you feel. There you were in that car, heart torn apart, and we didn't even know it. I wouldn't have gone out with Aunt Jillian if I had known this." I pace a few feet, steadily back and forth, an angry lioness with only enough patience to plan an attack.

"But, Mom, my heart wasn't torn apart," Faith says calmly, sitting cross-legged on the bed.

Hezekiah takes a seat beside her, hands clasped. "Tell us what you mean, baby girl."

"Well, Grandma Darlene told me a long time ago that people would compare me and Joy, and that they would think Joy was prettier because of the history of this country."

Hezekiah's eyes meet mine and I can tell he's ashamed, as I am, that we never raised this issue head-on ourselves.

"And I could tell Grandma Patsy was one of those people just from the last couple of times I saw her." She shrugs again and lowers her head. "I could just tell she liked Joy better."

The pacing kicks in again. *I'm going to tell my mother exactly what I think of her.*

"But Grandma Darlene did a Bible study with me by e-mail. It started when we were in Chicago, maybe two years ago, all about who God is and who I am as a believer. She would give me verses to read and questions to answer and then we'd go back and forth about it. So I already know that God made me, and if He made me, I must be special. Grandma Patsy's opinion doesn't bother me." Then Faith adds, "But Mom, Dad?"

We look into her eyes.

"I don't think Grandma Patsy knows God. If I'm upset about anything, it's that. Can we pray for her?"

Hezekiah practically tackles Faith with his enthusiastic hug. "Girl! I knew God had given you wisdom but I didn't know He had His hand on you like *this*. My Lord! You could teach *me* a thing or two."

I see them smiling. I hear their voices. But I'm in my own space, in a bubble, floating past them. Hezekiah waves me over, and vaguely I understand that they are about to pray, but I'm moving on, down the stairs, grabbing my purse, starting the car, driving down 193, entering BWI Parkway again, this time going south. In a flash, it seems, I'm transported from Faith's bedroom to Patsy's doorstep. When she answers, I shove the door wider with my hand, storm past her, and before she turns, say, "How dare you say the things you said today to my daughter." My eyes bear down on her, everything familiar about this house a blur.

Patsy backs the door to a slow close. "Whatever I said doesn't give you the right to burst into my house in an ill manner."

"I beg to differ, and I'm sure you know what I'm referring to."

"Yes," Patsy says, folding her silk-shirted arms. "I do. You're referring to the bit of truth I shared with Faith about skin color in this world. What, pray tell, is audacious about that?"

"You told her she's not as pretty as her sister."

"Isn't it the truth?"

"You are hateful and heartless," I say, my voice rising and quavering out of control.

"Actually, I'm neither. I don't hate Faith; I rather like her. She seems to have a good head on her shoulders. And I've always held that it takes more heart to be honest. She needs to know what the world is like so she can realistically assess her options. If you won't tell her the facts of life, somebody has to. If you ask me, Faith is mature enough to handle the truth."

"Oh, stop talking about 'truth.' You don't know what truth is. The truth is that God says—"

"*God* says? What is this, Treva, Sunday school?" Patsy crosses the hardwood and my eyes follow her into the well-lit living room where she retrieves her wine glass from the antique side table. She takes two long swallows before turning around and I stare at her black-and-white striped silk shirt, black slacks, and pearl earrings, wondering if this woman ever lets down. I'm quite sure she came home from the brunch and changed right into this attire, including the heels, with nothing planned but an evening of reading and white wine.

She returns, sipping and showing amusement. "You've allowed Darlene to fill your head with some backward notions, and I know because she's tried it with me. Darlene is a hairdresser, Treva, not a fount of wisdom. Religion is a nice crutch if you need it but don't lose sight of the real world. You can't pretend that being dark doesn't make a difference. You know firsthand."

"It only makes a difference with *you*."

"Oh, really? Turn on the television, dear heart. When you see African-American women, what complexion are they most often? Who's in the anchor chair on CNN and the other news channels? Who's the love interest on the dramas? Who's the woman the R&B singers and rappers are lusting over in those videos? Who are the black Cover Girls? Go to the movies. How many dark-skinned black women do you see in starring roles? One or two, *maybe*, and the black magazines blow a trumpet because we've come so far. But who's the featured face more often? Who gets the guy? Who gets the close-ups? Drive down Silver Spring Avenue to a jazz club. Who's got the men around her? It's not just *me*, Treva. This is the world."

I could have given the spiel myself. She's spouting the very words I spout to Hezekiah. I wish I could call to mind his best arguments about how times have changed, though I know I couldn't sound nearly as convincing as he.

"Why get upset with me for telling Faith she's got to work a little harder," Patsy continues. "Black people know they've got to work harder than white people. Why can't we openly acknowledge that certain black women have it easier than other black women?" Patsy downs another swig. "Was Faith even upset? She didn't look it to me."

"She's too young to realize—"

"So she wasn't upset, was she? What, really, are *you* upset about, Treva?" A gleam enters her eye and she steps forward. "You're upset because I forced you to face yourself."

My eyes narrow. "I don't know what you're talking about."

"Well, let me make it plainer. What I told Faith today, that she's not as pretty as Joy, you've said it yourself, in your heart, haven't you?"

"You're crazy."

"Oh, am I? The difference between you and me, Treva Campbell Langston, is that I have the guts to say it out loud. But go ahead, prove me wrong. Do you think Faith is as pretty as Joy?"

My eyes falter from her gaze and recover. "I don't have to prove anything to you, Mother. And let me tell you why I'm upset, since you asked. I'm upset because I know what it's like to grow up receiving regular doses of 'the truth according to Patsy' and now you've made my daughter party to it. Well, no more. From henceforth, our lives are none of your affair."

"Your lives weren't my affair for the longest time anyway. You went years without calling."

"Oh, let's talk about that," I say, angry enough to finally broach the subject. "Let's talk about why I stopped calling. Could it be because of the bit of *truth* you shared the night before Daddy's funeral?"

"We've gone over that. I was grieving, for heaven's sake."

"*We* haven't gone over anything. You've never said a word to me about it, never even apologized."

"I don't even remember what I said."

"Well, it's still ringing in my ears so let me refresh you. You said Jillian was the chosen one and you wished I'd never been born. And I knew you felt that way while we were growing up. Don't even try to tell me you made comments about skin color to 'prepare' me for the real world. You did it out of spite. You never loved me. Admit it, since you're so fond of *truth*."

I've marched out on a limb, a weak limb, and it's too late to turn back. My entire body is shaking so I fold my arms, which steadies them, but does nothing for the twitching shoulders or the legs that are threatening to go limp and haven't the faintest idea what possessed my mouth to bring us out here.

"I can handle the truth if you can," Patsy says, draining her glass and returning it to the crystal tray atop the table. "Why don't you come in here and have a seat?"

"No, thank you, I'll stand."

"As you wish," she says, "but you'll have to stand in here because these bones need to sit."

Patsy takes a seat on the sofa and I move reluctantly into the living room, standing just inside, my legs crying out for me to give in and take the chair. But now is not the time for creature comforts. Standing helps me to maintain my lioness mindset.

Angling herself to face me, Patsy crosses her legs and says, "I still remember vividly the day you were born. When I woke up in the delivery room and they handed you to me, I argued with that nurse. Told her there was no way you could be my baby, that it was genetically impossible, and that they had better go get my baby from whomever they had given it to. When they, and Charles, convinced me that you were mine, I cried. Cried for days, couldn't even hold you, let alone look at you." Patsy hops up, takes the wine bottle from the decanter and refills her glass. "I'm not proud of my reaction but it's the way I felt. Pure shock. I kept thinking, 'How could I have birthed one of them?' Growing up, there was 'us' and 'them,' in my mind anyway."

"And in Grandma Vivian's."

"Yes, I guess she did affect me that way," Patsy says. "I don't recall there ever being a person with dark skin in our home, and the thought of me bringing one home to live with us...I'm not exaggerating when I say I felt that I was in the twilight zone. And as expected, everyone reacted with the same shock. Well, Charles's parents didn't. They acted proud that you had taken the likeness of Jupiter Campbell, whom I'd never heard of until they produced a picture as 'proof' that you were part of a legitimate heritage. They never liked me, by the way. Anyway, everybody else was shocked. Some asked if we'd adopted, though they'd seen me pregnant. Those first few weeks were the worst of my life. I considered giving you up for adoption but, Charles...he said he wouldn't hear of it. He never had quite the same viewpoints as I."

Patsy's eyes harden. "And lest you charge me again with being heartless, you must understand where I was then, Treva. I wanted a certain kind of life. My mother had told me about Washington's high society and I had seen glimpses of it now and again, but never did I behold it fully until I stepped on Howard University's campus. Those people, only in college and yet they had connections in boardrooms, in government, in hospitals and judges' chambers. The money, the places they summered, the camps they'd attended, the organizations they all seemed to belong to. I wanted that world, but I learned quickly that it wasn't easy to penetrate. I'd grown up in Washington but not in the right neighborhoods, didn't have the right family history. No one knew my mother or father's name or—"

"I'm confused. I thought Grandma Vivian was...." I stop because I don't know what I thought. No one ever discussed anything with me. I merely snatched bits and pieces of overheard conversation when I could. And of those bits and pieces I had assembled a grander picture of her.

"My mother knew how to put on airs around those who didn't know better, like you children. She, of course, had gone to Howard, too, and had met, most likely, some of the parents of the people I met. She sought inclusion, making overtures both then and later, but in one way or another was rebuffed, and she didn't have the thick skin I have." Patsy's eyes gleam again. "She kind of gave up, but always spoke of me going to Howard. When I did, and then married Charles, who's professional standing was much more impressive than the insurance job Daddy had, Mother got excited again about the possibility of this world opening up to her, through me."

Patsy sighs in remembrance. "I worked so hard. You wouldn't believe how I humbled myself to curry favor with these women, to gain access to the right social groups, the right parties, as if I were pledging, which I also did, of course. Alpha chapter had to be on my resume. So that's where I was. I knew I'd never be part of the old guard in Washington, but a life I could savor was in view. Charles was doing well at Brooks Donnelly, we had just snagged this house on the gold coast in upper Northwest, and...you were born." Patsy stares into her glass. "You said I never loved you. As you grew older, I came to appreciate your intellect and your pluck. I knew life wasn't easy for you, I knew *I* didn't make it easy, but you learned to soar anyway. I admired that."

Patsy looks at me. "But love you? It was hard to. In my heart I never truly accepted that you were my daughter." Patsy looks away and her diamond bracelets sparkle in the light as she raises her arm for another drink.

I wait to see if she's finished, her last words hanging in the silence, heavy and suffocating. When she doesn't speak or even turn back, I shift on my feet, feeling awkward, a stranger still in this house after thirty-eight years. I ought to respond, inform her what a despicable specimen of human being she is, but that's not foremost in my mind. Mainly, I'm satisfied. It's out. I know. We don't have to pretend.

I get back in my bubble and float out of her door, out of her life, longing for God to help me breathe, to help me…just help me…not remembering how to reach Him or why He left or why…a lot of things.

Chapter Twenty-Seven

"You shouldn't have gone over there. And, Hezekiah, you shouldn't have let her." Darlene's eyes bat between the two of us, not sure who she is more upset with.

"She was gone before I knew what was going on," Hezekiah says, exasperated still. "I thought—well, hoped—she had gone back to Jillian's to talk to her."

"And when he called and told me what happened, I knew where she'd gone," Jillian says.

"This is not good," Darlene says. "It should've been handled in a totally different way."

Darlene hasn't sat down since I walked in. The three of them pounced the moment I opened the door and refused to leave it until tomorrow, insisting I tell them right then, in full. I did, minus Patsy's insult about Darlene and the exchange over my own inner thoughts about Faith. Darlene stood the entire time, sometimes walking the floor, sometimes not, Hezekiah sat at the kitchen table with his chair facing outward, arms folded, with that look he had at the Dairy when I first told him of Patsy, and Jillian took a bar stool next to mine, dabbing tears intermittently, a loving grip on my hand, which was no longer shaking. I was calm. On the ride home I had felt it, a detachment, a freeing permission, granted by my mother, to cut her off completely.

"I don't like that she went over there either, Darlene, but I do think something had to be done," Jillian says. "For her to say that to Faith...."

"I think something had to be done too. A confrontation was certainly in order," Darlene says.

My eyes show surprise. "Really?"

"But not that kind," Darlene says. "Not when you're angry and in the flesh. You can't get a victory that way. You didn't even have any prayer coverage, and it doesn't sound like you were praying yourself. The enemy had you where he wanted you, filling your mind with more filth and lies.

"No, that's not the kind of confrontation I had in mind," Darlene says. "And I did have a plan too. I was waiting for Treva to call me back so we could talk about it." Darlene scolds me with loving eyes. "I've been praying for Patsy for years, been trying to share the gospel, which has gotten nowhere, and since you all came back, I've just been feeling like the time was getting ripe, like God was doing something. When this thing happened earlier today, with Patsy dipping into the next generation with that poison, a bell sounded in my heart. It was time to act. My plan was that the four of us, and anybody else who's willing, y'all's Bible study group would have been perfect, would all pray and pick at least two days to fast together between now and Faith's party. And, honey, we were just going to believe God that when Patsy showed up, Treva would confront her, *in the power of the Holy Spirit,* and bring about a real change in both of their lives." Darlene stares for a moment above our heads. "I say we still do it."

"No. No. *No,*" I say, before Hezekiah and Jillian catch the wave. "How could you even suggest that she should still be invited to Faith's party? I never wanted her to come in the first place; no way now."

"Treva, I know where you're coming from," Darlene says. "That's a natural response. But remember what you said to me just one week ago? That it's not about you? It applies in this situation too. It's not just about you and your hurt. We've got to think about Patsy and *why* she's this way. We've got to love her and pray her into the kingdom."

"Fine, but she won't be coming here," I say.

"Didn't Faith tell me she already sent out the invitations?" Darlene says.

"*Oh,*" I groan, "she sure did. Yesterday. After tonight, though, there's no way Mother would show up…. But just to be sure—Jillian, will you call and uninvite her?"

Jillian cuts her eyes away. "I'm not calling. I can't even talk to her right now. I know we have to think of her spiritual condition and all that, but right now I'm disgusted. It'll take me awhile to deal with her again. It always takes awhile. I'm with you, though. She wouldn't come anyway."

"I'll call and uninvite her."

I stare incredulously at Hezekiah, who hasn't said a word since I told what happened.

"Hezekiah!" Darlene says.

"Ma, I'm the one who said we should invite Patsy, and that God might want to use Treva in her life, but now I don't see any good that would come from her being here, only more hurt. I'm all for praying, but I'm for keeping the peace in my home too."

Darlene studies the three of us. "Well, isn't this special, all three of you ready to write Patsy off?"

Hezekiah throws up his hands. "I said I would pray for her!"

"And I'm not writing her off," Jillian says. "I just need time."

"Well, I'm writing her off," I say.

"Treva, you're upset, and understandably so," Darlene says. "But in the light of morning—"

"Ma, I *might* get to the point where I can pray for her—I'm not even there right now—and I know God would have me forgive her—not there yet either—but once I get to those places, that's as far as I'm going. And I don't see a problem with that. We don't need to masquerade as mother and daughter. She's never felt it, nor have I. I'm through."

Darlene nods slowly, eyes lowered. "Okay…well…okay," she says, crestfallen.

Yawning, Jillian says, "I'd better be going. It's getting late." She hops up and gathers her purse and jacket. "Treva, I'll see you at church tomorrow, and I'll be praying for you, that all that filth you heard doesn't sink into your spirit. Whenever it comes to mind, cast it down right away." Jillian pulls me out of my chair and into her embrace. "Remember who loves you, and who adopted you into His family. You're *His* daughter, and there's nothing better."

"Amen to that," Darlene says, grabbing her things as well. "I'll walk out with you, Jillian." Darlene hugs me and says in my ear, "You know I'll be praying for you, baby."

Hezekiah and I walk them to the front door, hand in hand, and when they're gone, he holds me there for long, long seconds, and he knew I needed this better than I because in his strong, warm arms, the steely calm I had found leaves and tears roll in its place, quickly turning to sobs. Hezekiah tightens his grip as I bury my head, memories flying of childhood, of my mother, of Faith in various stages of her life, of Patsy's words tonight…those words… all those words, and now, of Jillian's car, just this afternoon, seemingly eons ago, when I was caught up in another realm and nothing else mattered, only God, and it was glorious. *Heavenly places.* My heartbeat quickens. That's where I was. That's what it's like. And *that's* where God says He's placed me? Permanently?

I want to go there again, without a song having to catapult me. I want to dwell there.

<hr />

The following week flies by as I need it to, moving me from one thing to the next, farther and farther away from Saturday night. I made Monday an errand day, taking the car for an oil change, picking up dry cleaning, stopping by the plant nursery, which turned out to be a boon since they'd just received a new shipment and I was able to snap up three tall floor plants and four full bunchy ones to fill up empty, sun-filled corners in the house, all to be delivered by week's end. And finally, I

shopped for groceries, a much more strategic exercise now that I'm train-
ing myself to plan meals and have a list in hand.

On Tuesday I did my duty as room mother in Hope's kindergarten
class, which had been scheduled for a half day but spilled over into most
of the afternoon because I was actually enjoying the enthusiasm and
wide-eyed wonder of the little people. Arms shot up in the air when Mrs.
Troyer asked a question, minds and hands focused immediately when
given a task, some more adeptly than others, which was where I sometimes came in, to help the lagging ones. And when Mrs. Troyer gathered
them around for read-aloud time, every eye stayed riveted on her. The
morning passed quickly, and since it seemed a shame to miss art, when
Jimmy Lyles would paint the mask he had worked so hard at sculpting
the day before, a process he described in detail to me during the morning
break, I decided to stay until well after lunch. My primary motivation
was, of course, Hope, who was thrilled to have me in her world, though
not nearly as thrilled as Jimmy about my seeing her finished mask.

On Wednesday I decided to shop for winter clothes for the girls and
drove out to Tysons Corner in McLean, Virginia. After buying a few fleece
tops and pants, sweaters, and corduroys, the excursion livened up when
I happened by a display of dishware in one of the department stores. I
can safely say my heart had never skipped a beat before over dishes,
glassware, and silverware, seeing them as necessary, not exciting, but I
got beside myself that day browsing styles and patterns. Thanks to
Hezekiah, we have an extensive line of cookware—several surgical stainless steel skillets and pots of various sizes, Dutch ovens, etc.—but we
have one set of everyday dishes and spying those displays sparked a
desire within me to set the table nightly and breathe some variety into
the setting. Ordinarily when I shop I politely refuse the help of store
personnel, finding them a bother, but this time, when the woman asked
if I was looking for anything in particular, my clueless stare welcomed
her, and we got along famously as she tutored me in stoneware and china
and the finer points of stemware. When I left, stimulated, arms loaded
down with handled paper shopping bags, my main thought was that a

changing of the guard was taking place in that kitchen. It was becoming mine, infused with my personality and ideas. I liked that. When Hezekiah came home that evening, he liked it too, commenting that he would have never picked cobalt blue and fiery orange dishes but it looked fabulous. Next week I'll break out the glazed green setting.

I volunteered at Grace Bible Fellowship Thursday, my first time, and helped with the clothes drive to supply suits, shirts, and skirts to men and women in need of work. For two Sundays I had half noticed the call for help in the bulletin, but this past Sunday my mind said, *What about you? What will you be doing that day?* I signed up and brought a few suits of my own, including a couple of the freshly laundered ones I'd picked up from the cleaners on Monday, which wasn't my initial intent but was apparently God's since I don't know how else I could give up stylish suits that fit me perfectly well still. I have to say, though, that when a woman's eyes filled upon seeing them, saying she had never had a designer anything and only came because her mother told her she'd be blessed, I believe I might have had the bigger blessing.

I'm on my way to Monique's now, glad it's Friday and glad Carmen and I decided at the last Bible study to ride together today. Seeing her reminds me that others have endured pain and overcome. Her life gives me hope. Her chatter now makes me smile.

At Monique's, unlike last time, I feel warmed as I walk in. They're all here and their voices lift me, each one distinct and personal and comforting.

"I was thinking about you this week," Monique says, hugging me and taking my jacket. "I started to call you just to see what you were doing."

"You should have," I say, meaning it.

"Hey, Treva. Hey, Carmen," Asia says, approaching us with a big smile. Hugging her, my heart suddenly aches. She's so young and sweet, and this bustier, which before would have evoked disdain, is awakening in me a desire to talk to her, as a big sister, as a sister in Christ. *Lord, I believe You're giving me Your heart for this girl. I pray You would open up an opportunity for me to speak with Asia, in love.*

"Hey, you," Willow says, coming up behind me, slipping her arm around my neck, Zoe in the other. I lean in and we embrace. "I thought about you this week too," she says, "and I did call but I didn't leave a message. I wanted to find out how the brunch went."

"I meant to ask you about that myself," Carmen says, and a semicircle gathers around me.

Jillian and I exchange glances and she walks up beside me, half prepared in her sisterly concern, I think, to speak in my behalf.

"All week I tried not to think about it," I say, and for the most part I was successful. Only a couple of times was the memory of Saturday triggered, both by seeing Faith, and in those moments a voice whispered in my ear—*Do you think she's pretty?* I couldn't tell if it was Patsy's voice or mine or both as I forced it out. I never need to dwell on what I think about the way Faith or I look.

"Uh-oh," Monique says. "Doesn't sound good."

"It wasn't," I say, and though I don't want to talk about it, it seems easier to get it out and be done. "Long story short, my mother told Faith she wasn't as pretty as her sister. When I confronted her, I got that plus the added tidbit that she never loved me." I shrug. "Nothing I didn't already know."

Every mouth but Jillian's drops and heads begin to shake. Willow breaks the silence. "Okay. You should have called. We should have gotten together. We need to talk, we need to pray, we'll just take the time now and—"

"You know, I would rather just get started with the study," I say, plopping down on Monique's sofa. "I've already moved on."

They remain standing, eyeing me warily. "Don't you want to talk about it, Treva?" Asia says. "You've got to be hurting."

"I was," I admit, "and if I think or talk about it long enough, I'm sure I'd be hurting again, so I'm not going there. Faith is fine and I will be too."

"But Faith is fine because she doesn't believe—"

"Jillian, it doesn't matter why she's fine or how she got there. I'm going to get there, too, my way, by divorcing myself from Patsy Parker Campbell and, in time, hopefully, all that she stands for." I unzip my Bible cover and look up at everyone, palms tilted upward. "Well, what are you all waiting for? Aren't you ready for some Ephesians 5?"

Willow groans, staring down at the Bible in her hand, and I bet I know why—the same reason I didn't groan during this week's homework. God had already whipped me into shape for it with Titus Two. I chuckle and pat a place next to me on the sofa. She collapses into it.

"Oh, Willow, it's not that bad," I say, teasing.

She rolls her eyes.

"Hmm, we need to talk about this. We need to pray," I say, sounding Willow-esque.

Monique laughs outright.

"I guess we all know what the focus is this week," Jillian says, taking a seat on the carpet. "Dr. Lyles says in the notes that if men are in the group, to follow the discussion notes on 'husbands, love your wives,' if women—"

"Wives, be subject to your husbands," we singsong in unison.

"Very good," Jillian says, as if to two-year-olds, then chuckles. "The first thing he says to ascertain is whether anyone has a problem with this command. And you know Dr. Lyles—he has 'command' in bold type."

Willow waves her arm unabashedly. "I know it's not right, but I do have a problem with it. What about when the husband does not study the Word, does not pray like he ought to, and basically sleeps on the things of God? That's Damien, and I'm sorry, but I don't see why I should submit to that."

I lean away from Willow to get a better look at her and raise my eyebrows. "What happened to laying your will on the altar?"

"Don't even try it, Missy. From what you've said, Hezekiah does all the things I'm talking about. You don't know what it's like to have a husband like Damien."

"Is he saved?" Asia asks.

"Says he is," Willow says.

"Willow!" Carmen says. "You're making Damien sound awful. I met him and he seemed like a very nice guy, very respectful."

"I didn't say he wasn't nice. I wouldn't have married him if he were an ogre. I love him, don't get me wrong. He treats me well, he's great with Zoe, he goes to church. But he's not stepping up as the spiritual head of the household. Let me give you an example. Giving. Throughout our marriage, we have argued about this issue because he has not given but a pittance to the church from his paycheck, even though I've been making a decent wage. He does not trust God with the finances. I told him the other day, 'Now that I won't be working, I guess you won't want to give anything at all. You need to have faith.' Of course he got mad but what am I supposed to do? Sit back and let him do that?"

"What else can you do?" Carmen says. "I understand your frustration, I really do, but you can't make him give, and causing strife over it makes it worse."

Willow shakes her head and expels a sigh. "That's just one example. And the root of them all is his lack of a strong personal relationship with God. I cannot see subjecting myself to his lead in the marriage and trusting him to make the right decisions when I never see him crack open a Bible."

"Maybe that's it. You just don't see it," Monique says.

"No. *He* says he doesn't study, says he doesn't have time."

"Okay," Carmen says, "look how he agreed to let you leave the firm. He made the right decision in that instance."

"You mean God hit him over the head. Remember, it was after we prayed."

"Ahhh," Jillian says. "So you haven't forgotten."

"Come again?" Willow says.

Jillian smiles at Willow. "God and prayer. When you submit yourself to Damien, it's God you're ultimately trusting. Just like He led Damien to that one decision, He can give him a heart to give, and to do whatever he needs to do as head of the household, *as you pray*. Dr. Lyles was ready for you, girlfriend. Right here he quotes Proverbs 21:1: 'The king's heart is like channels of water in the hand of the Lord; He turns it wherever He wishes.' If God can handle kings, He can certainly handle Damien. God can establish His will in your home *through* Damien, because He's God. Damien has some growing to do but don't forget you do too. You said Damien needs to trust God with the finances; you need to trust God with Damien. You have a strong personality; you like to be in control. God wants you to humble yourself, trust Him, and obey His Word. Let Damien lead. You might be surprised at what he'll step up and do if he sees you giving him the reigns."

Willow pushes back against the sofa, eyes downcast, thinking. Moments later, she nods, still looking down. "You're right. I know you're right. Of course you're right." Her fingers run tracks through her long curls. "Okay, God, I have to trust You. I have to trust You," she says in a light voice. Then looking at us, the sass returns. "So am I the only one who has a problem in this area?"

"I sure can't say I'm problem free," I offer.

"Me neither," Monique says. "And I really tripped when I saw that we had to submit *in everything*."

Asia sits forward in her chair and in her small voice, says, "I have a question about the *in everything* part." She sinks back as if reconsidering, then, "First I'd better give some background. About my husband."

Chapter Twenty-Eight

I shift my body and point my knees toward Asia, as do Willow and Monique, the three of us eager to gain insight into this husband about whom Asia has rarely spoken. Jillian and Carmen wear bare sympathetic smiles. They must already know.

Asia twists the dangling ties on her bustier. She begins, "My husband and I started dating, if you want to call it that, in middle school, though he was a grade ahead of me. He was everything to me, so different from the other boys—sweet and considerate. He would wait for me after class, walk with me down the hall, spend time with me, not caring that the other guys teased him because of it. We would talk on the phone till all hours of the night. He told me all the time that he loved me, and he never pressured me to do anything with him...you know, sexually.

"But when he was in the tenth grade his mother died in a car accident and his world was just shattered. He loved his mom so much. She was a Christian woman and taught him about the Bible and took him to church. After she died, he went to live with his aunt and had to go to a different school. It was awful. Everything changed. He still called but we rarely saw each other and when we did, he started pressuring me, saying if I really loved him, I would show it. And he wasn't even trying to be sweet about it; he was kind of mean, in tone anyway. My mother gave me grief because she saw him changing too. He dressed differently, talked differently, wasn't respectful anymore. I tried to break up with him a couple of times and he would change for a while, tell me he loved me. And I loved him so much that my heart would melt every time he said it."

Asia looks up and into our faces, as if checking to see if we're with her still. When she sees she has our rapt attention, she continues. "We got married as soon as I graduated, only a year and a half ago, and we did it without telling anyone. My mother was so disappointed with me. By then, he was on the fast track in the hip-hop world. I couldn't even tell you how he got the connections he got or met the people he did. Next thing I knew, his songs were being played on WPGC, WKYS, all of them. The changes in him after his mother died were nothing compared to how he acted then. His head blew up and he thought the world revolved around him, and it kind of did. He got attention everywhere we went, like he was a real star or something. And because other people let him tell them what to do, he thought he could tell me what to do, like what I should wear. He said he had a bad boy image and my clothes were too lame. I needed to be edgier, sexier, if I was going to be seen with him. And of course I wanted to be with him. I wanted all those groupie girls to know he was taken."

Asia sighs and tears start in her eyes. "I don't want to wear this stuff," she says, flipping the ties from her hands. "One day I came home and all of my clothes were gone. He had replaced them and acted like I was supposed to be proud because he had gotten a hookup with some hip-hop designer. When I told him I didn't want to wear these clothes, he said I needed to submit to my husband, that that's what his mother had taught him about the roles of husbands and wives. He said I'd be sinning if I didn't do it."

Asia breaks down and I rush to her side and fall on my knees, just beating Jillian and Monique. "Is that true?" she asks. "Would I be sinning if I didn't submit to my husband and wear this?"

"No," I say forcefully, instinctively certain. "I don't know all the ins and outs of submission but I know you don't have to wear that."

"Asia, I never knew all of this," Jillian says. "I knew you were having a difficult time in your marriage, and who your husband was and all, but I didn't know he made you wear these things. Ephesians five says to submit *as unto the Lord*. You don't have to submit to anything that's contrary to what God has commanded, and dress is one of those things. The Lord would have you dress modestly."

"Who does he think he is?" Monique says. "So what he can rap! I can't stand when these men treat their woman any old kind of way. All this worrying about his image and he probably won't even go far. D.C. then bust." Monique rolls her eyes.

"His song is in the top ten," Carmen says.

"Top ten what?" I say, turning to her.

"Top ten in the country."

"Who is he?" Monique says.

Asia lifts her head. "To me, he's Ned. To the world, Eloquence."

"Are you serious? Eloquence?" I say, slumping from my knees onto my bottom, flabbergasted.

"Since when do you keep up with rappers?" Jillian says.

"I don't. Isaiah was talking about him when he came over. He works for Eloquence."

"What?" Jillian says, waiting for more. I'll fill her in later.

"Do you know him, Asia?" I ask.

Asia tilts her head slightly, her tears having eased up. "Isaiah? Might be familiar. When Ned's home, there are so many people coming through the house. It's like a zoo all times of the day and night."

"Hmph," I say. "This one should stand out. He's probably twenty years older than everybody else."

"Oh," Asia says. "I know who you're talking about. How do you know him?"

"He's my brother-in-law. Small world."

Willow stands. "Okay, my initial shock is over. We've got to do something."

"I'm thinking the same thing," I say, and I know what strikes me. Picturing his smug face on that T-shirt makes me want to wring his little neck. But looking at Asia rights my focus. Standing to my feet, I say, "I think the first order of business is to plan a girls' day of shopping."

"Ooh, I'm down," Monique says.

"Count me in too," Willow says.

"Me three," adds Carmen.

"Then it's unanimous," Jillian says.

"I don't know," Asia nearly whispers.

"What?" Monique and I ask, heads snapping toward Asia.

Asia's head moves slowly side to side. "I can't just show up in new clothes. I don't like the way Ned is now but I still have to live with him. What if he puts me out? What if he separates me from DeRon?"

"He's not that crazy, is he?" Monique asks.

"He might be. That's the thing. I don't know. Seems like the more fame he gets the crazier he acts. Remember that day he said I couldn't use the car? He's big into control these days."

My eyes skitter across the pictures on Monique's fireplace mantel, my mind darting all over. "I have some ideas, but can we have an extended prayer time after we finish the study and watch Dr. Lyles? I really want to make sure we hear from God on this one."

My stomach has never tied itself up in this many knots, not even in my most difficult moments with Patsy. With her, my mental and emotional state were at risk. Right now, I am convinced that my life may be at risk. Asia said herself she didn't know what Eloquence—Ned— might do. To go meddling in his personal life like this….

Yet I have to go. There is no way I could *not* go. When Asia shared her burden on Friday, it became mine, and for two days it has weighed me down, waking me up at night, moving me to pray. I now understand Carmen's visit when she said she'd been burdened by my life. When God gives it, you can't shake it. I only hope it's God leading the way this evening, and that this Eloquence keeps a cool head.

Darlene's not the least bit worried. I told her he'd changed and was unpredictable, but she insists she remembers little Ned. I haven't the foggiest what that has to do with anything but it satisfies her at least. She did have definite ideas, though, about how she wanted to proceed. She forbade Hezekiah from coming with us, though he (and I) protested much, because she said a man would appear threatening. She also said Jillian and the rest of the women needed to stay home, believing a crowd would also appear unnecessarily threatening.

So she and I, alone, clear the guard gate and wind through the neighborhood that now makes total sense to me as one where Asia and her husband would live. The house is dark when I cut the headlights in the driveway and I wonder if our information was correct. Isaiah, who knew Eloquence's schedule better than Asia, said he'd be away Friday and Saturday, and back on Sunday afternoon. He was reticent to tell us, treating Eloquence's whereabouts as that of a CIA agent, but Darlene got it out of him by utilizing guilt. She'd never asked Isaiah for much, she told him, never complained when he forgot her birthday or Mother's Day, but now she needed this one thing from him. When Isaiah asked why, Darlene said he didn't need to know everything God was up to, and I suppose the mention of God, on top of the guilt, produced this top secret information. When I passed it on to Asia she said it was a good plan, that the house had the least traffic on Sunday. We set a time of seven o'clock.

Darlene walks ahead of me, her legs carrying a woman on a mission, and rings the doorbell. Though she's never met Asia, I think God has transferred some of this burden to her. As we wait, Darlene says, "I didn't know they made houses this big around here. I thought yours was huge."

I gaze around at the broad silhouettes of the nearby houses, illuminated by extensive landscape lighting. "Our realtor told us about these; we didn't even bother to look inside one. Exorbitant."

When Asia answers, trying to smile a welcome for her guests, Darlene groans a tender, "Ohhhh, look at this baby," and hugs her immediately. I hug her next and as we move just inside the door, I keep an arm around her and introduce the woman I've told Asia about.

Asia, who told me she was embarrassed about what my mother-in-law would think of her, says, "Thank you for coming."

"It's my pleasure," Darlene says, her voice emanating love and the seriousness of the issue that brings her. "When Treva told me your situation, and that your husband was Ned...." Darlene puts her palm to her chest and drops her jaw. "I couldn't believe it. That boy was the nicest little thing."

Asia nods her head, remembering.

"I don't know if I can be of any real help," Darlene says, "but I do know that God is your very present help and He delights in showing His power. We've been praying that He'll show Himself strong on your behalf."

"I've been praying too," Asia says. She rubs her bare arms up and down and tries another smile. "I'm really nervous."

"Is he here?" I ask.

"Mm-hmm, he's in the basement studio."

"Don't you have a baby?" Darlene says. "Where's he?"

"I just put him to bed. It's early for him but I kept him up all day so I could. I thought it would be best if he was out of the way."

As Asia tells Darlene more about DeRon, I take in the surroundings, wondering whose mark this is, Asia's or Eloquence's. The stretch of living space before us is enormous, featuring at its center a leather sectional whose shape and color I never happened upon in my furniture hunts here or in Chicago. It's sleek to be sure, the love child of a contemporary designer, one obviously fascinated with concentric circles. I find my head tilting as I follow its sweeping lines and curves, figuring these must be modules arranged in a custom manner. It's stunning actually, if one could get past the orchid color. I don't imagine that this was the only color available. Someone chose it, thought it worthy. That and the glass circles tiered and white frosted, posing as a coffee table. That's it in the room, two intriguing pieces in a sea of white carpet. Maybe they're still pulling it together. Maybe they've pulled it together, a minimalist approach.

"Is that John-John and them?" a voice yells, accompanied by footsteps bounding up the stairs. "I heard the doorbell through the intercom and nobody came down yet."

My body stiffens. Asia gives us both a quick glance but doesn't respond to her husband. She waits.

"Asia!" he yells, then steps into view.

I'm struck by how slight he is. No muscles apparent anywhere, though he seems to need some to support the white ribbed tank T-shirt that's hanging on his upper frame. Definitely needs something to support the sagging jeans. And honestly, I thought the afro with the pick positioned inside was a Jackson Five era deal. I'd be amused if the air wasn't so tense.

"Who is this?" he says, his upper lip raised in offense.

"This is my friend, Treva, from my Bible study—"

"Mm-hm," he says, and sucks his teeth.

"—and her mother-in-law, Darlene."

"What do they want?" He keeps his dark brown eyes on us.

Asia sighs. "Ned—"

The eyes flick to Asia. "Girl, stop doing that. Eloquence. All the way."

"Well...they came to talk to me." Asia's eyes fall. "And you."

"Aw, nah." He utters an expletive. "I ain't got time for this. What you been telling them, Asia? I knew I shouldn't have let you go to that Bible study."

"First of all, young man," Darlene says, jerking his head her way again, "there won't be any more foul language while I'm standing here, and second, the problem was evident before Asia said anything, by these little bitty threads she wears." Darlene stares him down and he turns to Asia.

"This is my house and they need to leave. Now. Or I'm calling security. I can't believe they snuck up in here 'bout the only time Big Mob ain't here."

"Ned, I knew your mother," Darlene says, taking a step toward him.

His jaw tightens. He turns his head toward the Spartan furniture. "Lots of people knew my mother."

"Do you remember when you were about eleven or twelve and your mother got sick and I brought her some homemade chicken soup and then took you back to the house with me so she could get some rest? And my husband gave you a glove that belonged to one of our sons and played ball with you in the backyard. You ate so much of my fried chicken I told you I had no idea where you had put it in that tiny body of yours." Darlene smiles at the memory.

Eloquence turns and looks at her, as if for the first time. "Mrs.…Mrs. Langston? I still…I still got that glove." He quickly shakes his head, as if willing away words, thoughts, a feeling, and draws himself up to his full height. "Look, I don't go there," he says, shaking his head again. "I don't think about those times…I don't think about my mother. I just don't."

"Well, you should," Darlene says. "You would remember how wonderful she was and the things she taught you—" Darlene bends her head to meet his eyes, which have fallen downward. "—about how to treat people. You would remember that she wasn't treated well by your father and had to raise you by herself, and taught you how to treat your future wife one day, and I know she did because she told me. She said you would be different. And if you took the time to think about her, I know you'd remember that your mother was a Christian woman, and that her godliness showed through to every facet of her life, including how she dressed. She was stylish, and she wouldn't have been caught in anything like this." Darlene's thumb angles toward Asia. "And, if your mother had known the way you would one day treat your wife and the clothes you would charge her to wear, she would have whipped your tail then in anticipation of it."

Eloquence gives Asia a very brief once-over, then says, with little conviction, "It's just the style. If she's got a nice body, why not show it off while she's young?"

Darlene twists her lips and her full body, gazing at Asia, who's face is contorted with tears. "Style? Baby, ain't nothing changed. It's the same now that it's always been. Trash." She moves closer to Eloquence and takes both of his hands. He draws his arms back a touch, but not enough to wrest himself from her grip. "Your wife is a precious jewel, sweetheart. She's your crown. Why would you even want other men to be able to feast their eyes on her? She deserves to be protected, nurtured, cherished, in every way. She deserves what your mother never had. A real man."

Eloquence removes one hand from Darlene's and in a quick reflex, brushes a lid, his jaw managing to remain firm.

Darlene finds his stray hand again and swings them both, as with a child. "Ned, don't forget the most important thing your mother taught you. God loves you, even in the midst of this path you've chosen—I'm told your music is very raunchy—and He's waiting for you to turn to Him. I realize it may take you some time, and that's between you and God, but we're here to secure some changes *today* regarding this baby's wardrobe." Darlene waves Asia over and drops one of Eloquence's hands in favor of one of hers. With them both at her side, Darlene says, "We're ready and willing to take Asia shopping and replace these clothes with some that your mom would be proud to see on a daughter-in-law of hers."

Asia lifts her red eyes to him cautiously, her free hand rising every few seconds to swipe a new tear.

I watch Eloquence shift his macho stance from one foot to another, looking at none of us, his hardness betrayed by the hand that still rests in Darlene's.

"You just had to bring my mother into this, didn't you?" he mumbles, glancing over at Darlene. "You can…," he says, his mumble dying to a hoarse whisper.

"I didn't catch that," Darlene says, leaning her ear.

He clears his throat. "I said, 'You can use my credit card.'"

"Oh, Ned, thank you," Asia says, throwing both arms around his neck. He says nothing this time about her use of his boyhood name in front of us. "Can we go tomorrow?" she says, wisely offering him a say.

"Might as well, I guess," he says, patting her half-exposed back.

Asia looks around at us, and I've never seen her smile so bright. The doorbell rings and Eloquence straightens, wipes the back of his hand across his nose and, gently displacing his wife, walks to the door.

"What up, dude," he says, clasping hands with a bigger man. "Y'all should have been here a long time ago. Where you been?"

"Working, man. For you. Tour starts Wednesday. Remember?" The man rolls through the door and heads straight for the stairs.

Another follows behind. "Big Mob," Eloquence says. "Figures you'd show up after the fact."

"After what? What's up? Something happen?" Big Mob shifts his weight about, looking around, past us harmless women, after acknowledging us with a nod of the head, for the problem Eloquence is speaking of. He's at least two hundred and fifty pounds yet he, too, found a pair of oversized pants to hang from his derriere.

"Nothing, man," Eloquence says, sliding us a look.

Three more guys lumber in carrying fast-food bags and they each file downstairs. Eloquence closes the front door and ambles in the direction of the stairs, slowing up as he nears us. Stopping by Darlene, he says, "Mrs. Langston, I remember another time when some boys in the neighborhood were picking on me and you came down the street and yelled that you had to talk to me, like you were mad 'cause I had done something, and soon as they left you invited me in for some chocolate cake." He turns his head aside, then back. "I know I can't repay you for what you did for me and my mother. You don't want free tickets or a CD or nothing like that, and you probably wouldn't take my money." He gives her a sideways glance to make sure he's right. "But if you ever need anything, I want to know about it."

"Will do, baby," Darlene says.

"And Mrs. L—remember I used to call you that?" Darlene smiles. " I feel funny asking you for something but…I don't know, I just feel like it would be nice to know that you were praying for me, like…like my mother used to do."

"You got it, sweetheart," she says, and holds forth her arms. He walks into them and lays his head down on her shoulder. A couple of seconds later, he pops it back up and makes his way downstairs.

I stare after him. "Do you think he's changed, just like that?"

"No," Darlene says. "God touched his heart for our purposes but it's hard to change a lifestyle. He'll go out on tour and be Eloquence and rap those lyrics and do what only God knows they do on those tours. But in time and with prayer, I believe God will draw him. I don't know why; I just do."

"Mrs. Langston," Asia says, "Treva told me you and Ned's mother were neighbors but I didn't know you had actually interacted with him the way you had. I don't think this would have worked without that connection. I haven't seen that side of Ned in years."

"God is good, isn't He?" Darlene says. "He's always blessing. He was working way back then, for today."

Darlene starts toward the door and I follow, then stop, telling her I'll meet her in the car. She hugs Asia and walks out of the door as Asia gives me a questioning look.

"I have to confess something, Asia," I say. "In my mind you were a tramp because of the clothes you wore, and I'm sorry for judging you that way."

To my surprise, Asia waves it away. "How can I blame you? I would think the same thing of someone dressed like me. And, really, I owe you an apology too. I judged you the same way Monique did. I thought you thought you were too good for everybody else, but when you shared your background, I knew my first impressions didn't do you justice. They never do, do they?"

I smile. "No, I guess they never do."

"Thanks, Treva, for everything you did to arrange this." Asia hugs me. "This was just beyond—"

"What you could ask or think?" I say, and we laugh. "Shopping tomorrow?"

"Are you really going with me?"

"Wouldn't miss it," I say. "And I bet I'm not the only one. Let's talk in the morning."

I step into the cool night air and my mood plummets in a nanosecond. Asia's happy, problem solved. The problem was *able* to be solved. Why can't mine be that type, solvable?

I sigh, feeling ungrateful. God has done so much for me. He's given me the Bible study and new friends. He's given me a change of heart that is helping me to appreciate my husband and daughters more and more each day. I even understand now that He did close the door on my working at a big firm here, and remarkably, though some days are better than others, I'm beginning to appreciate that too. I know I would never have experienced these blessings had I continued in the vein that consumed me in Chicago.

Why can't these things be enough? Why do these feelings clobber me out of nowhere, causing me to focus only on the things He can't change?

Will these feelings never cease? Will a part of me be perpetually unhappy?

Chapter Twenty-Nine

"Only three days until your birthday, Faith!" Hope says, entering the kitchen like a herald into the town square. Each morning this week she has greeted Faith with a countdown. Her hair looks cute still in the twists I put in over the weekend. It took three hours, and there are so many I didn't count, but they're full and pretty and versatile. Monday and Tuesday she wore them pulled to the top of her head. Today they're hanging down. I think tomorrow we'll try the front half pulled together, the back half down.

"I know when it is," Faith says, easing a forkful of eggs into her mouth. I almost chuckle at her attempt to be nonchalant, knowing her insides are about to explode over this passage into teen-hood.

"Mom," Joy says, her hair in two long braids, "is it true that Faith gets to go to bed later when she turns thirteen? 'Cause that's what she said."

"Actually, it's quite the opposite. She will have to go to bed earlier," I say, sipping my coffee at the table with the same nonchalance.

Faith gasps and her hand, holding toast to her mouth, flings to the table.

I continue, "The teenage body needs more rest to function properly with all the new hormones raging."

Hezekiah pads down the steps, handsome in blue slacks and a striped polo shirt.

"Daddy, is this true?" Faith says. "Do I have to go to bed earlier after my birthday?"

Hezekiah catches my eye and furrows his brow in seriousness. "Absolutely. When I turned thirteen, my bedtime went from nine o'clock to seven o'clock."

Faith busts up with laughter, her fears subsiding. "Daddy, it did not! I'm gonna ask Grandma Darlene."

"Well, you know, she's getting up in age and her memory isn't what it used to be. You might not get accurate information."

"I'm gonna tell her you said *that* too," Faith says.

Hezekiah chuckles. "You'd better not."

"Daddy, I've got a word for you. I saw it last night in a book I'm reading," Joy says.

Hezekiah tucks his plate into the microwave. "I'm ready."

"Pabulum. And it's food," Joy adds before he asks.

"P-a-b-l-u-m," he says.

"Wrong," Joy says.

"It is not wrong."

"Wrong, babe," I say.

Hezekiah joins all of us girls at the table and eyes us as if a conspiracy has been hatched against him. "I suppose Joy told you the spelling?" he says to me.

"I didn't tell her anything," Joy says.

"I suppose you think you *know* the spelling, then?" he says.

"P-a-b-u-l-u-m. Pabulum," I say, taking another sip of coffee.

"Well, see, Mom said the word differently," Hezekiah says. "Joy, you pronounced it 'pablum' but Mom just said, 'pabyelum.' I would have gotten it right if you had pronounced it right, Joy."

"Mm-hmm," Joy says, openly doubting.

"I've got one for you," Faith says.

"I'm not worried," Hezekiah says, spreading jam on his unbuttered wheat toast.

"Phlegmatic—having an unemotional attitude," Faith says.

"P-h-l-e-g-m-a-t-i-c," Hezekiah says.

"Ugh, you got it," Faith says.

"Good job, Daddy," the little cheerleader, Hope, says.

"Okay, you won't get this one," Faith says. "Piranha—a dangerous fish."

"Oh, this should be easy," he says, his eyes traveling upward. "Okay, okay, p-i-r-r-a-n-h-a."

"One 'r' dear," I say.

"Got him," Faith says in triumph.

"Don't you all have to get to school?" Hezekiah asks.

I recline my head on his shoulder and pat his back. "It's okay, sweetheart. Nobody expects a math man to know how to spell anyway."

"That's what I'm going to do," Hezekiah says, nodding his head. "We'll start having math problems at the table."

The girls groan as one and hop up to put their plates in the sink and get ready to go.

Hezekiah, still eating, leans over with lips puckered. Mine meet his. "So what's on your agenda for today?" he says.

"Nothing, really." Immediately my thoughts flit to earlier this morning when I cut short my time with the homework, reasoning I'd get back to it after I return from taking the girls to school, which I often do. But today I'm not looking forward to it at all. I lift from my thoughts and look at Hezekiah. "This is our last week in Ephesians and this chapter is kind of difficult for me."

"In what way?"

"I don't know. It's just…difficult."

"Okay…," he says, stretching the word.

"I can't explain it. We're into spiritual warfare and demons and all of that. Every time I start the homework this wave of dread comes over me. Who wants to think about all the forces of evil that are out there and what they could be up to? It just makes me uneasy."

Hezekiah takes his last bite and pushes the plate away. "I can understand that. Think about it this way—God wants us to be aware of what we're up against. It's not meant to make you uneasy but to spur you to stay prepared and focused on God."

I nod my head, gazing forward.

Hezekiah kisses my cheek and pushes back his chair. "I hate to leave the conversation like this but I've got to get to a nine o'clock meeting. Let's talk about it this evening when we have more time."

I stand as well. "I don't know. We'll see." I doubt I'll want to talk about it. I'm kind of relieved that there's no time to explore the issue right now.

I stare down at my Bible at the words I've marked with colored pencils. Three times in chapter six I see the admonition to "stand firm" in bright red, but what I need to stand firm "against"—a word that appears a haunting six times, colored now in brown—is what grips me.

*"Finally, be strong in the Lord, and in the strength of His might. Put on the full armor of God, that you may be able to stand firm **against** the schemes of the devil. For our struggle is not **against** flesh and blood, but **against** the rulers, **against** the powers, **against** the world forces of this darkness, **against** the spiritual forces of wickedness in the heavenly places. Therefore, take up the full armor of God, that you may be able to resist in the evil day, and having done everything, to stand firm. Stand firm therefore...."*

In my mind flashes statements Darlene and others have made about the enemy but I never knew there was a whole hierarchical host of powerful demons organized *against* me. And when I saw where they are—*in the heavenly places*—my spirit collapsed within me. This entire study I've been thinking about what it means to be seated in heavenly places and now I see that demons occupy that space too. Out of habit, I colored "in the heavenly places" in the same metallic gold to match the ones in chapters one and two but it doesn't shine as the others did. The phrase has lost its luster.

And I know the point of these verses is to focus on God's protection but how can I? For the life of me I cannot understand what these pieces of armor really mean. I'm told to stand firm in a belt of truth, a breast-plate of righteousness, and shoes of peace, plus take up a shield of faith, a helmet of salvation, and a sword, which all sound vital, each piece indispensable. And this picture in Dr. Lyles's notes of an ancient warrior so dressed shows why such a person would be able to stand firm in ancient battle. But how to make effective use of these pieces against a host of demons in my present-day life is beyond me. Couldn't the apostle Paul have spelled it out plainly rather than in metaphor? What do I *do*? I'm coming unglued, unable to decipher the good, fully comprehending the evil.

The anxiety is only worsened by the other verses to which Dr. Lyles directed us in the homework. Thanks to him, I've read all there is to know about the devil from Genesis 3 to Revelation, about his days of beauty when he was created, his rebellion against God, and his downfall. I know he's defeated. But I also know that he hasn't been cast into the lake of fire yet, and that he's superhumanly powerful. He's roaming, seeking to devour.

Dr. Lyles expected us to rejoice once we compared the verses about the devil with those that show God as infinitely more powerful. And they did help. But only a bit. Because even as I read God's proclamation of His power in the last chapters of Job, my mind kept taking me back to the opening chapters where the devil smote Job with boils from his head to his feet and took all the man had. Dr. Lyles made sure we understood that Satan had authority over Job only because God gave it to him and trumpeted this as "good news." I'm sorry, it didn't warm me. What if God allows the devil and his host to come against me like that?

The next thought paralyzes me.

What if they've already come against me? What if they've been coming against me my entire life? I pin my eyes to the verse. "For our struggle is not against flesh and blood, but against the rulers, against the powers...." I rise from my seat, considering it. My lifelong struggles have revolved around Patsy and skin color. Maybe skin color more than Patsy. It's the reason for my problems with Patsy—the reason she never accepted me. It's also the reason I was excluded while growing up. The reason I've tried so hard to prove myself worthy. The reason I didn't think initially that God loved me. The reason, today, that I find it hard to trust totally in His goodness toward me. No, demons couldn't be responsible for all of that. They didn't make me dark. I back wearily against the counter, heaving a sigh. I don't get this. I don't want to get all of this. Is this supposed to help me, to know that my real problem may be a host of demons? That's infinitely worse!

Put on the full armor of God, my heart whispers.

I don't know what that means!

Nor do I know what difference it will make. The armor won't lighten my skin.

Chapter Thirty

"We are in warfare," Dr. Lyles says, staring resolutely into the camera. It strikes me that this is the first time he has started the DVD session with a close-up, without any levity, and as the six of us look around at one another with eyebrows raised, it's clear we all sense a new intensity with the lesson. He has grabbed our attention at the outset.

"I'll say it again, slowly, just in case you didn't hear me. We are in warfare. The first three chapters of Ephesians told us who we are and what we have in Christ. Chapters four, five, and the first part of six tell us how to walk in the light of who we are and what we have. Now we get to the part that tells us that we who are richly and eternally blessed have an enemy—the serpent of old. And why, you may ask, is he our enemy? Because we are caught in the middle of a supernatural and age-old battle between Satan and God. Satan, a created being, wanted to be like God and was cast from heaven. He became an enemy of God. And because he's an enemy of God, he's an enemy of everyone who belongs to God. His kingdom is opposed to God's kingdom.

"He's a liar, he's a deceiver, he's a destroyer, and he's a murderer, but he's also crafty, subtle, cunning, and powerful." Dr. Lyles backs up to his stool and sits on it. "Let me ask you, did you feel burdened this week as you studied? Distracted? Were you thrown into confusion? Depression? Was it hard to keep your focus on the Lord of Hosts?"

"Oh, my Lord," Monique says, covering her mouth. "Carmen, can you pause it?"

Carmen reaches for the remote and clicks Dr. Lyles to a standstill.

"I'm telling y'all," Monique says, a light dawning in her eyes, "I could not do the homework this week. I know, I know, I didn't do it that other week but that was different. I had just neglected to do it. But I've been faithful about it since then. And every week I've been getting more and more excited about it because I can't believe I'm actually learning. But this week, every time I tried to study, I had some kind of problem. Either I was falling asleep—I have *never* fallen asleep while I'm studying—or I had a million interruptions. One day I sat down to study after the boys went to school and normally the whole day is quiet. First the phone rang off the hook until it got to the point where I had to unplug it, then the doorbell started ringing, which I tried to ignore because I figured it had to be a solicitation. It was my next-door neighbor and she'd gotten locked out of the house and had to wait for her husband to come let her in." Monique tosses her eyes in the air. "Y'all, she was at my house all day.

"The next day, I kid you not, got myself all settled in, had my cup of colored pencils—did anybody else get the box of fifty?"

Willow and I raise our hands, chuckling at the pencil fetish.

"—and in walks my husband from work. Do you know he said soon as he got there, he felt sick with the flu and had to turn around and come home? I spent the entire day dealing with a big baby. I was like, 'I can't believe this!' Now I can't believe Dr. Lyles is talking about this."

"I know," I say. "I had my own share of difficulties. Not interruptions but as I did the homework I was just feeling…." I exaggerate a shiver, letting my body say what my mouth can't find the words for. "I can't believe Dr. Lyles is saying this either. I have a feeling he's going to say a lot of interesting things today."

Jillian nods. "That's for sure."

When all eyes turn back to the television, Carmen says, "I guess that's my cue." She finds the button and pushes it, and Dr. Lyles's voice fills the room.

"I wouldn't be surprised if each of these hit you at one time or another this past week. Distracted one day, depressed the next. The enemy doesn't want you to learn about him. He wreaks his havoc under cover of darkness and ignorance, so the less truth you possess about him, the better. He'd like you to be in one of two camps. In the first, you have such an overblown view of him that you think more about his power than God's. In the second, you're not cognizant of him or his schemes at all. Either way, you're out of balance and he's got you. So when you endeavor to study and grow in wisdom and discernment, and in particular to study *him,* don't be surprised if he attempts to derail you. If you're watching this DVD, I commend you for hanging in there to the end of the study."

We look at each other and smile, noting that none of us has missed a meeting.

Dr. Lyles is saying, "I can't wait to move my focus higher, to the omnipotent and all-merciful God, but I need to touch on a couple of more points about Satan. I've got to make sure you understand this. First, he doesn't operate alone. When he rebelled, one-third of the angels went with him and together they comprise a formidable demonic host. I don't say that to scare you, just to let you know that you, in yourself, do not have the power to stand against them. Second, we talked a lot in chapters one and two about being seated in heavenly places and being blessed in heavenly places. Chapter six says this demonic host is in the heavenly places, but please don't get confused. Oh, how the enemy would love to confuse you on this one! The heavenly places where demons dwell are *not* the heavenly places where we dwell."

Everyone is quiet, paying close attention, but in the event anyone should utter anything to cause me to miss one word that Dr. Lyles is about to say, I scoop my Bible from my lap and plop right on the floor in front of the super-wide, high-definition screen. My adrenalin is pumping, recognizing the need for me to master this one point.

"Who are we seated with?" Dr. Lyles asks, giving his audience time to answer.

With Jesus, I say to myself.

"Where is *He* seated?"

At the right hand of the Father.

"Where is that?"

Tears dart to my eyes and I close them, the moistness seeping through my lashes. *Far above all rule and authority and power and dominion, and every name that is named, not only in this age but also in the one to come.* I recite these verses every day around the house now that I've memorized up to the end of chapter one. It makes no sense that it didn't come to mind while I was studying. This must be the confusion Dr. Lyles spoke of.

"So let's be clear," Dr. Lyles continues. "Because Jesus is seated far above the demonic rulers and powers, you also are seated above demonic rulers and powers. It doesn't mean they cannot come against you; it means their power is no match for the power that is at your disposal." A broad smile spreads across Dr. Lyles's face and he rubs his hands in delight. "This is our segue to that matchless power, the Most High God who rules over all, who accomplishes His will among the host of heaven and the inhabitants of the earth. Oh, if you would just consume yourself with Him. Nothing else would matter."

I know this DVD is prerecorded and this man doesn't know me, but he has stepped squarely into my life today, addressing thoughts, concerns, and desires I've had the last couple of weeks. I know it's God. *I know it,* I repeat in my heart, overwhelmed. *Thank You, Lord, that I can see now when You're working.*

After Dr. Lyles makes sure we understand that we have to be strong *in the Lord,* and not in ourselves, he walks over a few feet to a life-sized cardboard statue of the same ancient warrior that was in our notes. "When taken together," Dr. Lyles says, sweeping his hand from the statue's helmet to the upraised sword in his grip, "the full armor of God means knowing the truth and obeying it. That's why the apostle Paul spends the second half of Ephesians telling you how to walk. And because much of spiritual warfare takes place in the mind, it means we must be continually renewed in our minds, replacing old under-the-devil's-influence thinking with God's truth. Beloved, I promise you, if you walk in truth—and by that I mean you know it, believe it, and obey it—you are prepared in this war.

"Now, to the actual pieces of armor...."

When Dr. Lyles finishes his session, the longest of the series, the blue screen appears but no one moves to turn it off. We are each in contemplation, heads bowed or angled away.

After a few moments have passed, Carmen says, "I wish we could visit Dr. Lyles personally for one-on-one ministry. Can you imagine the wisdom he could impart into our lives?"

"I was thinking the same thing," Monique says. "He is so on target in his sermons; if he could only help me apply the messages to my own life."

"Isn't that what God wants to do?" Asia says. "He's probably the reason the sermon is so on target."

Willow chuckles. "Ain't no 'probably' in that. God is definitely leading that man." She tilts her head toward Asia. "You're getting wiser and wiser every week, with your cute self."

Asia smiles, slightly lowering her head. "You all stop embarrassing me."

We've been making a big deal of Asia since we got here. She wore the outfit we all thought looked so adorable when she tried it on—and we made her try everything on, as tickled as we were with the outing. We were quite a bunch with the six of us, DeRon, Zoe, and even Malcolm since Carmen's mother had a doctor's appointment and couldn't baby-sit, all filing through just about every store that sold Asia's size. We went to Tyson's Corner since I had just been out there the week before and knew exactly where we should start, having seen some clothes I thought would look great on her. We shopped for three hours, stopped for lunch, then went for another hour and a half before the babies cried us out the door. We were pleased by then, though, with our productivity. Asia had, in her arms and in the arms of three others, a full and becoming wardrobe.

Today she's wearing a simple gray velour hoodie and pants but on her petite frame, and given, no doubt, what we're used to seeing, she couldn't be any cuter. Her hair is darling, too, after a trip to Darlene's salon. I do a double take every time I look at her, not used to the shorter length of her own hair.

Asia surprised us yesterday when she called to propose a change of venue for today's meeting. Since Eloquence had departed Wednesday for his tour, she wanted to open up her home to us. When we arrived, an hour earlier than normal at her request, she presented each of us a rose in thanks, she said, for our support. Then she led us to the kitchen, an open and airy space with two islands and a dramatic wall of tall white-lacquered cabinetry, made festive by the floral bouquets and aromas that greeted us. She had prepared an array of breakfast casseroles and home-made pastries, including croissants—another surprise since we didn't know young Asia could cook. I made a point of jotting down a few of her recipes.

We adjourned to a downstairs area after breakfast, one of many from what I could tell, this one featuring several deep-cushioned leather chairs, all a surprising sedate toffee brown, positioned before a flat-screened television that covers and appears part of the entire length of one wall. It looked as if Dr. Lyles was in the room with us.

Carmen expels a loud sigh. "Y'all, I can't believe this is our last Bible study meeting."

"I know," Jillian says, sighing herself. "It was infinitely better than I anticipated. God showed up each and every week."

"I actually got teary eyed thinking about it as I dressed this morning," Monique says. "Y'all are like my, well, you *are* my sisters."

"Excuse me," I say, hand partway raised, "Who said it was ending?"

Their faces tell me they are each considering this.

"I don't know," Carmen says.

"I just thought…I don't know, either," Jillian says. "I guess I didn't want to assume that everyone could commit to another. I was thrilled just to get this one off the ground."

"What else do you all have to do on Friday mornings?" I ask.

A string of "nothing" sounds around the room.

"Good. Because I really don't know what I would do without you all." I turn my head aside as I experience a weird rush of emotion. "I'm sorry," I say, dabbing my eyes with my finger. "I don't know where this is coming from. I'm just overwhelmed, I guess, by what you all have meant to me. In a few short weeks I suddenly can't spend a Friday morning without you." I laugh as tears trickle from my eyes.

"A-*men*," Willow says. "I don't know what Carmen, Jillian, and Monique were talking about anyway. I intended to be right here next week, or in another one of your houses, or you were going to be at mine." Willow laughs.

"I know," Asia says. "I thought we would just choose the next book of the Bible we want to study and get the materials ordered. I was looking through that booklet Jillian handed out at the first meeting and I've got my eye on enough studies to last us for years."

"Anybody opposed?" Willow asks, daring us to say so with an evil eye.

I fold my arms and the others follow suit.

Willow bangs her fist on the arm of her chair. "Resolved, therefore, that these six women will henceforth continue as one in study, fellowship, and prayer, for as long as the Lord says the same."

"Amen!" booms from us all.

"Since this group means so much to you, I guess you'd better thank Hezekiah," Jillian says, elbowing me as we stand for closing prayer.

"For what?" I say.

"If it hadn't been for him, you'd be in Potomac somewhere, and you know you wouldn't have been driving all the way to P.G. for a Bible study with women you didn't know."

I toss my eyes upward, traveling back to August and September. "You're right. I wouldn't have been here."

"Girl, you were thinking about Potomac?" Willow says, widening our twosome to a beginning circle. "You know you need to be over here amongst the folk."

"Don't trip now, Willow," Monique says, grasping her hand. "It *is* nice over there. Sometimes I drive to those areas just to look at the houses."

"I hope you look at the price tags hanging on them too," Carmen says.

Asia laughs. "Even Ned, who likes the hype, said it made more sense financially to live here. He grew up in P.G., though. I don't think he'd live anywhere else."

The circle formed, hands linked, a thought springs to mind. "You know what?" I say. "I just realized why you all are so important to me. You're part of my armor. You keep me focused on God and growing. You set me straight when I need to be, and you pray for me. I didn't know prayer was part of warfare until this chapter. Well, I didn't know much about warfare, period, until this chapter." I curl my lips in contemplation. "I have a prayer request. I learned a lot today but there's so much I still don't understand with respect to my own life. I have to admit, a one-on-one with Dr. Lyles sounded good to me, too."

"Do you want to talk about it, Treva?" Jillian asks.

I shake my head lightly. "No. The main thing I need right now, and I feel it strongly, is prayer. These last couple of days I've felt such a foreboding. Maybe I really am in warfare. Maybe it's what Dr. Lyles said, that the enemy doesn't want me to learn about him, although I don't know that there's much left to learn. The homework had us dissecting him pretty well."

"What you need now is discernment," Carmen says. "He doesn't want you to be able to apply what you've learned, to recognize his fingerprints in your life and in your thinking so you can change." She pauses. "You've been on my mind a lot this week, Treva. I've been praying for you."

My heart leaps at this, seeing that God must not have lifted the burden he gave Carmen for me. I'm grateful for it now. It gives me hope that He might be up to something in my behalf. "What have you been praying?" I ask.

Carmen doesn't hesitate. "For a breakthrough."

Chapter Thirty-One

Not just anybody can be a ballerina. They'd never put you on stage; you're too dark. Be realistic about your goals.

I shift under the covers for the hundredth time.

We are in warfare.

My heartbeat is racing, as if I'm running, something great and terrible on my heels.

You can't pretend that being dark doesn't make a difference. You know firsthand.

I turn and lift my head to look at the clock, hoping I fell asleep at some point and the night has almost passed. The digits laughingly pronounce, *2:13* A.M. My head slaps the pillow.

You're too dark…You're too dark…You're too dark…

He's a liar, he's a deceiver, he's a destroyer, and he's a murderer, but he's also crafty, subtle, cunning, and powerful.

I try to picture Dr. Lyles, try to stay with him, his voice. I allow his words to ring in my ear, wanting them to rock me to sleep.

This is not my world, Treva. This is the world.

I can't take this. I've got to do something. I want to wake Hezekiah. But I don't know…He's so hard to awaken, and he'll kill me when he sees the time.

In my heart I never truly accepted that you were my daughter…

"Hezekiah."

"Hmmm?" he says, with the clarity of a snore.

Heartened, though, by a reply, I prop myself up on an elbow facing him. "Are you asleep?"

Inaudible.

I shake him. "Hezekiah?"

He gives a start. "What's wrong?"

"I can't sleep."

"Mm," he mumbles. "What's wrong?"

I launch right into my question. "Do you think my upbringing and the way I view myself have anything to do with the enemy?"

"Mm-hm," he says.

I shake him again, lest he think he's venturing anywhere near sleep at this point. "You've got to say more," I tell him. "I've been trying to understand this for two days, how he could have been at work in all of that. Dr. Lyles was saying today, well, yesterday, that when we believe in Jesus Christ, God delivers us from Satan's domain and transfers us to His kingdom, and Satan becomes our enemy. But when I was growing up, I wasn't a believer. Was he my enemy then, anyway?"

Hezekiah remains silent, then kicks his legs up under the cover, sending his torso upright in an instant. "Put some clothes on. We're going outside."

"We're not going outside, Hezekiah. It's cold out there tonight."

"Better dress warmly, then." In his bed-wrinkled athletic shorts and red Maryland Terrapins basketball shirt, he moves with an unsteady gait to the bathroom, his body questioning waking movement at this hour. I follow close behind.

"Hezekiah, we can talk right here in the bedroom. Why in the world would we go outside?"

Brushing his teeth, he mutters, "You asked a cosmic-sized question. I think it deserves a cosmic-sized answer."

Layered in silk long underwear, a turtleneck, extra warm fleece pants, a wool sweater, and a down coat, I grab Hezekiah's arm as he leads us out the back door. Before he steps out, he surveys me. "You think you're back in Chicago? It's not that cold."

"We'll see what you say when you've been out there awhile."

I smile inside at the safety I feel, now that my husband has taken up my cause. I snuggle up closer, realizing I'm shivering, and not yet cold.

Hezekiah stops in a clearing without trees and looks up into the night. "What makes the sky beautiful?" he says.

I look up, then over at him, wondering where the question came from, and what the right answer is.

"Is it the stars?" he asks. "The moon? Is it the clear blue of daytime? Or maybe blue with puffy white clouds? Sunrise? Sunset? All of these things make the sky beautiful, don't they? Variety—from sky blue to dusky oranges and reds to the black of night. But I think it's more than that." He drops my hand and spreads his arms upward. "It's beautiful because the God of heaven made it. *He* is beautiful."

A biting wind whips around my face and I wish now that I had dug out my scarf. "Hezekiah, I agree with all you've said but, come on, did we need to see the sky right now? It's cold and you're not even answering my question."

Hezekiah, looking strangely refreshed, beams and reclines his neck fully. "Really, think about it, Treva. How could anything His hands have made be less than beautiful?" Then, looking at me, "How could anything He has made *in His image* be less than beautiful?" He comes within an inch of my face, his breath warm and minty. "He doesn't fellowship with the sky, Treva, as beautiful as it is. He made man for fellowship. He actually chose to fellowship with man. We're His crowning achievement in creation. He made the stars and the animals and all the other things He made and called it 'good.' He made man and called His creation 'very good.'"

His words are stirring and soothing, and I know he means for me to think better of myself because of them, but I can't. Not with this road-block in my way. "Hezekiah," I say, slowing my speech to drive home my desperation, "you agreed rather quickly that the enemy had an impact on my upbringing and the way I view myself. What leads you to that conclusion? Please. Explain."

"That was my next point," he says, and leads me by hand to the gazebo, putting us farther outdoors. When we're seated, cuddled together, he finally continues. "So, God creates the world and His crown-ing achievement, humans, and He's enjoying fellowship with them as intended. But Satan is opposed to God, so he sets out to destroy the fellowship by tempting man to sin against God in the garden." Hezekiah is animated, his hands telling the story "Through Adam's sin, that fellow-ship was broken and the whole of mankind fell under Satan's dominion." Hezekiah's hands pause as he leans his face before mine, bringing my gaze from the distance to him. "You with me?"

I nod. "I'm with you. That's Ephesians," I say, glad to understand *something.* "We're under the enemy's influence until we're saved."

"Right," the hands say. "So if the enemy of God gets mankind under his influence, what is he going to do?"

"Everything that's opposed to God," I say.

"Exactly. All kinds of foul and wicked mess, all with the aim of keeping man separated from God and ultimately doomed to hell. So we fast-forward to the part of history that we're intimately familiar with. In Satan's ongoing quest to destroy man, he used one group of humans—Europeans—to come against another group of humans—Africans. And he accomplished this by putting the arrogant notion into their heads—pride is his specialty—that white skin is better than dark skin. That lie, together with greed, also of Satan, ushered in hundreds of years of slavery."

I sigh and watch white mist seep from my mouth. "And the slaves with the lighter skin got better treatment than the slaves with the darker skin."

I see Hezekiah's head nod in my peripheral vision. "Of course, once it got entrenched, it was tempting for some of us to believe the lie ourselves," he says, bringing his hands to his pocket now, "that light skin and finer features are just better. And it did seem better because many of those people were doing better. Definitely had more advantages, well after slavery ended." He shrugs, in resignation it seems. "Treva, Satan's lies are weaved everywhere in the fabric of our existence. That particular lie about skin color has endured a long time, and you happened to be raised in an environment where it thrived. It's not that the enemy had you singled out specially for attack while you were growing up. It's just that he's the god of this world and we can't escape his influence, one way or another. It's really that simple."

I stand and walk a little ways, seeing what I've never seen, as if God put a wide angle lens on the whole of my existence, showing me the view from above. The cosmic view. I agree. It's simple. Why did it take me so long to see it?

I turn. "Why haven't you shared all of this before?"

Hezekiah puts his forearms on his thighs and looks up at me with his deep brown eyes. "You never asked, sweetheart. And you never like to talk about your past. As I think about it, you've never been comfortable talking about the enemy, either. But I always told you what I felt you needed to know—that you're beautiful."

I close my eyes and turn away again when the word hits me. "Beautiful." It's still foreign. *It's still foreign. I hoped the truth would set me free.* Tears spring to my eyes as I face my reality. I'm a casualty of the enemy's lies, and seeing the cosmic view doesn't alter this earthly spot I'm standing in, unable to look at my husband, not while he's looking at me. Not while the chasm is yawning between us again, making him very light and me extremely dark. I can't help but wonder whether he fully escaped the world's influence. Has he secretly envisioned someone else on his arm, one with fine features, acknowledged by the masses as beautiful?

I jump at the touch of Hezekiah's hand on my shoulder turning me to him, brushing my tears with the back of his finger. "I wasn't finished with my cosmic-sized answer," he says. "Did you think I'd leave it on that note, with the god of this world front and center?"

He attempts to lift my chin with his finger but I resist, unwilling still to face him. He kisses my cheek instead, reaches inside his leather jacket, and pulls something out. When I hear pages turning, I lift my chin on my own, puzzled. It's the monogrammed pocket Bible Darlene gave him for one of his birthdays.

Finding what he wants, he suspends it in front of my eyes and says, "So, you studied this, right? Just finished, what, yesterday?"

I stare at him, past the "Ephesians" title, wondering how in the world he could have what appears to be a half smile on his face. I answer with an expression that makes clear that I am not in the mood for flip, rhetorical questions.

"Okay, so help me out," he says, returning the page to his view. "You know that you've been blessed with every spiritual blessing in the heavenly places." He turns an ear and leans forward to draw out a response but I'm not in a heavenly place so I stare past him. He puts his eyes to the page again. "And you know that you were chosen before the foundation of the world and that you have a rich inheritance." He flips the page. "You know that you were saved because of God's great love for you, that you were raised and seated with Christ in heavenly places." He looks up again, knowing it's my favorite verse of the book. I avert my gaze. He flips the page again.

"Ahh, I know you know He is able to do exceeding abundantly, beyond all that you ask or think, according to the power that works within you." Flip. "You know He's given you His armor and that you only need to stand firm in His strength and truth. So—" He makes a show of turning back a couple of pages. "—if I'm understanding correctly, the only thing you haven't grasped in the study is chapter four, verse twenty-three."

Unable to resist, I respond, making sure my voice is flat. "Which is what?"

"Be renewed in the spirit of your mind."

I decide to speak up for myself. "I wouldn't say I haven't grasped it. I couldn't have begun making changes with you and the girls if my mind hadn't been renewed in that area."

"Amen to that," he says, planting a kiss on unpuckered lips. Then, wagging a finger, "I like the way you put that. You said you couldn't have made changes if your mind hadn't been renewed *in that area*." He lays hold of my arms through the bulky coat. "There's one area you've struggled with your entire life—the way you look. Right? And you're still struggling with it. Let's just be real. I saw the way you turned when I called you 'beautiful,' no different from the reaction I got from you the first time I said it. You couldn't receive it. So your mind has not been renewed *in that area*. Is that a fair statement?"

"No, it isn't a fair statement," I say, emotion upping my voice an octave. "My mind *has* been renewed in that area." I throw my hands up. "Isn't that what we've been doing out here tonight? Renewing my mind? Well, hallelujah, it's *totally* renewed now. I know exactly why I've struggled so long with the way I look. I've been caught in a cosmic battle. It really wasn't Patsy's fault at all! She's off the hook. I'm still dangling." I move my eyes off of him.

He moves them back with a finger to the cheek. "Knowing why is a start, but if that's all you walk away with, you're right, you're still dangling. You're no better off. Renewing your mind doesn't mean recognizing the devil's lies and wallowing in them. It means recognizing them, *rejecting* them, and replacing them with God's truth. But you've got to believe the truth, sweetheart. You've got to believe in the beauty of *all* of God's creation. That's what I was trying to say to you when we first came out here but you weren't hearing me." His voice trails off, his attention turned aside. I watch him curiously. Is he praying? Or…listening?

He turns back, nodding to himself, a secret smile easing onto his face. "You weren't hearing me," he says again, "but that's okay. I've got something else for you." He tucks the Bible back into his coat. "I'm going to help you see the cosmic view—of yourself."

My eyes remain fixed on Hezekiah now as he grazes my forehead slowly with his hand, saying, "You were fearfully and wonderfully made—you studied that, too, didn't you?" His smile is electric. "Sweetheart, God created you deliberately and with care. He planned specifically how many centimeters apart your eyes would be, how wide they would be, how they would open like a flower in bloom, full and arresting, showing off the penetrating brown of the pupils. And He decided the exact point at which the eyes would slightly dip at the inside corners here—" He touches the spot gently and my body tingles.

"He planned the exact placement of your ears on your head, the angle of your cheekbones, the slope of the bridge of your nose, the exact thickness of your lips—" He kisses them, and they're puckered. "—and the distance they would be from your nose." Hezekiah's fingers light on each feature he mentions, sending chills, warm chills, through my being. "He planned how wide the corners of your mouth would turn up when you smile and how the smile would cause two distinct spots on your cheek to cave into a dimple. He planned how many hairs would be in your head, your eyebrows, and your eyelashes, and how those lashes would curve to a perfect thick arch.

"God planned the *type* of hair you would have," he says, running his fingers through my curls, "hair only a certain percentage of women on the planet were privileged to receive. Tightly curled versatile hair you could wear natural if you choose, in braids, twists, locks, a short afro, long afro, afro puffs, or you could relax it and wear it blow-dried, wet-set, wrapped, in more styles than you could try in a lifetime, and I know, 'cause I'm Darlene Langston's son. He planned the thickness of your hair, how long it would grow, how much moisture it would hold. He knew the very day that single gray strand would pop up."

Hezekiah glides his finger down the side of my face. "And He deliberately planned your skin. He made it deep and lush and so warm the eyes need to linger to get enough, to drink of its richness. I don't know why He chose to give only some such an intense and lavish stroke of vibrant color, but you were among them. You are among those on display throughout the earth who show *God's* richness and depth and creativity."

Hezekiah takes my hand and lifts it, moving me to a full-bodied turn as he says, "You, Treva Campbell Langston, are unique, one-of-a-kind, hand-wrought by the God of the Universe. You could be nothing other than beautiful. You *are* nothing less than beautiful."

He unzips my coat and his jacket and pulls me to him, sliding his arms around my waist and, for a long while, strokes my hair, neck, and back as I cry. I cry for the years of pain and rejection, the years of feeling invisible, marginalized, inferior, and self-conscious, years of ugliness and of feeling ugly. And I feel Hezekiah's lips on mine, drawing me to a slow, romantic, and consuming kiss, somewhere in the midst of which, miraculously it seems, the gap widens and I realize the tears that continue to dampen my face are for *her.* The old Treva.

My eyes pop open. *She's gone.*

I pull back and look at Hezekiah with eyes that are surely bloodshot and bleary but will just as surely do the job of making the introduction. He meets my gaze, then he meets *me* and picks me clear off the ground with a hoot of laughter. I throw my head back, peering at the stars that must be winking at me, knowing all along they'd provide the stunning backdrop to my celebration party. I laugh out loud as a voice within reminds me who the Guest of Honor is—a celebration not of me, but of the God who made me. I laugh again as Hezekiah sets me down. Just like God. Soon as I get a better view of myself, He puts the view where it should have been all along. On Him.

My legs, filled with energy, have to move. I take a victory lap, so to speak, walking along the cobblestone path, oblivious to the cold, shaking my head in wonder at what God has done since I moved back.

It seems now that it had all been building to this night. The Bible study, the prayers, the discussions—with Darlene, Hezekiah, Jillian, and every other member of the group—even the encounter with my mother, all building to this moment when I would step fully into God's love and trust Him. "Oh, I praise You, Lord," I say aloud, falling to my knees, arms outstretched, "for Your mercy endures forever. Lord, I praise You because as I think about Ephesians, and it's becoming so clear in my mind right now, Lord; You're making it clear—" I laugh in awe. " —that all the things You've done for me— blessing me, choosing me, redeeming me, forgiving me, loving me, protecting me—are all for *Your* glory. It's about You, Lord. It's all about You."

With a sudden spur, I spring to my feet, giddier still, an effervescence I've never known tickling my spirit. I begin to move, breezily, effortlessly, in a choreographed waltz, arms raised. I hear the music, a lively orchestra, playing for me and…and…*God* I'm dancing with *God*. I'm enjoying Him! *Oh, Father!* Tears and laughter gush forth as I revel in my glorious *moment* with the King of kings and Lord of lords. *Thank You, Father. Thank You.*

When I finally make my way back to the gazebo, I find Hezekiah in his own prayer moment, standing with head raised to the sky, eyes shut tight. *Thank You, Lord, for my husband. I pray to see neither of us as colors again, but as two whom You have made into one flesh.* I stand quietly waiting, gazing at him. When he's done, he sees me, walks over, and folds his arm around my neck. We head in blissful silence to the house and he pauses at the door, bends down, kisses me. "You're beautiful," he says.

I smile, tilt my neck to kiss him again, and we continue into the house.

Chapter Thirty-Two

"Happy birthday, sweetie!" I say, surprised to see Faith in the kitchen so early this Saturday morning—a definite testament to her excitement. No one else is awake yet.

"Thanks, Mom," she says, grinning, looking every bit a teenager in those capri lounging pants she loves from Old Navy, this pair a pink festival of fuchsia, salmon, and rose, all married in plaid, and a pale pink Old Navy-emblazoned shirt. Jamila's older sister put microbraids in her hair after school yesterday and they're swinging lazily around her face as she makes her way to me.

I move from my seat at the table to give her a birthday hug, but before I bring her to my bosom, my heart moves me to stare closely at her features—her naturally arched eyebrows, her lashes, thick like mine, the mole above her lid and the one above the left side of her lip, the way her eyes dance when, as now, she's bubbling with anticipation, and her silky milk chocolate skin. I open my mouth and tell her, "You are very beautiful, Faith."

Faith gives me a confused look. "Do you really think so, Mom? You've never said that before. Why now?"

"Never?" I ask, as if unsure. I'm more than sure. It was the best I could manage with the wind knocked out of me and my heart caving.

She does me the favor of crinkling her brow as if she might have been too hasty. Then, "No. Never."

My eyes fold to a close. *Lord, I've ruined my child.* I pull her to me, now needing the hug more than giving it. I thought my subtleties had gone undetected. I've never told any of my daughters that they're beautiful. Not Faith, because I didn't believe it, and not Joy or Hope because I had the sense to know that if I couldn't tell one, I'd better not tell any. But I nuanced—"you look beautiful," which, with Faith, meant the hair or the clothes or the combination, but was worded and conveyed in such a way that she could have taken it to apply to her person. I always felt guilty for not being able to say it outright—"You are beautiful"—but I would have felt guiltier saying what I didn't mean. In my mind the words were a great improvement over what I received as a child, which was nothing. I wanted to validate Faith. I thought I *was* validating Faith.

Hezekiah has always told the girls that they're beautiful, so Faith has grown up hearing it. But apparently her ears were fine-tuned to what she wasn't hearing, from me.

As I hold my precious daughter, fingering her braids, a pall of regret washes over me. How I wish I had seen her beauty before now. How I wish I could have told her.

And down in this mire, a worse feeling hits. I *could* have told her she's beautiful and meant it, had I prized the more excellent thing—her heart.

Sighing inside, I lift my eyes. *Oh, God, if only Your truths had overtaken me when Faith was younger. My failings keep smacking me in the face. First my failure to nurture a relationship with her, now my failure to affirm the way You made her. She has a forgiving spirit, Lord, but will that erase the damage? What could I possibly say to her?*

Ending our embrace, I face her finally and lead her by hand to the table, wishing she could sit on my lap, wishing she were young enough, young enough that a kiss and a lollipop could smooth the rough places. But this is my big girl, my teenager. My wise young woman. No lollipops for her.

With a sigh to muster strength, I look into her eyes. "Faith, you're right. I've never told you that, that…you know." I sigh again. *Oh, God, this is so hard.* "Your mom has had a lot of problems as a result of growing up in a home where God was not glorified. You already found out, unfortunately, that your Grandma Patsy favors light skin over dark. I grew up under that mindset, and as much as I hated it, it seeped in like poison and became my mindset. In my crazy mixed-up head, dark skin was a curse." '

Okay, Lord, this is awful. What am I saying to her? I didn't have to be this candid. It's one thing for her to know what her grandmother thinks of dark skin. But telling her what I thought about it? She'll have a worse complex. Please back me out of this, Lord. I shouldn't have even told her she's beautiful. I thought I was doing a good thing but given where it has led....

I search her face for signs of distress, of inward crumbling, but it's blank. Don't know what that means. I hang my head for a moment, not sure where to go. Given where I left off, I'd better forge ahead. I can't abandon those words.

"Sweetheart," I say, "I know now that that was a horrible lie but it took many, many years for me to know it. Believe it or not, it didn't sink in until the wee hours of this morning."

Faith's eyes perk. "Really, this morning? What happened?"

I consider my answer. "It won't make sense unless I start with what happened three years ago," I say. "I haven't been open about my spiritual life, Faith, and I really wish I had been." A dead chuckle escapes as my gaze shifts. "I wish a whole lot of things...." Looking upon her again, I say, "Do you remember when we came to your Grandpa Charles's funeral?"

"Yes."

"I accepted Jesus as my Lord and Savior while we were at the house, the night before the funeral."

"And that's why you started going to church with us every Sunday after that—well, almost every Sunday?" At my nod, she says, "I knew something was different but no one said anything. Being saved isn't supposed to be a secret, is it? Shouldn't we have done something special to celebrate?"

Her sweetness brings a smile to my face. "It's not supposed to be secret, no, and I didn't set out to treat it as one. It's just that I didn't want to think about the night I was saved because of other things that happened that night that upset me "

"Between you and Grandma Patsy?"

I stare at her with questioning eyes.

Faith shrugs slightly. "I could just tell. Everybody looked upset—not just you but Grandma Patsy, Grandma Darlene, Aunt Jillian, Daddy. And you and Grandma Patsy wouldn't even look at each other when you finally came downstairs."

A quirked brow joins the stare as I take a jet tour through years and situations. *What else has she picked up on?* Finding it best to move on, I say, "Well, the reason I brought up that night is because I want you to understand that it was the turning point of my life. That was when God made me alive, brought me into His kingdom, turned me from darkness to light, none of which I truly understood until we moved here, which brings me to the next turning point—this." I slide the Bible between us, its pages opened to Ephesians from my early morning study.

"God is so good, Faith. In the last three months, He has done such a work in my life that I don't even recognize myself. And the biggest thing He did was to get me into His Word." I caress her cheek. "Like I always see you doing. Now I know what a difference it makes. I began to see things as God sees them."

I sigh, this a contented one. "Which brings me to this morning."

"God did something, didn't He?" Faith asks. "He really can do miracles, Mom."

I look at her intently again, wondering at the statement, but my mind speeds me on to the scene, my husband's strong and gentle hands on my face, leading me to a new level of glory. I still get chills thinking about it.

"It was awesome, Faith. It sure seemed like a miracle to me. One moment I couldn't see it and the next I could, as if I'd been given new eyes. I could see the beauty of a dark complexion. And not only that," I say, amusement in my expression, "Daddy did such a good job of helping me see it that I almost believe God blessed you and me in an extra special way." I lean to her and whisper, "We'll keep that to ourselves."

Faith smiles, but I sober. "But, honey, the sad part is that it took me so long to see it. For all of your life up to this point I did not appreciate your beauty, and it grieves me. I am so sorry, Faith, for not acknowledging how beautiful you are, inside and out. I feel just awful."

Faith cocks her head, a mysterious gleam in her eye. "Mom, don't feel bad. I don't. I'm excited. God answered my prayer." She does a little shoulder dance. "I *love* it when He answers my prayers. This one definitely goes into the journal."

I collapse back into my chair. "What prayer?"

"I prayed that you would know you're beautiful—because you are, Mom—and when you told me I was beautiful, I just knew it had to mean you saw it in yourself. That's why I said, 'Why now?' I wanted to know what happened."

My body leans in. "Why were you praying that? How would you even know what I thought of myself?"

"Well," Faith says, "when Grandma Patsy told me I'm not as pretty as Joy—"

I close my eyes and cringe, still burning over the statement.

"—I knew she probably said the same thing about you and Aunt Jillian. And then I thought about how Daddy says, 'Hey, beautiful,' and you roll your eyes." She does the teenage shrug again, already a pro. "It didn't take a lot to put the two together. You never believed him because you'd been brainwashed. Hmm," she says, cocking that head again, "now that I think about it—I wonder if God helped me put it together. Anyway, I started praying the night of the brunch."

I rise from my seat as if it will give me a better perspective. "Unbelievable. Absolutely unbelievable." Standing over her, I search her face again, saying, "But, Faith, you are not made of steel, and I can't help but be concerned about you. You had to have been hurting inside over the years, given the mother you've grown up with."

Faith stands, tucks a few braids behind her ear, "Mom, I didn't need you to tell me I'm beautiful. That's not important to me. What mainly hurt was not knowing you, not being able to talk to you. You would be gone early in the morning and wouldn't get home until late at night. And when you were home, you'd be working. These last couple of months have been a turning point in my life too. I feel like I have a mom now."

"Faith, it's your birthday!" Hope announces, jumping down from stair to stair with both feet at a time.

"Happy Birthday, Faith!" Joy says, scurrying around Hope to make her way to Faith first.

A giggle erupts and Hope takes the last three steps at once as they break into a dash across the kitchen floor. They fall into Faith and she falls against the table, back arched, her sisters smothering her with vigorous hugs and kisses.

"Mom, help," she says, laughing, sticking out an arm.

I pull her forward and the other two come upright with her. Then I suddenly feel silly myself and thrust a bear hug upon them all, sending them flying back over the table.

"Mom!" they say.

"Nobody told me the party had started," Hezekiah bellows from behind. In a shake he's down the stairs throwing his arms around the pile and the pile tumbles to the floor, a collective 'Whoa!' crescendoing as in the first five seconds down the biggest hill of a roller coaster. Heads rise in laughter to assess our relative positions atop one another and the biggest kid yells 'tag, you're it,' hits *me,* and hightails it out of the kitchen.

Primed in Nike shorts and aerobic shoes, I dart after him, yelling, "Oh, no you don't. Don't even try it." The girls, forsaking the rules of the game, run after me as I run after Dad. I consider turning on them and tagging whichever is closest, but we all know the big fun is in capturing The Man.

We spot him in the living room and our posse attempts to trap him around the sofa but he's too fast. He runs us around the sofa again to shame us, then bounds up the steps off the foyer, down the hall, past the bedrooms, and down the stairs that lead into the kitchen. When he reaches the doorframe of the kitchen, with us in hot pursuit on the last steps, he does a quick Rocky celebration jig, arms raised, not noticing yet that Faith is not among us. She had doubled back down the first set of stairs and is now creeping up behind him. In a deft move, she knocks her knee behind his, catching him mid-jig. He buckles under, flailing in mock defeat to his knees.

I sashay over to the fallen. "He's so cute, isn't he, girls?" I extend a hand and help him up.

"Good thing it's your birthday," he says. "Otherwise I'd be planning severe reprisals, young lady."

Faith crosses her arms smugly.

"What's a reprisal, Daddy?" Hope says.

"It means it'd be payback time." He lifts Faith off the floor and gives her a big smooch on each cheek. "Happy birthday, baby girl. I love you."

"I love you, too, Daddy," Faith says, and as Hezekiah lets her down, she surprises me with an embrace. "And I love you, too, Mom." She squeezes tighter and so do I. "I thank God for you, sweetheart," I say in her ear, and it's all I can say as tears overwhelm.

Not to be outdone, Hope and Joy hug my waist as well, and we become one big pile again when Hezekiah enfolds us all.

When I get myself together, I say, "All right, family. We've got a birthday to celebrate and it starts now, with a celebration breakfast. Everybody out. I need to prepare."

When they all troop upstairs to get washed and ready for the day, I stand in the moment in the center of the kitchen. Thankful.

———

"Thanks, Cecil. I don't know what we would have done without you," I say.

Cecil fixes another lavender balloon onto the spout and zaps it with helium, fastens a clip on the end, and lets it fly to the now crowded ceiling. "You would have been exercising your jaws, sister," he says and chuckles. "When I saw all those balloons and no tank, I knew somebody had to make a run."

"I appreciate it," I say. "I had a long to-do list and renting a helium tank wasn't on it."

"It's my turn to do one, Daddy," David says, a limp balloon in hand.

"Treva, where's the punch bowl?" Jillian calls from the kitchen. "Don't you have one bigger than this?"

I look at Cecil and shake my head. "Girl, how am I supposed to know what 'this' is?" I yell, making my way from the living room back to the kitchen.

"Treva," Hezekiah's voice booms from the family room, "are you sure they didn't give you any other directions? This popcorn machine is not working."

When I get in the kitchen, I shout out, "That's all they gave me, babe."

"Then I need you to come in here when you get a chance. Didn't they show you how it works?"

I sigh. "I'll be in there in a minute."

I grab a step stool and find the punch bowl we need in a cabinet above the refrigerator. "Here, Jill," I say, handing it to her. "Which punch are you making?"

"The Sprite one."

"Ooh, I like that one. Thanks. You helping out too, Trevor?"

"Yes. Aunt Treva?"

"Yes, sweetie?"

"Can I have a cookie?" He looks at his mom and I can tell the matter has been discussed.

"What did your mom say?"

"She said I had to wait."

I chuckle inside. "Then I guess you have to wait, little man." I grab one from a plate and fold it in a napkin. "I'll put this really big one aside just for you, okay? We'll hide it right here behind the coffee pot."

Trevor's head bobs furiously. "Thanks, Aunt Treva."

I check the oven and the Crock-Pot and gaze longingly at a bar stool. How I would love to sit down. I've been hopping since this morning. When Faith came back down for breakfast, she entered a kitchen with streamers, "13" confetti sprinkled on the counters and table, gifts, and a dozen Mylar "Happy Birthday" balloons that I'd run to pick up while keeping breakfast warm. After eating and opening the gifts, I picked up her three friends and took them all to a matinee, then out to lunch, then to Amber's house where they could spend time doing whatever new teenage girls do, so we could have time to get ready. The party's not a surprise, but the decorative touches will be. Amber's mother will be dropping them here at six o'clock.

"Treva!"

I amble past the tempting bar stool and walk to the family room, finding a frustrated Hezekiah.

"Mommy, the popcorn won't pop," Joy says. "And this is the best part of the whole party."

"The world won't end if we don't get it to work," I tell Joy and myself. "There's always the microwave." I kneel down beside the contraption to see what might be the problem.

"Mommy," Hope says, "Should I put the Trouble game on this table and Uno cards on this one? Or should Trouble go in the living room with the chessboard?"

"Nooo," Hezekiah says, his head buried with mine. "Isaiah and I won't be able to concentrate with that thing popping every two seconds."

I laugh, then mutter to Hezekiah, "If he even comes...." Lifting my head, I say, "These tables in here are fine, Hopey. Thanks for helping."

Hezekiah figures out the problem and the tester kernels bring victorious cheers as they transform into yummy fluffs.

"Aunt Treva," Courtney says, "I can't find the Yolanda Adams CD. Joy said you have the latest one but it's not in here." I help Courtney find it and thank her for programming the CDs to play throughout the house during the party.

"Doorbell, Mommy," Joy says, setting "Happy Birthday" coasters on the tables.

I arrive in the foyer as Cecil lets in Darlene and Russell and an amazingly scrumptious aroma.

"Hey, Cecil," Darlene and Russell say.

Since both of their arms are full, Cecil hugs their necks and takes the deep stockpot from Darlene's hands as David and Trevor run to them.

"Hi, Grandma Darlene. Hi, Grandpa Russell," they say, flying to their waists. Jillian and Cecil's children may as well be blood, the way Darlene and Russell have adopted them.

"Hey, sugars," Darlene says, beaming.

"Let me get that, Pop," Hezekiah says, walking up. He takes the second stockpot and I get my hugs from both of them.

"Oh, Russell, look at this," Darlene says, her gaze upward. "The entire ceiling is covered with lavender and yellow. Faith will love this."

"You see that," Russell says, inclining his head toward the vinyl banner. It stretches from the top of one column to the top of the other and says, "Happy 13th Faith."

"How could I miss it? It's fabulous," Darlene says. She steps across the foyer and through the columns, peering into the living room. "The balloons are even more striking in here because the ceiling is lower." Moving further in, she says, "I was wondering what that was. Where'd you find those pretty candles?"

I peep my head in at the floating lavender '13' candles inside glass bowls on the tables and fireplace mantel. "I ordered them online. Aren't they nice?"

Hezekiah walks directly in front of us, gesturing with the stockpot.

"Oh, okay, baby," Darlene says with a chuckle. "Let's get those in the kitchen."

"Looks like we'll have enough food to feed an army," I say.

"And there's more in the car," Russell says, shooting a look at Darlene that says she did the usual—made too much.

"You said the guest list doubled, didn't you?" Darlene says, marching toward the kitchen.

"It's about tripled now," I say, following behind. "Faith's list of friends went from three to eleven, last count. And I told my Bible study buddies they might as well stop by if they can."

"Good, we'll have plenty," she says.

"Hey, Darlene," Jillian says from the door jamb, giving her a big hug.

"Jillian, you need to bring those kids by more often," Darlene says. "I couldn't even recognize them, big as they are now."

"Weren't we just by there a couple of months ago?" Jillian says.

"I guess you were, weren't you?" Darlene says. "They must be weeds then."

Darlene directs Hezekiah to put his pot on the back burner and Cecil to put his next to it. She turns the fire under both on low and slaps Hezekiah's wrist when he tries to investigate the contents. Hezekiah and Cecil retrieve three casserole dishes from the car, which Darlene puts on an empty rack in the convection oven. Their third-trip items go on the counter. Darlene has officially set up camp and I've no doubt she'll stick here all evening, making sure everyone is well nourished. I treasure the help.

After a few minutes, I notice no one is calling me and nothing immediate needs to be done. The men and children have stolen off somewhere. Darlene is chopping vegetables for a tossed salad, for which she has said she doesn't need help. Jillian is washing dishes that have accumulated, and she, too, has refused help. I slip quietly onto the bar stool and take a deep breath. My head falls on the counter.

Darlene and Jillian laugh. "Tired, huh?" Darlene says. "You need to get more sleep."

My head shoots up like a rocket. "Oh my goodness! I haven't had time to tell you two."

"What?" they say.

All I'm able to do is shake my head in wonder.

"What!"

"Everything you two have ever said about the awesomeness of God, and Jillian, everything you've ever said about Hezekiah being the best thing to ever happen to me—imagine those two things coming together in the middle of the night. Outside." I can't help shaking my head again. "It was the most amazing night of my life. So much has changed."

Jillian brings soapy hands closer to me and Darlene stops chopping. Both are hanging on whatever my next word will be and I oblige, from beginning to end. And at the end, we are all in tears.

Jillian almost knocks me off the bar stool with the biggest embrace I believe she's ever given me. When she tries to talk nothing comes out and she hugs me again. "Oh, Treva," she says now. "Oh, Treva. Oh, this is just...." Another hug. "Do you understand how many prayers...?" Hug.

"You know I've got to get in there," Darlene says, waiting her turn. Jillian uses the opportunity to grab a tissue as Darlene holds me, stroking my hair. "Oh, my daughter," she says. "I knew this day would come, the day when you would understand that you'd been set free from the mess of this world. You're not even of this world," she says, her voice rising with joy. "You're on top of the world. Breathe the free air, baby."

In heavenly places, I think to myself. That's exactly where I am.

Hezekiah happens into the kitchen and all eyes fall on him. He looks at us with suspicion. "What?" he says, backing up.

"Come here, my son," Darlene says. Tears start in her eyes again as she grabs his hands. "You have shown your wife the love of God, and I'm so proud of you. I'm so—" She leans her head into his chest for a moment, then lifts it. "Don't you stop loving her like that, you hear?"

Hezekiah's jaws tighten and he closes his eyes briefly, answering with a nod.

Jillian walks over to him and just looks at him, smiling and shaking her head. She still can't talk. They hug.

Hezekiah comes and kisses me on the cheek, gives me a five-second shoulder massage, kisses me again, and makes his exit, to preserve his emotions, I'm sure.

We ease back into preparations, making sure we haven't forgotten anything, all the while unable to leave what Jillian dubbed "the cosmic tale." Before we know it, Faith returns, with a horde of teenagers.

Chapter Thirty-three

"All right. I see you," Isaiah says, hunkered down. "I see where you're going. You won't get my queen, though."

Hezekiah stares him down, waiting.

"You two need some more dip?" I ask, making the rounds. "Punch?"

"Nah, I'm cool," Isaiah says without looking up.

"No thanks, babe." Hezekiah favors me with a one-second glance.

"How about you all? You okay?" I ask at the next table.

"I'm good, Treva," Cecil says.

"Mrs. Langston, are there any more of those meatballs? They were really good."

"Sure, sweetheart," I say, giggling to myself. He seems like a sweet boy, and I can see why Russell and Cecil thought they'd run all over him and his friend in a game of bid whist. I saw the sly look in their eyes when the boys said they could play. Now Cecil's threatening to dump Russell and take one of them as a partner.

In the family room the action is livelier. Faith jumps up when she sees me. "Mom, I am so glad Courtney and Sophia brought their Trouble game so we could have two. We've got a tournament going."

A roar goes up at one table. "Get on back home," Amber says. "That's all right. You'd better not get in my start because I'm coming right back out," Kelly says. Faith grins at me. "Can you believe it, Mom? Trouble? We have all these games and this is all they want to play." I smile as she hurries back to the table, thrilled that the game theme is such a success. It was what Faith wanted, and it appears her friends share the same love.

"You think people are ready to eat?" Darlene asks as I return to the kitchen.

"I doubt it," I say, arranging meatballs and other food items on a tray. "They don't mind eating hors d'oeuvres at the table but I don't think they want to get up. Everybody's pretty intense about the game they're playing." I laugh and say, "Although, your husbands might be eager to end it. They're getting beat up out there."

Jillian transfers more chips to a serving bowl. "That's what they get, trying to take advantage of those boys."

"We'll give everybody a few more minutes, then call them to eat," Darlene says. "Russell will thank me."

The doorbell rings and the air swells with talk and laughter.

"I know who that is," Jillian says.

"Me, too," I say. "I can hear Monique from here."

Jillian and I hasten to the foyer, where Hezekiah is introducing himself to Monique, Asia, and Willow.

"Where's Carmen?" I ask.

"She said she'd walk over and meet us," Willow says. "Her mother's out of town so she was waiting for Karl to get home to take care of Stacy and Malcolm."

"She could have brought them," Jillian says. "Our kids are here."

"She told me she just wanted to hang out tonight," Monique says. "She said we should have planned a pajama party."

All of our eyes grow wide. "She should have told us," I say. "That would have been fun."

Given the girl talk, Hezekiah flashes his palm to dismiss himself, saying, "We need to have you and your families over for dinner. The husbands need to get in on this deal, find out what you ladies have been talking about."

"Hey, I have an idea," Willow says. "Why don't the husbands get their own Bible study going? I'll sign mine up first."

Monique bumps Willow forward with her elbow and Hezekiah looks at me, wondering what's between the lines. He dons a devious smile. "If Eloquence shows up, I'm there."

"Hezekiah!" I say, eyeing Asia's reaction.

Asia bursts with laughter. "You and me both. That's the only way I'd believe it."

I shoo Hezekiah back to the living room with the tray in hand for the guys. Our group gravitates to the kitchen, and Darlene hugs Asia, then Monique and Willow as she meets them, making sure they all get a plate of appetizers.

When Monique takes a seat at the kitchen table with hers, she says, "Ooh, that popping is music to my ears. They're playing Trouble in there, aren't they?"

"Mm-hmm," I say, "been playing all evening."

"I might have to get in on that," Monique says. "That's my game. I love playing with my boys."

"Uh-oh," Asia says. "When you said Faith loved games, I bought Trouble for her because I remembered how much I used to like it. I didn't know it was still popular."

"It won't be a problem," I say. "Watch this." I walk to the top step of the family room and call Faith. After introducing her to everyone, I tell her Asia's dilemma.

"Oh! Can we open it now?" Faith asks Asia. "We have people waiting to play."

"You sure can," Asia says, handing her the gift.

"Thank you, ma'am!"

"Faith, please call me 'Asia.' I'm a teenager myself."

Everybody cracks up as Faith dashes back.

When Isaiah shows his face, Darlene says, "I've hardly seen you, Son. I heard the game was so intense you weren't ready to eat."

"Hez got my queen so I had to take a break. I'm ready to grub."

Isaiah sees Asia and they talk about what's happening on tour with Eloquence as Darlene, Jillian, and I move the food to the dining room. At Faith's request, her grandmother made fried chicken, barbecued chicken, baked beans, red beans and rice, potato salad, collard greens, and homemade rolls. On top of that, Hezekiah grilled hot dogs and hamburgers. My contribution was the appetizers—meatballs, fried mozzarella sticks, shrimp kabobs, and two kinds of dip to go with the assorted chips.

With some effort, we coax everyone from their respective games and gather around the dining room table. Hezekiah raises his hands to quiet the crowd, then puts his arm around Faith. "Before we pray over the food," he says, "I can't let the moment pass without saying a few words about my baby girl."

Faith blushes when a few of her friends chorus, "Awww."

"This is our firstborn, and I'm sure at least some of your parents can attest that there is a lot of trial and error with firstborns as the parents try to figure out how not to ruin the child's life." He turns Faith to him and scans her person. "She's still intact, I think; only a few nicks and bruises from that time we dropped her."

Faith lowers her head in embarrassment.

Hezekiah squeezes his arm around her. "But what I want to say in all seriousness is that we didn't know what we were doing. And I don't know if we've figured it out yet. But God has had her covered all along. By His grace, she has grown in wisdom as she's grown in stature, and I believe she has blessed me far more than whatever I've been able to do for her. In fact," he says, pointing, "one thing I *have* figured out is that

Faith and God have a thing going. If I want a prayer answered, I tell her about it." At the sound of chuckles, he says, "It's the truth!"

"I love you, sweetheart," he says, embracing Faith. Over additional "Awwws" and applause, Hezekiah meets my gaze and questions me with his brow. I nod and wait, standing directly on the other side of Faith.

When quiet comes, I say, "I don't know why I indicated to my husband that I would say a few words because I have no idea what to say. I just knew I had to say something." I crook my arm around Faith's neck and she allows her head to rest briefly on my shoulder. "My husband could not have said it better. It takes a while to figure out this parenting thing, and at the rate I'm going, I may have it figured before she graduates." I smile and let them chuckle. If they only knew.

"I have to echo something else my husband said." I chuckle myself this time. "It's a good thing he went first, huh? I would have really been at a loss for words. But, he said Faith has been a blessing to him and I had to also tell her openly what a blessing she has been to—"

Heads turn at the doorbell.

Willow waves us to continue. "I'll get that," she says, "It's Carmen."

I turn back. "—what a blessing she has been to me. I've learned so much from her about grace and forgiveness in action, and about prayer." I raise a hand in the air. "I can vouch for my husband—give this girl your prayer requests. I found out this morning one of her prayers for me had been answered." I look into her eyes. "You're a beautiful girl, sweetie. I'm blessed to be able to call you my daughter." I wrap my arms around her and the room applauds again.

"Grandma!" Faith says over my shoulder. "You made it."

I whip around and see her. In my house. At Faith's party.

Hezekiah takes note and quickly says, "Why don't we pray so you all can begin serving yourselves? I know you're hungry."

I bow my head, and when he's no longer talking, I assume it's over and slip into the kitchen. Jillian is right behind me.

"I thought Hezekiah called Mama," she says.

I stare off to my right, pacing slowly. "He did. He told her an invitation was in the mail but given what happened the day and night of the brunch, it would be best for all concerned if she stayed away. I was sitting right there."

"What did Mama say?"

"She said she would never want to be where she's not wanted. He talked to her a few more minutes, saying he hoped things could be amicable between us one day, and then hung up."

"Then what is she doing here?" Jillian says.

"Looks to me like we prayed her here," Darlene says, coming in on the tail end.

I stand still. "'We' who?"

"Remember I suggested we pray and watch God move at this party and not one of you agreed?"

Jillian and I remain silent.

"I left it alone, until I got an e-mail a couple of days later from Faith, asking *me* to join *her* in praying for her mother and grandmother." Darlene walks closer to me. "Treva, Faith said she and Hezekiah were about to pray for Patsy that night of the brunch and you left the room, then left the house. She knew you were upset, and she assumed where you went. I didn't verify it but she's a smart girl. She had two petitions, that you would come to love and forgive your mother and that Patsy would come to know the Lord. No, make that three petitions. She wanted us to pray specifically for a breakthrough of some sort at this party. I guess God said there's more than one way to skin a cat. If y'all wouldn't take the task, He'd give it to a child."

"Wow," Jillian whispers, obviously touched.

I'm not.

"So how did she actually *get* here?" I ask. "Did Faith call and invite her again?"

"Far as I know, Faith didn't talk to her," Darlene says.

I fold my arms and stare at the floor. *She's got to get out of here. I will not be vexed in my own house, and on such a special day.*

Willow strides in with the others behind her, including Carmen, faces fraught with worry. "Treva, did you know your mother was coming?" Willow asks.

"Nope." I look up for a second. "Hey, Carmen."

Carmen gives me a hug. "I just got here. Have you and your mother spoken yet?"

"Nope."

From the corner of my eye I see the others looking tentatively at each other. "Maybe we should pray," someone says in a low voice. I think it was Asia.

Slowly the feet of Darlene, Jillian, Asia, Willow, Monique, and Carmen shuffle toward me and surround me. I hear words such as "power," "strength," "peace," "armor," "love," and "glory" coming from each of them in turn. As Darlene sums up a prayer, a voice tops hers.

"So the party's in here? Or is it church?"

Darlene pauses, drops her hand from Monique's, and extends it to Patsy. "You're welcome to join us."

"No, thanks. I'll wait." Patsy moves fully into the kitchen, exploring, distracting with her heels.

The heat rises within me. I back from the center of the circle to the perimeter, clutching the hands of Jillian and Asia.

"Lord, have Your way," Darlene says. "You are all powerful. You are sovereign. All things are possible with You, and we thank You, in Jesus' name. Amen."

Jillian goes immediately to our mother to greet her and ease the tension. Darlene is with her. Seems lovely. Voices are easy. Mother's laughing.

343

What's left of the circle begins to drift that way. Carmen, ever the beam of light, extends her hand. Give me a break. *Introductions?* When Willow and Monique make it over there, I snap.

"Mother, I need to speak with you. In private." I brush past their fellowship gathering and take the back stairs, refusing to look back. They can eat, they can mingle, they can pray about my inability to cope. I don't care. I'm not pretending this can work. She's got to go.

I hear Patsy's steps behind mine, and as I enter the hallway, I consider taking our meeting into the guest room but I haven't furnished it the way I would like yet. I don't want her in my bedroom either, but design wise, it's the best choice. And I cleaned it yesterday.

I step inside the sitting area and watch her stroll in with her half smile. My body tenses as I close the door. *Will I be able to handle another confrontation?* I fold my arms to feel brave. "Why are you here?"

Her eyes flash around the room, and I am not sure whether she's assessing the place or measuring her response. Finally, "For Faith's party."

"Hezekiah told you it would be best that you not come."

"And I didn't intend to," she says. "But I had a gift—"

"You could've mailed it Thursday. Would've gotten here today."

"Listen, Treva, I know you don't want me here. And I wasn't chomping at the bit to come. I can't explain it. I just felt that I needed to deliver the gift in person, for Faith's sake."

"For *Faith's* sake? You don't care about my—" I let my head drop, and slowly roll it back up. *I'm not going there.* "The gift is delivered. Thanks. You can go."

Patsy eyes me. "This is a sore spot with you but I have to ask. I heard a curious thing when I walked in. You were telling Faith she's a beautiful girl. Do you think that's wise?"

Strength unlooked for spreads through my bones as I remember the point at which Patsy arrived. *Lord, Your timing is perfect.* Smiling inside, I say, "Excuse me?"

"I know these black women's magazines say we need to tell our daughters they're beautiful, whether they are or not. They've been peddling that psychology for years but I never subscribed to it. Why fill a child's head with false notions? Frankly, I was surprised to see you subscribing to it. Do you think it's wise to be untruthful to your daughter—being a Christian and all?"

I almost tell Patsy that I was speaking of internal beauty in my words to Faith but I decide to use the opportunity to make a different case. "I don't subscribe to that philosophy either," I say.

"It's obvious you do."

"No. I don't subscribe to the philosophy of telling our daughters they're beautiful. I subscribe to God's philosophy of *believing* our daughters are beautiful because they're made in His image."

Patsy smirks. "I can see why you need that, Treva. I'm sure it helps."

In a blink of an eye, I say, "You need it too."

"Need what?"

"To see yourself as made in God's image."

"Please."

I take a step toward her. "What is your strength, Mother? Your fair skin? Your straight, sandy-colored hair? Oh, the lovely European nose and hazel eyes. That's it. And that mighty Rolodex. How long will those things last? You won't outrun the wrinkles forever. Your eyes will dim. Your friends will die. *You* will die. Nothing you trust in will last forever."

"That's life, Treva."

"No, it isn't," I say, my composure waning. "No, it isn't. That's *death*. You've never known what it means to live."

She throws her head back in amusement. "And I suppose you do?"

"As a matter of fact, I do. God saw me beaten down, *by you*, three years ago. He saw me writhing in the blood you'd spilled, and He said to me, 'Live.'" The voice breaks, tears spill. "He said, 'Treva, live.' And He picked me up and cleaned me off. He gave me beauty for ashes and joy for mourning." I wipe my face. "And I didn't even understand it. I'm still learning what it all means. But I know I'm alive. And I'll be alive. Eternally." I step closer. "*That* is not what matters," I say, pointing to her face. "Your earthly body will decay. The question is, 'Will you get another one, a better one?' You need to see yourself as made in God's image because you need to know there's more to you than what you see. You have a spirit that needs to be connected to God, that needs to be made alive."

I want badly to grab a tissue from my nightstand but my mother's stare seems crucial to her, as if she's longing to see into my soul. She swallows hard a couple of times, looks to the left, then right.

"You've got a nice house, Treva," she says, walking to the window. "You've decorated well." Her head nods slowly. "You've done all right for yourself, career notwithstanding. You, you have a good husband. The way he looks at you, touches you. I've noticed." Her head bows slightly. "Charles never, well, he wasn't that way. I used to wonder sometimes why we married. We were never very happy. He was gone long before he died.

"And your children," she says with a light laugh I've never heard. "Couldn't stop talking about you at the brunch. They sure love you." She glides a finger along a dusty horizontal blind. "Of course you know I never had that either. You and Jillian…I know you don't like me."

"And you know why. You pushed me away. You said yourself you never loved me."

"I *couldn't* love you, Treva. I knew I was being mean when you were a child, but even when I wanted to be nice, something inside me…I just didn't know how." She holds herself, staring out of the window.

I sniff, and sniff, wanting badly to blow my nose, sensing I shouldn't move, feeling that I *can't* move, as if God's hand is firmly on my shoulder, fixing me in this spot.

"I've been lonely for years. Decades," she says, and I wonder if she knows I'm still here. She seems in conversation with herself. "And I know it's my doing." She shrugs limply. "I ran everyone away."

She turns to face me, taking me by surprise. "I think that's why I came," she says. "I didn't realize it until now, but I think I came today because I needed to be around you and Jillian and your families, see you smiling." She casts her glance aside. "See how family life is supposed to be. You actually talk to each other. You encourage one another. Just seeing you and Hezekiah standing with your arms around Faith. And Cecil had his arms around Courtney and Sophia. We never had that closeness. We just…kind of…existed."

"You might think you came to be around our families," I say, "but I think Darlene had it right. God brought you here."

Without a change of expression she faces the window again.

I breathe in deeply and exhale quietly, not sure what to think of this Patsy. This reflective, vulnerable Patsy. A second later I realize I'm not to think at all; I'm to pray. So I do. I close my eyes and pray, and the weight of it reduces me to sobs. I know instantly that God is giving me a burden for her. Letting me feel her vacuous existence, her desperate void.

Minutes later, I take tentative steps forward and reach for her shoulder. She turns easily, tears drenching her face, tears from eyes that no longer appear hazel. Just lost.

"Treva," she says, and her face shows her anguish. "Oh, God," she wails, covering her mouth, then her chest. "Oh, God." Her hand returns to her mouth, trembling. "What is happening to me? I'm calling on *God*."

I stand inches away, wide-eyed, unsure of what to do or say.

She takes in the breadth of the room as if questioning her whereabouts, her eyes landing on me once more. But, pained it seems, they close again. "Treva," she says, her eyes unfolding, "I don't blame you for hating me. I wouldn't blame you if you hated me the rest of your life. But I want you to know that I'm sorry. I'm sorry for the horrible way I raised you. I'm sorry for the horrible things I've said. I know I made your life a living hell. I'm sure I will never fully know just how much I burdened you. I'm just…." She throws her hands up, shaking her head. "It's not enough. Two words. How is that enough?"

Her head falls into her hand, and the mother I have never before seen in tears is weeping uncontrollably. My mind cycles back to some of those horrible things she referenced but God won't let me stay there. He takes me instead to Faith, to the grace and forgiveness she extended to her flawed mother.

I reach for my mother again and bring her to me. She clings fast. Softly in her ear I say, "I forgive you."

She leans back to face me. "How? Why?"

"Because God forgave me. And He'll forgive you."

"You spoke of God and life and…I can't remember it all…."

At this moment I remember that my Bible, which I normally leave on the kitchen shelf, is on the nightstand. I brought it upstairs to memorize the next couple of verses as I dressed to take Faith and her friends to the movie. I walk over and grab it and the tissue box, and I invite my mother to sit next to me on the sitting room sofa.

I open to Ephesians, the only book of the Bible I'm truly familiar with. As I flip past the other books, it strikes me that there is so much treasure in those pages that I have not yet mined, but as God would have it, right now, Ephesians is all I need.

Chapter Thirty-four

My mother and I descend the stairs almost three hours later. Faith, in the kitchen eating cake, stands as we approach and smiles cautiously.

"Where is everyone?" I ask.

"My friends have left."

"What's that popping I hear?"

"Miss Monique's been in there for a while. She got your friends to play with her."

I chuckle. "And Dad?"

"He and Papa Russ are playing Uncle Isaiah and Uncle Cecil in a card game. Trevor and Hope fell asleep, and the rest of us are trying out some other games I got today. I came to get another piece of cake. I hope that's okay."

"It's fine, sweetie. I'm sorry I missed the rest of the party."

"That's okay, Mom. It was great. And, I guess, you were busy?" Her eyes travel between Patsy and me.

"You could definitely say I was busy."

Darlene walks in with empty plates and cups and halts with them.

I place an arm around my mother. "You two, meet your new sister in Christ."

Darlene lets fly a whoop, tosses the plates and cups on the counter, and congratulates Patsy with a long hug. When Faith hugs her, Patsy says, "I understand you were praying for me and I want to thank you."

She looks at Faith. "I also want to apologize to you for the things I said at the brunch. I have a lot of making up to do. How about we go to lunch next Saturday?"

"Yes, ma'am," Faith says, delighted. Then, "Grandma?"

"Yes?"

"I'm so happy for you."

Patsy hugs her again. "I'm happy for me too. Happier than I've been in a long time." She looks over at me. "I hadn't realized how empty my life was until today."

"Darlene, should I start bringing the food into the kitchen?" Jillian yells from somewhere.

"I think you should bring yourself into the kitchen," Darlene shouts back.

When Jillian sees Mother's face, emotion overtakes her immediately. She grabs us both for a three-way hug and buries her head in our chests. "This is what I always wanted," Jillian says through tears. "For us to love each other. Thank You, God. Thank You, God."

Jillian pulls back and looks at me, wanting to know what happened.

"Girl, it'll take a long while to tell this story," I say, smiling at Patsy.

"Did somebody say all-nighter?" Willow says, as the crew enters from the family room.

"I am *down*," Monique says.

"I already told Karl I might not be back tonight," Carmen says.

"Mom's got DeRon at her house for the night," Asia says.

"Excuse me a moment, you all," I say, my heart heavy. "I want to make proper introductions. Please meet my mother, your sister, Patsy Campbell."

They throw their arms around Patsy and she seems genuinely overwhelmed by the warmth and acceptance. We bring the food into the kitchen, not to put away but to enjoy, and the eight of us women carry on until past midnight, when Russell drags Darlene out the door and

Patsy makes her own tearful exit. The remaining six adjourn to the family room, play Trouble, pop popcorn, eat cake, dance the electric slide without music, to Monique's lead, and gab and laugh until the sun rises.

───※───

"I'll get that," I say, laughing as I pick up the phone.

"Treva," Willow says.

"Hey, Willow, what's going on? You sound hurried."

"Excited is more like it. I'm sorry to bother you on Thanksgiving—"

"Girl, please."

"—but I had to call you. Listen. The producers of 'Asked and Answered' are planning to pilot a new show to air nationally on their business cable network. It'll be sort of a hip legal show where they'll have youngish lawyers breaking down the hyped cases in the media, you know, not the old codger type that normally do the legal punditry."

I chuckle. "You're the youngest one on your show, aren't you?"

"Yes, and there's about a twenty-year difference between me and the others. Anyway, this show will focus on business law instead of criminal and they asked me a while back if I could recommend someone well-versed in business law who would also be engaging and well-spoken on air and I told them about you."

"What? Why?" I move into the dining room to focus and process what she's saying.

"You'd be great, Treva. You certainly know your stuff. Graduated top of the class, clerked for a federal judge, worked for one of the top firms in the world—"

"Didn't make partner, unemployed...."

"Neither of which matter," Willow states emphatically. "I already told them so I could gauge their reaction and it wasn't a concern. All they cared about was whether you had brains, a way with words, and, being television, the look."

An ache erupts in the pit of my stomach. How could I advance myself as a candidate for a position that overtly favors universal appeal?

"So get this," Willow continues. "They just called. They said they're fast-tracking the show because several cases are heating up in the media. They'll be here *tomorrow* at the local NBC affiliate and they want to meet you."

"What?"

"Yeah, isn't that exciting?"

"I don't know, Willow. Even *if* I were to get it, and that's a huge 'if,' what would it entail? When will it air? Would I have to commit my evenings to it?" I have other thoughts. Will I still be able to share in my girls' after-school exuberance? Will I hear the fresh tales of friendships forged or feelings hurt on the playground? Faith's been open about the changes she's seeing in other girls, how they're gaining in fascination with the opposite sex, and the openness is greatest right after school.

What about my dinners? Will I still have time to experiment with lavish meals? To get ideas from Giada, Paula, and Rachel on Food Network? Would the schedule upset the dinner hour itself? Our time around the table, a table the girls and I have had great fun in using our creativity to set, has become a highlight of the day for me.

"Honestly, Treva, I don't know all the particulars but I do know that it will air once a week, unlike my show which airs every weeknight. I think it's just the nature of criminal cases—murder entices people. They'll be able to tell you more themselves."

I think a moment. "I guess it wouldn't hurt to meet them."

"Fantastic!" Willow says. "I'll call you back with the details."

I re-enter the kitchen and hang up the phone as my mother, Darlene, and Jillian follow my movements.

"What was Willow talking about?" Jillian asks.

I relate the conversation as well as my concerns, deciding to even be open about the concern that I wouldn't have "the look" they want. I look briefly at Patsy when I disclose the latter, remembering what she said about the type of black women one sees on television.

"That's an incredible opportunity, Treva," Jillian says, drying the fine china for our meal.

"It really is," Darlene adds, transferring the gigantic perfectly roasted turkey onto an ample platter. "The good thing is, sounds like you'll find out pretty fast whether it'll work out."

My eyes slide sideways to Patsy, who brought a cute apron to wear over her silk threads as she prepared cornbread stuffing and mashed potatoes. She pauses from taste-testing the potatoes. "Whether you get the position or not, Treva, you're blessed. And from what you all have been telling me, it seems that if God wants you to have it, you'll have it. Right?"

A river of joy splashes through me at the reminder of who's in control and what He has done in my mother's life. In *our* lives. Raising us all to heavenly places.

Epilogue

Three months later.

"Consumers may not be a party to this lawsuit but you can be sure they're watching it closely," I say, jumping into the discussion. "The digital music downloads market is hot and MelonCorp has had the largest share of the market to date, but their own consumers have said for some time that they want choice as to where they buy their music online. RealRhythms is saying, 'Consumer, we're on your side. We've figured out a way for you to buy and play our music on MelonCorp's I3 player.'"

"There's just the tiny little matter of it allegedly violating the Digital Millennium Copyright Act," Robert Lowe says, finger pointed in the air, chuckling.

"Exactly," I say. "When RealRhythms figured out how to make its music files compatible with the I3 player two years ago, MelonCorp fired a shot across the bow, telling them their actions amounted to nothing more than illegal hacking. They quickly updated the I3 software to render RealRhythms' technology obsolete, but here comes RealRhythms again, undeterred, with its own update. Hence the lawsuit."

"I'll tell you what," Wendy Minor says, crossing her legs, "my money's with MelonCorp. They've built a clever and lucrative market niche by tying together the I3 and the I-Music Store. They'll bring out the big guns to protect this investment."

I nod my head. "And they have deep enough pockets to force a small company like RealRhythms to back down or lose its shirt in litigation.

But if RealRhythms finds the wherewithal to hold out financially, they might just stand a chance. There are many who believe that application of the DMCA to these facts is tenuous."

The host, Neil Gordon, gets the signal to wrap. With a barely perceptible nod, he says, "While all of this is being sorted out in court, I assume it is legally permissible for the I3 user to download Celine Dion from the RealRhythms online music store?"

Sean Thompson gestures agreement. "Or Springsteen."

I smile. "Or Cece Winans."

Neil chuckles. "Fair enough." Then, turning to the camera, "Coming up, the case viewers can't seem to get enough of. Our panel will analyze the latest developments in the tale of the contestant who sued American Idol for intentional infliction of emotional distress. We'll be back, live from the nation's capitol. This is 'Civil Judgment.'"

"Mommy, you were great!" Hope says when I enter the green room.

"Thank you, sweetheart," I say, rubbing her back as we embrace.

"Can I get one of those I3 you were talking about, Mommy?" Joy asks, eyes raised.

"I don't even have one," Faith says.

I look at my seven-year-old to see if she's serious. She is. "No," I say, tousling her braids.

"Great job, babe," Hezekiah says, leaning over Hope and Joy for a kiss. "Ready for lunch?"

"Sure am. That hour goes by fast but I'm starving by the end of it."

"Are we going to Grandma Patsy's after lunch?" Faith says.

"It's becoming our Saturday ritual, isn't it? Breakfast at home, studio, lunch, Grandma Patsy's."

"We didn't plan it but it's been nice, making this a family day," Hezekiah says. "'Civil Judgment' airing on Saturday mornings couldn't have been more perfect."

I'm nodding before he's finished. "The perfect time. The perfect workload. And because I'm able to research and prepare at home during the week, it's really the perfect position."

We smile to ourselves at the same time, then at one another. We both say it. "Exceeding abundant."

Reading Guide

1. "I'd prefer privacy to cookies," Treva says. When do you prefer space and solitude to companions and fellowship? What are the pros and cons of privacy? When is a desire to be alone healthy—and when is it not?

2. "That's what they all are for the moment. Colors. Whenever I see Patsy I receive the same gift: her magnified lens." Treva's mother's lens perceived value in skin tone and hair texture. With what lens do you perceive people? How have you been perceived and valued? What does 1 Samuel 16:7 mean to you? What does it say about God's lens?

3. What makes you feel good about yourself? What is "as good as you can feel"? How does your faith help you overcome the negative messages people, culture, and past experience have sent you—about your looks, your intelligence, your personality?

4. "With me, the disconnect comes in the doing," Treva admits. She hears what her loved ones and even her own conscience say, but the challenge is *doing* (see Romans 7:14-25). What's your disconnect? Hearing, understanding, doing, following through? How might you overcome it?

5. Treva describes her interactions with God as cathartic, not victorious. How would you describe your relationship with the Lord? When have you experienced a sense of *enjoying* God?

6. If you were in a Bible study group such as the one Jillian has formed, which book of the Bible would you vote for? Why?

7. Read Ephesians 1, and then read it again. What does it say to you—about God, about you, and about who you are in the Lord? How do you respond to Psalm 139's assertion in verse 14 that you are fearfully and wonderfully created by God?

8. Treva recalls wrestling with the question of children and how having a young family would impact her career. When have you wrestled with similar issues? What choices did you make? What were the consequences—for better and worse?

9. Read the Scriptures Darlene suggests to Treva: Proverbs 14:1, Deuteronomy 6:5-7, and Titus 2:3-5. What would it look like for you to apply those biblical principles in your life as wife and mother?

10. How do you answer the question, not of "whether" to work but "how"?

11. When have you experienced the kind of prejudice that Treva and Monique describe—whether because of how dark you are or how light you are? How did you respond then? How do you respond now?

12. What's your dream—big or small? At home, in ministry, in a career? Are you willing to surrender that dream to God and subject your plans to the Lord's will? Why or why not?

13. "I'm not brave enough for that kind of prayer. I can't even truthfully say that all I want is God's will," Treva confesses. When have you wrestled with that kind of resistance—to prayer or studying the Word in pursuit of God's will? Why do you resist?

14. "Ask God if he wants to use you in Patsy's life." What is God asking *you* to do?

15. Describe yourself. Where do you start—with your appearance (height, eyes, hair, build), your job, your family, your talent? What does that starting place say about how you answer Treva's question, "Who am I?"

16. Jillian's Bible study group looks at Ephesians 5, focusing on verse 21. Be sure to read the entire chapter, particularly reading verse 21 in the fuller context of verses 20-33 and even Ephesians 6:1-9, which continues the "household code" begun in verse 20. What do you have a problem with—and why?

17. How would you respond to Treva's question: "What if God allows the devil and his host to come against me like that?"

18. When you enjoy a dance with God, what music do (or will) you hear?

19. When have you been forced to confront a deep wound such as Treva's? Who inflicted it? Have you been able to forgive that person? Why or why not? What would it take for you to shoulder their burden, as Treva shouldered Patsy's?

20. What does your "heavenly place" on earth look like? Feel like? Sound like? Who is there to share it with you?

Prayer of Salvation

God loves you—no matter who you are, no matter what your past. God loves you so much that He gave His one and only begotten Son for you. The Bible tells us that "...whoever believes in him shall not perish but have eternal life" (John 3:16 NIV). Jesus laid down His life and rose again so that we could spend eternity with Him in heaven and experience His absolute best on earth. If you would like to receive Jesus into your life, say the following prayer out loud and mean it from your heart.

Heavenly Father, I come to You admitting that I am a sinner. Right now, I choose to turn away from sin, and I ask You to cleanse me of all unrighteousness. I believe that Your Son, Jesus, died on the cross to take away my sins. I also believe that He rose again from the dead so that I might be forgiven of my sins and made righteous through faith in Him. I call upon the name of Jesus Christ to be the Savior and Lord of my life. Jesus, I choose to follow You and ask that You fill me with the power of the Holy Spirit. I declare that right now I am a child of God. I am free from sin and full of the righteousness of God. I am saved in Jesus' name. Amen.

Compelling New Fiction!

The Taste of Good Fruit

First time author, MaRita Teague, tells the story of two sisters and their close friend who become wrapped up in unforeseen and devastating circumstances. Is their faith in God strong enough to weather Sydney's dream husband's untimely death, the devastating secret revealed from Sherese's past, or Chanel's seductive mistake that may cost her everything she loves? Drained of joy, Sydney, Sherese and Chanel decide to take a road trip to clear their heads, to search for assurance, and learn that in faith, there is hope!

Coming Spring 2008
The Taste of Good Fruit by MaRita Teague
Paperback, 978-1-57794-858-2

The Good Stuff

From the author of *Boaz Brown* and *Divas of Damascas Road*, Michelle Stimpson reveals a story about two marriages on the verge of divorce. Sonia and Kennard have the "perfect" life, but Kennard's emotional distance from the family makes Sonia believe that a good marriage is more than financial security. Adrian couldn't love her husband Darryl more if she tried, but he seems more interested in making money than babies. Theses two women are heartbroken and ready to call it quits when a common friend, Miss Erma, invites them to a prayer group. They discover marriage is more than wedding dresses and happily ever after—it is compromise, sacrifice, and patience. *The Good Stuff!*

www.walkworthypress.net
Coming Fall 2008
The Good Stuff by Michelle Stimpson
Paperback, 978-1-57794-856-8

Glory Girls Reading Group

Enjoy reading great books that glorify God? Join the thousands of women who belong to Glory Girls: Reading Groups for African American Christian Women Who Love God and Like to Read. For more information, visit **www.glorygirlsread.net**.